Checkered Scissors

Douglas Schwartz
Copyright 2013 by Douglas Schwartz
Smashwords Edition

v1.1

October 2013

ISBN 978-0-9860554-0-9 (eBook Edition)
ISBN 978-0-9860554-1-6 (Print Edition)

www.checkeredscissors.com

Published in 2013 by Douglas Schwartz

Cover art by Douglas Schwartz

To Julie, Wendy, and Joe.

CHAPTER ONE

Birth of a Salesman

The room of many swimming pools amazed Ed, but the most captivating pool hung sideways across the wall. If it weren't for the people swimming by, the pool on the wall could have been mistaken for a cloudless and horizonless blue sky. The pool spanned twenty feet from floor to ceiling and nearly forty feet from wall to wall. What amazed Ed the most was the lack of glass separating the pool water from the room. The water's surface suspended vertically across the wall, with the swimmers' heads breaking the surface as they played Marco-Polo. It should have flooded the room, but didn't. Instead, the water and its swimmers defied gravity the way a child refuses to eat vegetables – with absolute certainty.

Alternating squares of light and dark shades tiled the floor, ceiling, and walls of the stately, aquatic ballroom. Smaller oval and rectangular-shaped pools interrupted the room's checkerboard pattern. Another, thinner pool, on the far side of the room, stretched up the wall from floor to ceiling, turned ninety degrees, and continued for several more feet across the ceiling. People took turns walking into the narrow pool affixed to the wall, then swam up to the far end on the ceiling. Positioning themselves above the circular pool below, they gripped the sides of the pool to pull themselves out of the water to the point where gravity took over, then dropped to splash down on the floor.

"Polo," said a female voice behind Ed. He turned and looked toward the large, wall-sized pool behind him. A young brunette wearing a yellow, two-piece bikini glided by. She smiled and waved at Ed as she swam past. Ed recognized her as a girl from school. He had seen her several times before, but never knew her name. She might be in a grade or two above his. He returned a smile. She smirked at him, dove under the water, and swam away, disappearing beyond the lip of the pool.

Ed felt the urge to dive into the water after her. The pool was so inviting, and the young woman tempted his teenage urges. Ed reached out a hand and touched the water clinging to the wall. He pulled his hand back and looked at his wet fingertips. He pondered the impossibility of this pool.

"I once sold a pool to a family of otters," said a voice.

Ed swiveled his head around. The voice belonged to a lanky man standing uncomfortably close behind him. Ed was taller than many of the other kids in his high school, but this man stood more than a foot taller than Ed. The man's wild, messy hair made him appear even taller. The man could have passed as Uncle Sam if he grew a beard and wore a red, white, and blue top hat and suit. The man's voice was soothing with kindness and patience, and he had a simple, carefree smile. He wore a slightly baggy suit that reminded Ed of his favorite, most comfortable pair of pajamas. A satchel hung from his shoulder with the strap crossing his chest and back. Similar to Ed's other dreams where he knew things without being told, Ed understood the man's true profession was selling these impossible swimming pools, even though his appearance made him seem more like a street magician than salesman.

"Your pools are amazing," Ed said, looking once again at the swimmers on the wall. "How does the pool stay vertical like that? Shouldn't the water spill onto the floor?"

The man stepped forward. He stood beside Ed and observed the swimmers playing Marco Polo. He folded his arms behind his back and contemplated Ed's question. He shrugged and said, "I suppose each pool holds its own gravity."

Ed understood how gravity normally worked. The water should have flooded the room. Ed accepted the answer anyway, because he couldn't think of a better explanation.

"Would you like to try one on? I always carry a spare," he said.

"Of course," Ed said.

The man lifted the flap in the satchel hanging from his shoulder and pulled out a cylindrical tube. The satchel did not look deep enough to contain the tube, but Ed wrote this off as one of many impossible things.

The white tube, a cardboard container about a yard long and three inches in diameter, was capped at both ends. Ed looked at the tube and saw shapes form into letters on the side. The shapes were lucid but meaningless. He couldn't see the letters as clearly as the pool water, but understood them to read "M P P".

As if reading Ed's mind, the man said, "M. P. P. 'Max's Portable Pools'. I'm Maxwell Spyne, and this is a sample of one of my portable pools," Max said, pointing at the pool on the wall with the tube.

When Ed looked at the tube again, the writing had changed to something that seemed to read "Max's Port-a-Pool". He wondered how a portable pool could fit inside the tube? Would Max pour a magic liquid onto the floor that would spread into a new, refreshing pool?

Max popped the cap from one end of the tube; it was dark inside. He tipped the tube over, but nothing came out. Max tapped the container, and a smaller tube of black paper slid slowly out of the end.

Max knelt on the floor and unrolled the black paper. The black backing gripped the floor, as if by static electricity. On the other side of the paper, blue water sparkled. Max flipped over the corner to show the black back side. He tapped the black side, which resisted his fingers. Solid. He flipped the corner back down and dipped his hand up to his wrist into the clear-blue water. Liquid. Max pulled his hand out of the pool, shook the water from his hand, and then dried it on his baggy suit.

"Impressive," Ed said.

"Portable pools. Take them anywhere. Go for a swim anytime you'd like," Max said.

"Cool," Ed said.

"No. Pool, with a P," Max corrected.

Ed shook his head and smiled at Max's bad joke. Max's portable pools were amazing, and Ed wanted one. He asked, "How do you make these?"

"It's a secret," Max said, waving to one of the wall swimmers. Then, he stood up leaned in close to Ed, and said conspiratorially, "But for you, I'll show you how. Follow me."

Max left the tube and the partially unrolled pool on the floor. He walked to the edge of the large, wall-sized pool. Firmly grabbing the rim, Max slowly walked the length of the room and peeled the swimming pool from the wall. The pool crumpled to the ground to the annoyed cries of the swimmers within. The swimmers grumbling faded away as Max revealed a set of double doors hidden behind the pool. He opened the doors and disappeared inside. Ed, careful not to tread on the crumpled pool littering the floor, followed Max into the next room, leaving the room of impossible pools behind.

Max led Ed into a roundish room. The book-filled shelves lining the walls gave the room the appearance of an office or a study. Built-in shelving aside, no other furniture occupied the room. Ed thought the room looked familiar, as if it belonged to one of his parents' friends or a distant relative, but the room he remembered also had a window seat, sofa, and desk, too. When he looked around the room again, these furnishings popped into existence, as if they were there the whole time, but sadly unnoticed.

Max closed the double doors and locked them. Normally, if a stranger locked Ed into a room, it would be cause for panic. Max had a soothing nature about him. Something about Max's relaxed personality reminded Ed of his favorite uncle, Adam. Ed remained perfectly calm, anticipating the secret of Max's portable pool trade.

Max pulled a pair of scissors from his satchel. A black and white checkered pattern decorated the scissors, similar to the tiles of the other room. The scissors had the smooth, polished surface of porcelain.

Max held out the scissors and hesitated. Ed wondered if Max would give him the scissors. Max had an internal argument, but then shook his head and carefully laid the scissors in Ed's hands. The scissors felt light, but solid.

"Each pool is handmade using these scissors," Max said.

Ed slid his fingers and thumb into the loops of

the checkered scissors and made a couple of snips in the air. Nothing happened.

"Here, let me show you," Max said.

Max took the scissors from Ed. With one hand, he delicately held nothing in front of him. With his other hand, he steadied the scissors, snipped at thin air, and produced a small sliver of water. He pinched the hole closed again, and then offered the scissors to Ed, and said, "Now you try."

Ed held out his hand and grasped at nothingness. Even though he couldn't see anything, this time the air felt like a thick sheet of invisible fabric in his hand. With the other hand holding the scissors, Ed cut at the nothing, and another seam opened in midair.

In the excitement of his success, Ed turned to Max and saw he wore a frown. Max looked concerned about the hole he allowed Ed to cut.

Ed turned back around to look at his hole again. Unlike the sparkling blue of Max's pools, the hole Ed cut was dark. It needed to be bigger for Ed to look through, so he steadied his hands and cut some more.

"I'd like my scissors back, please," Max said nervously, and held out his hand.

"I'm not done, yet," Ed said, and continued to cut a bigger hole.

"My scissors, *please*," Max said, and tried to reach around Ed to take them back. Ed fought him off with his elbows, head, and shoulder, while he cut the hole even larger.

The hole was the diameter of a frisbee, but he continued to cut it bigger. As he cut, Ed looked through the hole and saw someone asleep in a darkened room. Both the person and the room were very familiar. Ed used the scissors to cut a small portal to voyeur his own bedroom. He wondered what would happen if the hole was large enough for him to fit through. What would happen if his dream self suddenly appeared in the waking world?

Max grabbed at the scissors, and Ed did his best to cut the hole larger while fighting off the pool man. When the hole was big enough for him to fit through, he handed Max his scissors and swung one leg through the portal. In his bedroom, the hole hovered near the ceiling. Ed prepared to lower himself down gently. He feared the sudden drop might wake himself up. Then again, what would happen if he woke himself up?

"Where are you going?" Max asked.

"Through the looking glass," Ed said.

"I don't think that's a good idea," Max said.

"Then stop me," Ed said.

And, Max did.

As loud as he could, which was unnaturally loud, Max bellowed, "Wake up!"

The volume woke the real Ed with a start, and the dream Ed vanished the instant the real Ed opened his eyes.

From bed, Ed thought he saw a hole in midair near the ceiling with Max peeping down at him. He rolled on his side and turned on the bedside lamp.

11

When he rolled back and looked again, the hole was gone. He wondered if the hole was ever there, or if it was all part of his vivid dream.

Like he had done dozens of times before, Ed groggily reached for his journal sitting next to the lamp. He clicked on the light and squinted his eyes, keeping one shut tight and the other open enough to see. He propped the journal on his stomach and opened it to where the pencil had marked his spot. The last entry read, "The poker dealer's dance of confession." On the next blank line, he wrote a dash followed by, "Max's Portable Pools; Checkered Scissors; Hole in the dream".

Ed closed his journal with the pencil marking his spot. He turned out the light, rolled over, and fell back to sleep.

Life went on for Edwin Black. He continued to write more and more entries in his journal. He had started the journal in middle school after getting in trouble daydreaming in class. His parents asked him what he was thinking, and Ed, thinking they were asking about what he daydreamed about, shared bits of his imagination with them. His father, the plumber, and his mom, the accountant, were not creative people. They were not concerned with the details of Ed's daydream. They were more concerned that Ed spent too much time with his head in the clouds and often told him not to be ridiculous. Instead of sharing his thoughts with his parents, Ed decided to journal them. He took one of his old school spirals, one that should have been used more for class notes, and tore out the few, used pages, and began jotting down notes of his random thoughts. As he grew, progressed through school, and let his mind wander further and further (especially during the boring subjects), he slowly filled more and more pages of the spiral. Ed flipped back through the pages and read and reread the entries. Occasionally, he wondered what he would do with all these notes, and figured maybe he could one day write a story using some of them.

The journal entry and the dream were not the last of Max, his portable pools, and the checkered scissors. In another layer of the universe, apart from the one in which Ed updated his journal, Max stood in the staging area and clasped the checkered scissors within his hand. He swept his other hand across his tangle of hair and stared at the scissors as if it were a smoking gun.

The scenery faded and Max stood by himself in an empty, white room. The image of that impossible hole was etched into his mind's eye. Something about seeing the dreamer and the sleeper together felt incredibly and terribly wrong. Even though he was not the one who cut the hole, he felt guilty.

"Maxwell? Are you with us?" said a woman's voice behind him.

Shaken from his thoughts, Max turned around to a young woman with dragonfly-like wings folded neatly down her back. She had her hair pulled tight into a ponytail. A look of mild concern crossed her stern facial features.

"Sorry. Yes?" Max said. He pulled his eyes away from the scissors and focussed on the woman.

"My name is Karol. I'll be your integration specialist," she said.

"Integration specialist? What does that mean?" Max asked.

"I am here to go over your integration into the dreamer's world. Are you ready?"

"Um, yes? I suppose so," Max said still clinging to the scissors.

"I have been told to inform you not to use your scissors for anything," Karol said, then flipped through her paperwork, "other than creating swimming pools. Is that understood?"

Max nodded his head and said, "Yes, but I didn't …"

"Is that understood?" she repeated.

"Yes, ma'am," Max said, and slid the scissors into his jacket pocket.

"Good," she said. "Follow me. I'll lead you to orientation."

As Max walked toward the door indicated by Karol, he stopped and asked, "Hypothetically, what could happen if the scissors cut another hole in the world?"

"You and the scissors could be purged from existence," she said, "But, you wouldn't do that, would you?"

Max swallowed hard and shook his head. She forced a smile, then motioned him to the door, again.

Max walked to his orientation in silence. Like a good portable pool salesmen, Max was determined to obey Karol's warning. Yet, the thought lingered of the dream in which he witnessed a hole to another world.

After orientation and integration, life went on for Maxwell Spyne. Unlike Ed's parents, Max didn't mind Ed's wandering mind. The more Ed's imagination expanded, the more places Max could travel. The more places Max could travel, the more people he could find to sell his portable pools. As the world of Ed's imagination expanded, so did Max's portable pool business. Everywhere he went, he demonstrated his portable pools, and everyone wanted one. As much as he sold the portable pools, Max was not a rich man in the traditional money sense. He didn't charge as much as he could for his pools and spent much of his earnings traveling in style. Max did not consider himself wealthy in the monetary sense, but he grew rich in experiences and knowledge. And, this suited him fine.

Business bloomed as more people heard about his incredible, portable pools. Then, one day, business took a dive almost as bad as the boy who injured himself diving into one of Max's pools and missing. Trying to show off, the boy missed the pool, hit the hard floor on which the pool was spread, and became seriously injured. Even though the accident was not Max's fault, he extended his kindness and helped the family with the medical expenses and lost quite a bit more of his savings.

Around the time of dealing with the boy and his family, Max began to realize the difference between people and customers. People were often friendly, and he enjoyed talking with them and hearing their stories. When people wanted to buy his pools, they turned into customers. Then, the friendliness faded. The customers became demanding or indecisive, which often made Max's job more difficult and not as pleasurable. Max tried to bring the pleasure back into his business by finding the person hiding within the customer.

Sales recovered from the one tragedy, and then took another hit by another disaster. While a wrestler was swimming laps in his portable pool, he was attacked by a shark. He had no idea how the shark got into his pool, but he was attacked and severely bitten before he could get out of his pool. Rumors and doubts spread, and many customers canceled their orders. Max lost many customers and nearly lost his business.

Sales slowed to a trickle, yet Max stuck with his career. He enjoyed the travels and seeing the sights. He enjoyed finding new people within the crazy or selfish customers. He pinched his pennies a little harder and learned of cheaper ways to travel. Time passed and Max continued to trek across the growing land of Ed's imagination, working through his list of back orders – at least the ones people didn't cancel. Throughout his career and all his travels, Max still thought about that hole in the world and how his scissors could have possibly cut that impossible hole. No matter how many times he used the scissors, Max could not cut anything other than pools.

CHAPTER TWO

Hammond Eggs

Fifteen years after Ed dreamed of Max, the salesman and his portable pools were a distant memory and a brief entry in his journal. Ed flipped through this same journal, tattered from years of use. He skimmed the entries of dreams, quotes, ideas, and other bits of randomness. A brief memory or mental image flashed across his mind with each entry.

Ed clicked his mechanical pencil to extract more lead. Reaching the next blank line after the most recent entry, "Sunken submarine sandwich," he added a new line which read, "Chickens frying steaks".

Ed closed his journal and sighed. He set the journal on the coffee table and plopped down on the sofa. He stretched out his long legs and rested his feet on the coffee table, careful not to spill soda onto his journal. He rubbed his eyes with the base of his palms, and then ruffled his light brown hair with his fingers. Burt Hammond, Ed's college buddy, sat upside down on the matching love seat with his bare feet bobbing up and down over the seat's back.

Ed kept his apartment sparsely furnished which fit his solitary, bachelor lifestyle. Ed bought the sofa and matching love seat from a couple who moved out from upstairs. The wooden coffee table, with several deep scratches, dents, water stains, and in need of another coat of varnish, he had found on the curb. The television, one of the few furnishings he bought, perched on a smaller table he had since college. The DVD player did its best to balance atop the TV, while a plastic crate held an unorganized mix of DVDs, a few books, and a CD jam box. Other crates and cardboard boxes held more books and movies. His apartment wasn't much, but it suited Ed fine.

Ed's living room was not too different from the apartment he shared with Burt during their last couple of years of college. Their neighbors had come to the mistaken conclusion Ed and Burt were brothers. Even their friends at college had this impression. From the moment they met in college, they became fast friends. At that time, they did look a bit alike. Both stood around six feet tall. Both had brown hair, except Ed's hair was lighter and straighter, and Burt's hair was darker and became wavier the more he needed a haircut. In college, they both had a similar body build, but now Ed kept his thin physique, while Burt added more muscle mass. Like the brothers they were mistaken to be, they remained inseparable. Even now, hours after Ed was let go from a job for the third time, Burt was there for his best friend.

Burt fiddled with Ed's well-worn Rubik's Cube. In response to Ed's sigh, he said, "I hear you. Multi Site's no party, either. It sucks Vanguard laid you off."

"Yep. At least they offered a decent severance package. Eight weeks pay, plus unused vacation and sick time. Better than most places."

"No kidding," Burt said. He twisted the puzzle and got as many as three sides solved, but each time he worked on a fourth side, the other sides got out of order again. "Damn this cube!"

"You want me to solve it?" Ed asked.

"No," Burt huffed, "Have you told your parents yet?"

Ed shuddered, sighed, and said, "No. That's a drama I don't want to deal with again." The last time he had been laid off, Ed hung up on his parents after they speculated he was let go for being lazy and for spending too much time with his head in the clouds. "I think this time, I'll wait until I have a new job, or I'm desperate for money."

"Don't blame you," Burt said, "At least while you look for another job, you can work on that game of yours. How's that thing going anyway?"

"Meh. It's alright," Ed said. "I set it on the back burner to work on other stuff."

Ed had worked on the same pseudo-role-playing card game since he and Burt met in college. After eight different generations that Burt and friends helped play test, Ed still couldn't get the mechanics of the game just right. In the first version, the game had too many moving parts and was too confusing. He simplified the next version, and then the game lost most of its flair. He tweaked and adjusted through six more iterations before losing steam. Ed set the game aside and picked up one of his many other side projects. Ed never ran out of projects and kept thinking of new projects all the time.

"What other stuff?" Burt asked.

"I'm just fiddling with some code right now. Nothing solid. Just trying to get a handle on things. Train myself up a bit for my next job," Ed said.

"If you're worried about finding another job, don't. You're a brilliant guy. You'll find something else," Burt said.

Ed sighed and said, "I don't want another job. I'm tired of doing other people's work. I'd love to work on my own stuff."

"Blast it! Here! You do it," Burt said. He gave up on the Rubik's Cube. He tried to toss it onto the coffee table, but missed. Ed bent over, picked the cube off the floor, and began twisting the sides. In college, Ed had memorized the solutions guide and solved the Cube to clear his thoughts and relax.

"It'd be nice to have a job where I could get paid to work on my own projects," Ed said.

"No kidding. If you could get paid for all your ideas, you wouldn't have to look for a new job. You'd be set for life," Burt said.

"You know I can't be the only one thinking this.

Tons of other people out there work on their own side projects while working for 'The Man'," Ed said, air-quoting the last couple of words. He set the solved cube down on the coffee table. Burt rolled his eyes.

"Oh, you know there are people like that," Burt said.

Ed sat up, looked at Burt and asked, "I wonder if anyone ever started a company where the employees work on their own projects."

Burt shrugged and nearly slid off the chair backwards. "If there is a company like that, I've never heard of it."

"Even if everyone worked on their own projects, with enough people with diverse talents, they could scratch each others' backs in the areas where their expertise lacked."

Ed stood up, grabbed his can of soda from the table, and began to pace.

"Uh oh. What are you thinking?" Burt asked. He'd seen Ed like this only a few times before. Usually, it ended with a random act of mischief.

"What if we start our own company like that?" Ed said.

"Okay, first," Burt said as he struggled to sit right side up, "We don't know anything about starting a company. Second, where do we find the money to start a company? Third, what projects could we work on that would actually generate enough money to both sustain a living and build a company like that? And, fourth ... We? No offense,

22

but I already have a job."

"Yeah. A job you hate."

"True," Burt said, then hung his head and nodded. It was true. How many times did he and Ed complain about their jobs, bosses, office politics, co-workers, and so on? Some days it seemed they worked more at complaining about the companies than they did the actual work for the company they complained about.

"We can look into how to start a company. As for projects? I've got a long list of ideas and unfinished side projects. One or two must be somewhat profitable, at least as a starting project. The money? What about my severance package? That might be enough to start something."

"We can't use your severance. What are you going to live on?" Burt asked.

Ed brushed the thought aside. Being a single guy living the life of a semi-minimalist, he had a decent cash buffer built up in savings.

"I don't know, " Burt said, "I don't think it can be done. If it could, it seems like someone would have done it already."

"Maybe other companies did start this way, then gravitated towards a single product. Only difference would be ours will be based on a variety of ideas, not just one. Think about it, Burt. Don't give up on the dream yet," Ed said.

Ed didn't give up on the dream and wouldn't let Burt give up that easy, either. Ed spent part of his time searching for another job working for "The

Man," and most of his time focused on a plan to pull off his own company with Burt. Ed encouraged Burt to spend lunchtime at Ed's apartment with the motive of brainstorming the idea some more. Ed also enjoyed Burt's company. Not having anywhere to go or anyone to talk to depressed him, so Ed often invited Burt over for lunch.

The two of them bounced around more and more ideas. With each pessimistic "What about ...?" from Burt, Ed thought of a solid counter-point. In under four months, they started their dream company. They called it Hammond Eggs, the name Burt would have used if he ever started a band, which he would never do, since he was mostly tone deaf and couldn't play an instrument.

Hammond Eggs started in Ed's apartment, where the idea of the company first originated. They hired on a couple of their closer, mutual friends with whom they worked and knew their work ethic well enough. Others joined, too, but Hammond Eggs was exclusive. They decided they couldn't let just anyone work there. Ed thought up the rules and guidelines for the company, while Burt tweaked them.

First, at the Egg (as it was soon nicknamed by Burt, who hated repeatedly saying his last name), everyone needed his or her own project - and not just any project, either. The project must be a potential money maker worthwhile for anyone working on the project. Those applying for a job had to hard sell their idea to the Egg. Some applicants were hesitant to share their idea, for fear that the Egg would steal it. Interviews ended immediately for anyone asking the Egg to sign a non-disclosure agreement.

Even Ed struggled with this first rule. He had several projects, but not many potentially brought in enough money to make them worthwhile. TimeFactor, Ed's first project and the first official Hammond Eggs product, mainly sold to law firms and contracting companies. TimeFactor evolved from a timesheet program he wrote for a class his senior year in college. Burt, who handled more of the business relations and financial side of the company, used TimeFactor to track how much time each person spent on each project and how much revenue each project generated. TimeFactor also determined how much each employee netted after the company's take, a small overhead percentage. Also, it kept employees honest and forced them to spend more time on their own projects and not everyone else's.

Second, everyone needed a set of skills beneficial to the company as a whole. Sure, someone might have the unique ability to juggle hamsters, but if that talent did not benefit the completion of anyone else's project, it was not considered a valuable skill. For example, Ed's artistic skills, fountain of creativity, and experience as a programmer assisted Burt when it came to marketing the Egg's first line of products. And, although the Egg might have been Ed's brainchild, it would never have worked without Burt's keen business sense.

Third, all employees supplied their own equipment and materials. Ed and Burt shared their older desktop computers and space at Ed's coffee table, kitchen table, and kitchen counter with the new employees. If anyone needed better equipment, it came out of his or her own money. Most made do with what they had or could afford. Some took on second jobs, usually part time or contract work, to earn a little extra. This was common in the early days of the Egg. Burt, who once was skeptical, but now was a true believer in the Egg, switched to half days at his other job until the Egg got off the ground. Ed earned money on the side tutoring basic computer skills to children and senior citizens.

Lastly, when one employee needed help with his or her project and another employee had the skill required to complete the project, that person was obligated to help with the project, while the owner of the project was obligated to share a portion of the project's net income. Some employees, for example, were stronger programmers, while others were better artists. Every once in a while, the Egg attracted multitalented people, but dealt out small portions of their projects, so they could concentrate on their strengths. Ed was one of the few multitalented people at the Egg, but tended to gravitate more towards the creative aspects of projects rather than the programmatic or analytical side.

Similar to Ed working on TimeFactor, many of the first employees expanded upon projects which once were school assignments or stalled pet projects. One project, Cash Back, was a point-of-sale and inventory program that the Egg sold to smaller retailers, online stores, and independent sales consultants. The first non-software product was a container for comic book collectors, which Burt discovered were perfect for libraries to use for their periodicals. Ed's second product was the network of company websites, both internal and external, which shared project information with both the other employees and those external to the company. Burt found customers who helped fund projects with pre-purchases or investments, which drove the employees to bring their projects to completion sooner and with higher quality.

Together, Ed and Burt developed the Egg. Over two and a half years, the company grew to 72 employees, with hundreds of projects bringing in revenue. Once word began to spread about Hammond Eggs, other people wanted to work there, too. Those turned down for a job blogged harsh words about the snobbiness of the Egg, then attempted their own, often failed, versions of the company. Accept no imitation eggs. The imitators lacked Ed's creativity and imagination to keep the company moving forward. Ed's creative drive made him and Burt successful entrepreneurs. This trait was what first attracted Lydia Huston to Edwin Black.

Lydia heard very little of Hammond Eggs, and like many people, had no idea what they actually did. Since she had no idea what the company did, she paid little attention to the two men who ran the company. She correctly assumed one of the founders had either the first or last name of "Hammond," but wouldn't have been able to pick either out of a crowd or even recognize their picture. Since she lacked this knowledge, she embarrassed herself when she first met Edwin Black, cofounder of Hammond Eggs, at a mutual friend's party.

Ed rarely went to parties. He didn't drink, but never minded tagging along with his friends to be the designated driver. They considered Ed the designated, designated driver. On this particular evening, his neighbor and her boyfriend persuaded Ed to tag along with them. The party reminded Ed of the ones Burt dragged him to on the occasional Friday or Saturday. The kind where partiers hung out at someone's house and drank various alcoholic beverages from a collection of mismatched plastic cups collected from various fast food restaurants. The only difference between parties during their college days and this party were refined tastes in beverages, instead of drinking a cup of the cheap stuff. The other difference between this party and the college ones was the music played at a more respectable level where it lingered like background noise, most likely due to the homeowner dealing with an HOA. Neither flavor of party suited Ed. His idea of a "party" would be to invite over a few friends, sit around socializing, and play cards or board games.

Groups of people mingled around the house and backyard. Some people played a drinking game called "Get Barbara" at the kitchen table. The game made little sense, and the number one rule was that no one wanted to be The Barbara. Ed watched for a while, but figured Get Barbara was one of those games best understood when one wasn't thinking clearly.

On his way to the living room, Ed discovered the whiteboard in the kitchen. He nursed his plastic cup of Dr. Pepper, picked up a marker, and doodled a picture on the whiteboard just as Lydia entered the kitchen to forge for some munchies.

Lydia was slightly shorter than Ed with long, straight, black hair that fell across her shoulders. She wore a brightly colored shirt and "high fashion" jeans, the kind with holes purposely torn in them. She was the kind of girl who looked dressed up even when dressing down.

With her hand full of pretzels, Lydia walked up behind Ed and looked over his shoulder as he sketched and erased. She crunched on a couple pretzels and watched for a moment or two, couldn't make heads or tails what it was supposed to be, and then left to mingle some more. A couple minutes later, she excused herself to refill her drink to wash down the dry, salty pretzels, and returned to the kitchen.

After refilling her cup, Lydia walked up behind Ed and said, "Okay. I'm too curious. What's that supposed to be?"

Ed looked over his shoulder and saw Lydia. He smiled and asked, "You can't tell?"

Lydia shook her head and said, "Not really."

Ed stood back to stand next to Lydia, and said, "I thought I was a better sketch artist than that. Maybe it's the dry erase markers. It's supposed to be a picture of a man standing beside a flagpole."

"Why is he naked?"

"Because, all his clothes are flying from the flagpole."

"Oooo-kay. Why?"

"What do you mean?"

"Why are his clothes on the flagpole?"

"It's art," Ed said simply.

Lydia shrugged and said, "I guess I don't have an eye for art."

Neither Ed nor Lydia knew at the time, but Ed would tell the Hammond Eggs' resident photographer about his doodle, who would find a local celebrity to model for the picture, and within two months time, *Fully Dressed Salute*, would sell at a charity fundraiser for $1,200.

Before she walked away, Ed said, "I'm Ed. What's your name?"

"Lydia," she said, and offered her hand.

"Nice to meet you, Lydia," Ed said. He juggled the marker into the hand holding his soda, then shook her hand. "What do you do?"

"I work in sales. What do you do?"

"This," he said, and turned to display his whiteboard doodle like a spokesmodel.

30

"What? You draw comic books or something?" she asked.

"Comic books? Interesting," Ed said. He set down the marker and drink and whipped a small notebook out of his pocket and jotted something down.

"What's that?" Lydia asked.

"A list of ideas," Ed said, then put the notebook away again in a flash. He looked back up at Lydia and said, "I'm not a comic artist. I guess you could say I'm more of a thinker."

"A thinker, huh," she said, and checked her watch, "Okay. I'll bite. What do you think about?"

"Lots of things. That's why I have the notebook," he said, patting his pocket.

"What kind of company pays people to doodle and think?"

"Hammond Eggs."

"That sounds more like a breakfast platter," Lydia said.

"Yeah. It reminds me of Dr. Seuss," Ed said. "Ever heard of us?"

"I've heard of them. What do they do, I mean, besides doodle and think?"

"Breakfast platters," Ed said with a smile. Lydia grinned, too, which she quickly tried to suppress. Ed sensed he hadn't made a strong impression on Lydia, but she was either curious enough or bored enough to keep talking to him.

"Actually, we pay people to make their dreams come true," Ed said.

"If you don't want to tell me what you do, you don't have to make stuff up. Your imaginary job sounds more Disney than day-job," Lydia said.

Ed could tell that he frustrated Lydia. At that moment, Ed's neighbor entered the kitchen to put more ice in her cup.

"Imaginary, huh?" he said to Lydia. Over the noise of the party, he called to his neighbor, who was digging in the freezer looking for more ice. "Hey, Penny. What do I do for a living?"

Penny shrugged, as if the answer was common knowledge and said, "You and Burt run Hammond Eggs."

"You *run* Hammond Eggs? Are you like the CEO or something?"

"Co-founder. Penny is exaggerating. Burt runs most of the business. As I said, I'm more of a thinker. I think up different projects to work on."

"What kind of projects?"

"Ever heard of TimeFactor or Cash Back?"

"A friend of mine uses Cash Back for her cosmetics business. You thought of that?"

"Not that one, but both products are from the Egg," Ed said, and went on to explain how he and Burt co-founded Hammond Eggs. This time, he made a stronger impression on Lydia.

Ed took a picture of his doodle on the whiteboard with his phone. They took their conversation from the kitchen to the back porch, where they found a wooden bench swing and lawn chairs with a few others escaping the increasingly crowded interior of the house. The conversation drifted away from Hammond Eggs and veered towards their connection with this particular party. Ed explained he had tagged along with Penny and her boyfriend, Mike. Lydia knew a few people at the party, but was supposed to meet her co-worker and his girlfriend. As the night grew later, it was more and more unlikely they would show up. Mike and Penny joined Ed and Lydia on the porch, and the conversation soon detoured again into religious and political territory.

When strong words and opinions grew too heated, Penny declared, "It's late, and I need to get up early tomorrow."

On cue, Mike stood up and offered his hand to help Penny out of her lawn chair.

"You ready, Ed? Or, do you want to stick around?" Penny asked.

Ed gave an apologetic look to Lydia, and said, "They're my ride."

"I should be going, too, but I'm too drink to druve," Lydia said, and then stared into the distance as if trying to figure out what was wrong with what she just said. She shrugged, pulled her car keys from her pocket, and then handed them to Ed. "Do you mind?"

Ed took the keys, shrugged, and said, "Um, sure. No problem."

Lydia stood up, wobbled a bit, leaned into Ed, and said, "But, you can't come in, because my place is a piggy sty."

The thought occurred to Ed that Lydia was about to invite him to stay at her place, but he was too sober and too much of a gentleman to take advantage of the situation. He breathed a sigh of relief when she uninvited him.

"You take Lydia home in her car, and Penny and I will follow you. We can take you home from there," Mike said.

"It's settled. Let's go," Lydia said, and strode forth into the house. She said her goodbyes and gave hugs to friends and a couple strangers as they wound their way through the house.

Ed helped Lydia into her black Mustang and assisted her with buckling her seatbelt. Ed asked Lydia for directions, but got confused when she switched up her lefts and rights. Mike grew impatient and flashed the lights of his car at them. When Lydia finally let slip the name of her apartment complex, Ed feigned understanding of her scrambled directions. He was familiar enough with the whereabouts of the complex, and they were on their way at last. At the apartment complex, Ed walked Lydia to her apartment while Mike and Penny waited in their car in the parking lot.

"Didn't I tell you not to come in? It's a pigsty. Piggies everywhere. Here a pig. There's a pig. Everywhere a pig, pig," Lydia said, then sang in a voice much too loud for an apartment complex late at night, "E-I-E-I-Oooooooo!"

Ed did his best to shush her and hurry her to her apartment. He was lucky to have the apartment

34

number written on her key. Whenever he mentioned her apartment, it only led to her explaining how messy it was.

Opening the door, Lydia was not kidding about the apartment being a mess. It wasn't that the place was dirty, smelled, or had piles of dishes in sink. Clutter speckled the surfaces, from countertops to tables, and clothes littered the floor, coffee table, and sofa. If it weren't for the glow of the monitor, Ed might not have seen Lydia's roommate at her computer in the corner.

"Hey girl. Have fun?" Lydia's roommate said without looking up from her monitor.

"A little too much," Ed said, easing Lydia through the door.

Lydia's roommate quickly looked up, patted down her hair, and adjusted her clothes. She said, "Oh! I didn't know we were having company."

"Shelley, this is Egg. He works at the Ed. Egg. Shell," Lydia said. She paused and swayed, then broke into hysterical laughter at what she had just said.

"Hi. Are you, uh, staying?" Shelley asked, treading carefully around the implications of the question.

"No worries. Just helping her home," Ed said.

"I told you the place was a mess," Lydia said, attempting not to stomp on too much of the mess with little success. Shelley rolled her eyes and turned an embarrassed shade of pink.

"G'night, piggies!" Lydia said before falling

onto the sofa. The moment Lydia hit the cushions, she was quietly snoring.

Ed covered her with a blanket, then asked Shelley, "Excuse me. May I trouble you for a glass of water?"

"Second cabinet next to the fridge," she pointed, once again with her eyes transfixed on her monitor.

Ed poured a glass of water from the kitchen sink and walked back to the sofa. He cleared a spot on the coffee table to set down the glass of water. He pulled his pen and notepad from his pocket, scribbled a note, and tore off the page. In the morning, when Lydia awoke, she would see a glass of water with a note reading, "Drink this and call me in the morning," followed by Ed's name and phone number.

Ed excused himself from Lydia's apartment, let himself out, and found Mike and Penny in the parking lot. Since all were exhausted from the evening, it was a quiet ride home.

"Lydia seems nice," Penny said.

"Yep," Ed said, daydreaming. Ed agreed Lydia was nice. He thought Penny was nice, too. Penny lived in the apartment next to Ed. Ed thought Penny was pretty, but still within his league. Intelligent, but not so much that she flaunted it or dominated conversations. Quirky, but in an eccentric kind of way. As nice as Penny was, she was with Mike, and Ed respected their relationship. Ed thought it was fortuitous they invited him along. He may not have met Lydia. Lydia was not quirky, but listening to her debate Mike's political and religious views at the party, Ed could tell she was intelligent. That was a trait Ed found very attractive in Lydia. As for pretty, Ed considered Lydia a woman who had natural beauty. Penny was not available, but He assumed Lydia was single. Why else would she hang out with him and his friends?

On the ride home, he never mentioned the note to Penny or Mike, and wondered if Lydia would ever call him. The sentiment of the note made a strong impression on Lydia — strong enough for Lydia to call Ed at work two days later and ask him on a date.

On their first date, Lydia picked up Ed at Hammond Eggs in her car and the two drove downtown for shish kabob. They talked about their jobs. She told him about her job in sales and claimed it really was more exciting than she could describe. Ed rattled off the list of projects he completed, which ones were currently in the works, and a few that had yet to begin.

After dinner, they walked two blocks over to a little hole-in-the-wall coffee shop and talked some more. Most of the people had their noses in books or laptops. Ed spotted the shop's calendar and noticed it wasn't open mic or live music night, which was good since they wanted to talk and get to know each other better.

"I like to cook," Lydia said as she sipped her latté.

"Meals or desserts?" Ed said.

"Both. I've always liked cooking, especially since my parents gave me free rein in the kitchen. I like playing card games, Hearts and Spades mostly. I get that from my parents, too. What about you?"

"I like playing card games, and video games. I read a lot. Watch TV. Watch movies. That sort of stuff."

"Sounds lonely. Don't you get out much?"

"Sometimes. I got out tonight."

"Only because I dragged you out," Lydia said, with a smile.

"Burt and I hang out. Not as much as before the Egg. Maybe that's because we see enough of each other during the day."

"Maybe. You should get out more. Socialize. Connect with people."

Ed shrugged. She was a career sales gal, socializing was a major part of Lydia's life. Ed's job was thinking, which didn't always require much social interaction beyond people at the Egg. It wasn't that Ed was antisocial. He just didn't always fit comfortably in social situations. Lydia sensed Ed's discomfort and changed the subject. The two talked some more, and both had a great time. Lydia drove Ed back to Hammond Eggs and pulled up next to his car.

She looked at his ancient two-door, compact car. The car was so old and well-used, that it looked like faith held it together and it ran on unleaded miracles. Lydia said, "No wonder you don't get out much. If I drove that thing, I'd be worried I might not make it back."

"Ha, ha. I've had it since college. It's the first car I bought myself. It may not look like much, but it's a sturdy little car that still runs fine," Ed said, defending his set of wheels.

Lydia shrugged. She was thankful she didn't have to drive it and prayed she would rarely need to ride in it. She asked, "Ever thought about getting a new one?"

Ed shrugged and said, "I've considered it."

They shared an awkward hug over the gear shift in Lydia's Mustang. They mumbled how nice the date was and muttered how they should do it again sometime. Ed climbed out of Lydia's car. He opened the door to his car, slid into the driver's seat, and started the car. He waved as Lydia drove off, and then said aloud to himself, "I like my little car," and patted the dashboard.

Days passed and Ed and Lydia saw more and more of each other, although neither acknowledged they were dating exclusively. Although she could be critical when her tastes collided with his, Ed liked Lydia. Ed was a geyser of ideas and flip-flopped between projects more than a perpetually bored teenager channel surfing. Lydia brought focus to Ed's projects. With her encouragement, he felt he actually chipped away at several items on his lengthy, ever-growing To Do list.

One Friday night, Ed invited Lydia over for dinner and a movie. Ed prepared Santa Fe Pasta (one of his favorites) and strawberry shortcake (one of

Lydia's favorites). She was impressed with how well he could cook.

After dinner, Lydia sat on the sofa as Ed prepared the movie. She looked around his apartment, then asked, "Ed, do you ever treat yourself?"

Ed turned around, gave her a quizzical look, and said, "Of course I do. I go out to dinner a lot. I treat myself to new books and movies all the time."

Lydia looked warily at the stacks of books, CD cases, and DVD boxes stacked strategically around the apartment as if they would creep up on her and avalanche her at any moment.

"Isn't it time you afforded some real shelves?"

"I've been meaning to do that for some time," he agreed.

"You know, you could even upgrade your old CD player. Stuart, you know, that guy I work with? He was telling me about his new MP3 stereo. Even if you don't want to convert all your music, they have CD changers that hold 200 to 300 discs," Lydia said.

"That's true," Ed agreed.

"I'm not knocking your collections. I think it's wonderful that you have so many books and movies and things. I just think the co-founder for the Egg might want to update his image a bit. Anyone with enough money to start a successful business should be able to treat themselves to some shelves and a new stereo."

Ed stood silently and looked around his apartment. The place was very much a bachelor's apartment. Lydia made a valid point. How many people ran companies and had an apartment with teetering stacks of books and movies? He invested his own money in the Egg, and he earned it back with interest. Ed made a face.

Lydia said, "What? Don't be mad at me. I'm just saying."

Ed said, "No. You're right. Let's go out tomorrow and splurge a little."

Lydia smiled.

><   ><   ><

The next day, Ed and Lydia borrowed Burt and his truck for the Day of Shopping. First, the three set out to replace his plastic crates, cardboard boxes, and teetering stacks with shelving to help organize his growing collection of DVDs and books. Lydia suggested a set of real wood shelves, stained a dark mahogany. Ed preferred the cheaper particle board style since it had adjustable shelves, and the real wood shelves did not. Plus, he chose white over the darker faux-mahogany. In the end, practicality won over aesthetics. Ed bought two shelving units each standing seven feet tall and three feet wide, and another unit standing at half the height of the others. Mentally unpacking Ed's things onto the shelves, Lydia couldn't understand why he needed that much space.

Next, Ed hunted for a new entertainment center to occupy the shorter of the shelf units. Both Lydia and Burt encouraged Ed to buy the fancier stereo, the kind that included all the bells and whistles and a musician to play all the bells and whistles. Ed settled on the 300 disc changer with an accompanying receiver and speaker set. It was not top of the line and was a purchase that would eventually cause Ed a series of headaches. If he went with the higher end model, Ed would still have a series of headaches; only the headaches would have been more expensive.

Burt dropped Ed, Lydia, and all his purchases off at Ed's apartment. Burt stayed long enough to help Ed construct the new shelves, which were sturdier than the display shelves at the store. They left the backing off the shorter unit so the cords for the TV and stereo equipment could connect through the back without the need to drill holes.

At the kitchen table, Lydia sorted Ed's CDs in preparation for the disc changer. Ed owned just over 200 discs. She tried sorting the music by genre, but his collection was so eclectic, she ended up placing a quarter of the CDs into a miscellaneous group.

Ed and Burt completed the two taller sets of shelves before Lydia finished sorting CDs into the new changer. Once they completed construction on all three units, Ed placed all three along one wall of the living room with the small one in the middle so that the three formed an angular U-shape.

Ed and Lydia followed Burt out to the apartment parking lot when he left.

"Thanks, Burt, for all your help today. I'll buy you lunch on Monday," Ed said.

"No worries," Burt said, getting back into his

truck. "I know where you work."

They waved to Burt as he drove off through the apartment parking lot and out of sight.

"Speaking of lunch ... Can we eat? I'm starving," Lydia said and headed towards her car.

"Sure, but I'm driving," Ed said.

"It's okay, I can drive," Lydia said. She discovered she didn't mind riding in Ed's car; it was comfortable enough. She still didn't have as much faith in the car as Ed did.

"Come on," Ed said, and opened the passenger door of his car for Lydia.

"Okay," she caved.

After an early dinner at a local diner that quickly became one of their favorite spots to eat, Ed announced he had one more place to shop on the way home. They already had done a decent job upgrading Ed's living room, and Lydia wondered what else they could be buying. Surely, he wasn't going to buy more books and movies to fill the abundant shelf space. Or, was he?

To Lydia's pleasant surprise, Ed slowed down and pulled into a Mini Cooper car lot.

"A new car? Really?" Lydia asked.

"Sure. Why not? I've been thinking about getting one for a while now. I know you don't like this car. Plus, the Day of Shopping isn't over, yet. So, I thought, 'Why not?'"

"Oh boy!" Lydia exclaimed.

Already knowing what he wanted, Ed chose the convertible compact. The dealer had a friend in the auto detailing business who could paint cars to almost any shade imaginable. Ed chose Twilight Grape — a deep, rich, purple color. If purple's a royal color, this shade of purple would be crowned king and rule over the entire box of crayons.

When it came to the paperwork, Lydia stepped in, took charge, and quickly gained the upper hand. Ed could not have come anywhere close to Lydia's haggling of extras and perks. Not only were the usual things, like floor mats and the mysterious sealants and undercoatings included at no additional charge, but she also had a satellite radio thrown in and the paint job for free, plus, somehow, she managed to knock an additional $1000 off the sticker price.

After signing the last form to officially buy his dream car and trading in his old car, Ed turned to Lydia and said, "I love you."

Lydia looked smug and said, "I know."

✂   ✂   ✂

Back at the apartment, Ed shelved books while Lydia picked up where she left off stocking the CD changer. Lydia discovered Ed had three large boxes of books tucked away in the bedroom closet, each filled with books, which explained why he wanted so much shelf space.

Shelving the books was strenuous, with all the bending up and down and hauling stacks of books to the upper shelves. Despite the effort, Ed was pleased with the new arrangement and smiled.

Lydia, sitting on floor, looked up at Ed and

chuckled. She asked, "Why are you grinning?"

Ed said, "Oh, you know. I was just thinking about how good life is. My job is perfect. Soon, I'll be driving my dream car. And, I have a wonderful girlfriend who takes care of me and treats me so well. Life is great. Can't get much better than this."

Ed knocked on the veneer-over-particle-board shelves. It was the closest thing in the vicinity he had to knocking on real wood.

"Yep. It's all downhill from here," Lydia said with a grin.

Ed lightly tapped her knee with his foot.

"Don't kick me," she said.

She closed the CD changer and moved onto organizing the stacks of DVDs. Without looking up, she said, "You finally acknowledge I'm your girlfriend?"

Ed stopped what he was doing. He looked down at her with a quizzical look and said, "Well. Yeah. You are. Right?"

"Of course," she reassured him. "Today was also the first time I heard you say you love me."

"Oh, that. That was because of your incredible negotiating super powers."

"Oh? So, you only love me for my 'incredible negotiating super powers', huh?"

"That, and your mad cooking skills," Ed said. He pretended to be thinking hard about something, then added, "Negotiating super powers and mad cooking skills. Mm hm. That's it. Nothing else to love."

Ed smiled down at her. She scrunched up her face and slapped him across the calf with a DVD case.

"Ow! I just thought of one more. I love it when you get crazy angry at me. Ow! Stop hitting my toes!"

The two of them laughed and went back to what they were doing. When Lydia was done alphabetizing the DVDs, she stood up and stretched.

"Need any help?" she asked.

"No thanks. I got it," he said.

"I'm already done with the CDs and the DVDs. What's taking you so long?" she asked.

"I'm organizing my books."

Lydia looked at the books. They were mostly in alphabetical order, except for the groupings of large collections of certain, favored authors. She noticed most were right side up, but occasionally, randomly, Ed shelved a book upside down.

She reached up to one of the upside down books and said, "You put this one in upside down. Let me fix it."

"Stop!" he said, and held back her hand. "It's all part of the organization."

She looked at the books again. It still made no sense to her why a certain few were upside down and others not.

She tossed her hands up and said, "Okay, I give. Explain."

"The books that are right side up are all the books I've read," he said.

"And, the upside down books are the ones you haven't read."

"Exactly! That way, if I want to read a new book, I can quickly scan the shelves of books and easily spot the ones I haven't read, yet," he said shelving the next book right side up.

"What about that one?" she said, pointing to the book he just shelved, "I was with you when you bought it last week. Have you already read it?"

"Yes and no. I read it several years ago, loaned it to someone at work, and never saw it again. I bought this one last week, because I enjoy it and want it for my collection. So, yes I've read it, but not this copy. Since I've already read it, it's right side up."

"You know I love you for your crazy organization skills?" Lydia asked, admiring Ed's new literary trophy case. She added, "Crazy organization skills, and that's about it." He nudged her, and she kissed him in return.

✂   ✂   ✂

Lydia hung out at Ed's apartment instead of her own after work and on most weekends. For a bachelor, he kept his apartment tidy. Her apartment, on the other hand, was much more of a mess, largely due to her roommate, Shelley. Lydia and Shelley got along like sisters. Both thought of their apartment more as a place to store their things. Lydia explained that she and Shelley agreed if they kept their apartment somewhat of a mess, but not too messy, they considered that a good enough excuse why not to invite over guests, which gave them reason to leave the apartment more and socialize. Lydia gave this excuse to Ed as to why she preferred hanging out at his apartment. Since Ed had seen Lydia's apartment, he believed this to be true, but enjoyed Lydia's company no matter where they were.

Ed didn't need her excuse. He enjoyed being a homebody. Besides, even though the Day of Shopping cut into Ed's savings more than he originally intended, the new purchases helped make his apartment feel more comfortable. With more organization of his new shelves, he appreciated his living space even more. With his collection of books prominently displayed, Ed found himself reading even more. When he read, he liked a little background noise. His routine became turning on and shuffling a block of music, selecting a book, and laying on the sofa to read. However, soon, after settling into this ritual, the headaches started. In the weeks that followed, Ed began what Lydia called "The Episodes."

Ed's first Episode, a minor one, happened one afternoon while he read *The Lion, The Witch, and the Wardrobe*. The problem with reading while lying down, was that Ed sometimes read in bed to wind down at the end of the day, and it often made him sleepy. As Ed read about Edmund finding his way through the wardrobe for the first time, Ed's mind began to wander. He reread several sentences as his mind strayed from the book. When the stereo began to play Jefferson Airplane's *White Rabbit*, Ed's thoughts strayed from Narnia to Wonderland. In his thoughts, Edmund and Alice orbited the lamppost to the beat of the music while the Cheshire Cat curled up and slept on top, enjoying the warmth from the lamp. The two children walked around and around the lamppost examining each other, while the shadow of a creature in the woods watched them all.

Lydia typed on her laptop at the kitchen table trying to finish a report for work when she heard Ed mumbling to himself from the sofa. She couldn't hear what he was saying since he mumbled very quietly and the music from the stereo drowned out his whispers.

"What's that?" she called over her shoulder.

When Ed didn't answer, she saved her work, stood up, and walked over to the sofa. Ed's eyes were closed, and the book had slipped out of his hands and onto his chest. She carefully took the book off his slowly rising and falling chest and laid it on the coffee table. As she turned her back, she heard him mumble again. She leaned closer to see if she could understand what he said.

Ed mumbled, over and over, "Curiouser and curiouser."

Lydia didn't know if she should wake Ed, or let him be. She decided to let him sleep. Since he was asleep, she figured he wouldn't mind her changing the music to something else. Lydia walked to the stereo and stopped the shuffle of music.

"Hi there," Ed said behind her.

Lydia yelped and turned around quickly. Ed

was still lying on the sofa, but was completely awake. He didn't even look remotely groggy.

"Hi," she said. "Did you have a good nap?"

"I guess so. The last thing I remember was listening to music and reading my book. I guess I passed out."

"You sure did. You even talked in your sleep."

Lydia turned on the Eagles, one of her favorites in Ed's collection.

"I didn't know I talk in my sleep. What did I say?"

"Don't know. Something like 'curious and curious'."

"Curiouser and curiouser?"

"That sounds about right."

"Hm, that *is* curiouser and curiouser," Ed said, and tried to sit up.

"Ooo! My head," Ed said. He scrunched up his face and massaged his temples.

"What's wrong?" Lydia asked.

"Ugh. Headache. I must have been lying weird. Either that, or I'm not drinking enough water."

Ed got up to get some water and medicine for his headache. He survived the first of many more strange headaches yet to come.

CHAPTER THREE

A Helping Hand

Max strode his barstool at the Jack of Diamonds Pub with the tips of his shoes brushing the floor of polished wood. The stool wasn't really his, but he occupied it often enough to claim ownership. The pub's bar lined the back wall of the pub. The right end of the bar opened to the main sitting area, while the left side curved to the wall next to the archway of the hallway leading to the back rooms and restrooms. Bar stools, spaced a foot or so apart from each other, dotted the long edge of the bar with Max's stool on the far left side. Max preferred that corner so he could watch the people coming and going down the hall. The other regulars smiled or nodded in Max's direction. Some ventured over to him to exchange brief pleasantries the way regulars do.

Max considered the Jack of Diamonds Pub his favorite hangout and home base for when he returned from his travels of cutting portable pools. The pub usually held a steady flow of people, but today the crowd was thinner. A couple groups sat in the booths lining the walls, and another group gathered at a table in the middle of the room. Although only two others occupied stools at the bar, Max set down his satchel to reserve the one next to him.

The pub currently had no smoking customers, but a faint smell of smoke lingered like a cigarette ghost waiting to cross over. The bar, booths, and tables were all wooden, and stained black. It made the room dark, small, and cozy. The owners of the Jack of Diamonds constructed their pub from an old building on the edge of town. The Diamonds lived upstairs above the pub. How they got up there was a mystery to the patrons, including Max. Individual rooms in the back, designed in different themes, were available to reserve for private parties and functions.

Jack and Jackie of Diamonds, the owners and head bartenders, mostly stayed behind the bar. They were a two-sided playing card with Jack on one side, Jackie on the other. Each side of the card was like a frame to a living diorama. Though the edge of their card was paper thin, it had an inward depth in which Jack and Jackie's full bodies lived. If someone was taking in the full view of the card, they had complete bodies trapped within their card frame, from head to toe. Luckily for them, they were not like traditional playing cards that displayed mirrored twins conjoined diagonally across the waist. Growing up like this, Jack and Jackie worked together well, constantly balancing and swiveling their card frame around in a flat ballet. At work, both wore white, bartender aprons around the waists of their regal, playing card clothes. Since their birth dream, many arguments broke out regarding who was the front of the card and who was the back. Most people would agree Jackie was the better half, while Jack was the backside.

Max drained the last of his beer and set the empty mug on the bar.

Jack swiveled around, picked up the empty mug, and asked, "Care for another?"

"I didn't know you had free refills," Max replied with a grin. "I should probably wait. I don't want to be too far gone before he gets here."

"He's late, isn't he?" Jack said, swiveling around with the mug. Jackie frowned and added, "He's not always punctual. Go on. Relax and have another."

"Since you insist," Max said.

Jack grabbed another frosted mug and poured another beer on tap. Shelly, the rollerskating waitress, zipped up to the counter with her circular tray under her arm. She stopped and steadied herself with the brass bar encircling the counter.

"I need two Pink Jimmies and an Uptown Camel for booth three," Shelly said. She turned to Max and said, "Hey Max. How's work?"

Max let out a groan followed by a sigh, "Same old, same old. I had some doozies this week. One woman kept changing her mind between a circular pool and a rectangular pool. She finally settled on something pill-shaped, like a rectangle rounded at the ends. Another one wanted a snowflake. I couldn't fold it over like cutting a paper snowflake, because I can only work on a single edge at a time. I had to do it all in stages."

Max let out a sigh of disgust, then, in a mocking tone, "Then, he's like, 'This isn't detailed enough. That's not symmetrical enough.'"

Jack set another beer in front of him. Max muttered a thanks and took a sip.

"Bet you wanted to make his face asymmetrical. Huh?"

"Seriously," Max took another swig of the beer. "Then, the last one … I thought it was going to be simple, but, ugh, you know how customers can be. They wanted two pools. No problem. I got them two pools. Nope. They wanted the pools for a garden, and wanted one to waterfall into the other. They didn't understand you can't do that. If the water flows out of the pools, it defeats the purpose of them being portable. So, they got all bent out of shape."

Jackie placed Shelly's drinks on her tray, and Shelly zipped away to booth three. Jackie turned and faced Max. Her hands reached beyond the frame, took Max's hands in hers, and gave them a gentle squeeze. "You seem to be happy, though."

Max held his head high, smiled, and said, "I am happy. Customers aside, I enjoy what I do. I love traveling this great, big world we live in. Business hit some bumps, but sales are still going strong. I have a list of backorders to keep me busy for a while. It's my life, and I love doing what I'm doing."

"Good for you," Jackie said.

"And now, I'm going to take some time, kick back, and relax with a friend," Max said. He looked over his shoulder at the door and added, "If he'll ever get here."

"You rest up before getting back to the grind," Jack said.

"I plan to."

"So, no more sharks?"

"Jack. Don't burst Max's bubble," Jackie said.

"No worries, Jackie," Max said, "I weathered that one fine. Sure, people kept an eye out for fins for a while. That shark was one incident, and no one has seen as much as a guppy since. As for that kid ..."

Max nursed his beer and continued, "He's still paralyzed. Most of my customers don't blame me for that. The kid was showing off and took a swan dive into a marble floor. Did you know, even though I covered his medical bills, he and his family still hate me?"

The card flipped around. Jackie reached out and placed her palms on Max's cheeks, and said, "Aw. Who could hate such an adorable face?"

Max blushed.

"Let them hate me. The rest of the world loves me," he said, and took a big gulp of beer.

"That's the spirit. Everyone loves your portable pools," Jackie said.

"Damn straight. Those pools are out of this world," Jack said. Jackie nodded in agreement.

"They're out of this world, alright," Max said in a slow and deliberate way, as if he was carefully examining each word. The words brought back memories of his birth dream. He remembered seeing the creator lying in bed, looking up at him. Max tried and tried but never could cut a hole to anything but water.

The card flipped back around. Jack said, "I'm serious. Those pools really are out of this world. I mean, where does all that water come from, anyway? It's so blue and clear. Have you ever seen a place with that much clear, blue water? It's like it's all from another world. Maybe it's another planet."

Max shrugged and finished his beer.

"Did I hear you right? You make out of this world pools?" a voice inquired.

Max turned towards the voice and saw a reversed mermaid with the head of a fish and the body of a man. Max traveled far and wide in this world of dreams. He saw many strange creatures, but typically ones with better fashion sense. The fish-man wore a red turtleneck sweater, a yellow and purple polka-dotted kilt, and bright green, rubber, rain boots.

Max straightened up as best he could after two beers, held out his hand, and said, "Max's Out-of-this-World Portable Pools. Max at your service."

"Yes, I gathered," said the fish-man, ignoring Max's hand. "I'm considering a gift for my boss. I hate to break up your party, but I wonder if you wouldn't mind demonstrating your pool-making

56

abilities."

"Portable pools make excellent gifts. I can set up an appointment with your boss and customize one to his liking. Who is your boss?"

"That would be super. My name is Kasper, and I work for Michael Pinkerton."

Max sobered up, and nearly slid off the stool sideways. Jack and Jackie's playing card body stiffened. Even the noise level of the rest of the bar dipped at the mention of the name.

"Did you say Pinkerton?" Max repeated.

"Yes. Do you think you are up for the job?" Kasper asked.

Max's beer-muddled thoughts swam with ideas. He heard the stories of Michael Pinkerton, and as rich as the man was, Max had no interest in going anywhere near Mr. Pinkerton or his mansion. Enough thoughts collided into a single decent idea. He could delay his vacation time a bit and get this one job out of the way.

"Tell you what … If you can tell me what you have in mind, maybe I can create one now, and you can bring it back to him. My pools are portable," Max said.

"Unfortunately," Kasper said, and passed his hand straight through the bar top and out the bottom like a ghost, "I'll have a little trouble carrying it back."

"Oh," Max said, and swallowed hard, his throat suddenly dry.

"I'm sure I can have it delivered," Kasper said.

"Oh. Yes. Good idea," Max said with relief.

Jackie turned around, and said, "If you want, we have a room available in the back."

"Great. I guess I can get started right away," Max said, and shot Jackie a look.

Jackie shrugged and gave Max an apologetic look.

Max grabbed his satchel, and then he and Kasper followed Jack-Jackie to the back rooms. Each of the back rooms had its own unique style. Max and Jack exchanged looks, hearing the squeals of laughter and cheers coming from the bachelorette party in the edible, gingerbread room designed after the witch's cottage from Hansel and Gretel. A broken pipe was responsible for reconstruction in the pirate ship room. Jack-Jackie led Max to the vacant hilltop room.

The Hilltop Room was an enormous room shaped somewhat like a cube with the floor and ceiling domed upward. Each wall was at least fifty feet long and tall. Live flowers and grass grew across the hilltop room's floor from wall to wall. The painted walls looked like the bottom part of the hill stretching down and out to the horizon. The top portion of the walls and ceiling were painted like a blue sky. White clouds tumbled and blew from one wall to the next, across the ceiling and down the other wall. A security camera in one corner interrupted the illusion of the room's outdoorsy feeling, but was a necessary precaution to capture any incidents of intoxicated customers getting a little too rowdy.

Kasper trailed behind Max. By the time he got to the room, he no longer looked like a fish-man. A blue and green giraffe head replaced the fish head. Kasper remained the same approximate height, so the neck stretched downward to a short, stubby body of a baby doll wearing a fireman's jacket and a pair of plaid, golf pants. Max shook his head and wondered when the fashion police would arrive to make an arrest.

"I'll leave you to it," Jack said. He looked at Max, glanced at the security camera and back at Max. Max understood. He did not expect trouble from Kasper but knew what to do just in case. Jack-Jackie left the room and closed the door behind them.

Max set his satchel down on the side of the hill. He took off his suit jacket, folded it neatly, and then laid it next to his bag. After rolling up his sleeves, he pulled the checkered scissors from a deep, breast pocket of his vest. He preferred to keep the tool of his trade close to him at all times.

"What kind of pool do you think he would like? Lap pool? Triangular? A loop?" Max asked, drawing each shape in the air with the scissors.

"I was thinking something that really puts your talents to the test. How about a hemisphere pool that folds up like an umbrella?" Kasper asked.

"Hemisphere. Umbrella. Ok. Do you want the water on the inside or the outside?" Max asked.

"Inside, of course."

"Of course," Max said. "And, how big do you want it?"

"I don't know. Twenty? Thirty feet across, maybe?"

"Sounds good. I'll get started right away."

"Super! Mind if I watch?"

In order to concentrate on his craft, Max preferred to work alone. What was he going to do? He couldn't throw his client, a shape-changing hologram, out of the room. Max sighed, and said, "Sure. Just keep it to a minimum."

Max should have phrased his request for no talking. For Kasper, "keep it to a minimum" meant asking one or two questions every minute. Max thought he would hate to know what Kasper's maximum setting was. Despite the chatter, Max did his best to concentrate on the pool.

After all his experience, Max could do circular pools in his sleep. Hemisphere-shaped pools were more of a challenge but possible. The domed model of pools required constructing the pool in pieces, then attaching the pieces together. This was not the first spherical pool he created. One customer requested a sphere with water on the outside. He struggled with the concept at first and then modeled it after a globe dividing it into longitudinal divides, then blending the pieces together. The pieces blended better the more accurate adjacent pieces fit together side by side.

The Mobius Strip model was one of the most requested pools. Endurance swimmers and lap swimmers bought the Mobius in order to continually swim in one direction without the need to turn around. Most people requested the simple and traditional rectangular model, which could easily be rolled up and stored away.

Max ignored Kasper's questions as best he could, but Kasper persistently demanded an answer.

"Where does the water come from?" Kasper asked, again.

"I said, I don't know," Max said. He pinched at the fabric of space with one hand and cut into mid-air with the scissors in his other hand. A small window of clear blue water appeared suspended above the ground.

"I mean, it must come from somewhere," Kasper said.

Max's hand slipped. Kasper set his nerves on edge. He corrected his mistake by pinching the incision together. When the hole closed, he started again.

He was about to start cutting again, when Kasper asked, "Do you think the water is from another world entirely made of water?"

"It's possible," Max said, and began to cut again. He cut one edge of the curved section before Kasper interrupted him again by suddenly gasping. Max's hand slipped again, but after a quick inspection, he decided it was close enough.

"Oo! What if you could cut into other worlds?" Kasper said, and changed his appearance into a marionette wearing camouflage.

Kasper's question brought back memories of his birth dream. He still had no idea how his creator cut a hole to himself, but perhaps that was the ways of the creator — a mystery he would never know.

Before starting on the other edge, Max said, "That would be something, wouldn't it? Then, I could be a door-to-door door salesman,"

"Yeah! You could!" Kasper said.

Max was able to complete one section while Kasper was lost in this line of thought. Halfway through the first edge of the next piece, Kasper suddenly asked, "Where would you go?"

The suddenness of the next question made Max's hand jitter slightly, but he didn't care. He could fix it during the blend. At this point, he wanted to finish as quickly as possible.

"What do you mean, where would I go?" Max asked, over his shoulder.

"I mean, if you could travel to other worlds, where would you go?" Kasper clarified.

Max shrugged, and said, "I've been to a lot of different places in this world, and there are still a lot of places left for me to see. Why would I want to leave this world for another?"

"Some people might not like this world," Kasper said, frowning.

"If someone doesn't like this world, I'd say they don't get out enough," Max said.

"I suppose," Kasper said. His mood changed to that of deep thought and deeper sadness, as if upset or worried about something. Kasper's questions subsided. Instead of encouraging more conversation, Max took the opportunity to finish more strips. Standing in for the questions, Kasper complimented Max's work and offered words of encouragement, and even these comments were fewer than his questions.

Kasper, who no longer looked like a puppet, but appeared as a mannequin in a tutu, stood up and announced, "I need to go check in with the boss. I'll be back in a bit. You've been working hard. Why not take a break? Or, not. You can use the time to finish more pieces. Whichever. Whatever. Okay, bye."

And with that, Kasper left the room.

Max watched Kasper pass through the door, then looked at the pieces he set aside. He still needed four more sections, but he was tired of cutting and, in some cases, re-cutting pieces. That, and Kasper's relentless questions wore him out. For a moment, he considered taking a break as Kasper suggested, then decided against it. He could cut four more pieces fairly quickly. Besides, his friend, who must be delayed, would arrive any moment. When he did, Jack-Jackie would show him to the back room, and it wouldn't look good to be caught napping on a job. After a quick, internal debate, Max decided to finish the pool. Before cutting more pieces, he started the dome and blended together the finished strips.

It helped that the room's floor was domed, too. He laid out a couple of pieces side by side and pinched two pool pieces together. When he completed a quarter of the pool, he carefully turned it over onto its base, where it rocked on the side of the hilltop. From there, he attached the other pieces working his way around the side of the bowl. The rim needed a bit of trimming, as the pieces weren't all the same length, but that could wait until the end. With over half of the hemisphere constructed, Max picked up the scissors and began cutting the next piece.

The door opened. Instead of his friend, an intoxicated woman stumbled and swayed into the room. As she walked through the door, she sang a country song poorly and out of tune, but stopped when she saw the portion of domed pool. Her mouth fell open with a soft burp, and her glazed eyes boggled.

"And, I thought I drank a lot," she slurred, then hiccuped.

Max stopped cutting to look around the partially constructed pool at the woman swaying on the spot by the doorway. Out of habit when meeting a potential new customer, he patted down his messy hair and straightened his vest with a tug.

"Are you gonna drink all that? Can I have a sip?" she said, then erupted in drunken laughter.

"No, ma'am," Max said politely, "It's a swimming pool."

"A pool? Great! Who's up for skinny dipping?" she said, then tugged at her shirt as she unsuccessfully attempted to undress herself.

Max dropped the scissors, pinched the seam to the new slice of pool closed, then rushed over to the woman before she caused a scene.

"I don't think that's a good idea," he said.

"Sure, it is. Let's get naked!" she said, and erupted into more laughter.

Max did his best to prevent the woman from undressing herself or himself, and gently tried persuading her to leave the room. As Max batted at the woman's hands grabbing at his clothes and encouraged her to keep her own clothes on, a hand stretched out of the wall behind him, pulling the picture of the hillside and sky with it. The hand grabbed Max's scissors. A second hand stretched out of the ground. Grass and flowers tagged along for the ride as the second hand grasped at nothing, the same way Max grasped at nothing before cutting a wedge of pool. The hand with the scissors cut into midair. Instead of water on the other side, bright sunlight shone through the slice and fell across the floor.

"I can't get my pants off," the woman grumbled.

"That's quite all right. You don't need to do that," Max pleaded.

"Here. Gimme a hand," she said. She tried to focus on Max, but her glazed eyes slid off Max to what was happening behind him. "Never mind. Maybe I can use one of those," she said, and pointed.

Max rolled his eyes and glanced behind him. As he turned, the hands dropped the scissors and quickly sank back into the floor and wall.

From where he stood, Max was unsure of what

he saw. He walked over to the side of his partial pool, and looked down at sunlight shining on the scissors laying in the grass.

"You're no fun. Where'd that gingerbread house go?" the woman said, hiccuping, and then stumbling out the door.

From the door, it was difficult to see what, if anything, the hands had done. He thought they might have shredded a hole in his pool. Max walked around to look over his pool, but the pool was intact. On the ground, next to the pool, he found shredded bits of something that mismatched the grass of the room. He leaned over to get a better look at the scraps. That's when he found a ragged hole cut in midair next to his swimming pool. He knelt down and realized as he peeked through a hole shredded in the universe he saw sunlight illuminating a slightly different grassy field. Around the other side of the hole, Pinkerton's pool was perfectly intact. He looked down and saw his scissors laying near the pile of shredded bits of the alien sunset land.

Max called out, "Hello? Is anyone there?"

Quiet, high pitched laughter came out of nowhere.

"Hello?" Max asked, "Kasper?"

He crawled over to the new hole and poked his head through it. On the other side, the hole floated a couple feet off the ground above a field in what appeared to be a large park. He could not see any people, but could hear traffic driving somewhere in the distance.

He pulled his head back out and looked around the room. No more laughter. No Kasper. No Jack-Jackie. Not even the drunken woman. All was quiet.

In all the times he used his scissors, he could never cut anything other than water. The only other time he'd ever seen something other than water, was the one time he let Ed try the scissors in his birth dream.

Max decided to climb through the hole and take a quick look around. He climbed through the hole and dropped himself onto the soft grass. He stood up and looked around. He wondered if this was another part of Ed's world, or if it was somewhere completely different. He looked up. The stars were coming out, and a sliver of moon hung low in the evening sky. This was a different world than the world he was familiar with where huge planets and other moons hung above the world.

He looked back at the hole. From where he stood, he could see the corner of the room where the security camera attached. Two hands rose out of the floor's grassy, faux-hilltop on the other side of the hole. One hand held up his scissors, and shook them, taunting. The other hand pinched the hole together so it started to seal.

Once a hole started closing, it was near impossible to pry it back open. Max stuck his hand through the hole and grabbed at the scissors. The hole closed around his arm. He grunted as he exerted himself to pry open the hole again. It loosened enough to slide his arm and hand back through the hole. In seconds, the hole sealed completely, stranding him in this strange world, while his scissors remained back in the world on the other side.

"Oh, this is not good," Max said.

CHAPTER FOUR

Fish Out of Water

Max didn't know what to do. He stood and stared at the empty space where the hole was moments ago, hoping it would open again and let him back through. After a couple of minutes, he gave up hope and decided to figure out what to do.

For years, he had thought about his birth dream and the hole between worlds. Now, here he was. Once again, a hole had appeared in the world, and this time, instead of being cautious, he had crawled through and stranded himself. Worse than that, he had left his satchel and scissors behind. The satchel he was less worried about. It held a few odds and ends, but nothing of too much importance. On the other hand, without his scissors, he was out of a job. What was he going to do? The only life he ever knew was traveling and cutting pools. He didn't know what else he could do.

What about his friends? From the surveillance camera, Jack-Jackie would know what had happened to him, but he doubted they would be able to help him get back. His buddy was late for drinks. Would he wonder what happened to Max? Or, would he peek in the bar, not see Max, and leave? If and when he ever returned, he would have to try to explain his sudden disappearance. Max wondered if anyone else would miss him. The backlist of customers could just deal with his absence. Was there anyone else?

Max's stomach grumbled and gave him something new to worry about. Working on Kasper's pool made him hungry. He surveyed his surroundings for two reasons. For one, he wanted to remember approximately where the hole was, in case he needed to return. For another, he wanted to get his bearings. He heard the traffic in the distance and listened hard to figure out where the sound originated. If the traffic in this world was anything like his creator's world, people driving the cars needed to occasionally stop to eat, and restaurants typically were not too far from the road.

He didn't have his satchel, but he did have a fair amount of money in his pocket. He could buy himself a few of the essentials until he found a new job. After a ten-minute hike, Max found a busy highway. After another ten minutes, he found a diner.

The diner had an old fashioned aura about it. Speckled linoleum covered the floor. The booths, tables, and chairs were mostly chrome, red padding, and checkered table cloths. The jukebox was updated to play MP3s, but the look of it fit right into the scene. The only things missing were rollerskating waitresses, girls in poodle skirts, and guys in leather jackets.

Max sat at the bar and ordered a stack of pancakes. The seat at the end of the bar nearest the kitchen reminded him of Jack of Diamonds. He considered switching seats to some place less nostalgic, but old habits were hard to break.

As he shoveled pancakes with syrup into his mouth, he thought about his situation. He started with what he knew. First, he knew this world was not a world of dreams. The physics were similar, but not quite the same. Plus, the text was very static; in his world, much of the text was very fluid. Also, the constellations were definitely not the same. It was an undeniable fact Max was no longer in the same world, nor in a world built upon dreams.

Second, Max knew that he was dreamed into existence by Edwin Black. In his world, everyone knew the name Edwin Black. He figured if Edwin Black could create a pair of scissors that could slice holes in the universe, he might also know of a way back. And, if Edwin cut a hole in his birth dream to a world in which he slept, maybe this was that same world.

Max thought back to his birth dream and what happened afterwards. He recalled his integration specialist warning him not to do what he just did. Would someone really come to purge him from existence? Or, was it an empty threat? If they were coming for him, how long would it take for them to realize he was not where he should be? If and when they arrived, could he convince them his being in

71

this world was a mistake? The thought of being purged was almost enough to ruin his appetite … Almost, but not quite. He shoveled a large bite of pancakes into his mouth.

The waitress dropped off the bill for Max's stack of pancakes. Before she could walk away, he asked her, "Do you know Edwin Black?"

The waitress tugged at one of her earrings and said, "Honey, this is a big city we live in with lots of people. Lots of people come through here to eat. More than likely, if you sit in here long enough, you'll probably see your friend, eventually."

"Before you go, I'd like to pay my bill," Max said, and dug out a handful of other worldly currency. He managed to count out three dollars worth of alien coins before the waitress stopped him.

"Sorry, honey. We don't take foreign money," she said.

Max didn't understand. Money was money. In the world he came from, currency was like snowflakes. Each coin and bill looked different from another with only a slight better chance of duplicates. Even when found on the ground, it was still money. In some areas, the grass grew coins and the trees had cash for leaves. Money was always money, and most people in his home world took it, no matter what it looked like. He couldn't understand why this waitress refused his money. It was money!

"But, it's money," Max said offering it again.

"Not to us, it's not. Sorry," she said.

"What about an Owe-Me?" he asked.

"Owe you? You mean, you owe us. Hang on a sec. You wait right here. Let me talk to Gus. No running off," she said, and disappeared into the kitchen.

Max sat and sulked. He thought of his scissors again and pouted. He needed this world's money, and he couldn't get that without a job. Without his scissors, he didn't know what else he could do.

A moment later, the waitress returned with Gus. Gus was large, but friendly. He had a grandfatherly look about him.

"What's your name, son?" Gus asked.

"Max, sir. And, I'm guessing you're Gus."

"That's right. Liz tells me you're a little down on your luck and can't pay your tab."

"I'll say. You might say I lost my job and my way, and kind of got stranded here. I stopped in for a quick bite. I thought you could take my money, but it is from another land. I don't mean to stiff you. You just tell me how I can repay you," Max pleaded.

"I appreciate your honesty and not running off like others might have done. There's a stack of dishes in the back that need washing and a couple bags of garbage to take out. You clean that up, and we'll call it even. Deal?"

"Deal," Max said. He and Gus exchanged a handshake, and Max got to working off his debt.

Liz showed Max to the kitchen and showed him the sink. She threw him a pair of pink, rubber gloves and showed him how to use the sprayer. Max jumped right in and whistled as he washed. The tune he whistled was a song he heard somewhere a long time ago that got stuck in his head. He never figured out the song's name, but often whistled it as he cut pools.

An hour later, the dishes were washed, dried, and stacked neatly away. Max took the garbage to the dumpster out back, then broke down a few boxes and stacked them neatly in the storage room. As he swept the floor of the kitchen, Gus entered to see how things were going and was pleasantly surprised by what he saw. Gus invited Max to the dining area and asked him to take a seat in a booth. As Max slid into the booth seat, Gus and a woman sat down across from him.

"Max, meet my wife, Cheryl," Gus said.

"How do you do?" Max said, and shook Cheryl's hand with gentle firmness.

"So polite and not afraid to give a lady a nice handshake," Cheryl said.

"I told Cheryl your predicament," Gus said. Max didn't offer Gus much but wondered what he told her.

"Gus tells me you lost your job. What line of work did you do?"

Max had a suspicion he should keep the details to a minimum, so he said, "I'm in sales. Swimming pools, mostly. Also, I help design them."

"How lovely. I bet you're very good at what you do," Cheryl said.

"Yes, ma'am," Max said, and left it at that.

"So polite," she repeated.

"How did you come across our diner?" Gus asked.

Max thought quickly about how to answer the question. "I got dropped off at a park not far from here; now I'm kind of stranded here. I walked over here for a quick meal, and then I was going to look for Edwin Black. Have you hear of him?"

Gus and Cheryl exchanged looks, then both shook their heads.

"Doesn't sound familiar. Is he a friend of yours?" Gus asked.

"I met him once long ago. I thought he lived around here and was hoping to find him. You might say he's my key to getting home."

"I take it you're far from home," Gus said.

"Yes, sir," Max said. *You have no idea.*

"You seem like a good man, Max. As I said, I appreciate your honesty, and I appreciate the work you did in the kitchen. You went beyond payback," Gus said.

"What my husband is saying, is that we know times are tough, and we want to help," Cheryl said.

"Oh no, I don't think you ..." Max started to say. He didn't know how they could help him get back home.

"We have a room above our garage. You're welcome to stay there until you can get back on your feet and earn enough to make your way home. You can repay us by working here at the diner and maybe helping a bit around the house, too," Gus said.

"I couldn't," Max said.

"We insist," Gus said.

"We believe the Lord works in mysterious ways and brought you to us for a good reason. Please say you'll stay."

Max never considered Edwin Black any sort of ruler, lord or otherwise, but he did agree his creator did some pretty mysterious work. First, there was the miracle of the holes between worlds. That was very mysterious. Now, here Max was stranded in another world when a job and a place to live were practically handed to him on a platter. How mysterious is that? Without worrying about food or shelter, he could work on trying to find the mysterious Edwin Black. How could Max refuse?

"Okay, I'll stay. I appreciate your generosity," Max said.

✂   ✂   ✂

"Again," Michael Pinkerton demanded.

Michael Pinkerton, one of the world's most influential people, sat in his wheelchair and grinned. Unlike Max, Pinkerton was nightmared into the world. A man in a wheelchair was not what frightened a young Edwin Black. A half man, half machine in a wheelchair with detachable whirling blades where one of his hands ought to be was terrifying to a young Edwin Black. And so, Pinkerton was born into Ed's world as half man, half machine, and all monster.

Michael Pinkerton never thought of himself as a

monster. Does a shark with its multiple rows of teeth think of itself as a monster? Does a lion eating a gazelle on the Serengeti think what it's doing is wrong and suddenly go vegetarian? In the nightmare, he recalled chasing after Ed wanting something from him and Ed running away. He didn't remember what it was he wanted. He didn't think that the whirling blade was menacing. Whatever it was he wanted became irrelevant.

Once integrated into the world, neither the chase nor whatever it was he chased Edwin Black for mattered. Everywhere he went, people ran from him. They developed a global understanding of a new monster coming to town. In his loneliness, the bitterness for the way he was made grew. Using what he had — a deep understanding of biological, mechanical and electrical components — he experimented on animals with the goal to figure out a way to make himself a better, more human person. When he showed people what he could do, the angry villagers put a stop to his creations, and took away his toys. His menagerie of mutated animals became exhibits in the City zoo. People thought his experiments were hideous, not ingenious. One of his creations, Quirk, a cat with the head of a chicken and miniature bull horns, fled with Pinkerton into reclusion. He never wanted to be a monster, and that was the only thing people saw about him. His anger and hatred intensified.

In private, he experimented more, then secretly gave his creations to the world. Everyone loved what he contributed to society. When he leaked to the people who the originator of these wonderful creations was, no one believed it. No monster could ever make such useful and beautiful things. They believed Pinkerton, the monster, stole their creator's ideas and claimed them for his own. Pinkerton knew the truth, and grew rich off the public's blindness to see only what they wanted to see. When he realized the public could never see him as anything but a monster, that's when Pinkerton decided it was time to leave.

If people considered him a monster and mad scientist, he didn't bother to change his appearance. In fact, he improved upon his monstrous look. He blended his body with his chair so no one other than himself knew where his body ended and the mechanics started. He kept his head shaved and carved himself two spiral-shaped scars along each side to give the illusion of horns. For special occasions, he trained a swarm of hornets to swarm along his jawline like a buzzing beard. He installed two rings of metal around each eye so that different lenses could magnetically be fixed to his face without the need for glasses. In a final act of self-mutilation, he carved a skull and crossbones into one of his canine teeth.

Pinkerton invented an assortment of useful attachments for his mechanical hand, including the original collection of whirling blades from his birth nightmare. He enhanced his wheelchair and even created other models of mobile chairs for traveling across different terrains. He put these attachments and enhancements to use and scoured the world for something to help him leave.

Now, in his remote mansion, Pinkerton sat next to Tellis Pripen, the media mogul. Tellis Pripen was one of the few people to see beyond Pinkerton the Monster and focused on Pinkerton the Businessman. Together, Pinkerton and Pripen built the communication empire of Pripen Communications. Pinkerton needed widespread surveillance for his quest, and Pripen strived for total media control. Tellis sat at the controls of an impressive array of monitors and surveillance equipment, compliments of Pripen Communications. Kasper, Pinkerton's assistant, paced nervously nearby in the form of a rat in a nun's habit.

Tellis Pripen turned a knob and backed up the surveillance video. He stopped it and replayed it for the seventh time. Once again, the hands stretched out of the floor and wall and cut a ragged hole in the universe. A moment later, they watched Max return to the pool, the woman stumble away, and Max crawl through the hole. The hands appeared again to take Max's scissors and strand him in the other world. Mr. Pinkerton laughed again at the surprised and desperate expression on Max's face as the hole sealed shut around his hand.

"I love his expression. Bye, bye, pool boy," Pinkerton said, and laughed again.

"See? I told you it was like those scissors cut into another world," Kasper said.

"Yes. So you keep saying," Pinkerton said. "How do you know the other side of that hole isn't another part of this damn world?"

Tellis said, "I've compared the image through the hole with our satellite topography and can find no matches. With the fluctuations and embedded pockets of this world, it's not 100%, but I'd say there's a good chance it's alien terrain."

"Alien, as in another planet? Or, another world outside this universe?" Pinkerton asked.

"Another world outside this world's universe," Tellis said.

"How can you tell? The sky is full of forkin' planets."

"The planets and stars you see in the sky of this world are projections. An illusion of sorts. Our universe is not much bigger than the planet we walk upon, but it is an enormous planet. The likelihood the hole is linked to another planet in this universe is highly improbable," Tellis said.

"Hot damn and a side of bacon! That's good enough for me," Pinkerton said.

Pinkerton turned his wheelchair to face Kasper. Pinkerton reached up and tugged on his earlobe with the fishhook earring. His sour face contorted, and he said, "Why couldn't you tell me any of this sooner?"

"The pool was going to be a surprise. I didn't know what happened to him. I left for a moment to check in with you and order him some food. When I got back, he was gone. I had no idea what happened to him," Kasper said.

"He disappeared days ago. Why didn't you tell me sooner? Why keep this secret to yourself?" Pinkerton said.

Pinkerton polished a small, red button with his finger on a remote attached to the side of the right-hand armrest of the wheelchair.

Kasper shook his head, and said, "No. Please, don't. I didn't know. I thought he got frustrated and walked out. I didn't know. I didn't know!"

Pinkerton pressed the button. As he held down the button, Kasper burst into a series of random images, body parts of various creatures cycling by in an instant, never settling on one. His clothes were a flurry of fabrics of every color and texture. Kasper screamed and pleaded for him to stop.

"Why didn't you tell me, Kasper? Why? Sure, you told me it looked like it cut into a different world. Why did you leave the room? You could have stuck around to watch the man succeed at what I've been longing to do for so many years. You could have watched and learned how. Why weren't you there to track down those scissors? Why?" Pinkerton said, torturing Kasper in the only way he knew how.

"I don't know! Please! Stop it! Tellis, please, help me!"

Tellis Pripen sat nearby, helpless and emotionless. Pinkerton was a loose cannon. He knew not to be on the wrong side of that cannon when it was loaded.

Pinkerton released the button. Kasper, a jumble

of spare body parts and a patchwork of clothing, collapsed to the floor. It took time, but he eventually sorted himself out. He settled on the appearance of a boy in a mustard yellow school uniform. It was one of his more normal appearances.

"Okay. The pool boy's gone missing. The more important question is where are those scissors?" Pinkerton asked.

Pinkerton looked at Kasper, who shook his head and refused to look Pinkerton in the eye. Behind him, Tellis cleared his throat. Pinkerton spun his wheelchair around to face the media mogul.

"I can field that question as well," Tellis said.

Tellis snapped open the video remote and unfolded it into a full keyboard. Resting the keyboard on one hand, he typed at the keys with the fingers of his other hand. In seconds, the surveillance of Max's disappearance minimized to the bottom of the screen and a queue of videos appeared along the top edge.

One after another, Tellis showed the videos as he narrated, "I did some research and discovered a series of other thefts performed by the same, or similar, set of hands. There doesn't seem to be any connection to the kinds of objects this thing takes. Here is a baseball from a game in progress. Here's a block of cheese from a restaurant. And, so on.

"As you may or may not have noticed, each time this thing takes an item, it pulls the item into the ground. A slight mound remains, revealing the hand and stolen item's whereabouts. This mound then makes a b-line to what we can only assume is its lair or nest. Again, using the topographical information of each of the scenes, we can follow it home. As you can see from the satellite images, all roads lead to this rural area right here. We contacted the locals of this area and asked if they'd seen anything unusual. Locals are aware of the anomaly and refer to it as the 'Yabowak'," Tellis said.

Pinkerton clapped one hand of flesh against his other, artificial hand, and said, "Now, that is an answer."

Pinkerton swiveled around to face Kasper, who raised his head to watch the videos, but quickly cowered under Pinkerton's gaze.

"We have an idea of where this Yabowak might be. And, more importantly, I now know the possible whereabouts of those scissors. What are we waiting for?"

✂   ✂   ✂

Days turned into weeks, and weeks into months. Max's fear of being purged faded, and was replaced with a frustration of being stuck. Max was no closer to finding his creator than he was finding his way home. He asked the diner patrons if they had heard of Edwin Black, and no one had heard of him. Eventually, he gave up looking for him, but often wondered the whereabouts of his scissors. Did those strange bodiless hands still have them? Or, did someone else stumble upon them? Whoever had them, did they take good care of them? Did that person take over as the world's traveling pool salesman? Or, was that person hopping from one universe to another through poorly cut holes? He worried more about his scissors than whether anyone missed him or not.

Max dried the last dish and placed it on top of the stack. He pulled off the gloves and left them draped over the edge of the sink. Carefully hefting the stack, he carried the dishes to the front. Max set the dishes down behind the bar next to the refrigerated display case of cakes, pies, and other sweets. He poured himself a glass of water, and watched people as he drank.

The bell above the front door jingled as two boys tumbled in, arguing all the way to the bar where their mother sat.

"Mom! Jesse tore my costume! Now, I can't be in the play!" yelled one boy.

"It's not my fault! Mom told you not to wear it until we got to the school. It's his fault he tripped over it and tore it!"

"It is not!"

"Is too!"

Mom calmly set her fork down next to her plate, swallowed her food before chewing it properly, and said, "Bobby, I told you to be careful. And, I told both of you to settle down. What were you doing? Wrestling again?"

The boys looked sheepish.

"Never mind. How bad's the damage? See now? You tore the hem. I don't have time to mend it. You'll just have to go on as you are."

"But, Mom! I'll look like an idiot on stage!" Bobby said.

"That's 'cuz you are an idiot," Jesse said.

"I could help mend it," Max said, setting down his glass of water.

"We don't have much time. And, I'm afraid I don't have anything to mend it with," Mom said.

"We've keep a needle and thread here behind the counter to mend the table cloths," Max said.

"I hate to trouble you," Mom said.

"No trouble at all," Max said.

He pulled out a small spool of white thread, a needle and some utility scissors. He lead Bobby to one of the vacant tables and sat down.

"Now then, Bobby, was it?"

The boy nodded.

"Bobby, sit down and put your feet up on my leg so I can get at that hem," Max said.

Bobby looked at his mother, who shrugged and gave him a nod of encouragement. Bobby sat down, leaned back, and rested both of his dirty shoes on Max's pants.

Max surveyed the damage, while the rest of the diner watched Max. He pulled out a strand of thread from the spool and snipped it with the scissors. He threaded the needle on the first try and tied a small knot at one end. Max's fingers did a rapid ballet as they twiddled around the hem of Bobby's costume. It didn't look like he was doing much but wiggling his fingers, but in no time, the costume's hem was perfectly mended.

"Whoa! You fixed it!" Bobby said.

"What do you say?" Mom prompted.

"Thank you, mister," Bobby said, and gave Max a hug.

Max stood up, ruffled Bobby's hair, and said, "Now, listen to your mom, and have fun tonight."

"Great, now my hair is a mess," Bobby said, trying to straighten it again.

Bobby's mom slid off her bar stool and said, "Thank you so much."

She leaned up and gave Max a peck on the cheek. Max blushed. The diner clapped, causing Max to blush even more.

"Alright, alright," Max said, "This isn't dinner theater. Show's over."

Max returned the sewing supplies back underneath the counter.

"Excuse me, young man," said a voice as Max stood up again. An older woman smiled at Max from the other side of the counter.

"Yes? May I help you?" Max said.

"I hope so," the woman said, "My name is Nancy Hitchcock, and I'm with Roaming Thunder, a traveling theatre troupe. I'm the group's seamstress and costume designer. I couldn't help but notice how quickly you mended that boy's costume. I don't suppose you'd like to join us? These hands aren't as precise as they once were, and I could use the help."

Cheryl set down a pot of coffee and walked over to Max and Nancy.

"Are you thinking of leaving us, Max?" Cheryl

asked.

"I don't know. Do you travel a lot?" Max asked Nancy.

"All the time, and all over the place," Nancy said. "Travel's not a problem for you, is it?"

"No. I used to travel with my previous job. Then, I found myself working here for Cheryl and Gus," Max said.

"We probably can't pay you much more than you earn here," Nancy said.

Max brushed aside the comment and said, "It's not that. I'd love to get out and travel, again."

"No need for references. The work you did on that boy's costume is good enough for me."

"So, you are leaving us," Cheryl said.

"Hands that can work sewing magic shouldn't be washing dishes," Nancy said.

Cheryl nodded in agreement.

Max turned to Cheryl and said, "You and Gus have been more than kind to take me in. I appreciate all you've done."

"Well, I know Gus will hate to see you leave. He hates saying goodbye, especially to good help. We really appreciated all the work you put in. We might have to hire two of the local kids to make up for one of you."

Cheryl gave Max a hug.

"When do we leave?" Max asked.

"In the morning," Nancy said.

"Oh! And, I don't know if this is going to be a problem or not, but, um, I'm not exactly local, if you know what I mean. As for as working legally, they kind of pay me under the radar, so to say," Max said, dancing around the truth of him being an illegal alien, not only to this country, but to the world in general.

Nancy shook her head and smiled, "No worries. Roaming Thunder pays everyone in cash. Believe me. You're not the only one."

Max doubted anyone else with Roaming Thunder was an alien of this world. Of the country, maybe, but not of the world.

Max finished up his work for the rest of the day. At closing time, Gus came by to wish Max luck with his new job. He and Cheryl knew he was there for a reason and knew the opportunity was too good for Max to pass up. They paid Max out of the register, gave him two good home-cooked meals, dinner and breakfast, and drove him to the diner early the next morning.

A large bus with "Roaming Thunder" painted on the side was parked outside the diner. A small group of people waited with Nancy in the parking lot. Nancy introduced Max to the troupe, and they welcomed him with open arms and many hugs. With his few belongings in a new backpack, Max was off. He waved to Gus and Cheryl out of the troupe's bus window. Max might not have had his checkered scissors, but he was happy to be traveling once again.

CHAPTER FIVE

Music and Mayhem

Life got curiouser and curiouser for Ed as the episodes continued. Each episode started with the same routine: Music, book, sofa. Similar to the first episode, the next time Ed clearly stated in his sleep, "I smell dinosaurs." This sudden announcement scared Lydia, who nearly spilled lemonade on her laptop. Again, Ed awoke with another headache, but claimed it was only on the right side of his head. He wrote it off as a sinus headache.

The episode a couple days after did not give Ed a headache. Instead, he awoke with the odd sensation that his teeth were fizzing like a carbonated beverage. The rest of the day, Ed licked and prodded at his teeth with his tongue to make sure they were all accounted for.

The next episode happened with Ed completely awake. He and Lydia sat side by side on the sofa. Ed made notes in a spiral for his projects at work, while Lydia read her magazine.

Lydia jumped when he suddenly yelled, "Beans!"

He didn't just yell "Beans!" once. He yelled it over and over, each exactly eleven seconds apart from the last. His eyes were opened, and he continued writing between outbursts as if nothing happened.

"What are you doing?" she asked.

"What do — Beans! — you mean what am I doing? I'm making notes. What are you doing?"

"I was reading my ..."

"Beans!"

"I was reading my magazine, when you started yelling, 'Beans'."

"What?" Ed chuckled, "I — Beans! — yelled what?"

"I'm calling the doctor. You're scaring me," Lydia said and stood up.

"Beans!"

Ed could see Lydia was serious. She had no idea who to call, nor how she could even explain what Ed was doing. She picked up the phone to dial 911. When she turned off the stereo, Ed stopped.

"Who are you calling? I'm fine."

"You are not fine. You were yelling 'Beans'," she said, her voice cracking.

"I'm sorry. I don't mean to laugh. But, what do you want me to do about it?" he asked.

"Go see a doctor. Please. I don't know what you were doing. It was like you were having some kind of bizarre seizure or Turrets or something. You've been having a lot of headaches lately. What if it's a tumor? Aren't you concerned?" Lydia asked.

Ed could tell whatever happened clearly shook up Lydia to the point she was trembling with either fear or outrage. He held her and calmed her down.

"Shh. You're okay. I'm okay. Everything is fine. I'll go see a doctor. I will. I don't have a tumor. I don't know what frightened you, but I'll go. Okay?" he said.

She took a deep breath, smiled, and nodded.

✄   ✄   ✄

The trip to the doctor was uneventful. After both Ed and the doctor laughed about the Beans story, he checked all of Ed's vitals and ran several tests, including an MRI. They even brought in the resident neurologist. They found nothing wrong. Ed appeared to be perfectly healthy. He told Lydia this the next time he saw her.

"Sudden outbursts like that are not normal. If they can't help you, then go to a psychiatrist," Lydia demanded.

"Hold on. Even though he couldn't find anything wrong, the doctor did suggest a couple of things. One thing he suggested is that it might be stress related. The other thing is that it might be some kind of environmental factor triggering the episodes. He told me to make a note of what's going on when it happens: What I'm doing at the time, the time of day, what I've eaten, and so on. There may be a common factor. As for the headaches, I might try cutting back on caffeine and drink more water."

"That's it? Take notes and drink water?"

"The neurologist said the brain still holds a lot

of mysteries. She thinks it could be something like a combination of hypnosis and talking in my sleep."

"But this last time, you weren't asleep. You were wide awake and yelling, 'Beans!' every few seconds. How is that healthy? It's weird and crazy and I don't like it!"

"And, you think I do? You're telling me I'm having random outbursts I don't remember and can't control."

Ed took the episodes less seriously than Lydia. She was concerned, for Ed's health and her own safety. Since Ed hadn't said or done anything violent or offensive in his outbursts, he just wrote it off as a new quirk in his personality.

The episodes continued to happen. After taking copious notes, they discovered that it might have something to do with the stereo, specifically the CD changer. Ed thought this was ridiculous but couldn't deny the common factor was listening to music.

At a small party at Ed's apartment to celebrate the release of another fine product of Hammond Eggs, Ed had his first public episode. Other than Lydia and Ed, no one else had experienced one of Ed's episodes, until that night.

Ed mingled with his co-workers as the CD changed and played a shuffle of pop music through the ages. Suddenly, Ed began to speak only one word.

"I think it's great that you pickles pickles pickles," Ed said.

Beth, the co-worker he was talking to at the time, froze and said, "What was that last part?"

"Pickles pickles pickles. Pickles pickles, pickles pickles pickles," he said.

"Uh. Lydia? Burt? A little help, please?" Beth called over her shoulder. She held her gaze at Ed in case he did something dangerously unexpected.

"Pickles? Pickles pickles?" Ed said. He looked concerned, more for Beth than himself.

"And, hurry," she added.

Lydia and Burt joined Beth and Ed. Other people turned to see that Beth was okay. When they realized she was neither bleeding nor on fire, they returned to their conversation.

"What's up?" Burt asked.

"It's Ed. He's only saying, 'Pickles,'" Beth said.

"What?" Burt asked.

"Pickles?" Ed asked.

"Oh no," Lydia said.

Lydia made her way to the stereo.

"Pickles pickles pickles to worry about. Okay?" Ed said to Beth and Burt as Lydia turned off the stereo.

"No. Not okay. That was weird," Beth said. She finished her drink, collected her purse and her date, and made a hasty exit.

Lydia turned the radio on instead of the CD changer. During their experiments, it never seemed to trigger any sudden episodes.

The other guests watched Beth go, then went about their business. The party continued. After

93

much pressure from Burt, Ed caved and filled him in on his series of episodes.

"That is so messed up," Burt said.

"Tell me about it. And, the weird thing is that it didn't start happening until after I met Lydia and we got that new stereo," Ed said.

"What if it's not the stereo? What if it's Lydia?" Burt asked.

"No. I don't think so. We think it's something to do with the CD changer. I really do," Ed said.

"And, you don't remember anything afterwards?"

"Sometimes, but not always."

"What if these episodes happened before Lydia and you never realized it?" Burt asked.

"I thought about that, too. But, Lydia has been over here before, and neither of us can recall anything odd happening. I'm telling you, it's the CD changer. I stopped saying pickles when she stopped the music, didn't I?"

"That's true. That is so weird. I've never heard anything like it."

The party eventually wound down and the guests went home, including Lydia. She was too embarrassed by Ed's public outburst and was too tired to get into another argument so late in the evening.

✂   ✂   ✂

After the party, Ed and Burt tried some experiments. During one experiment, they noted the playlist of songs that triggered an episode, then replayed it elsewhere, like on the MP3 player at work. Simulating the same scenario produced different results. Ed was perfectly fine at the office, in the car, and at Burt's place. They queued the same list of songs in Ed's CD changer, had him repeat what he was doing, and still could not trigger an episode.

They exchanged the CD changer, too. The episodes continued with a new CD changer, both of the same make and model, and with another brand.

Since they couldn't reproduce the results reliably, Ed didn't know what to think or do about it. He shrugged it off despite Lydia's persistence about needing another professional opinion. If he wouldn't seek help, she encouraged him not to listen to the CD changer.

Ed continued to listen to his shuffle of music in private when Lydia was away. Like television sets, he discovered a sleep timer could be set to turn off his stereo after a given time. When he was alone, he set the timer before turning on his music. That way, if he did begin to have an episode, it would end a short while later. This seemed to work. Ed recalled having a few episodes, and realized they did end when the music suddenly cut off.

Ed made a point never to listen to the stereo when Lydia came over. They realized they could still listen to the radio or single CDs, but definitely not the CD changer. The lack of episodes made Lydia happy, and Ed was content to find a compromise that allowed him to continue listening to his music.

Or, one might say he was content until the day his episodes got worse. Up until this point, the episodes were limited to him uncontrollably saying random things aloud. Then, he began losing motor control, too.

It happened one evening as Ed washed the dishes. He only had a single set of dishes, and they were all dirty and in the sink waiting to be washed. As the music played in the background, and his hands were sudsy with dish soap, the episode started.

Ed half listened to the music as he washed the cups and glasses. As Elvis Costello sang the story of Veronica, Ed tried to remember the name of an oldies song about a woman waiting for her sailor husband. Something like Mandy, or was it Brandy? His thoughts took a tangent and began thinking of sea monsters and pirates. Then, the pirates in his imagination encountered the Sirens, and the episode consumed him.

In a gruff, pirate-like voice, Ed said, "That lady be golden!" then picked up a dinner plate and smashed it on the edge of the counter. He went through the whole set of eight dinner plates.

"That lady be golden!"

Smash!

"That lady be golden!"

Crash!

And, so on.

When he ran out of plates, a whirlpool captured the pirate ship. The pirate ship in his mind turned into an enormous rubber duck. Ed slowly turned in a circle where he stood, stepping on the broken bits of plates and quacked like a duck at the top of his lungs.

The timer ended. The music and the quacking stopped. The sink's faucet still ran, so he turned it off. He heard a knock on the door, which, at first, he mistook for his rapidly beating heart.

That was different, Ed thought.

He looked down at the pieces of broken plates. He heard the knock at the door, but wasn't sure if he wanted to open it. The episodes elevated to a new level of out-of-control-ness, and he felt flustered.

Whoever was at the door knocked again. He thought it didn't sound urgent, so he decided to see who was there. Ed crossed the apartment and opened the door. It was Penny, his friend and neighbor.

Her eyes were red and puffy, like she'd been crying.

"Penny. What's wrong?" Ed asked.

"Was that you quacking like a duck?" she asked.

"Oh. You heard that. I was goofing around," he said.

"May I come in?" she asked and sniffed.

"Of course. Come in. I've got this mess, but ... What's the matter?"

Penny came inside and sat down at the kitchen table. She saw the pile of broken plates on the floor. She sniffed, pointed at the mess, and asked, "What happened?"

"Nothing. I just broke some plates," Ed said, shrugging it off like it was nothing to break a whole set of plates while talking like a pirate and quacking like a duck. He had yet to tell Penny about his episodes and didn't want to try to explain it.

He asked her, "Were you crying?"

Penny chuckled and said, "Yeah, as if you can't tell. I'm a mess."

"I guess that makes two," Ed said. He grabbed the broom and dust pan to clean up the bits of broken plates in the kitchen.

"Mike broke up with me," Penny said. She frowned and began to cry again.

Ed stopped what he was doing, stepped over the mess, and walked over to give Penny a hug. She burst into heavy sobs the moment he held her. He comforted her like a mother consoling a hurt child. Penny tried to explain what happened between sobs, but Ed gently shushed her and told her everything would be okay.

When she settled down, she helped Ed clean up the broken plates. They dumped the pieces into the trash can. Afterwards, Ed fixed Penny a glass of ice water, and the two sat on the sofa.

Penny explained what happened between her and Mike. Ed had met Penny a few days after moving into the apartment. The two instantly hit it off like old friends. He and Penny would have made a good couple. But, as long as he'd known Penny, he knew she was dating Mike. Now that she was no longer with Mike, Ed was dating Lydia. And, Lydia was good for Ed. She kept him grounded and focused on his work. She also helped elevate his lifestyle. Penny, on the other hand, always seemed like a free spirit and a bit of a dreamer, like Ed. He thought Mike was good for Penny the way Lydia was good for him. Ed knew more about Penny than he knew about Mike. Mike seemed like decent guy. It came as a surprise to Ed, too, when Penny told him Mike found God, quit his job, and wanted to live a celibate life to continue his journey in his newfound religion.

"He what?" Ed said, "I'm always tickled when I hear about people finding God. Why do people assume he's missing, and then suddenly find him? It sounds like, 'Oh! Here He is! He fell into the sofa cushions with a bit of broken pencil and some spare change. Well, that's another mystery solved.'"

"Seriously," Penny said, smiling, "You know, each time I open my junk drawer, I keep a look out for Him in case He shows up all tangled in a rubber band. You know, you never can tell with rubber bands."

The two had a good laugh at all the places God could misplace Himself and then suddenly be discovered by some unsuspecting person. Places like behind the drier wearing one of the missing socks, or on a playground with kids playing hide-and-seek.

"You always know how to make me laugh," Penny said, "Now tell me the real story behind those broken plates."

The smile dropped from Ed's face. He didn't want to, but couldn't help it. It was Penny, his neighbor and buddy. He explained the episodes, starting from the nonsense phrases and working up to his recent uncontrollable plate smashing. He told her about the experiments with Burt. He told her he had no idea why the CD changer seems to trigger the episodes, and why he couldn't reproduce them elsewhere. He told her what the doctors said. He even confessed his covert, timed sessions that Lydia knew nothing about.

Penny said, "To me, it sounds like one of two things. Maybe even a bit of both. I know these may sound a little farfetched, so just bear with me. Part of it sounds like hypnosis. You know, like when people receive a triggered response. I don't know how your music could be giving you hypnotic suggestions, though. The other part sounds like possession, like a spirit enters your body and causes you to do things. I've never heard of someone being possessed by music. I agree, though. It's definitely unusual. What are you going to do now?"

"I don't know. I'm still a little shaken by the plate smashing. Do you have any suggestions?"

"I'll run your situation by my moms. They might be able to suggest something," Penny said.

Two mothers and no father raised Penny. One interesting thing about her moms, which was a common misconception, was that neither of her moms was lesbian. They were two females, best friends, who grew up together, enjoyed each other's company, and always wanted to share their lives together. Their relationship had nothing to do with finding each other sexually attractive. In fact, occasionally, they would date and bring guys home. Neither found any man as interesting as her best friend, so neither wanted to get married. One day, they decided to raise a child together as co-parents, and that's when they adopted Penny.

The other interesting thing about Penny's moms, is that they were practicing Wiccans, or, more commonly known, witches. Her moms joined a local coven and practiced witchcraft in the privacy of their own home. Penny didn't practice with them and rarely joined them at coven gatherings, and that was fine with her moms. The moms were very open about their religion. If anyone questioned or criticized their belief, they were more than willing to enlighten them and often suggested they were willing to attend a religious session of someone else's faith if they were willing to attend one of theirs.

"Thanks, Penny. It helps getting an outside perspective," Ed said.

"And, thank you for listening to me vent about Mike."

"What are friends for?"

Penny looked at her watch and said, "Almost five o'clock. I better get home and feed Oscar-Frank."

"Five o'clock?! Lydia is coming over tonight, and I need to go buy a new set of plates."

Penny stood up. Ed got up, too, and pulled on his shoes.

Penny walked up to him, gave him a big hug, and said, "Thank you. You're the best friend and neighbor anyone could ask for."

Ed hugged her back and asked her, "Are you okay?"

Penny nodded into his shoulder.

The door to the apartment opened and in walked Lydia.

"What's going on?" Lydia said.

Penny and Ed broke apart.

"Penny needed a sympathetic ear," Ed said.

"Mike and I broke up," Penny said.

"Hmm. I'm sorry," Lydia said. It was clear by her tone that she didn't really mean it. Lydia did nothing to hide her jealousy of Ed's friendship with Penny.

"Why are your shoes on? Where are you going?" Lydia asked Ed.

Penny snuck around behind Lydia, waved to Ed, and slipped out the door. Ed waved to Penny around Lydia, then answered her questions.

"I was going to the store. I broke the dinner plates. We need to buy new ones."

"You broke the dinner plates?"

"Yep."

"All of them?"

"Yep."

"I can't leave you alone for a moment, can I? Breaking all the plates. Caught embracing the girl next door. What's next?"

"Wild orgies and erotic poetry readings," Ed said.

Lydia didn't smile.

"I'm kidding," he said. "What are you doing here so early? I thought you couldn't come over until seven."

"The meeting was canceled, so I thought I'd surprise you. And, good thing I did. I caught you with your girlfriend."

Ed looked puzzled and said, "But, Penny's not my-."

"Are you sure?" Lydia asked, "You seem guilty about something."

Ed figured he probably did look guilty. He wasn't worried about him being caught hugging Penny. He was more concerned about what would have happened if Lydia had walked in on him breaking the plates in the kitchen. Or worse, if she found out he had been listening to the CD changer in her absence.

"I'm only guilty of breaking a stack of plates," he half-lied.

"Yeah, how did you manage to do that?"

"I'm a klutz with buttery fingers," he said wiggling his fingers at her.

He put his hands down and said, "Speaking of butter ... Where do you want to have dinner? While we're out, we'll buy more dishes."

They decided to go to an Italian restaurant a half mile away from a superstore where Ed could buy more dinner plates. Talking with Lydia about her day and hoping that Penny's moms could help sort out his episodes, Ed relaxed more and more as the evening progressed.

✂   ✂   ✂

Over the next couple of weeks, Ed didn't listen to any of his music. He listened to the radio or turned on the TV to a low volume if he wanted some other kind of background noise. It wasn't fair. He missed listening to his own music.

Eventually, he warmed up to the idea of trying another couple of experiments. He tried shortening the cutoff timer, but his body still lost control, though not as much as the Dinner Plate Incident. When he listened to single CDs he seemed fine. Even though he felt fine, he continued to use the cutoff timer, just in case. Because Lydia claimed that in the early days of the episodes, Ed said things he was unaware of saying, part of him wondered if he still had episodes when listening only to single CDs, too.

Ed wondered why the music only affected him. In the earlier days of the episodes, Lydia was present, too. Why didn't the music affect her the same way it affected him? Was it because it was his music? What would happen if the changer was filled with Lydia's CDs?

The thought of switching his CDs with Lydia's gave him another idea. What if he jumbled the CDs? One afternoon, he took all the CDs out, shuffled them, and put them back into the player in no particular order. He listened to the CDs on shuffle (still keeping the timer on), but in a few days, the episodes returned. When Lydia asked why the CDs were not in the same order, Ed lied about trying to find a particular CD to listen to in the car, and getting them all out of order when he put them back in. The lie was a bit farfetched, but Lydia didn't question him further.

✂   ✂   ✂

One Thursday, Lydia needed Ed's place for an important dinner party. When he asked why she couldn't have the dinner at her place, she said her dining table was too small.

It was true. Two people barely had enough room to eat comfortably. Plus, Ed's dining table was the one piece of hand-me-down furniture Lydia liked. Ed acquired it from Burt's aunt, who was moving across the country to a retirement home closer to Burt's parents. By itself, the square table was roomy enough to feed a family of four. With the leaves added, the table could seat eight people comfortably.

Since Lydia needed Ed's apartment, he took the day off to clean. The apartment complex was quiet during the day with most tenants away at work. Ed turned on the TV but was often suckered into watching whatever was on. He turned on the radio but couldn't pick up any of the local stations he liked. He chanced the CD changer. He set himself a playlist of five CDs of good, mindless cleaning-the-house music, and started doing the list of chores

Lydia left for him. He figured with a set playlist of five non-shuffled CDs, he didn't need the cutoff timer. So, he didn't set it.

He dusted and vacuumed without a single episode. He pushed the coffee table against the shelves to make room for the dining table, which would need to be moved farther into the living room when he added the leaves. As he pushed the coffee table, the edge nudged the stereo and switched on the all disc shuffle.

Ed left the apartment and returned with the basket of clean laundry from the apartment laundry room. He set the basket on the floor, propped his back against the edge of the sofa, and began to fold laundry. With only six garments left to fold, another episode took control of Ed.

They say a butterfly flapping its wings in Central Park can cause a thunderstorm in China. For Edwin Black, a tiny scratch on his Iron Butterfly CD apparently caused him to uncontrollably perform the chicken dance.

As if the song In-A-Gadda-Da-Vida wasn't long enough, running at seventeen minutes and two seconds, Ed felt compelled to stop folding laundry, leap up, and chicken dance after about forty-seven seconds into the song. Roughly a minute more, the song skipped and repeated the chorus over and over and over again. Fifty-eight minutes later, nearly three and half times the length of the song, Ed continued to chicken dance.

Sweat dripped from Ed's hair into his eyes. It

stung his glazed-over eyes with each drip, but Ed was too busy flapping and clapping to wipe the sweat from his face. His arms ached from flapping. His hands cramped and blistered from mimicking chicken beaks and clapping. Searing pain throbbed in Ed's calves at the extreme aerobic workout with no stretching ahead of time. Ed smacked his lips while his tongue craved a sip from the cup of water resting a mere six feet away on the kitchen counter. Despite the pain and exhaustion, Ed continued to chicken dance.

When it came to the parts in which he would skip around in a circle, first one way, then the other, Ed paid no attention to his feet, which knocked over and trampled the piles of what once were neatly folded shirts and pants. Ed was oblivious to everything else. The only thing that mattered to him were iron butterflies and dancing chickens. He never heard the phone ring a half an hour before an enraged Lydia stood and stared from the door of the apartment.

"Ed!" Lydia yelled over the music, "What are you doing?!"

Ed did not respond. He only chicken danced.

Lydia stormed into the apartment, over to the kitchen, slammed the grocery bags on the counter, picked up the remote, and powered off the stereo. The moment the music stopped, Ed crumpled to the floor.

Ed caught up with reality faster than his breath, and said, "Whew! What a workout!"

"What in the holy Hell was that?" Lydia demanded, her arms akimbo.

Ed gasped for more air and said, "If I'm not mistaken, that was about an hour long chicken dance."

"Which explains why you didn't answer the phone," Lydia muttered to herself.

She looked around the room. The clean and folded laundry became kicked-around-the-room-and-splattered-with-droplets-of-sweat laundry. She blinked her eyes as she stammered to find the words. Her hands clenched and flexed to control the anger swelling inside.

She exploded with, "You chicken danced for an hour?! We have guests arriving in less than an hour and a half, and you still haven't folded the laundry. Or, the dishes."

"The dishes need folding?" Ed said.

Lydia froze Ed's childish grin off his face.

"Oh, come on. It was a joke," he said.

"Do you see me laughing?"

Ed thought about giving Lydia a hug, but changed his mind when he realized how sweat drenched he was. Lydia muttered to herself and put the groceries away. Ed crawled around the floor, collecting the laundry into the basket. With a grunt and a groan, Ed stood up with the laundry basket and hobbled over to the kitchen.

Ed looked at Lydia, but she was too mad to look at him. He said, "Look. I'm sorry. I don't know what came over me."

"No. Don't start," Lydia said, slamming down a loaf of French bread on the counter.

"Start what?"

Lydia glared at Ed, and said, "If you're going to blame this on one of your little ... episodes, I'll ... I'll ..."

Ed waited patiently for the response.

Lydia drew a deep breath and changed gears. She said, "No. I'm the one who's sorry. I'm nervous about tonight. This is a big deal for me. I appreciate you letting me entertain my co-workers at your place."

Ed kissed Lydia on the cheek and said, "No worries, love. Let me set this basket down in the bedroom, and I'll finish cleaning up in here while you prepare dinner. Once this is all cleaned up, I'll clean myself up. Everything will be fine before they get here."

As promised, everything was ready before the first guest arrived. The living room was spotless. They moved the dining table into position. The dishes, except the ones containing the evening's meal, were cleaned and put away without as much as a chip or a nick. The laundry waited patiently in the bedroom to be re-cleaned and folded another day.

✂   ✂   ✂

Stuart was the first guest to arrive. Ed met Stuart once before at Lydia's company picnic. He and Lydia shared an office. Like Lydia, they both were successful members of the sales team. Ed knew he and Lydia had been working hard on this proposal together, putting in several extra hours. Ed hoped all their extra effort would pay off.

Next, Helen and Mel arrived, who were Lydia's boss and her husband. Mel's head was completely bald, not from hair loss, but by choice. Lydia speculated that it was not Mel's choice, but Helen's fetish for bald men. In private, Ed referred to the couple as Helen and Melon, and fought the urge to greet them as such as they entered the apartment.

Kyle and his date were the last guests to arrive. Kyle was another member of Lydia's team of co-workers. He was young and cocky: a real loose cannon. Kyle had a way with words, but unfortunately, he often used inappropriate words at inopportune times. As Ed understood it, Lydia included Kyle because of his incredible sales numbers. Kyle's numbers didn't lie, and Helen and her superiors looked at the numbers critically.

For some reason, Kyle brought Penny as his date.

"Penny? This is a surprise," Ed said. Penny walked in behind Kyle and gave Ed a half hug.

Lydia walked up and whispered into Ed's ear, "What is she doing here?"

Ed shrugged. Penny, standing only a few feet away and who heard the question, leaned towards Lydia and whispered, "I'm here to keep Kyle in check. I've known him since college, and know how he can be. I also know how important this dinner is for you, Lydia. I wouldn't want Kyle to blow it for you."

Ed could tell a rapid debate battled within Lydia's mind. Finally, she said to Ed, "Fine. She can stay."

Everything was fine through dinner. Lydia proposed her idea to Helen, while Stuart supported her by filling in the finer details. When necessary, Kyle quoted the numbers and statistics to back up Lydia and Stuart. And, Penny tamed Kyle like a professional to keep him from making the presentation more colorful than necessary. Ed and Melon sat idly by, absorbing the conversation, but neither participating nor interrupting.

Dessert, on the other hand, was a disaster. The desserts, strawberry shortcake parfaits, were delicious and a huge success. The conversation wasn't too bad, either. The soft music playing in the background triggered the disaster.

Lydia set the CD changer to play the soft, soothing tones of what Ed referred to as the "light mix."

"What are you doing?" Ed whispered to Lydia.

"What could go wrong with a shuffle of new age, jazz, and classical music? No words. No subliminal messages. Besides, I'll keep the kill switch next to me if there is any funny business," Lydia said, taking the stereo's remote with her back to her place at the table.

Lydia kept an eye on Ed, but soon got pulled into a conversation with Helen. The music seeped into Ed's mind and took hold. Ed zoned out. His eyes stared at nothing. All he could think about was the sweet, smooth tones playing in the background. Lydia glanced at Ed and mistook his vacant look for loving admiration.

Stuart, who sat on Ed's left, asked him, "What projects are you working on these days?"

Ed never heard the question. A tranquil hint of a smile rested on his lips. His fork hovered above his dessert. He must have registered at some level that Stuart addressed him. He turned his head, eyes as glazed as donuts, not quite focusing on Stuart.

"What? What are you staring at? Do I have whipped cream on my face?" Stuart asked and dabbed at his face with his napkin.

No one paid much attention to this strange exchange between Stuart and Ed, especially Lydia, who should have been watching him more closely. She and everyone else were so engaged in their own conversations they almost missed what happened next.

Ed stood up slightly and leaned into Stuart. Stuart wiped his mouth with his napkin when Ed stuck out his tongue and licked across Stuart's forehead.

Stuart shoved Ed away from him and shouted, "Dude! What the Hell?!"

Ed fell backwards over his chair and into Mel, who choked on a spoonful of parfait. Ed got stuck between his chair and Mel's. The music stopped and everyone stared at him.

"What's everyone staring at?" Ed asked.

"Oh, Edwin. How could you?" Lydia growled, with remote in hand.

"Why did you lick me?" Stuart asked, his face a mix of rage, confusion, and disgust.

"Sorry, Melon," Ed said to Mel, then winced as he realized what he just said.

Ed unwedged himself from between the chairs. Helen walked around the table to tend to her husband, who sipped water between coughing fits.

Ed asked, "I licked Stuart?"

He looked around the room for an answer. Lydia, tense and with clenched fists, tried to calm Stuart down and convince him to stay. Helen rubbed Mel's back, while Mel retold his version of what he saw happen. Kyle scraped the bottom of his parfait glass, licked his spoon, and looked around the table wondering who was not going to finish their dessert. Penny looked at Ed and nodded. She tilted her head to suggest he might want to step outside. As if reading her thoughts, Ed took it as a good idea. He stood up, walked across the room, and left his apartment. No one, but Penny, watched him go, but everyone knew he left.

Ed felt horrible. He knew how important this deal was to Lydia, and now, one of his little episodes might have blown the whole deal. He deserved the fight to come later that night. Lydia did not deserve to miss a career-advancing opportunity because of him. He wanted to blame her for turning on the stereo, but knew everyone else would blame him.

Ed slouched on the curb outside the apartment

and watched cars and people come and go. Once again, he contemplated why he had these bizarre episodes. His doctor found nothing physically wrong with him. He wondered if another signal broadcast through his CD changer, layered in the shuffling music. Was there an extra layer to the music in the disc changer? Why only affect him and not anyone else? Why couldn't it happen to Kyle or Stuart?

"I think you were possessed by the ghost in the Machine," said a voice behind him.

Ed turned around. Penny walked up and sat down beside Ed.

"I don't have any proof, but I think your stereo is haunted," she said.

Ed snorted a laugh.

"Let me ask you something. When the episodes happen, does it only happen when the shuffle is on?"

Ed nodded.

"When the changer is shuffling all the music, does it tend to gravitate towards certain types of music? Like more country than rock? Or, more slow songs than fast? Or, more quiet songs than loud?"

Ed hadn't considered this. He tried thinking back through his various episodes, especially the bigger ones. His collection of music was eclectic, and now that he thought about it, it did seem like the shuffle gravitated towards one genre or artist over others. Even tonight with Lydia's pick of the light mix, he did recall more of the slower, dreamier songs. It seemed too weighted to be completely random.

"Maybe you're right. Maybe my stereo is haunted," he said.

"You might want to consider having someone to exorcise your apartment," she said.

"Why? Do you think it's getting too fat?" Ed asked with a smile. Penny punched him playfully on the shoulder.

"Do you know someone who can cast out the demons? Can your moms do it?" Ed asked.

Penny asked, "What about me?"

"You?" Ed asked. He was unaware his neighbor was an ordained minister trained to exorcise demons out of dwellings.

"I can't really do an exorcism, but I do have a divining board."

"A diving board without a pool?"

"No, wise guy. A *divining* board. Like a Ouija board, but homemade. I learned a bit from my moms. They can help, too. We can perform a seance to see what kind of spirit we're dealing with."

"I don't know. Not until this thing with Lydia blows over. I hope I didn't botch things up for her," Ed said.

"No worries. What happens, happens. Right?" Penny said, and gave Ed a one-armed hug.

Lydia cleared her throat from behind Ed and Penny. Penny took her arm off Ed. Lydia stood in the doorway, showing the guests out. Ed could tell she was annoyed with him; he didn't want to drag Penny into the oncoming storm, too. Ed stood up and walked back to his apartment.

Still embarrassed by his behavior, he hung his head, mumbled "goodnight" to the guests, and busied himself with clearing the table and washing the dishes. Ed was up to his elbows in suds when the last guest left. Lydia walked to the kitchen, her arms folded.

Here it comes, Ed thought. He stopped washing dishes, turned off the water, and carefully set down the partially soapy plate.

Lydia did not yell. In fact, she spoke with a very level voice, "I want you to know, I am still very, *very* mad at you."

"As you should be," Ed said.

"Do not interrupt me," Lydia said. Ed shut his mouth and listened.

"Even though I am very mad at you," she continued, "you should also know about my proposal. Helen said she was on the fence. She thought my idea was intriguing, but costly. After seeing the way you acted tonight ..."

Oh no, Ed thought. He winced.

"... Helen accepted the proposal. She figures I could tolerate a bit of time away from you and your 'shenanigans,' as she put it."

"That's great! I'm so happy for you. I was worried I screwed it up for you," Ed said.

"Yeah, well, I think we all did. Except for Kyle, who just wanted seconds."

Ed turned the water on and continued to wash dishes.

"I'm not staying here tonight," she said.

Ed nodded, and said, "I understand."

Lydia gathered a few of her things and slipped into her shoes. Ed watched her from the kitchen.

"Goodnight, Ed," she said at the front door.

"Goodnight," he called. The closing door interrupted him telling her, "I love you."

CHAPTER SIX

Exit, Stage Left

Michael Pinkerton rolled through the gallery of Pinkerton Mansion among the exhibits of his collection. He paused by each exhibit and recalled the moment he claimed each prize for his collection.

The first exhibit was a large, blue, police box he found abandoned and partially vine-covered in the ruins of an old castle. He hauled it back to the mansion, and spent months cracking open the lock and figuring out the controls. When he took it for a spin, it took him to various places in time and space, but not where he wanted to go.

The next exhibit hung on the wall behind the tall, blue box. A tattered, blue and black map of sorts framed behind glass. A small band of little thieves sold him the map, which exposed various portals that opened in the fabric of the universe. None of the portals took him to where he wanted to go either.

Pinkerton rolled over to the next exhibit and touched the polished wood with his hand of flesh. He claimed the wardrobe from an estate sale of an old professor who passed on and had no other family. The wardrobe led to a small pocket of a fairytale land of mystical creatures and medieval warriors. It was definitely not where he wanted to go.

The next exhibit was a toy car and tollbooth he found in a secondhand store. The toy car was almost big enough for two child-sized passengers and barely big enough for Pinkerton himself. He didn't care about the car. He wanted the tollbooth. Having his own vehicle of sorts, Pinkerton had deposited the coins that accompanied the tollbooth and transported himself to another pocket land filled with grammatical and mathematical puns. He found this place more annoying than the last.

Pinkerton stopped when he reached the next exhibit, a large mirror positioned over a fireplace mantle. The mirror was another portal to another pocket fairytale land of insane creatures and talking game pieces. He rolled away from his collection. Looking at his collection only irritated and disgusted him even more.

His collection of odd portals and conveyances frustrated him because of all the time, money, and energy he wasted on collecting each item. Each took him to fantastical places, but not one of them took him to where he really wanted to go. Each took him to other places within the universe of the same creator. He despised his creator. Since he was nightmared into existence, he hated his creator and wanted nothing to do with him or his world. He had been looking for a way out for a long, long time. As much as his collection frustrated him, he still had hope. He placed his last bit of hope in the pool man's scissors. If the pool man could leave the world, then so could he.

He hated his creator for making him half man, half machine, and all monster. He never wanted to be a monster, but that's how he appeared in the dream. The dream defined him. In one of Ed's dreams, he was a wheelchair-bound, menacing man who chased Ed with various mechanical attachments to his one artificial arm. Because of this nightmare, he was born as some kind of monster.

After he arrived in the world of his creator, he wondered why he was chasing Edwin Black in the first place. Was it to scare Ed? Because he scared Ed, others in the world also knew to be scared of him. No matter how he tried to reach out to other people in the world, he intimidated them and frightened them. Because the people didn't want to be around him, he became more and more of a recluse and hid away in his mansion.

Michael Pinkerton had no friends to speak of until Kasper, his shape-changing, holographic assistant. Kasper wasn't a friend. He couldn't stand Kasper and his changing appearances, but tolerated him because Kasper wanted to help him. Being a hologram, Kasper wasn't afraid of much, including Michael Pinkerton. They tolerated each other and appreciated each other's presence.

Tellis Pripen, the world's media mogul, was Pinkerton's next closest thing to a friend. Pinkerton could tell that he intimidated Tellis, too. Tellis did his best to set his fears and intimidation aside for business. Tellis Pripen was a businessman who appreciated Pinkerton's brilliance. Without Pinkerton, Tellis Communications would never have become the expansive media empire it had become.

Pinkerton wanted more than two acquaintances. If he must exist, he wanted to live out his existence in a world where nobody knew he was the monster his creator deemed him to be. He wanted a fresh slate — a new beginning.

"Excuse me, sir," Kasper said, poking his head through the wall of the room. Kasper's head was well groomed and had the right colors, size, and shape of a normal human head.

"Enter," Pinkerton said.

The rest of Kasper stepped out of the wall and normalcy exited through the window. The rest of Kasper appeared in a camouflaged clown-suit with grass growing on his large, floppy (and squeaky) clown shoes.

"I found them," Kasper said.

A smile spread across Pinkerton's face, pushing his dark thoughts aside. He said, "Great. Where are they?"

"In an old farmhouse buried under the floorboards. The Yabowak wasn't there. At least, I don't know if it was or not. It didn't show itself."

"Do you think the scissors are safe?"

"Safe enough. The locals don't go into the old farmhouse. They all think it's haunted," Kasper said.

"Before anyone else finds those scissors, let's go catch a ghost and claim its treasure."

"How are you going to capture that thing?" Kasper said.

Pinkerton patted the device attached to the side of his chair, and Kasper winced.

"Oh, that's how," Kasper said, and shied away from looking at Pinkerton in case he got the urge to press the button.

Pinkerton knew Kasper was all too familiar with the device. While Kasper was away on reconnoissance locating the checkered scissors, Pinkerton made a few modifications to the device.

"I'm not going to push the button. You've done your job. Come. Lead the way to those scissors," Pinkerton said with a smile. He couldn't help smiling. He knew throughout his flesh and mechanical body he was close to leaving this time. Without a doubt, he knew the scissors would take him to where he wanted to go.

✂ ✂ ✂

"Annabelle, stop fidgeting," Max said.

"Sorry. I've got the butterflies, Max," she said, shuffling her feet.

"There's nothing to be nervous about. You're going to be great tonight. I promise," he said, stitching together the cuff of her costume's pants.

"You think so?"

"I know so. Now, hold still."

Her legs shook as she stood on the stool before Max. She flapped her arms to try to ventilate the armpits of her pig costume. She didn't want it to get too sweaty before opening night, but her fidgeting wasn't helping.

"Are you almost done?" she asked for the eighth time.

"Nearly there," Max said, checking the length one more time.

The rest of the cast crowded the dressing room. Everyone had his or her own little pre-show ritual. Some paced around or teamed up to practice lines. Others fought over the mirrors to primp and prepare themselves. One of the cast sat back and listened to music through earphones to clear her mind.

"What if I drop a line?"

"You? Drop a line? Never. I think you have the whole script memorized. During rehearsals, you've been reminding other people of their lines, too. It's not going to happen. There," Max said. He stood back to get the full view of Annabelle's pig costume. He nodded and said, "Finished. What do you think?"

Annabelle carefully stepped off the stool with Max's assistance. She walked over to the mirror to see herself in her pig costume. For years she travelled with the troupe as Linda Jefferson's understudy, until Linda was arrested for serial shoplifting. Tonight, Annabelle would take the place of the star role as Priscilla Pigg in Roaming Thunder's production of *Swine Women and Song*, a farm-themed, musical, love story.

"I've never looked in the mirror before and

123

been so pleased to see such a pretty piggy. Thank you, Max," she said, and stretched up to kiss him on the cheek.

Angie, another cast member, pinched Max on his other cheek (not the one on his face). She said, "We've never looked better, Max."

"Yes, Angie, even with you dressed as a pig, I agree. You never have looked better," said Nancy. The rest of the cast laughed and pointed at Angie, who stuck her tongue out at them.

Without Nancy, the crew wouldn't be costumed at all. She designed all the costumes. Max stepped in to lend her a hand on getting them all done in time. With his help, they both had time to add that extra bit of zing to bring more life to each character's appearance. Nancy knew Angie really understood who was the master designer. She also knew Angie had an eye on Max the moment he stepped onto the Roaming Thunder bus.

Angie cornered Max and whispered, "You've worked your magic before the show. How about you let me work some of my own after the show?"

Max side-stepped Angie, pretended to look over everyone's costumes, even though they were all perfect, and told Angie, "Gee. I don't doubt your prestidigitationary skills, but I already have plans this evening. Thanks. Maybe smother time."

"Did you say 'some other', or 'smother'?" Angie asked.

"Yes," Max said, and slipped out of the dressing area and quickly walked to the venue's front lobby.

With a sigh of relief, Max snagged a cup from the concession stand and filled it at the water fountain. Minutes later, Nancy joined him, rolling her eyes and laughing about Angie throwing herself at Max.

The two sat in a couple of high backed chairs and relaxed. For now, their work was done. That is, until some of the outfits needed mending post-show.

"You're looking good," Nancy said.

"Please, don't you start," Max said.

"I only meant you look much happier traveling with us than you did at that diner," Nancy said.

"Oh. Thanks. It is good to be traveling again," Max said, settling into a faraway sigh.

"Going somewhere?" Nancy asked him, pulling him back to the here and now.

"Just thinking about home," he said.

"You don't talk about home much. Where are you from?"

Max shrugged, and said, "Doesn't matter. It's not like I'll ever be going back there, anyway."

"Of course it matters. Home is what defines us," Nancy said.

"You can say that again," Max said.

"What was your home like growing up? Tell me about your mom and dad. Do you have any siblings? What were you like as a kid? Give me something," Nancy said.

Max remained quiet. How could he tell her about his home? How do you tell someone you have no parents? How could he explain that he was dreamt into being, that one moment he wasn't, the next moment he was? How would Nancy react to knowing he was born more out of an idea than by natural childbirth?

"I'd rather not talk about it," Max said.

Nancy frowned. Her eyes begged Max to open up.

"I'll tell you this, though. When you go outside at night and look up into the sky, what do you see?" he asked.

"The moon. A few of the brighter stars. Venus. Sometimes Mars," she said.

"Where I'm from, it's like you can see the whole universe. There are so many stars and planets in the sky. They seem so close, you feel like you could almost touch them."

Max looked at Nancy, who looked like she was trying to imagine a night sky like that.

"And, the people there ... There is so much life and diversity. It's just ... I don't know how to describe it. You think Roaming Thunder is a wacky bunch of people. No harm meant, but they're nothing, *nothing*, compared to the people there."

"You miss them?" Nancy asked.

"I miss it all," Max said.

"Then, why don't you go back there?" Nancy said. Max could tell she was both frustrated and confused. He guessed she was thinking his home was someplace a person could just hop on a plane and fly there.

"It's not that simple. I once thought that if I could find Edwin Black, he could figure out how to get me home. But, I don't know where to begin looking for him."

"Edwin Black? Who is he?"

Max couldn't tell Nancy that Edwin was his creator. He still wondered, even if he found Ed, could he get Max home again? Did Ed even have the ability to do so?

Max looked up at the clock on the wall, then stood up.

"Show's about to start. Let's go grab some seats," he said, and stretched out his hand. Nancy took his hand, and he helped her up. The two went arm-in-arm into the theatre and took seats towards the back of the house.

CHAPTER SEVEN

Ghost in the Machine

Over the next couple of weeks, Lydia's job kept her at work many evenings. Lydia said it was necessary to finish preparations in time for the consumer expo in Las Vegas.

With Lydia away most evenings, Ed fell back into his single life ways of zoning out in front of the TV or playing video games late into the night. One evening, Ed stretched out across the sofa and read *Life, the Universe, and Everything*. He considered listening to music, but ever since he licked Stuart's forehead like an envelope, he wasn't inclined to do something else stupid under the influence.

Ed's eyes drooped shut and the book he read fell from his hands and onto the floor with a soft thud. His thoughts drifted away from the book and towards dreams of Invasion of the Body Snatchers - The Musical! He dreamed that arms and hands reached out of the stereo and grabbed at him to pull him in.

The phone rang and startled him awake. Ed reached down for his book, picked it up, and then placed it on the coffee table. He shuffled over to the phone. He cleared his throat before answering it.

"Hello?" he croaked.

"Did I wake you up?" Lydia asked.

"I was reading and fell asleep on the sofa."

"Sorry to wake you. Should I let you go?"

"No, you're fine. You saved me from a bad dream, anyway."

"Oh?"

"I don't remember what happened," he lied. He didn't want to concern her with his dream. "So, what's up?"

"My preparations are all done. Everything is ready for Vegas. I'm very excited."

"That's great! I know you've been working hard. I've hardly seen you the last few weeks. Are you coming over?"

"I can't."

"Really?"

"I just wanted to call to let you know I leave Friday afternoon."

"So early? But, the expo doesn't start until Tuesday. And, you'll have all day Monday to set things up."

"I know. But, I have some things I want to do in Vegas before dealing with work. Sight seeing and stuff."

"That's cool," Ed said, "Oh! Hey! I have something to ask you."

"What's that?" Lydia asked.

"Okay. I know you don't really hit it off with

Penny ..."

Ed heard Lydia sigh, but he ignored it and continued, "She mentioned the other day about having a seance to see if the apartment is haunted. Her mothers agreed to help her and are going to be in town. I was wondering if they could come by tomorrow night. Would that be alright?"

"Tomorrow night? Thursday?" she asked, and sighed again.

"Yes? Are you okay with that?" Ed asked, and added, "I'd like you to be there, too."

"That's the night before I leave. I'll need to pack."

"Well, you just said you don't leave until Friday afternoon. You could pack in the morning. If you want, I'll take the day off and help you. Besides, it'll only be a couple hours."

"Promise?"

"Of course."

Lydia paused, and said, "Okay. She can have her little seance. But, I'm bringing Stuart, too, for moral support."

"Sure, he'd probably get a kick out of it," Ed said.

"Rather a kick, than a lick," she said.

Ed smiled at her little joke.

"Listen. I gotta go," Lydia said.

"Ok, have a good evening. See you tomorrow."

"See you tomorrow."

"And, Lydia?"

"Yes?"

"Thank you."

"No problem," she said and hung up the phone.

✂   ✂   ✂

Thursday afternoon, Ed left work early to help Penny and her mothers, Chloe and Zelda, set up for that evening's seance. Ed helped Zelda move his kitchen table into the living room. Chloe spread a black table cloth over the table. Penny and Ed set the chairs around the table, while the moms set candles close to the corners of the table. Each candle sat upon a small dish with a high lip to catch any dripping wax.

Ed asked, "Why does the table need to be moved into the living room?"

Chloe explained, "Penny tells us music from your stereo might be what is triggering you. We're setting up in here to be closer to the source. We're going to need the stereo on, so hopefully, you will connect tonight."

Zelda added, "But, no music. Just static. We'll need to tune the radio to a non-station."

Chloe continued, "Yes. No music. We don't want you, or anyone else, to be fully triggered. Just connected."

After they completed the preparations, Ed followed Penny and her moms to Penny's apartment for a pre-seance dinner. Zelda prepared vegetarian sandwiches of cream cheese on wheat bread with bean sprouts, raisins, walnuts, shaved carrots, and cucumber slices. Ed, being more of a carnivorous omnivore, found the sandwiches surprisingly

131

delicious.

Oscar-Frank, Penny's dachshund, begged Ed for part of his sandwich. Like Penny, Ed refused to feed him table scraps. Chloe and Zelda were more sharing, and offered Oscar-Frank some of the left over carrot shavings. To show his thanks, Oscar-Frank brought the moms his tattered stuffed-animal octopus.

"Not now," Penny said, and put the octopus away in the closet so everyone could finish eating in peace.

Ed felt nervous about the seance. He looked it, too. Usually, his episodes happened without him thinking much about it. Tonight, he felt as if he were performing. Knowing there would be an audience and not knowing what he might do, Ed did not know what might happen. He wasn't worried about doing anything dangerous, to either himself or to others. There would be enough people present to stop him from doing anything too harmful. After his last episode of nearly ruining Lydia's dinner, he worried more about embarrassing himself ... Again.

On the other hand, if this seance could stop him from having these outbursts, he was all for it. He had tried doctors. He had tried his experiments. At least Ed could definitely link it to music. But, why music from his stereo in his apartment? Why nowhere else? Ed had a hard time believing it really could be a ghost haunting his apartment. Then again, he had no idea who else lived, or possibly died, in his apartment before him.

Chloe and Zelda put Ed at ease. He felt as comfortable around them as he did around Penny. Ed helped Penny carry plates to the kitchen after dinner, and then joined the moms in the living room. Penny sat nearest the window to keep an eye out for Lydia and Stuart.

"How long have you been performing seances?" Ed asked.

Chloe looked at Zelda, and asked, "How long has it been?"

Zelda squinted and guessed, "Seventeen, maybe eighteen years?"

"They've been 'practicing magic' longer than that," Penny said, emphasizing her words with air-quotes.

Zelda looked at Ed and said, "Penny doesn't believe in our magic."

Chloe added, "She thinks magic is like what you see on TV."

"I do not. But, it's not what you two do," Penny said.

"What is it you do?" Ed asked, "Besides seances."

"We tell people's fortunes," Zelda said.

"Which is just psychiatry and story telling," Penny corrected.

Chloe rolled her eyes, and said, "We make potions."

"Otherwise known as herbology and fancy cooking," Penny added.

"And, cast the occasional spell," Zelda finished.

133

"Poetry and showmanship," Penny concluded.

Zelda said, "And, now that Penny's given away all our secrets, you can see you have nothing to fear tonight but a little razzle-dazzle."

"I told you she thinks magic is like stuff on TV," Chloe said.

"Mom, hush. I do not," Penny said.

"You don't believe in magic?" Ed asked.

"It's not that. I know there's some magic in the world. But, a lot of what they do is based on some form of science."

"Science, perception, and a willingness to accept the unusual. That's real magic," Zelda said.

"I think real magic has a bit of mystery to it. Like how Oscar-Frank got his octopus," Penny said.

Everyone looked down at Penny's dachshund who was chewing and pulling on one of the octopus's legs. When he saw everyone staring at him, he smiled broadly with his tongue hanging out as if immensely proud of his accomplishment.

"Didn't you put that in the closet during dinner?" Zelda asked.

"I thought I did. Maybe I didn't close the door tight enough," Penny said.

As Penny stood up to check the closet door, she glanced out the window and saw Lydia and Stuart pull into the parking lot. Penny let her moms and Ed know they should go and greet Lydia and Stuart at Ed's apartment. When Lydia saw Ed with Penny and her moms leaving Penny's apartment, she did nothing to conceal her look of disapproval, but kept her comments to herself. They all followed Ed into his apartment with Stuart trailing behind.

"Have you eaten?" Chloe asked Lydia and Stuart. "We have more fixings if you'd like us to make you a sandwich."

"No thanks. We grabbed a quick bite on the way here," Lydia said.

Ed, Lydia, and Stuart stood around the black-clothed dining table in Ed's living room, while Penny and her moms made last minute adjustments. Even though the moms walked Ed through what to expect earlier, he looked just as lost as Lydia and Stuart as to what they should be doing.

"If you'll take your places around the table," Zelda said. "Ed, sit at that end closest to the stereo. Chloe and I will sit on either side of you. Lydia, you sit there with Stuart sitting across from you. And, Penny, you take the other end of the table."

Everyone except Zelda took their seats as instructed. Zelda turned on the stereo, followed by the CD changer.

"Um," Lydia said, and shook her head.

"It's cool. She knows what she's doing," Ed said.

Lydia looked skeptical, but settled back into her chair. Zelda shuffled the music but turned the receiver to the radio tuner. With a little adjustment, she found static between stations. She turned the volume way down so only a hint of white noise could be heard in the background.

As Zelda took her place at the table, she and

Chloe lit the two candles at Ed's end of the table and muttered a sort of quiet prayer. Chloe motioned to Penny, who lit the other two candles as they did. Penny, too, silently spoke the prayer.

"This is the divining board," Zelda said, indicating the handcrafted divining board centered on the tabletop. It was a large, square board made of polished wood with the alphabet, numerals, and other symbols inscribed strategically around the surface.

"And, this is the planchette," Chloe said, holding up a smaller object made of the same kind of wood. The planchette looked like a wooden heart with a smaller heart-shaped hole punched through it towards the pointed end.

"Did you make this one?" Ed asked Zelda and Chloe.

"No, my Aunt Sue made this," Chloe said.

"It's beautiful," Lydia said, admiring the details on the board.

"Thank you. I'll pass along your compliment to her," Chloe said.

Zelda cleared her throat quietly to get everyone's attention and said, "This is how it will work. Chloe and I will each hold both of Ed's hands and place our free hand on the planchette. Lydia and Stuart will do the same with both of Penny's hands. We should all stay connected and form something that looks like an infinity sign through the divining board via the planchette. It's okay if you need to scratch your nose should the need arise. Please return holding hands or the planchette as soon as you can to keep the connection the strongest."

Chloe added, "From what we were told, Ed is affected by the CD changer. We've turned it on to appease the spirit we believe is trapped inside his stereo. We set the radio to static. It seems the selection of music plays a key role in the spirit's ability to control him. Hopefully, this will connect the spirit to Ed, but not control him."

Zelda nodded, and said, "We ask that Chloe and I do most of the talking. When you are ready, please join hands."

Chloe and Zelda were ready to take both of Ed's hands, which he had resting palm side up on the table. Stuart scratched his chin and left ear before taking Penny's hand, while Lydia took another moment to trace the designs on the divining board with her finger.

Once they all held each other's hands and the planchette, Zelda and Chloe said in unison, "We open the board to communication. Let our hands be your mouth so that you may speak. Let our eyes be our ears so that we may listen. Join us now so that we may talk."

Slowly at first, then gaining a little speed, the planchette moved lazily around the board in no particular fashion, but did not stop at any of the letters.

"Cool. Are you doing this?" Stuart asked quietly to Lydia.

Lydia giggled and said, "No."

Penny smiled and gave Lydia and Stuart a gentle squeeze. She nodded toward Zelda, who gave the two a stern look and shook her head. Lydia stifled her giggles, and the two focussed on the planchette, still lazily meandering around the board.

"We invite the one who lives among Ed's music to talk with us. Are you there?" Chloe asked.

The planchette drifted around the board and eventually settled on "Yes". Then, after a few seconds, it went back to wandering aimlessly.

"What is your name?" Chloe asked.

The planchette spelled out, "G-L-I-C-K"

"Glick?" Ed asked. Everyone shrugged.

"Why do you live among Ed's music?" Zelda asked.

The planchette spelled out, "L-O-S-T".

"You are lost?"

"Yes," it said.

"Can we help you find your way home?"

"Yes," it said.

"What can we do to help?"

It spelled, "W-A-N-T-Y-O-U-R-B-O-D-Y."

At this response, Ed momentarily blacked out, but had a flash of other people's emotions rush through him. He felt Penny long for someone Ed could not sense, possibly her ex-boyfriend, Mike. Lydia expressed jealousy mixed with desire. Stuart gave off a wave of primal lust. He felt a stronger sense from Chloe and Zelda, who each expressed concern and curiosity that the other might want something more than a platonic relationship. The strongest feeling originated from an unknown source and felt as if it wanted to wear Ed like a puppet. As quick as this happened, it faded again and Ed was once again aware of everyone at the table. No one at the table appeared phased by what happened, and it didn't seem to happen to anyone else.

As if to clarify, Chloe asked, "Whose body?"

It spelled, "E-D-W-I-N."

"Well, duh," Lydia said under her breath.

"Yes," it agreed.

"Is there any other way we can help you get home?" Zelda asked.

"No," it said.

"How do you know?"

"L-O-G-I-C," it said.

Ed saw Chloe and Zelda give each other a quizzical look.

"Why do you look puzzled?" Ed asked.

"Ghosts are like shadows of emotions, not based on logic," Chloe said.

"Right. They exist out of remnants of fear, anger, sadness, even nostalgia. But, not logic," Zelda said.

"I've never heard of a logical ghost," Chloe said.

"No," it said.

Chloe and Zelda looked at the planchette, then back at each other.

"Are we wrong about ghosts?" Chloe asked.

"No," it said.

"Then, why did you say, 'No'?" Zelda asked.

"N-O-T-A-G-H-O-S-T," it said.

"Not a ghost? Then, what are you?" Zelda asked.

"L-O-S-T," it repeated.

Stuart, cleared his throat and asked, "May I ask a question?"

"Yes," it said.

Chloe and Zelda looked at the answer, shrugged, and nodded.

"If you're lost, then I assume you're trying to find your way home. Right?"

"Yes."

"Is Ed your home?"

"No."

"Then, why take over Ed's body?"

"V-E-H-I-C-L-E."

"Where is home?" Lydia asked.

"J-A-I-U."

"Jaiu? I've never heard of it," Penny said, and looked to her moms, who shrugged and shook their heads.

"Where is Jaiu?" Penny asked.

For several moments, the planchette wandered around the board.

"Are you still there?" Chloe asked.

"Yes," it said, "T-H-I-N-K-I-N-G."

It wandered a bit more, then spelled, "O-T-H-E-R-S-I-D-E."

"The other side? Like, crossing over to the other side."

It shot directly to the "Yes".

"How is using my body as a vehicle going to
140

take you to the other side?" Ed asked.

"S-T-E-P-1."

"Taking my body is the first step?" Ed asked.

"Yes."

"What's the next step?" he asked.

"C-A-L-L-F-O-R-H-E-L-P."

Stuart snorted, and muttered, "Doesn't sound like much of a plan."

"Think about it," Zelda said, "Right now it's a bodiless entity. Its functions are limited but could be enhanced with the extras that a body has, like hands, feet, or a mouth."

"Yes," it said.

"I don't mind helping you find your way home, but do you need to take complete control of me? Can't you just hop in and I'll take you where you need to go? Like taking a taxi?"

The planchette wandered.

"That was a lot of questions," Zelda said.

"Why take the bus when you can jack a car," Stuart said.

"Yes," it said.

"Gee. Thanks," Ed said. "Only, it's not your car it's jacking."

To the restless spirit, Ed said, "I will try to find a way to get you back to this Jaiu place, if you try not to completely take over my body. Do we have a deal?"

The planchette wandered.

"I guess it's thinking," Chloe said.

"No," it finally said.

"No? We don't have a deal? Fine. Then, I'll never listen to shuffled music. I'll go back to listening to single CDs or go back to listening to my old CD player. No music, no body," Ed said.

"No," it said.

"Oh yeah? What are you going to do about it?" Ed said.

"F-I-N-D-A-W-A-Y."

Ed didn't doubt it probably could find a way. It found a way to take over his mind. It found a way to control his body. Could it find a way without the use of music or the stereo?

"This conversation is over," Ed said and pulled his hands away from Penny's moms.

He turned around, turned off the stereo, then turned back to the table.

"What now?" Penny asked wiping Stuart-sweat from her hand.

Ed shrugged, and said, "Life goes on."

"That was ... interesting," Stuart said, then to Lydia he said, "Ready?"

"Yep," she said, and stood up.

"Not going to stick around?" Ed asked.

"No. Big day tomorrow. Stuart said he'd take me back to my car. No reason for you to get out," Lydia said.

"What time should I come by?" Ed asked.

Lydia looked confused and asked, "What?"

"Tomorrow? I offered to help you pack? Remember?"

Lydia shook her head and said, "Oh. Right.

Why don't you come by around 10, 10:30?"

Chloe and Zelda used their snuffer to put out the candles and set them on the kitchen counter. Penny moved the divining board, then folded up the table cloth. Ed followed Lydia and Stuart to the door. He gave Lydia a kiss on the cheek.

Ed said, "Thanks, Stu, for driving Lydia. I know this wasn't your typical evening. I appreciate your support."

"No sweat, sport. Thanks for not licking me. Tonight was … different. Don't let anyone snatch your body," Stuart said, then crushed Ed's hand in a handshake more firm than necessary.

"Bye," Lydia said.

"See you tomorrow," Ed said. He watched Lydia and Stuart walk back to his car.

Penny and her moms returned the table back to the dining area.

Chloe put a motherly arm around Ed, and asked, "What are you thinking?"

"I'm thinking about having some ice cream. Do you want some?"

"I meant about the seance. And, yes, I'd love some."

Ed walked to the kitchen and fixed four coffee cups of ice cream. He and Penny sat on the kitchen chairs while Chloe and Zelda sat on the sofa.

"You still haven't answered my question," Chloe said.

"I don't know. This kind of stuff is new to me. I try to keep an open mind, but I'm not sure what to think. I would be skeptical, but with the episodes, I've had firsthand experience with weirdness. So, I'm apt to believe anything these days."

"I don't think you're dealing with your typical spirit. Logic? That's not right," Zelda said.

Chloe licked her spoon, and said, "Jaiu? That's something else I've never heard of. We need to ask around."

"I guess for now, until I decide to move from this place, I'll listen to one CD at a time. Plus, I'll continue to use the timer."

"Just be careful," Chloe said. Penny and Zelda nodded in agreement.

They changed the subject and talked of other things for another hour or so before calling it a night.

✂   ✂   ✂

The next day, Ed went to Lydia's place a little after ten in the morning. By the time he arrived, she only had a few things left to pack. Lydia went over her checklist and double and triple checked that she had packed everything.

Ed helped load the luggage into his car and drove Lydia to the airport.

Along the way, Ed said, "That was nice of Stuart to come over."

"What?" Lydia asked.

Ed thought her mind was elsewhere. He said, "I was wondering if Stuart would poke fun at the whole thing, but he was cool. I'm glad he took it so well."

"Oh. Mm hm," Lydia said, and looked out the

window.

"We should have him over some time, but in a more normal social setting. What do you think?"

"Sure," she said, sounding preoccupied.

"You okay?" he asked.

"Fine," she said, and patted his leg. "A lot on my mind."

"I'm sure you'll do great in Vegas," Ed said, and flashed a quick smile at her before moving his eyes back to the road.

At the terminal roundabout, Ed helped unload her luggage and gave her a hug. When he tried to give her a goodbye kiss, she turned her head so that he kissed her cheek.

"Good luck!" he called.

She gave him a thumbs up as she walked across the sidewalk to the terminal doors. The automatic doors swooshed to let her through, then swooshed shut again behind her.

With Lydia safely dropped off at the airport, Ed drove to work with his head full of thoughts of the seance.

CHAPTER EIGHT

Worst. Week. Ever.

Ed's weekend was uneventful. With Lydia not just gone, but out of town, the apartment seemed extra quiet. With too much quiet, Ed felt tempted to listen to music. He occupied himself with activities that took him out of his apartment, like going to the movies, the store, a walk around the park, and so on. No music equaled no episodes.

Monday was also uneventful compared to the other days of the week yet to happen. This Monday might have been interesting to someone else, but not for Edwin Black, who spent most of the day at work. It turned out to be one of those slow lazy days at work in which not much happened, but he still felt somewhat accomplished by the end of the day. To be an uneventful day is saying something for Mondays, which usually get a bad rap. On Tuesday, things took a left turn into the unexpected.

Tuesday morning, Ed strolled into Hammond Eggs around nine in the morning, as usual.

"Hey, Ed!" a voice called from the office next door.

Ed poked his head into the office and said, "Morning, Burt. What's up?"

Burt held out a tin box of hard candies. The candies were symmetrical, flower-like shapes, lightly dusted with powdered sugar. Burt said, "Do you want any more of these?"

"Any more? I couldn't finish the one piece you gave me yesterday. I still can't get the taste of orange and licorice out of my mouth. Sorry, but I had to throw it away. No offense," Ed said.

"None taken. I had a piece which was, I think, the flavor equivalent of body odor. That was enough for me. I guess I'll toss the rest of these," Burt said. He gave the candy a shameful look and wished for a box of chocolate instead. "I don't know what Aunt Lynn was thinking. You know I got this box of candy because she thought it was my birthday? My birthday is still four months away. What was she thinking?"

"Happy be-earlied birthday?" Ed said.

"I guess," Burt said. He closed the lid to the box of candy like a casket, then tossed it into the garbage pail where it landed with a solid "thunk!"

"Are you sure you don't want to keep the box? At least the tin is nice," Ed said.

Burt shook his head in a way that suggested if he kept the tin, the candy might come back to haunt him.

"What are you working on today?" Burt asked.

"I don't know. I'll look at my notes and figure something out," Ed said, "What about you?"

147

"Ashley's project is nearing completion, and I still need to find her the right kind of suction cups."

Ed nodded and said, "Can't help you there."

Ed adjusted his backpack and said, "Listen. My shoulder's about to fall off. I'm gonna go set my stuff down."

"Hey, Ed. Before you go, do you mind doing something for me today? Sarah and Matt are still arguing over hours. Do you think you could sort things out?"

"Aw, Burt," Ed said.

"I've tried, Ed. You know how stubborn Sarah can be. Please?"

"Okay. Sure. But, you owe me a lunch."

"No problem. Your choice ... within reason."

Ed walked to his office next door and dropped his backpack onto his desk chair. He walked down the hall to the vending machine to get a diet soda. Taking the long way back, he overheard Sarah and Matt arguing in Sarah's cube.

"Sarah, I just asked for a few pictures, not a whole art gallery," Matt said.

"If you don't appreciate my work ethic, you should have asked someone else to help you," Sarah said.

"You know your artistic style fits this project best. But, you've been pulling some unnecessary late nights. Plus, you gave me way more pictures than I asked for. I'm not taking that much extra time out of my cut."

"There's Ed. We'll ask him what he thinks,"

148

Sarah said.

Ed cringed.

This was not the first time Sarah consumed more hours of another coworker's project than she should or needed. Sarah, being the workaholic-perfectionist, often put in more effort than what was originally requested. Someone could ask her to make a clay ashtray, and she would return with a Michelangelo.

"Ed wishes you two could work this out on your own," Ed said. He wanted to keep walking back to his office but remembered his promise to Burt.

"Tell me what's wrong," Ed said, "Matt first."

Sarah, acting like a child, folded her arms and pouted.

"I asked Sarah for a dozen pictures for the educational software I'm working on. I gave her the details in the spec. She gave me forty seven. That's way more than I asked, and I'm not going to allow her to charge that many hours."

"Did you get what you needed?" Ed asked.

"Yes," Matt and Sarah said together, then glared at each other.

"Jinx", Ed wanted to say, but instead, held up a hand to indicate Sarah should be patient.

"Yes," Matt repeated.

"Could you use any of the additional pictures?" Ed asked.

Matt did a quick mental calculation and said, "Maybe a few."

Ed turned to Sarah, and asked, "Forty seven pictures? Really, Sarah? That's a little excessive, don't you think?"

"I gave him what he asked for," she said.

"That's not what I asked, and that's not how many Matt asked for," Ed said, "Do you think giving Matt nearly four times what he asked is excessive?"

"Just because I put a little extra effort into what he asked for, I don't think I should be ...," Sarah started to say before Ed held a hand up to stop her.

"Let me ask you another question. How long did it take you to work on all the pictures?"

"I only asked for eighty hours," she said.

"Tell you what ... Matt, give her two hours per picture," Ed said.

Calculating the numbers in his head, Matt said, "That's ninety four hours! I'm not giving her that!"

Sarah gloated.

"You didn't let me finish," Ed said, "Give her two hours per picture, but only for the pictures you decide to use for your project."

Sarah's jaw dropped, and said, "That's not fair!"

"It's fair for what he asked for and for what he'll use," Ed said.

Matt beamed and said, "Thanks, Ed."

Matt returned to his cube. Sarah glared at Ed as he walked out of the cube farm and down the hall.

Ed passed by Burt's office. Burt was on the phone, but waved him in and gestured for him to take a seat.

"That's right. If you could email a quote by this

afternoon, I'd appreciate it. Right. I understand. Okay. Thanks. Bye," Burt said, and hung up the phone.

Ed slouched in the chair across the desk from Burt.

"Ugh. Suction cups. Who would have thought it would be this difficult?" Burt said.

Ed shrugged.

"How are things going with Matt and Sarah?"

"Oh, you know. The usual."

"Sarah's eating habit, again?"

"You guessed it. I told Matt to charge two hours per picture, but only for the ones he needs. He seemed content. She wasn't."

"I'll talk to her about that later," Burt said,

"I better finally get some work done," Ed said, and stood up.

As Ed walked to the door, Burt asked, "Before you go, is Lydia off to Vegas yet?"

Ed turned back around, and said, "Yeah. She got there late Friday. She called me when she got in."

"Is she having any fun, or is it all work?"

"I guess she's having fun. I haven't heard from her since. I figure she's probably busy with the trade show."

Ed left Burt to track down the suction cups. He returned to his office and shut the door. He moved his backpack from his chair to the floor and sat down. He slid his laptop computer out of his backpack, set it on his desk, and turned it on.

As he waited for the laptop to boot up, he

thought about Lydia. It was quiet without Lydia, but he knew she was busy. Even if she wasn't there to work the trade show, Las Vegas is one place where time melts away. Ed felt guilty they spent her last night in town holding a seance at his place. He should have postponed it and taken her out to dinner instead.

When the computer fully awoke, Ed pulled up his To Do list and officially started his work day.

Ed tried to work, but his mind drifted to thoughts of whatever haunted his stereo. He browsed the web looking for articles regarding possessions and hauntings. Anything that sounded remotely like his episodes were all works of fiction. He couldn't find any solid proof this kind of thing really existed. Then, he looked for a priest who could really exorcise his apartment or some kind of ghost hunter to remove it. Most asked for incredibly high prices, or had charlatan written all over their websites.

Someone knocked at the office door. Burt opened the door a crack, poked his head inside, and asked, "Ready for lunch?"

Ed looked at the time on his laptop. It read twenty 'til noon.

"Already? Wow. Lost track of time," Ed said.

"Speaking of lost ... Have you seen the tin of candies?" Burt asked.

"No. Why?"

"They've gone missing. I thought about saving the tin, but tossing the candies. When I looked in the trash, it was gone. I wouldn't be surprised, but I hope it didn't walk off by itself. The only person in my office this morning besides you was Sarah. I asked her to stop by to talk about her excessive charging. I didn't see her take them. I've had a couple of meetings this morning. Someone might have taken them while I was out. Weird."

"No kidding. Who'd want to steal those things? Again, no offense to your aunt, but those things were nasty."

"Let's talk about something more appetizing. Lunch?"

They walked out to the parking lot. Burt filled in Ed about the conversation he had with Sarah and the details of the two meetings. Something distracted Ed from their conversation. He tapped Burt's arm and pointed.

Two large moving vans were parked across the parking lot. Workers hauled office furniture out of Inkwell-Framington's section of the building. Inkwell-Framington owned the building and sublet a portion to Hammond Eggs.

"Wonder what that's about," Ed said.

"Don't know. Switching out furniture, maybe? I'll pay them a visit later and see," Burt said.

Ed and Burt left for lunch. Burt drove and paid for lunch at a soup and sandwich place a few blocks away. Like all their social lunches, once the food was ordered, all work-related topics were off limits until they returned to work.

When they did get back, Ed walked with Burt

next door to Inkwell-Framington. They followed a mover into the lobby. No one sat at the receptionist's desk, because the lobby had no desk for the receptionist. They peeked into the cube farms and saw workers dismantling the cube walls.

"Oh, this is not good," Burt said.

"Nope," Ed said.

"Looks like I need to make some calls," Burt said.

"Yep," Ed agreed.

The two headed back to the Egg. Ed hardly saw Burt until the end of the day. Burt spent the afternoon in his office, making phone call after phone call. The only time Ed saw Burt was when he asked Ed to attend a meeting for him.

By the end of the day, Ed felt like he hadn't accomplished much at all. He poked his head into Burt's office and said, "I'm taking off. Any news?"

"Not yet. I can't get ahold of anyone at Inkwell-Framington. I've left messages at the other locations, and no one's returned my calls. I'm even trying to track down the number to the landlord. Hopefully, no news is good news ... For us anyway."

"There's always tomorrow," Ed said.

Ed left for the day. He looked forward to going home. It had been a day when he didn't want to think about anything. He wanted to lie on the sofa, turn on the TV, and turn into a couch potato.

When Ed arrived at the apartment complex, a package sat on the doormat. He hated when delivery services did that. What if someone came by and walked off with his package? Seems like it would have been easier to leave it at the front office. Then again, the apartment office always had crazy hours. No telling when he would get his package.

The package was a padded envelope. The only name and address on the envelope was his own. There was no return address anywhere on the envelope. The only indication of who sent the package was the postage meter stamp that indicated it was sent from Las Vegas. From Lydia? He wondered why she had sent him a package. What could be so important it couldn't wait another few days until she got home? Ed was eager to see what she sent.

Ed brought the envelope into the apartment. He tossed it onto the kitchen table and dropped his backpack onto one of the chairs. After checking the answering machine for messages, which there were none, he sat down to open the unexpected package.

He tore open the envelope and dumped the contents onto the table. A disc in a sleeve tumbled onto the table. The sleeve had "A DVD for Edwin" printed on it with a black Sharpie marker. Nothing else. The envelope contained no letter of explanation, only the lonely disc.

Ed popped the disc into the DVD player. He turned on the TV and switched it to the DVD input. He walked back to the envelope on the table and peeked inside for anything else that might have got stuck inside. Nothing. Not even a stray Post-It note with words of love from his love. This DVD from

Lydia intrigued him. It seemed like a very un-Lydia thing for his otherwise very practical girlfriend to do.

Seconds later, a video started starring his lovely Lydia.

"Hi Ed," she said. He saw her only a few days ago, but he realized how much he already missed her voice.

She sat on the edge of the bed in what was presumably her hotel room. Behind her, lights of the other Vegas hotels blinked and flashed through the partially drawn curtains. She was casually dressed in a t-shirt and jeans. Lydia's attire was plain, but Ed still thought she looked beautiful.

"If you are watching this, it means the package arrived okay. Hopefully, this doesn't fall into the wrong hands and end up on YouTube.

"The conference is going well. Originally, I planned on returning in a few days, but I decided to stay a while longer for reasons I'll explain in a moment," she said. She drew a deep breath and continued, "I needed this trip, Ed. I needed a break. From work. From life. From you."

At this point, a tear trickled down her cheek and her voice cracked, "I can't do this anymore, Ed. I can't put up with your antics anymore. I'm tired of your little episodes. At least I never had to deal with any in public. Do you have any idea how embarrassed I am by them? It's not the life I want. But, I know what I do want."

Lydia motioned at someone off camera to come

156

sit beside her on the hotel bed. That someone was Stuart.

"You're dumping me for Stuart?!" Ed yelled at his TV. He didn't know what to expect, but this was not it. He didn't know how to react. He managed a half laugh, half snort. He was too shocked to look away from his own train wreck of a relationship.

"I don't need to do introductions. I know you know Stuart."

"Wassup, Ed?" Stuart said, and waved at the camera.

Lydia continued, "I know we've been together now for over a year. But, Stuart and I have been seeing each other for the last three or four months."

Three or four months? Ed thought. *I'm such a chump. Why didn't I see this coming?*

"And, that's not all," Lydia said, then looked lovingly into Stuart's eyes. She gazed at Stuart, the way she gazed at Ed once upon a time when they first dated. To see her give that same look to someone else made Ed feel like his heart dropped into his stomach, got tied in knots, then beaten thoroughly in his stomach's back alley.

"That's not all?!" Ed asked aloud. "What else, you cheating cow?!"

As if in response, Lydia held up her left hand to show the sparkling, diamond ring. "Stuart and I got married here in Vegas on Saturday evening."

Lydia and Stuart, the happily married couple, kissed in front of the camera. Whether or not she had anything more to say, like she was pregnant with

Stu's baby, or really from the planet Fbleeping Beeyotch, Ed didn't care. He cursed very loudly at his DVD player to eject the disc. Once the player finally spit out the disc, he took it to the kitchen where he smashed it over and over with the kitchen's meat mallet, yelling, "Die! Die! Die!"

When Ed finished pounding the disc into hundreds of sharp shards and damaging the countertop with numerous dents, he still heard pounding. The pounding confused him. Was the DVD like the tell-tale heart continuing to beat long after it died a brutal murder? Was his racing heart about to burst out of his chest? No. Someone knocked on the door.

Ed stormed over to the door, tore it open, and barked, "What?"

Penny looked shocked and a bit frightened at Ed with the mallet still clutched in his white-knuckled fist.

"Uh, Ed? Is everything okay?" she asked.

"No. Why?" he barked, again.

"I heard a lot of loud obscenities and pounding. I wondered if you were okay, or if you were having another spell."

Ed drew a deep breath and forced himself to relax. "Sorry, Penny. Do you want to come in?"

"I don't know. Is it safe?" she asked, peeping around Ed.

"Yes. Yes, it's safe. I just ... UGH! I just received some bad news," Ed said, standing aside for Penny to pass.

"What bad news?" she asked, and took a seat on Ed's sofa.

She looked at the TV, which displayed an all blue screen, and asked, "Don't tell me the television is talking to you now."

Ed found telling someone what happened so difficult that he broke into tears. He sniffed and sobbed, but managed to say, "Lydia broke up with me."

"Oh no. Oh, Ed. I'm so sorry," Penny said. "Do you need a hug?"

"No. I'll be alright," he said, and sniffed back his runny nose as he reached for a tissue.

"When did this happen? I thought she was in Vegas. What happened? Did she call? Or, was it something on the news?"

"Yes, she's still is in Vegas. And, no, not a phone call and not the news. She broke up by video."

"She wha–?"

"By video. She sent me a break up DVD."

"A what? Who breaks up with someone that way?

"That's not the worst part," Ed said, and managed a slight chuckle.

"What could be worse than a long distance break up by video?" Penny asked.

"She married Stu."

"Get! Out!"

"No, you get out. This is my apartment."

"She married Stu?!"

"On Saturday."

Penny sat in stunned silence. Her mouth hung open, and she shook her head side to side in disbelief as if the craziness would fall out one ear to make room for something more sane. Finally, she said, "No wonder you were cursing. But, what was all the pounding?"

"Oh. Meat mallet meets DVD. Film at eleven," Ed said.

He found it comforting to tell someone what happened. Even though it had been several months, it seemed like only days before when he had comforted Penny when she and Mike broke up. Lydia expressed her dislike at Ed comforting Penny, but he and Penny had known each other for a few years prior to Ed meeting Lydia. What was she to do? Ed and Penny were long time neighbors in the same apartment complex. It wasn't as if they could avoid each other. Now, none of that mattered. Ed was glad she stopped by.

Penny stood up to view the remains of the DVD. With eyes wide, she said, "Wow. Part of me wished I could have seen the video. You know, it's one of those things you almost have to see to believe."

"Believe me," Ed said, "It's also one of those things I wish I could un-see."

"Are you going to be okay?" she asked.

"Yeah, Pen. I'll be alright," he said.

"I was coming home when I heard you. Thought something was up. I need to go feed Oscar-Frank and let him out, but I can come back later if you need me," Penny said walking to the door.

"That's alright. Thanks for dropping by," Ed said, and showed her to the door. Ed considered visiting with Penny, but changed his mind. He only wanted to decompress.

"If you need anything, you know where to find me," she said.

Ed nodded and shut the door behind her. He always had appreciated Penny's kindness.

The rest of Tuesday was not nearly as exciting. Ed fixed and ate a small dinner, moped in front of the TV, and fell asleep on the sofa before ten o'clock.

✂   ✂   ✂

The next morning, Ed took his time getting to work. Instead of his usual nine o'clockish, he pulled into the parking lot around 10:30. The lot was full, which forced him to park towards the far side.

In the building, he crept past Burt's office, shuffled into his own office, and shut the door behind him.

Seconds later, moments after dropping into his desk chair, he heard a gentle knock on his office door.

Ed sighed and called out, "Come!"

Burt opened the door, poked his head in, and said, "What's the matter, bud? Why so late?"

Ed sadly shook his head, sighed again, then said, "Lydia dumped me last night."

Puzzled, Burt said, "I thought she's still in Vegas."

"She is," Ed said.

"She broke up with you over the phone?"

"Nope. Via DVD."

"Seriously?"

Ed nodded.

"Ouch. That's cold, man. You're better off without her. I'm sorry. I'd treat you to lunch, but I'm meeting with the landlord today."

Ed perked up a bit, and asked, "Really? Any news?"

Burt shook his head, and said, "No. I caught him at a bad time. He was in a rush and couldn't go into the details, but agreed to meet me for an early lunch. I'll let you know how it all pans out."

Burt excused himself and left Ed's office, closing the door behind him. Ed pulled out his laptop, booted it up, and dove into his work. Focusing on a project or two helped keep his mind occupied. He channeled his anger towards Lydia into his work. His cell phone rang and interrupted his furious streak of work.

On the phone, Burt said, "I'm on my way back. Send out a message that there'll be an all hands meeting at two o'clock."

Before Ed could ask him anything, Burt cut him off and hung up the phone. Ed sensed tension in Burt's voice. Whatever the news, it didn't sound like it was going to be good. He and the rest of the company would find out in less than an hour.

Ed sent out an email to everyone at the Egg about the all hands meeting. His stomach grumbled. He had forty-five minutes before the meeting, which was just enough time to grab a quick bite.

Ed stood up checked his pockets for the usual suspects: wallet, cell phone, and keys. He hurried out the door and across the parking lot. When he saw his car, his customized purple car, he stopped cold; someone had vandalized it.

He found the missing hard candies from Burt's aunt. They spelled out words across the hood of his car that read, "I ran over the candy man." Not only that, whoever did it added more hard candies to make a mangled, stick-figure man, with Xs for eyes, across the windshield. Whoever stuck the candies to his car either sucked on them first or soaked them in water, because each hard candy glistened with moistened stickiness.

Ed swore under his breath. He didn't have time to clean off his windshield and grab lunch. He stormed back into the building, grabbed a quick lunch of potato chips, cupcakes, and a soda from the vending machines, stormed into his office, and slammed the door.

Livid about the vandalism of his custom car, Ed tried to write another company-wide email expressing how precisely upset he was while still sounding somewhat professional. Before he could send anything, Burt popped into his office and asked, "Have you seen your car?"

Ed just glared at Burt, who responded, "I take that as a yes. I'll say something at the meeting."

"Thanks," Ed said, and deleted his strongly worded email.

Ed worked a little more on his project and at his junk food lunch while Burt sat in his office preparing what he was going to say. A few minutes before two, they got up and headed for the Living Room.

The Living Room was the official name of the lounge located in the center of the Egg's portion of the building. The lounge was a large, open area with two sets of twin three-seater sofas facing each other. Coffee tables separated each set of facing sofas. The Living Room was where they held their all-hands meetings as it was the only area, besides the parking lot, large enough to hold all the employees. Besides meetings, they could entertain guests or have small company socials in this comfortable lounge area. On some occasions, members of the Egg cleared their heads by taking quick catnaps on one of the sofas.

Sarah exited the restroom as Burt and Ed passed. Her face looked pale and nauseous. Ed stopped while Burt went on ahead.

"Are you okay? You look like you're going to be sick," Ed said.

"I just had something that disagreed with me. I'll be fine," she said.

Ed walked with her to the Living Room. By the time they got there, almost everyone was there. With sixty to seventy people standing in the Living Room, it was pretty crowded. People socialized and wondered what the meeting was about.

Sarah sat down in a chair at the back. Ed leaned against the wall next to her.

Towards the middle of the room, Burt carefully

stepped up onto the coffee table.

"I hope my mom's not here to see me do this," he said.

Everyone chuckled.

"Can everyone hear me okay?" Burt asked.

Everyone nodded.

"I see a few people who might be out today, or may be still at lunch. I'll send out an email after this is over, but if you could give them a call, just in case, I'd appreciate it.

"I have some unfortunate news to share with you today, that I, myself, just found out over lunch. This came as a big surprise to me, as I'm sure it will surprise you, too. As you may know, the Egg sublet this portion of the building from a company called Inkwell-Framington. Inkwell was evicted from the building yesterday for not paying their rent. What you may not know is that the Egg pays our portion of rent to Inkwell, who should have paid Guardian Park, the owners of this group of office buildings. Guardian Park was unaware Inkwell had been subletting our portion. The movers also didn't know this, or else they would have been hauling our furniture out yesterday as well. So ... what does this mean for the Egg? Unfortunately, it means we need to leave the premises."

The Egg employees grumbled and muttered, and some raised their hands. Burt quieted down the group and continued.

"We do not need to be out of here today. I've had lunch with Bob Lincoln of Guardian Park, and he's agreed to give us a few days without the need to pay extra rent. We've already paid Inkwell. I have the sublet contract and the check stub for our rent to prove it. I agreed to support Guardian Park's fight against Inkwell. Bob is giving us until the end of this weekend to vacate the building. He and I will do a walkthrough for our portion.

"I will have moving boxes and packing material by tomorrow morning for you to use to clean out your cubes and offices. I will also handle packing up inventory and finding temporary storage. I'm sorry this will mean a slight delay to many of your projects. If it's any help, I'll print out the latest contact list and have those also available tomorrow morning. I know this news is a major pain in the backside. This affects all of us. Any questions?"

"Can't we rent this building?" someone asked.

"I did inquire how much it would cost, or if we could continue to rent this portion of the building. The current rates are much higher than we were paying Inkwell. Instead of taking out a larger cut for the Egg, I'm on the lookout for another location. I'm sure everyone would agree with that decision. Anyone else?"

"What do we do in the meantime?"

"We telecommute. It might be a little awkward to coordinate some things. We won't have the liberty of dropping by someone's desk, at least, not for a while. But, we'll manage. The Egg is full of brilliant people. We wouldn't be as successful as we are without the brilliance of each and every employee. It

166

might be tricky, but we can weather this. I'll be as quick as I can finding a new nest for the Egg, and we'll be back to normal in no time. Any more questions? No?"

Ed cleared his throat.

"Ah yes," Burt said, "Someone vandalized Ed's car earlier today. Someone at this company. If anyone has any information or wants to vent a grudge against him, please stop by and see one of us, so we can talk things over. I don't want any bad blood between us, especially with the situation we're about to weather. Okay? Good. Dismissed."

Burt's meeting sucked the energy out of the crowd. Everyone meandered out of the Living Room and back to their desks, except for Sarah who looked more green than pale and went straight back to the women's restroom. Ed also headed towards the restroom, but not to "do his business." He searched for cleaning supplies to clean the candy from his car.

The only paper towels Ed found were ones from the automatic dispenser. He checked the closet for cleaning supplies, but the door was locked. He asked the next person heading into the women's room, which happened to be Sarah yet again, if any supplies were available in there, but he had the same unfortunate luck.

Next, Ed tried the break room, but all he found was one roll of paper towels on its last three sheets. He checked each of the cabinets, but couldn't find any more spare rolls. Because of what happened to his car, he didn't feel too guilty about taking the last three sheets.

As a last resort, Ed went from cube to cube, office to office, asking people for spare napkins to donate to the cause of cleaning off his car. Finally, with three sheets of paper towels and a sizable stack of paper napkins of various shapes, sizes, and restaurant logos, Ed headed to the parking lot to clean candy from his car.

The afternoon sun shone bright and hot on the parking lot. Ed felt the heat radiating upward from the pavement as he trekked across the lot.

As he reached his car, his shoulders slumped, and he nearly littered the sizable stack of napkins. The hot sun melted Aunt Lynn's candy. Long, sticky tendrils of what once was questionably sugar drizzled across the hood of his car. That wasn't the worst of it. Hundreds, if not thousands, of ants crawled among the candy runoff.

Ed clutched the stack of napkins in a tight fist and cursed aloud. He stormed back to the building, into his office, and slammed the door. He threw down the stack of napkins, which fluttered across his desk and all over the floor. He let out a loud howl of rage.

Burt immediately appeared in the doorway of Ed's office, and asked, "Now what? Candy not coming off?"

Ed shook with extreme rage. He clenched and unclenched his fists. He attempted several times to speak, but managed to sputter and grunt instead.

"What?" Burt asked, looking very concerned.

Ed forced himself to take several deep breaths until he could speak. After composing himself, he asked, "Do you know anyone who can exterminate a car?"

Burt's eyes grew wide and his jaw dropped. "Oh no. The candy attracted bugs?"

Ed closed his eyes and nodded, "Ants."

Burt said, "They say candy's not good for you. I bet no one thought it would apply to cars, too."

Ed cracked. He couldn't resist laughing. This was the worst week of his life, and all he could do was laugh. The week started at bad, progressed to worse, and now sat in a comfortable throne at comically tragic.

Burt made a few calls to help Ed find someone who could exterminate ants from his car. One exterminator postponed all his other appointments because this was one thing he had to see to believe. Arriving within the half hour, the man took one look at Ed's car and said, "I've never seen anything like this. I don't even know what to charge. Tell you what ... I'm gonna cut you a break and do this one for free."

Ed appreciated the exterminator's generous offer. He and Burt stood back as the man fumigated his car inside and out. He lifted the hood and sprayed the engine. He opened both doors and sprayed the interior as well.

The man finished the job in minutes. He pulled down his mask, and said, "Those little buggers got all over. You're gonna need to vacuum it out. Plus, that candy seeped under the hood, and those ants were all over your engine, too. You might want to start 'er up, and see if she still works."

Ed slid into the driver's seat and sat among dead ant carcasses. Even with all the windows down, his poor car reeked of bug spray. He put the key in the ignition. It was not a good sign that the car let out a whimper to let him know the door was still open. When he turned the key, the engine struggled to turn over, then quickly died. He tried three more times before giving up.

The exterminator left and he called out a mechanic. The mechanic took a quick look and noticed the ant carcasses scattered among the engine. Plus, the exterminator's bug spray left a thin residue over everything, some of which had a reaction to the grease, creating a sticky sludge. Plus, some of the ants, in the short time they had feasted in Ed's car, had chewed into the wire casings and rubber hoses, causing all sorts of leaks and poor electrical connections. The mechanic said that a whole new engine replacement might be easier than repairing what remained.

The candy on the hood was another issue. Aunt Lynn's half-melted candies ruined the custom paint job on the hood. Smudgy black polka dots speckled his hood. The car would need to be repainted. Since the color was unusual, it might be difficult if not impossible to find an exact match to the rest of the car. It would be easier to repaint the entire car to ensure the uniformity of its color.

The mechanic left, and Burt called a tow truck. He waited with Ed until his poor, purple Mini was hauled away for engine repair and detailing. Ed frowned as they towed it out of the parking lot and disappeared around the corner. Burt put his arm across Ed's shoulders to let him know everything was going to be okay. Burt drove Ed home and said he would return in the morning to pick him up.

Thursday arrived and Ed feared he couldn't face another day of bad fortune. He forced himself out of bed and got ready. Burt arrived in a cargo van stuffed with enough collapsed boxes and rolls of packing material for everyone at the Egg to pack up any items at their desks.

At work, before packing up the personal belongings from his desk, Ed called his insurance company regarding his car. He told them what had happened and the mechanic's suggestions. At first, the insurance company said it would not be covered, because the vehicle was not covered under major pest problems, which was another policy Ed could have purchased if he had known such a policy even existed. They did accept Ed's argument that the car was vandalized, which covers any damage to the car's body and covers any vandalism severe enough to render the car inoperable.

That satisfied Ed. Finally, he had a stroke of luck in an overwhelming week of misfortune. Getting off the phone with the insurance company, he called the auto shop to let the mechanic know everything would be covered and to start the repairs immediately. He hung up the phone and smiled.

Someone knocked softly on his office door. Sarah poked her head inside the door and asked, "May I come in?"

"Of course. Come in," Ed said.

Sarah took a seat across the desk from Ed. She said, "Um," then began to cry.

Ed grabbed the box of tissue and offered her one. She took three and buried her face in them to wipe her eyes and blow her nose.

"Are you okay?" Ed asked.

When she finally emerged among the tissues, she said, "I'm the one who put the candies on your car. I'm sorry. I heard about all the damage, and I'll help pay to have it fixed. I'm really, really sorry."

Ed said, "Lucky for you, the repairs are covered by my insurance. I could have you charged with vandalism."

"No! Please, don't!" she begged.

"Or, at the very least, fire you from the Egg."

Sarah shook her head, buried her face in her handful of tissues, and cried harder.

"I should, but I won't," Ed said. "I've had a crazy enough week, and my car is being taken care of."

"Thank you. I'm still so sorry."

"No worries. Just don't pull any stunts like that again."

Sarah nodded and said, "I was annoyed by how you handled the art issue with Matt. I acted irrationally. It was stupid, and I shouldn't have done it."

She buried her head again and sobbed.

Ed said, "It is what it is."

"If it makes you feel any better, those candies made me pretty sick yesterday," she said, lifting her head.

"You didn't lick each one, did you?"

Sarah nodded.

Ed said, "Urgh. I'm surprised you're not dead. Those things were awful. I'd be sick, too, if I licked the whole tin of them."

Sarah said, "I brushed my teeth eight times last night, and I still can taste them this morning. They didn't seem bad at first with the powdered sugar, but that after taste ... Yuck. It's like sweat socks soaked in sweet tea. No wonder Burt threw those away."

"If you licked the whole box of them, yeah, I'd say we're even," Ed said and smiled. He stood up, walked around the desk, and gave Sarah a hug.

"No hard feelings, okay?" he said.

"We're cool?" she asked.

"We're cool," Ed agreed.

"Since you don't have a car, if you need me to take you home, I can give you a ride," she offered.

"Thanks, but no need. I agreed to help Burt pack the inventory and take it to storage."

"Thanks, Ed, for taking it so well," Sarah said, and let herself out of his office.

The rest of the day at the Egg went as smoothly

as possible with everyone packing up their belongings and hauling boxes and their computers to their cars. Burt reminded people not to leave anything behind but the furniture, which was technically Inkwell-Framington's.

After a short lunch, Ed and Burt loaded the last bit of inventory into the cargo van and unloaded it in storage. By early afternoon, Burt dropped Ed off at his apartment on the way back to the office.

Ed walked up to the door to his apartment, carrying his two boxes of office supplies and desktop knickknacks. He nearly tripped on the small box sitting on his door mat. Resting the two boxes on his knee and careful to not step on the smaller box, he managed to open the door to his apartment.

Ed avoided the package on his doorstep. He had already opened one troubling package this week; he wasn't about to be surprised by another. Then again, he couldn't imagine what more could surprise him this week.

Too many Jack-in-the-boxes, Ed thought.

He carried the boxes from work into his apartment and dumped them in the living room. He stepped back out of the apartment and waved to let Burt know he was in. Burt honked twice and drove away.

Ed looked down at the much smaller box sitting outside his door. The box was wrapped like a birthday present in Sunday comics paper. It seemed harmless enough. He nudged it with his toe. Since it didn't explode and didn't appear to hold a wild animal, he brought it inside and set it on the kitchen table. He moved the larger boxes from work into his bedroom. Passing by the kitchen table, he shook his head and ignored the small box.

The last time someone left a package on the door step, it contained bad news. Ed couldn't imagine the week getting much worse. Even though there was no address, postage, or return address information, the box was not without writing. Whoever left it printed a simple, two word message in neat handwriting on a plain, white sticker on top of the box. In red ink, the message read, "Open me."

To the casual observer, the two words, "Open me," might not have much more meaning than a request to open the package. Those who knew Ed, who really knew Ed, understood the deeper meaning behind these two words. Ed held a fascination with Alice in Wonderland. Part of Ed always believed in the existence of holes in the universe that could whisk a person away to other worlds. Most items in Ed's collection of books and videos contained some kind of similar reference to such holes. Lydia, who had never read about Alice's adventures, most likely did not know of other Alice-related, two-word commands, like "drink me," "eat me," or "open me". These simple kinds of commands led Alice deeper into Wonderland.

Ed continued to avoid the box through an early dinner. He placed his plate and utensils in the sink and refilled his glass of ice water. He sat back down at the table, then pulled the package to him. He picked it up and gave it a gentle shake. The contents sounded like a box of cereal with a large, toy surprise inside.

He peeled the newspaper off slowly like a child prolonging Christmas morning. Beneath the paper was a plain, white shoe box. Ed lifted the lid and looked at the contents. Inside the box, he found a CD with the word "Hear Me" printed on top, a plastic baggie of a half dozen homemade chocolate chip cookies with the words "Savor Me" printed on the bag, and a cloth sack tagged with the words "Fix me." Ed pulled the CD out of the box and set it on the table. He lifted the bag, opened the draw string, and dumped out dozens of puzzle pieces into the lid of the shoe box. Next, he pulled out the bag of cookies and opened it. A burst of chocolate and sweetness filled the air. Ed breathed deep and sighed. He set the cookies next to the lid with the pieces.

Ed sifted through the puzzle pieces. The pieces were white and some had letters marked with the same red ink. He found a single, shiny penny hidden among the puzzle pieces. He picked up the penny and smiled. He knew who had sent the package, and all his worries about the contents melted away.

Ed popped the disc into the CD changer and pressed play. He skimmed through the fourteen tracks of eclectic tunes. The CD held a blend of new songs to add to his collection covering various music genres, from jazz to new age, from oldies to modern pop. He set the stereo's timer, started the CD over from the beginning, sat down, and sorted puzzle pieces into edges and centers. Ed tapped his toes to the beat and finished constructing the edges before the end of the first four songs.

The phone rang. Ed got up and paused the CD before answering the phone. He walked to the phone and glanced at the caller ID. Ed grinned, pressed "Talk" on the cordless phone, and said, "Hey there. Yes, I got it. Thanks. No, I haven't finished it. I was working on it while listening to the CD. Yeah, it's really good. No, seriously, I like what you gave me. Yes, of course I set the timer. No, I won't shuffle the music. Okay. Yes. Feel free to drop by after work. Okay, bye."

Ed started the CD again before sitting down at the table. The song continued where it left off. He took two cookies from the bag, set them on the table, and returned the rest to the shoebox. He didn't realize it, but the small act of pausing the music cleared the cutoff timer.

Ed let the new music wash over and through him. He took bites of a cookie and set the rest down when he found connecting puzzle pieces. From the inner pieces he connected, he found a couple reading "I'm sorry" and another block of four pieces that read "Love, Penny". This was the happiest moment of the week since unfortunate circumstances had taken a turn for the worst on Tuesday. He didn't think about Lydia. He didn't worry about his car being in the shop. He didn't fret about the future of Hammond Eggs. He no longer cared about much at all, including the message spelled out in the pieces before him. He hadn't even noticed the CD ending and the stereo changing to shuffle mode all by itself. Ed was entranced, and there was no timer that could help him this time. He didn't care because he couldn't.

The moment James Brown belted out about how good he felt, Ed became completely disconnected. His body slumped forward. Orphaned puzzle pieces leapt to the floor when his head slammed into the table. By the following song, the spirit arranged a little traveling music to transport its essence from the stereo to Ed's body ... It's new body. The following song completed the spirit's connection.

✂   ✂   ✂

Ed's body twitched on the ground beside the chair, but actually, the body no longer belonged to Ed. The body now belonged to Glick, the spirit previously inhabiting his stereo.

With the song's help, Glick connected to Ed's body and began the process of familiarizing himself with how Ed operated what once was his body. Several hundred years had passed since Glick had his own body, and it took time to feel comfortable behind the controls. Connecting himself to the body's brain, Glick ran through a system's check and tested movements of his new body. Arms and legs twitched and flailed briefly. The only Ed-ish thing remaining in the body were imprints of Ed's memories. Glick could no longer sense Ed's soul as he could when he resided inside the stereo.

Glick opened the eyes. Because he knew what to look for, Glick could see Ed's soul hovering above the chair where the body sat moments before. The soul looked like a clear swirl of colors, like an iridescent bubble with a thicker skin and a spark of light in the center. During the disconnection, Glick didn't know he completely pulled the plug. Recalculating his plans, he figured he could use the soul to bargain his way home. First, he needed to regain bodily movement.

Once a body learns the various ways to bend, move, and perform, it stores this information in the brain. Eventually, this information becomes so engrained that the mind no longer needs to focus, and the actions become second nature. Glick accessed this portion of the brain to take better control of bodily movement.

He moved the feet side to side and flexed his hands. It took longer than he realized, but he had spent centuries without a body; he could be patient enough to spare a few more minutes to work things out. He lay on the floor with his mind focused on his movements, the soul floating above him as a constant reminder of his goal.

Then, something unexpected happened.

If anyone else had been present in Ed's apartment, they most likely would not have noticed anything. Glick knew how to see Ed's soul, which most other people could not. Because he could see souls, he could also see the dolphin and its small rider swim out of nowhere somewhere close to the ceiling.

Glick swiveled the head around to see the dolphin circle the room before stopping in front of Ed's soul. The dolphin's rider, a petite woman, stood no more than three feet tall. She had a double set of wings, like a dragonfly, attached to the middle of her back. She looked at the soul with curiosity, and down to the floor at the body. Her brow furrowed, as she surveyed the body like a detective investigating the crime scene. She flinched when she saw the eyes follow her and blink at her.

The woman moved her attention back to the soul. She reached into a satchel slung around her shoulder and pulled out a device that resembled an ice cream scoop. She adjusted the size of the cup at the end until it was a little bigger in diameter than the soul. She reached out the device, flicked a switch, and caught the soul in the scoop.

As she placed the device with Ed's trapped soul back in her satchel, Glick wanted to reach out an arm and try to tell her to stop. Instead, the left arm flopped like a fish out of water, and he managed to say, "Nuh. Stah," instead of, "No. Stop."

The woman secured her satchel. She looked over her shoulder at the body lying on the floor, and then she and the dolphin disappeared once more into the nothing from which they had arrived.

Glick recalculated his plan. Now that he had a body, he could find other ways to return home. He only needed to find the right one.

CHAPTER NINE

To Catch a Thief

In the middle of an old, dirt road, the large rectangular box rose out of the ground. A bell dinged and the doors slid open. Pinkerton arrived in a rural part of the world he hated, and Kasper loyally followed.

"Where to?" Pinkerton asked.

In a field on one side of the road, cows grazed lazily in the field, inflated like balloons, bobbed around a bit to another portion of farmland, deflated, and continued to graze. On the other side of the road, a row of abandoned, dilapidated houses faced the field of overgrown grassland and overinflated cattle.

Kasper, who now looked like a person-sized, plastic, action figure with the head of a snake, looked around. His serpentine head twisted from side to side as he surveyed each broken house on the block. All the run down houses looked similar, from the chipped peeling paint to the broken windows. A ditch, dried and weed-filled, ran the length of the houses like a moat. Some of the driveways cracked and crumbled into the ditch, making it impossible for cars and trucks to venture up the driveways.

"Well?" Pinkerton asked.

"I don't remember. It's definitely the right street, but I can't remember which house," he said.

Pinkerton sighed and said, "Then we search them all."

Pinkerton rode his robotic spider chair down the dirt road to the first house on the corner. Each of the legs worked independently while keeping his chair perfectly level. The spider chair crawled across the road with a metallic clattering and clanging of feet. The chair crawled down and across the ditch to a wooden fence surrounding the ancient and forgotten home. The legs of the spider chair were not tall enough to step over the fence. Pinkerton paused a moment to look up and down the fence for a gate or a section that had fallen down, but had no luck. One of the legs pushed on the thick wooden beams of the fence. Despite its appearance, the fence was still solid and sturdy. Pinkerton took a moment to think.

Four kids from the least ghost town part of the neighborhood approached. They laughed and chased each other, punching one another playfully in the arms. They froze when they saw Kasper with the snake head and Pinkerton with a spidery body.

"Whatcha doing?" the eldest of the kids asked. The youngest kids cowered behind him.

"None of your business," Pinkerton said.

"You're lookin' for the Yabowak, aren't ya?" he

asked.

"Maybe I am. It's still none of your business," Pinkerton said, turning the spider chair on the spot to look the boy more eye-to-eye.

"You don't know where the Yabowak is, do ya?" the boy asked.

"Not exactly. My associate here forgot which one. If you happen to know, you could save me time and tell me," Pinkerton said.

"Why should I tell ya?" the boy challenged.

Pinkerton crawled to the boy. The other kids scattered, but the eldest boy stood his ground.

"Tell me which house," Pinkerton said.

"Make me," the boy said, and folded his arms.

Before the boy had time to react, Pinkerton swiped one of the spider legs behind his legs and knocked him to the ground. Another one of the chair's legs pinned him to the ground.

Pinkerton reached down to a compartment beneath the spider chair and pulled out an attachment for his artificial hand. He pulled off his hand attachment and set it in his lap. As he connected the new attachment, he asked the boy, "Have you ever seen *Texas Chainsaw Massacre*?"

The boy swallowed hard, shook his head, then said, "What's that? A home movie?"

The saw-blade attachment spun to life, and Pinkerton lowered it towards the boy's face. Even though his patience was thin with this child, he spoke with calmness, "The house. Which one?"

"Don't hurt him! It's that house, there!" one of

183

the other kids shouted.

"I wouldn't go in. It's haunted," shouted another kid.

The saw-blade whirred to a stop, and Pinkerton said, "Looks like you've got friends."

Pinkerton lifted the spider leg off the boy, and he quickly crawled away to join the other kids. Pinkerton took his spider chair over to the house. Another sturdy fence enclosed the yard of the house. His saw-blade hand buzzed to life once more. The kids screamed and ran back down the dirt road, tripping over each other to get far enough away fast enough. Pinkerton leaned the robotic spider legs towards the fence and proceeded to use his saw-blade attachment to cut down a section of the wooden fence large enough to walk the spider chair through. When the section was big enough, Pinkerton replaced the saw attachment with his mechanical hand.

Pinkerton followed Kasper across the yard to the house. Pinkerton did not hear much, except the crunching of dried grass beneath the artificial spider legs and the rustling the leaves of the solitary dehydrated tree in the yard.

He walked his spider chair up onto the porch of the house. One of the legs tapped on the door.

"Nobody's home," Kasper said.

"Are you sure?" Pinkerton asked.

Kasper floated through the walls of the house and returned a few seconds later. He nodded his snake head. Kasper said, "Not even the Yabowak."

184

"In that case ..." Pinkerton said. He brought four of the spider legs to the front door, two on each side. The remaining four steadied the chair. The four on the door pushed hard. The door creaked and groaned before the louder crack of splintering wood. The door and part of its frame slammed to the floor.

"Let's go in," Pinkerton said. "After you."

Pinkerton could not tell how large the inside of the house really was. On the outside, it seemed like a small, one-story house. Inside, rooms connected to rooms with no rhyme or reason, as if rooms of other houses were stolen and Frankensteined together to make this rustic house. The wood paneled living room connected through an opened archway to a master bedroom painted mint green. The master bedroom was connected to another bedroom with yellow wallpaper and a kitchen painted blue-grey. Even the floors were mismatched with one floor of wood, the next of carpet, the next of linoleum, and another tiled.

Kasper led Pinkerton through the maze of rooms towards the back of the house. Kasper stopped in another living room and pointed at the wooden floor.

"Its stash is under the floorboards," Kasper said.

Pinkerton adjusted one of the spider legs so the end became narrow and flat. He wedged the leg between floorboards and pried them loose as if using an enormous crowbar. The sound of splintering wood echoed through the empty rooms.

As Kasper claimed, they found the Yabowak's stash beneath the floorboards. The items were completely random and had no connection to one another other than the fact that the Yabowak stole them. They found the baseball and a hardened block of cheese from Tellis's surveillance videos mixed in with the Yabowak's stash. A sock, a toy doll with a deflated head, a brass doorknob, a cracked champagne flute, a torn seven of diamonds, and what might be a house key were only a few of the pile of the creature's treasured items beneath the floor. The checkered scissors lay wedged among them.

Pinkerton controlled one of the spider legs to reach down and pick up the scissors. Robotic pinchers delicately grabbed a ring of the scissors and the walls of the house roared with a high-pitched scream.

Two arms of the Yabowak erupted from the floor. One grabbed at the scissors, trying to pry them loose from the robot spider's clutches. The other grabbed at the other spider legs trying to bring Pinkerton and his chair down.

"I thought you said nobody was home," Pinkerton said to Kasper.

Kasper shrugged and said, "Oops?"

Pinkerton growled and firmly grasped the controls. He maneuvered the leg holding the scissors up and away from the Yabowak. The leg curled around the scissors like a protective snake and moved the scissors over Pinkerton's head.

"Come on. Come on," Pinkerton muttered. "Get it."

The Yabowak's two hands reached up as high as they could through the tangle of spider chair legs towards the one holding the scissors. The arms could not stretch much higher than where Pinkerton sat. The arms grabbed at spider legs and pulled towards the floor, but Pinkerton, in the chair, remained stationary.

The Yabowak's arms wrapped around two spider legs and pulled downward as hard as they could. The two legs obliged, but made no difference to the immobile Pinkerton.

"Take it, damn you! Take it!" Pinkerton spat.

The Yabowak gave up pulling on the legs, and its essence blended into one of the legs of the spider.

"Yes! Now, I've got you!" Pinkerton said, and slammed his finger down on one of the buttons.

The Yabowak moved up the leg towards the body of the spider chair, but was too late. The button detached the leg from the rest of the chair. It coiled into a spiral on the floor and a faint fog surrounded it. The Yabowak's hands pressed out of the coiled spider leg to the resistance of a force field, encasing it and the detached leg. A muted scream could be heard from within.

"What just happened?" Kasper asked.

"I caught me a Yabowak. It's a surface dweller. Once it transferred to the surface of the leg, I caught it with a slight modification to the same feedback I use on you," Pinkerton said with a smile.

He reached above him with his good hand and fiddled a control with his other. The scissors dropped into his hand. Pinkerton slid the scissors into a pocket on the front of his lab shirt and secured them in place with a loop of Velcro.

"Let's go," Pinkerton said.

"What about the rest of the stuff?" Kasper asked.

"It's junk. Let's go."

Once Pinkerton and Kasper were outside the house, the kids came back. The group sat on a section of fence but kept their distance from Pinkerton, just in case. Pinkerton's spider crawled across the front yard towards the hole in the fence on six legs. One leg carried the ensnared Yabowak, while Kasper trailed not far behind.

"Did you see the ghost?" one of the kids asked.

"See it? I caught it," Pinkerton said, "I left behind its stash of treasure if you want it."

The kids' eyes lit up. Their faces grinned broadly as they imagined a treasure of gold and jewels — not knowing of the pile of junk beneath the floorboards. On the other hand, kids who can turn a cardboard box into a palace might think the Yabowak's pile of junk is the most fabulous treasure ever.

Pinkerton taunted the kids with the captured Yabowak as he crossed back through the gap in the fence. The boys leapt down from the fence and cautiously approached the house. Pinkerton called another televator to pick them up.

As the metal box rose out of the ground, Pinkerton turned around and hollered to the kids, "I should probably tell you ..."

The kids stopped in their tracks and turned around.

"The ghost may be gone, but if you want its treasure, you might watch out for the fire," Pinkerton said, and cackled as he entered the televator with Kasper.

The kids looked confused. When they turned around to the house, smoke billowed out of the top. Fire crackled across the roof and smoke filled the air. One of the kids ran home to call the fire department, while the other kids pouted and watched as the treasure they imagined went up in flames.

Max sat on the curb outside the bus and sipped his cup of coffee. There was more drama than he wanted to deal with inside the Roaming Thunder bus. Gary, the troupe's boss, sorted out the details with the theater manager about extending the show.

Nancy stepped off the bus, shaking the day's newspaper over her head and rolling her eyes at Angie's antics. She sat on the curb next to Max.

"Have you read our review this morning?" Nancy asked, tapping Max in the arm with the paper.

"Not yet," Max said.

"They gave us four stars!"

"Is that good?" Max asked.

"Good? It's fantastic! Four-out-of-five is

sensational. I think they'd give Shakespeare only four-and-a-half. Here, read for yourself," Nancy said, and passed the paper to Max.

Max took the paper from Nancy and asked, "What page?"

"Page eleven, right above the movie times."

Max flipped through the paper one page at a time, skimming the headlines as he went. When he got to page seven, the technology section, he stopped. He nearly ripped the paper as he flipped the page around to read the article headlining the technology section. The headline didn't catch his eye, but the accompanying picture did. In a black and white photo, two gentlemen sat proudly on a couple of stools. He didn't recognize one of the two men but knew the other one to be Edwin Black. The paper had an exclusive article about the successes and struggles of Hammond Eggs.

"That's him!" Max said, pointing at the paper.

"Him who, dear?" Nancy said.

"Him! Edwin Black! I've found him! I finally found him!" Max said and leapt to his feet.

Max paced back and forth. He read and reread the article. Without a doubt in his mind, he knew the man in the picture must be the same Edwin Black. The article praised Edwin Black's creativity and inventiveness, which matched the description of him in Max's head.

"How far is Austin from here?" Max asked.

"A hundred miles? Maybe more, maybe less?" Nancy guessed.

"I need someone to take me there, to this, this Hammond Eggs place."

"I don't know what we can do. The bus is the only transportation we have, and if all goes well, we'll be at this theater another week or two. If not, our next planned stop is Coushatta."

"Then, I know what I have to do," Max said.

Max ran up the stairs into the bus. Nancy followed at a slower pace.

Max announced to the gabbing passengers, "Who wants to go to Austin?"

Everyone looked confused for a moment and looked between Max and Nancy. Nancy shrugged and pointed to Max. Then, they erupted into cheers and shouted, "Austin road trip! Woo hoo!"

Roaming Thunder drove to Austin, Texas, leaving Gary behind. They gave him a call on the way. Max was the most excited of the bunch, but for different reasons. He had actually found Edwin Black. He renewed his faith in the mysterious ways his creator worked. If he didn't find the diner, he might never have mended the costume, which brought him to Roaming Thunder. If Roaming Thunder hadn't had a rave review in the paper, he might never have spotted the picture of Edwin Black. It took time, but he knew, somehow, Edwin Black did it. He couldn't wait for Edwin to send him back home.

CHAPTER TEN

New and Improved

Ed opened his eyes. He remembered eating cookies, working on a puzzle, and listening to music. He did not know where he was or how he got there. He looked around and saw pristine white walls all around him. He seemed to be laying on a table of sorts with his head slightly raised. Off to his side, a person in a lab coat hunched over a table of various instruments.

Ed cleared his throat and said, "Excuse me. Where am I?"

The person in the lab coat straightened up. His head was bulbous, grey, and completely bald. When the person turned around, he looked at Ed with two large, almond-shaped, black eyes. The tiny slit of a mouth curled into a smile, and in a deep male voice, he said, "Ah good. You're awake."

The appearance of the man did not frighten Ed. The man didn't seem strange or curious to him either. Ed wondered why none of this alarmed him. Why did he feel the situation was perfectly normal?

"Who are you?" Ed asked.

The man walked over and stood beside the examination table. He said, "I am Dr. Wilk, your reconstruction specialist. Do you know who you are?"

"Ed Black."

"Full name, please," Dr. Wilk prompted.

"Edwin James Black."

"Good," the doctor said, and smiled again.

"Where am I?" Ed asked.

"You are at the OmniCore medical facilities," the doctor said and returned to his table of instruments.

Ed said, "Oh."

Ed did not remember any place called OmniCore, especially a hospital or medical facility.

"Why am I here?" Ed asked.

"That's a deep question," Dr. Wilk said, and chuckled.

"I mean, was I in an accident?" he asked.

"You are here, because you died ... Essentially. As far as I can tell, you were not in an accident, but it certainly wasn't one of the normal ways to go," he said.

Ed said, "Oh," again.

He felt content with this answer and not at all surprised by the news of his own death.

The doctor turned around holding a metal rod in one hand about the length of a popsicle stick, but cylindrical instead of flat. In his other hand, he carried a clipboard.

"Sit up, please, and swing your legs over the

edge," the doctor asked.

Ed did as the doctor asked. Dr. Wilk said, "Good."

"If I am dead, how can I be sitting here talking with you?" Ed asked.

"You appear to be asking sound, logical questions. Good," the doctor said, and made a note on the clipboard. Then, he said, "You are here with me because we have created a new body for you based on the imprint from your soul. Now, please raise your left hand so your upper arm is perpendicular to your shoulder."

Ed said, "Oh," and did as the doctor asked.

The doctor took the metal rod and touched it to Ed's elbow. Dr. Wilk asked, "Now, please wiggle your fingers."

Ed wiggled his fingers, and asked, "Why am I not phased by any of this?"

The doctor looked at something on the rod and made a note on the clipboard.

He said, "You may put your arm down. Your emotions have been temporarily muted. Not to worry, not that you currently can worry, your emotions will all return in due time. Please, raise your left leg straight out."

Ed looked down as he raised his leg. For the first time since awaking in this strange medical facility, he realized he was completely naked and felt neither embarrassed nor shocked by this. Everything felt normal. His arms, legs, chest, and pubic area were completely hairless and nothing for him to worry about.

After placing the metal rod to Ed's knee, the doctor said. "Wiggle your toes."

Ed wiggled his toes and asked, "Why are emotions temporarily muted?"

Dr. Wilk said, "Leg down. We learned our lesson years ago in the early days after we revived the first few and they panicked so badly they died of fright. Quite a waste of new bodies. If you please, place both hands on top of your head."

Ed placed his hands on his head. His head, too, felt as bald as the doctor's head. The doctor placed the rod at the base of his sternum. Ed did as he was told, which was to breathe in and out, slowly and deeply.

Ed put his arms down when Dr. Wilk told him he could. Ed asked, "Where is OmniCore?"

The doctor made more notes on his clipboard and said, "You'll find out more during the orientation film."

"Did you say, 'orientation film'?" Ed asked.

The doctor said, "Mm hm," and continued making more notes on the clipboard.

"How did I die?" Ed asked. He thought he might have asked before but didn't remember getting an answer.

"It'll all be detailed in your death report. Are you ready to see your new body?"

Ed nodded. The doctor took Ed's arm and helped him into a standing position. Ed did not feel wobbly like he thought he might, so the doctor allowed him to stand on his own.

The table flipped up on the end and the doctor swiveled it around to face Ed. The underside of the table was a full length mirror. In the mirror, Ed saw he was completely hairless from head to toe. He almost didn't recognize himself. He ran his fingers over his body. He reached up to the side of his forehead. When he was alive and young, he fell off his bike, cut his forehead, and received several stitches. Now, the scar across his forehead was gone. He also noticed that all his freckles and moles were missing. Edwin Black was a new, pristine man.

"Your body has been reconstructed to exact middle age. Most people think this is the time approximately halfway between birth and death. Since death is an indeterminate time, all bodies are reconstructed to the halfway point between when the body is fully matured, but before the decline of old age. Like your emotions, the hair over your body will eventually return. Your body will stay this age until you decide to be absorbed."

"Absorbed?" Ed asked.

"It'll be explained in the film."

Ed examined his new body in the mirror a while longer. It looked mostly like himself, but not quite. Ed had a similar feeling when he bought his dream car, when there was a moment he couldn't believe he actually bought it and the car couldn't possibly belong to him. He felt the same about his new body – like the body couldn't possibly be his own.

196

Dr. Wilk handed Ed a hospital gown. He helped Ed wrap it around himself and tie it shut. The gown was patterned but seemed to do a better job at hiding his body than the gowns in the hospitals he'd known. Not that Ed felt any embarrassment. The doctor told him it was a courtesy to others working in the OmniCore's medical center.

Dr. Wilk showed Ed into the hallway, where a petite woman with dragonfly-like wings waited for him. She barely came up to Ed's waist.

The doctor shook Ed's hand and said, "Enjoy your new body, Mr. Black. I leave it in good hands. Good day."

The doctor bowed slightly to the woman, and then returned to his office.

"Hello. My name in Alaenia. I collected your soul. Normally, they send out one of the collectors, but this time they asked me instead."

"If you collected my soul, then you might be able to tell me how I died," Ed said.

Alaenia cleared her throat and said, "Your Death Report is still in progress."

"But, you do know how I died, right?" Ed asked. If he had his emotions, he was sure he would have felt frustrated or annoyed that no one gave him a straight answer about how he died.

Dodging the question again, Alaenia said, "The orientation film viewing room is right around the corner. I will finish your report while you watch the movie. Please wait in the viewing room, and I will escort you to the fitting area for your new set of clothes."

Ed looked down at his hospital gown and said, "It seems I should be fitted before the film."

"Under normal circumstances, yes. Unfortunately, the outfitters are all booked at the moment. We've arranged to have one available to you after the film."

They arrived at the door to the viewing room. Alaenia held the door open for Ed and followed him into the room. The room looked like a small movie theater. There were thirty seats arranged in rows before a big, silver screen. Ed looked up and saw the projector in the window up on top of the back wall. He asked, "Am I allowed to have popcorn?"

"No. Why? You shouldn't be feeling hungry," she said, concerned.

"No. I'm not hungry. It's just the whole movie theater experience."

When Ed saw her blank face, he added, "Never mind."

"I'll be back for you after the movie," Alaenia said.

Ed nodded and watched her leave the room before taking a seat. He sat down in the approximate center of the seats. A moment after he sat down, the lights dimmed.

A projector presented on the screen the words, "Are you ready, kids?"

Ed looked around. There were no children in the theater. In fact, he was alone.

The projector showed a new slide that

displayed, "I said, 'Are you ready, kids?'"

Ed said aloud, "Yes."

The projector changed, "I can't hear you. Are you ready, kids?!"

Ed hollered, "Yes!"

Instead of being the only one hollering, a chorus of children's voices accompanied his and screamed, "Yes!" followed by a crowd of kids cheering. The voices seemed to come from all around him, although no one was there.

The film strip started with the countdown. When it reached zero, fanfare music played and informed Ed the file was an OmniCore Production. The film's title popped onto the screen, which read, "Welcome to the First Day of the Rest of Your Afterlife."

After the title sequence and credits, the film showed a black and white film of angels and demons fighting. It looked like stock footage from a theatrical department with a very low budget. A few dozen people in handmade costumes fought with wooden swords overlaid with the sounds of battle.

A male voiceover announced, "Since the dawn of time, good and evil fought for the possession of souls. The battle raged over a long, long time, and many, many souls were claimed by either side, until ..."

The scene changed to a person in an angel costume approaching a closet door. He opened the closet, and hundreds of ping pong balls spilt to the floor. He picked up a ping pong ball, held it in front of him, and asked, "What dost one do with the soul of an aardvark?"

"Neither side knew what to do with the souls they collected."

The film switched again to an androgynous person working furiously over a writing desk. It lifted its head, shook it, crumbled up the piece of paper, then returned to writing like mad.

"Then, one day, someone had an idea that changed the universe forever."

The androgynous person held up its index finger, looked straight at the camera and said, "Golly! I know what to do!"

"Jaiu, the offspring of Mneme, the muse, and Lucien, a minion for the dream god, ended the war between good and evil when the idea was brought before the leaders of both sides."

The androgynous figure silently presented the idea to two people sitting upon oversized thrones: one represented a god in a flowing toga and halo resting on his head; the other was a demon with cut-out wings strapped to its back and horns on its head. When it finished the presentation, both throned people threw their arms up in surprise, and then hugged each other.

Ed no longer doubted why they temporarily suppressed the emotions of newbies. He knew he would laugh if he could. He also decided he didn't need popcorn; the filmstrip already had enough cheese to snack upon.

The next scene showed a lord and lady in

renaissance clothes feasting. The lord clasped his hands to his throat and said, "Ack! Chicken bone!" then proceeded to collapse onto the table piled high with food. The lady placed her hands on each cheek, tilted her head at the camera, and said, "Alas, my husband is dead. What will become of him?"

"What, indeed," said the voiceover.

The scene switched to a cartoon diagram, while the voiceover explained. The voiceover said, "When a living creature dies, its soul is collected and brought to Jaiu, a place named after its founder. Jaiu is also called the Wall of Worlds. You see, each soul is turned into its own world based upon the owner's life experiences. Then, the body is recreated and repopulated with the soul, and the creature lives in this world for all eternity."

The stock footage of the battle replayed on the screen, and the voiceover announced, "Another war arose over creative differences of how to construct the worlds. This resulted in the earlier worlds turning into chaotic, jumbled messes. This war would have raged on for a long, long time, if it weren't for OmniCore."

At the mention of "OmniCore", the film suddenly and drastically increased in production quality. Instead of fuzzy, black and white footage with bad actors, the screen now showed crisp, colorful images with professional actors. It reminded Ed of Dorothy's arrival in Oz, but instead of just going from black and white into color, it was like going from home movie to motion picture.

The video showed creatures walking the pristine, white hallways of OmniCore. These were not people in costumes, but creatures as they naturally worked in an ordered, well-run business.

The film dropped the deep male speaking the voiceover and replaced it with a smooth, female voice. She said, "Welcome to OmniCore. Let our superior staff of highly trained professionals assist you in your transition from life into death. Like the name suggests, OmniCore is the heart of everything. Every moment, our team puts our heart into guiding you every step of the way.

"Your journey began in Outworld, the layer outside of Jaiu, where your first body was born, lived, and died. At the moment of your birth, OmniCore began constructing your custom-tailored, afterlife world. The connection specialists monitor and secure the link between your Outworld soul and your Jaiuian world. The architects analyze your Outworld experience and strive to recreate every detail in your world.

"At the time of your death, the connection specialists work closely with the collectors to ensure your soul is brought safely into the OmniCore facility. Collectors carefully pass your soul to the reconstruction doctors, who grow you a new body. The integration specialists prepare and guide you and your new body into the world you helped create. These are only a few of OmniCore's team of hardworking professionals who want to welcome you to your new afterlife."

The film showed each of the OmniCore employees in action, showing each of the transitional steps. Ed understood that Dr. Wilk was the reconstruction doctor who provided his new body. He wasn't sure what role Alaenia filled. The film made it clear collectors and integration specialists were two distinct roles, but in Ed's case, she seemed to be filling both.

The smooth female voiceover continued to talk about other roles at OmniCore. The film never gave a concrete explanation of the location of OmniCore. Ed understood Outworld to be a sort of land of the living, even though he was technically dead, yet still existing in a new body. He grasped the concept of Jaiu being a collection of worlds, one for each living thing. The film displayed a visual representation of the Jaiuian Wall of Worlds as a wall infinitely tiled with squares, stretching in all directions. The picture gave the impression that each tile was an individual world associated with its own soul. Even with the visual, Ed had a hard time understanding where the wall actually existed or how it might be constructed. He pictured something like Heaven or Hell, only instead of up or down, the described concept seemed to suggest different layers. The voiceover's use of the term "layers" seemed to contradict the visual representation of tiles. Use of the term "layers" caused Ed to think of the universe as stacked like a deck of cards, but the visual made him think of a brick wall.

After introducing the facilities of OmniCore, the

film changed to existence in the customized worlds. A happy, animated figure provided a visual representation to help explain the different aspects of a soul living out eternity in its own world.

"Your world is created from your personal experiences," the voiceover said. "This not only includes your life experiences, but your dreams, imagination, and memories. As you continue to exist in your custom world, your world will continue to grow as big as your imagination. While in your world, the connection remains constant between your new body and the OmniCore facility, so our architects continue to make additions and modifications.

"Even though your soul remains connected to OmniCore, once integrated into your world, interaction and communication between the OmniCore facility and individuals will be limited. Should the case of additional deaths occur, OmniCore will provide you the option to recreate a new body vessel or become absorbed into the Essence. Death abuse is not tolerated. OmniCore wants you to enjoy your afterlife, and frequent deaths may lead to automatic absorption."

The film did not clearly explain the concept of absorption or provide a description of the Essence. Ed guessed it was a form of permanent death after death.

The film wrapped up, the credits scrolled by, and the lights grew brighter. As far as orientation films went, it was entertaining and somewhat informative. Ed sat, waited, and wondered about the content of the film. It seemed to be targeted towards a human audience. He couldn't imagine that cats or hippos or amoeba would watch an orientation film after their death.

Ed waited in the empty theater for Alaenia to return to escort him to the next station. He didn't bother to get up. He had no idea where he was or where to go outside the theater. He didn't feel curious, so he felt no desire to explore the facility. What if he got lost before having the chance to see a world tailored to his own imagination? He sat back and tried to imagine what his world might look like.

✂   ✂   ✂

Alaenia sat in her office and thought about what to write for Ed's Death Report. The section marked "Method of Death" stumped her. Ed's death confused everyone at OmniCore. Dr. Wilk's medical report stated "unknown" since his tests produced inconclusive results. The technicians claimed a double disconnection. Not only did his soul somehow become disconnected from his body, his soul also disconnected from OmniCore. At times, flaws disconnected one end or another, but she had never heard of a double disconnection. Luckily, the OmniCore technicians kept track of last known locations, which was how she knew where to retrieve Ed's soul.

Normally, Alaenia kept a tidy desk, but she had let things go and the paperwork piled up. She sifted through the other files and papers on her desk, searching for an idea of what to put in the report but resulting in making a bigger mess. She couldn't leave the section blank. He'd already asked more than once, and she avoided answering it each time. She couldn't use "old age" because Ed was in his mid-thirties. She considered "accidental", but the system prompted for more details, which she had none. In her search, she knocked over one of her pictures and pushed aside the gifts from her co-workers she didn't have the heart to throw away and didn't want cluttering up her home. She checked the time and needed to get back to Ed in the viewing room. Catching one of her child's drawings out of the corner of her eye, she got an idea. For his report, she entered something as a mental note to come back and fix it later.

She noted the method of Ed's death, and then straightened up her desk a bit. She returned the picture she had knocked over to its upright position. The picture showed a happy family of three on vacation: Alaenia, her husband, and their son. She brushed her fingers down the picture of her husband and sighed.

The anniversary of his disappearance was three cycles away. She vowed to herself to find him, no matter what. Even if she found him and learned he didn't want to return home, at least she would know he was still out there somewhere. She wanted closure. Not knowing where he was or what happened to him fueled her desire to continue searching.

Even though OmniCore frowned upon her obsession, they agreed to share all the information on the assignment where he was last seen. They granted her access to his world. For a while, they assigned others to aid her in the search. They even promoted her to Special Operations. Her husband was a real nowhere man.

Alaenia dreamed of the day she found him, of a time when they could be a happy family of three once again. Maybe they could even try to be a happy family of four or more.

A light rap on the doorway shook her from her daydream. She turned her head and forced a smile.

"Yeah, Fronz. What's up?" she said. Fronz was from the Integrity department.

"You asked me to run a check on Edwin James Black," Fronz said.

"And?"

"We still came up negative on why or how he disconnected. But, there's more to this guy than being unplugged. His world has a cold case regarding a reported hole a few cycles back."

"What do you mean by a hole?"

"Punched from his world right into Outworld," Fronz said, showing Alaenia the information packet.

Alaenia skimmed the information packet. Then, she reread it a second time, but more thoroughly.

"A hole to Outworld? How in Jaiu did that happen?" she asked.

Fronz shrugged.

"A disconnected soul ..."

"From both sides," Fronz added.

"From both sides, and a hole? Do you think it's a coincidence?"

"Quite a bit of time passed between the two events. I don't think they're connected. But, still ... Pretty odd, if you ask me. I've never seen either event, and here are two related to the same world. Are you up for a little investigation?"

"Investigation? Now? Black is in the middle of the orientation film. He's due for his fitting afterwards," Alaenia said.

"Karol said you're currently handling his case. You should be the one to investigate," Fronz said.

Alaenia did nothing to hide her disgust. She rolled her eyes and stuck out her tongue. And, Karol did nothing to hide her jealousy of Alaenia's promotion to SpecOps. Karol's mission was to make Alaenia's life miserable, hoping to force her out of SpecOps.

"First, I do her retrieval job, now this," Alaenia said.

"I know. But, since these cases have weird written all over them, and you're already handling his retrieval and integration, I'm asking for your help." Fronz said.

"No worries, Fronz. I'll do this because you asked, not her."

Fronz smiled, and said, "I'll let her know you're on your way."

"Yeah, yeah, yeah," Alaenia said, "Let me ask Vern to escort Ed to his fitting, then I'll meet you in the integration dock."

"Thanks," Fronz said, handing her the information packet and leaving.

Alaenia kissed her fingertips and brushed them against the picture of her husband.

"Another time," she sighed to herself.

Alaenia grabbed the packet and started flipping through the information inside. First a hole in his world, then a two-sided disconnect. She wondered if and how these two events could possibly be connected. Hopefully, it wouldn't end in total world absorption. She'd only heard of one other total world absorption, and that was many cycles in the past. She didn't want to be the one associated with another.

✂   ✂   ✂

Ed sat patiently in the viewing room. If he had his emotions, he would have been annoyed for waiting so long. Or, at least bored. He was neither. Then again, the room had no clocks, and he had no point of reference as to exactly how much time had passed.

Ed sat and thought about who and what he left behind. He wondered how his family would find out. The most logical person to tell them would be Burt. He pondered how well Burt would be able to continue the Egg without him. There were many talented people at Hammond Eggs, and Ed figured after a brief grieving period, the company would go on as usual. How would Burt discover his death?

Without a central location, it might be some time before Burt discovered his death. Even though Burt did a decent job of keeping in touch with Ed, it still might be a few days of unreturned calls before he thinks something was suspicious. Most likely, someone else would discover his body earlier. The landlady? Maintenance? Penny? One of the other tenants? What about Lydia, and would she even care if Ed died? At some level she might.

Ed searched his thoughts about anything embarrassing he might have left behind. Now that he was in the great beyond – and according to the film, the afterlife seemed pretty grand – would he ever run into anyone who discovered anything embarrassing left behind after his death? Would any of this embarrassing stuff follow him into his world? He figured probably so, especially if the world was based upon every detail of his life, including the embarrassing ones.

"Edwin James Black?" inquired a voice behind him.

Ed turned around and saw a large octopus standing in the doorway. It pulled itself up the doorframe to better see over the seats.

Ed stood up, turned toward the octopus, and said, "I'm Edwin James Black."

With a heavy, put-upon sigh, it said, "Follow me."

"I'm waiting for Alaenia. She asked me to wait here. Said she'd come back to take me to my fitting."

"Why do you think I'm here? And if you say for

my health, you'll find yourself slapped with at least half of my limbs," it said.

Ed might have been stripped of emotions, but he didn't care for this octopus's attitude. Since he didn't want trouble and didn't know where else to go, he walked up the aisle towards the door.

"I'm guessing you're here to take me to my fitting," Ed said.

"And, I'm guessing the doc remembered to install your brain. Yes, of course, that's why I'm here. Not like I have anything else better to do. Not like I have to rearrange my schedule. Follow me."

Ed followed the octopus out the door and down the hall. The octopus grumbled and complained about anything and everything. It complained that the floors weren't swept and his tentacles collected dust and grit. It complained about the brightness of the lights. It even complained about Ed's hospital gown.

"Having a tough day?" Ed asked, as they entered an elevator.

"There are no days here in the OmniCore facility. They're called cycles, not days. Saying days would imply planetary rotation, which there isn't one. And, no, I'm not having a bad cycle, but, thank you for asking," it said with condescending gratitude.

"What's your name?" Ed asked.

"The name is Vern. And, just because I'm telling you this, doesn't mean we're going to start hanging out. Okay?"

"Fair enough," Ed said, and rode out the rest of the elevator ride in silence.

Vern complained about the slowness of the elevator and the selection of background music. He even complained about how the doors opened.

They exited the elevator and trekked down the hallway of clothier rooms and proceeded to Vern's studio. Vern snorted and grunted at things down the hallway, but kept his comments to himself. He rolled his eyes as his other co-workers greeted them.

"Are you sure you're okay?" Ed asked.

They stopped before the door to Vern's studio. Vern pulled himself up the doorframe with his tentacles so that he was eye-to-eye with Ed.

"Have you ever met a talking octopod?" Vern asked.

Ed shook his head.

"We are very solitary creatures. We appreciate being left alone," Vern said.

Ed nodded once and said, "Ah."

"You should be glad Alaenia asked me and not André," Vern said pointing at another octopod at the end of the hall.

André swept the hallway in front of his door, but stopped long enough to give Vern an obscene gesture and make a clicking sound with his mouth.

"That guy is a real jerk," Vern muttered and shook his head.

Vern moved out of the doorway and showed Ed into his studio. He said, "Stand in the circle on the floor and disrobe."

The room was square and paneled in a light-colored wood. A hamper and trash can stood against the far wall. A broom and dustpan leaned against the wall next to the trash can. A blue circle, about four feet in diameter, was painted on the center of the floor. Next to the circle stood Vern's short worktable. The table was as long and wide as a dining table, but no more than a foot tall. Half of the table was padded with a measuring grid imprinted on it, while the other half was hard and off-white, like a writing desk. Vern's tools scattered across the surface of both halves.

Ed stood in the large blue circle. He took off the hospital gown and dropped it to the ground at his feet. Vern pulled himself over, grabbed the robe, wadded it up, and threw it into a hamper next to the wall.

"First, I'll take your measurements, then we'll discuss fashion," Vern said.

Vern grabbed a measuring tape, pencil, and clipboard from his desk and pulled himself to Ed. Tentacles reached up and around Ed as Vern took the various bodily measurements, while another tentacle took notes.

"What are you looking for in clothing? Comfort? Practicality? High fashion?" Vern asked.

"I don't know. I usually wear jeans and T-shirts," Ed said.

"Mm hm," said Vern as part of him took notes, "What is it about your jeans and T-shirts that you like?"

213

Ed had never given it much thought. He shrugged and said, "Comfort, I guess."

Vern took more notes.

"What size shirts?"

"Large or extra large."

"From your files, it didn't look like your old body was large or extra large," Vern said holding up a simulated picture of Ed's old body as it looked pre-death.

"It's not really the roominess that I liked. Although, that made it feel more comfortable. Less constricting. I liked the length. You know, so I can hold up my arms and not show off my bellybutton."

"Were you a modest person?"

"Sometimes."

"Hm," Vern said, and made several more notes. Then, he asked, "What about the jeans?"

"I liked the relaxed-fit jeans. Comfortable. Deep pockets."

"Do you keep a lot of stuff in your pockets?"

"No more than usual. Wallet. Cell phone. Key ring. Folded up scraps of paper."

"Hm," Vern said again. He made more notes, then looked over them.

After a moment, Vern said, "You want something comfortable yet functional. You appreciate coverage, but nothing constricting. Right?"

Ed nodded and said, "That sounds right."

"I can work with this. I'll be right back," Vern said.

Vern took the clipboard and pulled himself across the room. He pushed open a door that blended well with the wood-paneled walls. Through the door, Ed could see rows and rows of clothing racks and rolls of various fabrics.

While Vern was out, Ed looked down at the drawings scattered across Vern's desk. Vern had bits of outfits sketched on several scraps of paper. It reminded Ed of himself and the numerous notes he took on various ideas.

Ed thought about his notes, which led him to ponder again about what his world might look like. Ed's mind was a constant flow of ideas. When he was in school, he often let his imagination wander too far, and it sometimes got him in trouble for not paying attention to what he should.

Vern returned from the back room and brought Ed back from his thoughts. He returned holding a couple of hangers up with his tentacles. In one tentacle, Vern held up a navy blue T-shirt with a long torso. Another tentacle held a pair of folded cargo pants. In other tentacles, he held other various items, which Ed could not tell what they were from where he stood.

"Here," said Vern, "Get dressed."

✄   ✄   ✄

Alaenia opened an observation deck to the location noted in the report. The hole had been punched between Ed's world and Outworld and the deck observed the portion in Ed's world. The hole was long gone. The observation deck was designed like an invisible bubble inside one of the worlds. Invisible to the inhabitants of the world, but allowing complete freedom of movement for her within the bubble.

She looked around the room and took notes. The walls had a hillside and blue sky mural painted on them. She made note of the security camera mounted in the one corner. More than likely, the camera caught the entire event. She made note to replicate the surveillance videos, which was the kind of assignment the techno-geeks in the labs lived for.

The report also mentioned Max, the man who disappeared into Outworld. The report included a profile on Max detailing him as a portable pool salesman. A note appended to the report detailed his trade of cutting swimming pools out of thin air with a pair of scissors. Prior to the hole to Outworld, the pools were investigated, then considered a benign lead, since the scissors were only known to cut to a water world located elsewhere within the same universe.

Alaenia thought about the scissors. She figured if the scissors were still in this world, and they fell into the wrong hands, then other holes might occur. However, no other holes had been reported since this one event. Either the scissors were lost in this world, or whoever had them didn't know how to use them.

She also wondered if the scissors could punch a hole between worlds. Could the scissors also have severed Ed's soul from its world? In that case, Max might still have his scissors, and Max was in

216

Outworld. But, why would Max or anyone for that matter sever the link between a soul and its world? Nowhere in the report did it state that the scissors were missing from this world, too. She made another note to look for the scissors. Of course, the scissors and pool were no longer present in the room. It had been restored long ago to the state of being a peaceful hillside with no sign Max had ever disappeared.

Looking around the room, she noticed a small plaque mounted beside the door to the room. The plaque stated this was the Hilltop Room of Jack of Diamonds. If she ever walked among this world, she made a note of which establishment to visit to question the owner further. There was a slim chance she would get the opportunity to visit the world, however. Although it was common for OmniCore employees to vacation in some of the worlds in which they worked, OmniCore might block any visits to Ed's world under the circumstances. Since it now had two events associated with it, most likely it would become one of the taboo worlds.

Alaenia gave the room one last sweep, checked her notes, and left the observation deck. She glanced at the room as the door slid closed. A thought nagged at her that she had forgotten or missed something, but she couldn't think of what it could be.

When she got back to her desk, she dropped her notes on her desk. No sooner had she sat down when she checked the time and realized how late she was to meet Ed after his fitting. She quickly finished up the Death Report of Edwin James Black, gathered everything together in haste, and sped down the hall towards Vern's fitting studio. Vern was one of the more tolerable octopods and, in Alaenia's opinion, one of the best fitters, but no one deserved to be left alone with Vern longer than necessary.

CHAPTER ELEVEN

Pixie of Death

Penny arrived home late from work to her dark apartment. Oscar-Frank yipped as she fumbled the keys into the lock and opened the door. After rushing through taking the dog for a much needed walk, quickly changing her clothes, and snarfing down a meager dinner, she went to Ed's apartment. WIth Oscar-Frank under one arm, Penny knocked on the door with her free hand. Something banged back from the inside. Oscar-Frank looked at her, and she shrugged to her dachshund. She hoped Lydia hadn't sent a DVD sequel. She also hoped he didn't give her care package the same treatment Lydia's DVD. She waited until the banging stopped, then knocked again.

Glick, occupying Ed's body, answered the door and said, "Yes?"

"Ed? Are you okay?" Penny asked.

Glick paused, blinked, and said, "I am well, Penelope Nichols."

His response threw her off. Rarely did anyone call her by her formal name. Was Ed really well? She did not hear any music playing, so she figured Ed couldn't have been possessed by the spirit of the stereo. On the other hand, even Oscar-Frank became more fidgety and whined.

"Is now a bad time?" Penny asked.

Glick paused again before asking, "A bad time for what?"

"To visit?" she asked.

"To visit where?" he asked.

"Never mind. I can come back later if you are in the middle of something," she said.

Glick said, "I am in the middle of a project."

"Oh, okay. I don't want to intrude," she said.

Glick started to close the door when Penny's hand prevented it from shutting completely. As she had turned to go, Penny had caught a glimpse of the mess in Ed's apartment. One of the shelves lay on its back in the middle of the living room. The sofa was littered haphazardly with the shelving boards, and heaps of books scattered the perimeter of the room. The most surprising thing was a door off its hinges, leaning against the far wall.

"What exactly are you working on?" she asked.

Glick paused and said, "I am constructing a doorway to get to the Zephyrus."

Penny shook her head and said, "Okay. I'm sorry. I got as far as constructing a doorway. What is the Zephyrus?"

Glick said, "A marketplace."

Penny set Oscar-Frank down. Oscar-Frank sniffed at Ed, yipped once, then trotted into Ed's apartment.

"Oops! Looks like Oscar ran into your apartment. Silly dog. Do you mind? Thanks," she said, and pushed her way past Glick and into the apartment. Her intuition screamed at her to pay attention to Ed's exhibition of very un-Ed-like behavior. She figured she better watch him a while and make sure nothing happened to him.

Glick closed the door and returned to his work on the shelves while Penny cleared off the sofa to give herself someplace to sit out of the way. From the sofa, she could see the doorless bathroom across the room, as the door leaned against the wall beside her. Oscar-Frank sniffed at the shelves and inspected Glick with caution. He whined some more, joined Penny, and curled up against her on the sofa. Normally, Oscar-Frank loved belly rubs and would have begged Ed for some, and Ed would have obliged. For him not even to try asking for attention, Penny knew something wasn't right.

Glick picked up a hammer in one hand and a nail in the other. He nailed the bottom of the shelf unit to a Lazy Susan. Penny wondered what exactly he was hoping to accomplish by this. She guessed he would affix the bathroom door to the shelves, but wasn't sure about the Lazy Susan.

And, what was that about a marketplace called the Zephyrus? She admired Ed's creativity, but this new project of his was beyond her.

"Is this a new project for the Egg?" she asked.

"No. It is a doorway to the Zephyrus," he said.

"So you said. Do you need any help?" she asked.

"When I am done, you can help lift it. For now, no, I do not require your assistance," he replied.

Penny watched him finish nailing the shelf unit to the Lazy Susan. After that, he took the door hinges off the bathroom doorframe and attached them to the side of the bookcase. He didn't mention this project when she had phoned him earlier. She thought she remembered him saying he got her package and was working on the puzzle. Over the phone, he sounded appreciative of the package. She began to worry maybe giving him the care package was too soon after his breakup from Lydia. Then again, even if her act of kindness freaked him out, it wouldn't explain the bizarre project in his living room.

"Did you like the CD?" Penny asked, hoping he would catch the hint and talk about the package she left him.

"Yes. The music was most helpful," Glick said.

Helpful? Penny thought. Helpful was not her choice of words. Appreciated, maybe. But, helpful?

"Um," she said, "I'm glad it helped cheer you up. Did you finish the puzzle?"

"No. The puzzle is unfinished," Glick said, and pointed to the dining table.

Puzzle pieces sat ignored on and under the table. All the edges were put together, as were parts of the middle. Most of the puzzle remained unfinished, as he said. Even one of the cookies sat

222

partially eaten. Penny pouted.

"What made you want to build a doorway?" she asked.

"As I have said, to get to the Zephyrus."

"Which is the marketplace, right?"

"Correct."

She knew something was definitely not right about Ed but couldn't believe he had been possessed. The stereo was off. How could he be possessed without the music? Whenever Ed lost control, the music played, causing his episodes. It was clear Ed was not acting like himself. Was this some kind of post-hypnotic suggestion after the music ended? Ed didn't finish the puzzle or the cookie. He never would have treated his books in such a haphazard way. Plus, he would have been friendlier to her. Either the stress with his breakup with Lydia finally made him snap, or this wasn't Ed.

"What are you hoping to find in this Zephyr market?" she asked.

"The Zephyrus holds the key to get home," Glick said, screwing the second set of hinges to the shelves.

"And, where is home?" she asked, betting she knew the answer.

"Jaiu," Glick said.

Her stomach turned, and she felt like she was going to be sick. Jaiu was the same name the spirit had said through the Ouija board. Of course, Ed did not act like Ed because this person was not him. The stereo was off, probably because it already had served its function. He mentioned strange places she had never heard of. The only thing she could assume was the spirit had successfully taken over Ed's body, with or without music. She wondered if Ed was still inside his body somewhere.

"Um," Penny said. She fought back tears, cleared her throat, and struggled to get out her next question. "Where is Ed?"

"Taken," Glick said, his work uninterrupted by Penny's questions.

"Taken," she repeated. She swallowed hard, and asked, "Where did you take him?"

"I took his body. Someone else took his soul."

She did not know how to respond. The questions filling her head made her dizzy. What happened to Ed's soul? Who could take his soul? Where did they take his soul? Did this mean Ed was dead? What was going on?

"You didn't take his soul?" she asked, her mind spinning.

"No."

A tear trickled down her cheek, and she asked, "Who are you?"

"Glick," he said.

"Glick," she repeated. He gave the same name at the seance. "How was his soul taken?"

"When I took Ed's body vessel, I disconnected his soul from his body. A collector took his soul. I can only assume it has been taken to where I am trying to go."

"Which is this Jaiu place?"

224

"Yes."

"Oh, my stars," she said with a sad emptiness welling up inside her. She softly cried.

When Glick said the music was helpful, he must have used her selection of songs to finally gain control of Ed's body. She hated herself for helping this spirit take control of Ed. Did Ed shuffle her music? He knew how music affected him. If he shuffled her music, why didn't he use the timer?

Sorrow turned to anger. She found herself angry with Ed, with Glick, and herself. Penny leapt off the sofa at Glick. She slapped him and hit him on the back and cried, "Where is he? Why was he taken? I want him back! Bring him back!"

Glick turned around, undaunted by Penny's assault as she continued to smack him. Glick took all the hits without flinching or defending himself. With an eerie calmness, he said, "I did what needed to be done to get home. My goal was to use Ed temporarily to get to Jaiu. It was not my intention for him to be taken."

"Who took him?" she croaked.

"I do not know. One of the soul collectors. A pixie," he said.

Penny pulled herself away from Glick and slumped onto the sofa. Ed was her good friend. She wasn't ready to lose him. She couldn't lose him.

"No," she said.

Glick said, "I did not ask a question. Why did you say, 'No'?"

She shook her head and said, "No. They can't

take him. If he's still out there somewhere, I'm going to find him. I'm not about to let some pixie of death take someone I care about."

"The pixie did not cause his death."

"I don't care. If you're going to Jaiu, then so am I. I'm going to bring him back."

"I do not think that is possible."

"Don't talk to me about what is possible and impossible. We're going to find out. Now shut up and let's finish this doorway."

Glick nodded and returned to constructing the door with Penny at his side.

CHAPTER TWELVE
Eaten by a Dinosaur

Ed's new clothes fit perfectly. He had never worn clothes this comfortable. Although he was not one to follow high fashion, it was a shame he had to die to get an outfit so perfect. At least he would start his afterlife in comfort. The cargo pants covering his legs had a relaxed fit – not too baggy, but not constricting, either. The T-shirt hung down to just above his thigh, so even when he held his hands above his head, the shirt still covered his stomach. Unlike some of the extra-large shirts he wore when he was alive, this shirt was form-fitting, not baggy. Even the shirt's color complimented his new eyes as he checked himself out in the full-length mirror on the wall. Vern gave him a pair of footwear that had all the coverage of a shoe, with all the comfort and airiness of a sandal.

"This is perfect, Vern," Ed said.

"Of course it is," Vern said, cleaning up a few items from his workspace.

"Thank you."

Vern put the lid on the shoebox, turned, and

said, "You know, you're one of the rare ones to thank me for my work. It's been a while since someone thanked me. I know this job may look easy, but crafting a set of clothes to wear into the afterlife is not simple. I appreciate it, kid."

Alaenia appeared in the doorway out of breath. She gulped air into her lungs and said, "Sorry I'm late. Are you ready for Integration?"

"As I'll ever be," Ed said.

Before following Alaenia out the door, Ed turned and shook Vern's tentacle, which felt like a skinny tube of hamburger meat.

"Thanks again," he said.

"No problem. Take care," Vern said.

Ed followed Alaenia, who stood in the hallway ignoring André's crude comments and advancements. She escorted Ed back to the elevator and took him to the Integration department. The walls in Integration gleamed a flawless white. It reminded Ed of the reconstruction medical labs.

They walked passed a duck, nearly as tall as Alaenia, waddling quickly down the hallway in the opposite direction. The duck nodded to Alaenia, and she nodded back.

"Was that a duck?" Ed asked.

"Not just any duck. That's Gary, the Integration manager," she said.

"Oh," Ed said, then as an afterthought, asked, "Do you think Donald Duck has nightmares about wearing pants?"

Alaenia fought back a grin, and asked, "Who is

Donald Duck?"

"A cartoon."

"Cartoons don't dream. They have thought balloons," she said, looking confused.

"Never mind."

Alaenia opened the door to Ed's Integration room. Ed peeked through the door and saw nothing but more gleaming white.

"Before you enter your world, here is your Death Report. Hopefully, the report and the film answers all your questions," she said.

Ed took the binder from her and thanked her. He looked forward to reading his report to find out exactly how he died.

"Here's how Integration works. Once you go into the Integration room, I will shut the door behind you. The door will seal itself shut tight, like an airlock. When the door is completely sealed, the walls will turn from white to black. Don't worry. You won't be in complete darkness. There will still be plenty of light to read by.

"Over time, the walls will fade from black to transparent and eventually will dissolve completely. Once the walls are gone, you will be fully integrated into your world, and you're on your own.

"As Dr. Wilk should have explained, your emotions will eventually return. Sometimes they return during Integration; other times it takes a while longer. Don't worry. They will return.

"Normally, the Integrated soul is connected to their world. You are not completely connected, yet.

229

While our technicians are working on it, we will be monitoring you should any situations arise. Any questions?"

"Yes. What do I do if I need to contact you in the future?"

"You don't. You can try praying, but I won't be the one listening. Anything else?"

Ed shook his head and said, "Can't think of any more."

"Good. Off you go. Enjoy your afterlife," she said.

She motioned for Ed to bend down. He knelt down on one knee. Alaenia gave Ed a strong hug and whispered in his ear, "Your world is an amazing place."

She let go. As Ed stood up, he gave her a quizzical look. He wondered if she told everyone how amazing their worlds were, or if she had actually been to his world. He smiled at her, and entered the Integration room. The room was circular and not much bigger than ten feet in diameter. The moment Alaenia shut the door, the gleaming white walls instantly turned black. As she said, enough light shone from some unknown source so Ed could still clearly see himself and everything he carried.

Ed brushed his fingers across the smooth, black wall as he walked around the perimeter of the domed room. There was nothing to see but blackness. Ed sat on the floor in the approximate center of the room and started reading his Death Report.

He was disappointed to find out the actual reason for his death was "Eaten by a dinosaur." How could that have possibly happened? Everyone knows, with a few exceptions, dinosaurs were mostly extinct. In his last moments, he listened to music and put together a puzzle. He highly doubted a dinosaur snuck up behind him in his own apartment and ate him. If it wasn't a dinosaur, then how did he die? And, why would Alaenia enter something untrue in his report?

For the "Last thought" entry, the report claimed his last thought was, "There's a really cool smell in here." What smell was that? Musk of Tyrannosaur?

The most interesting pages in the report were the statistics, like how many times he breathed in his lifetime (one third of a billion times), or how many times his heart beat (1.3 billion times), or how much food he consumed (38 tons of food). He felt a hint of guilt when he saw what percentage of his life he spent sleeping (35% of his life, or just over 12 years worth of sleep). Ed thought about his guilt and wondered if it meant his emotions were returning.

Ed lingered on the pages of unfinished business. The report listed so many entries: activities to do, places to visit, restaurants at which to dine, movies and TV shows to watch, books to read, and so on. Each one he recalled making a mental note about, but never did anything about it. Many of them he completely forgot about, like travel to a remote part of the world to witness a total solar eclipse. He wondered how OmniCore knew these desires, like his dream to go to Australia. Now, he would never get the chance. He also wondered why OmniCore would detail this in the Death Report, especially if it was too late to do anything about it. Why tell people all the things they missed while they were alive? Was there a remote chance a person could fulfill these wishes in the afterlife?

The last item on the list of things undone was "Finish Penny's puzzle." He remembered the puzzle had letters on some of the pieces, but he couldn't think of what any of it said. Now that he was dead and living in his afterlife world, he would never know what it said. A single tear dropped onto the page and blurred a couple of items on the list.

Ed didn't want to read any more. His emotions were returning, and his Death Report depressed him. He closed the report and tossed it onto the ground. He looked up and could see faint images visible through the dome. He appeared to be somewhere indoors but couldn't clearly see any details.

Reflecting on his death and reading his report started to depress him. He thought of all the people and possessions he left behind. According to the video, all the people he ever met and items he ever encountered were somewhere in his world, so it wouldn't be as if he would never get to see them again. But, would the replicated people and things be the same? He could never call or visit his family again. Could Burt run the Egg without him? He started to think of all his friends and family left behind in Outworld. He thought of Penny and her care package. He wiped tears from his eyes and cleared his mind.

If he was dead, he needed to look more forward than back. He looked out the dome, but the view was still dark. Not thinking of anything else to do, he picked up his Death Report again and flipped through the pages. Still sitting on the floor, he noticed for the first time a blank page with handwritten notes listed down the page. The page was not attached to his report like the others. It seemed someone, possibly Alaenia, stuck the page into the report like a bookmark.

He read the list aloud, "Replicate security videos. Look for the pool boy and his scissors. Jack of Diamonds - Hilltop. What is this?"

He read it again a few more times and felt a brief wave of déjà vu. Ed wasn't sure if it was a nagging feeling about something he thought he should remember, or if it was a side effect of regaining his emotions. Something about two of the items on the list seemed familiar, but he couldn't put his finger on it. Why did a pool boy with scissors sound so familiar? Why did that particular playing card also sound familiar? Did Alaenia mean to leave this cryptic note in his Death Report? Why did she lie about his death, claiming he was eaten by a dinosaur? The Death Report seemed stocked with riddles.

Ed's death was a definite mystery. He wondered if Alaenia left this cryptic information as a hint to help investigate his own death, or if she accidentally left it in the report by mistake. How could he investigate his own death if his body was somewhere left behind in Outworld while he was somewhere in his own afterlife world? It didn't make any sense.

Again, he thought about his body laying lifeless in his apartment in Outworld. Who would find his body first? Maybe Burt would wonder why he was not showing up for work. But, that was wrong, because the Egg was temporarily out of an office. The landlady? No. Probably not. His rent wasn't due for another couple weeks. Penny, or one of the other neighbors, catching a whiff of his apartment full of the stench of rotted death? The thought sent chills down the spine of his new body.

He dropped his Death Report to the ground again, stood up, and paced in a circle around the perimeter of the dome. He felt like the new fish in an aquarium waiting to be let out of the plastic bag. He looked through the walls of the dome, and the room became more and more visible. It was like seeing the world through sunglasses that grew less and less tinted. Even the floor beneath his feet turned from black to wood-paneled flooring.

Before the walls dissolved completely, Ed concluded he was integrating into someone's personal library. Shelves and shelves of books lined the walls. Each shelf, the floorboards, and the crown moulding were all stained a deep bluish-black. Sunlight sparkled down through a glass pyramid ceiling. The room did not look familiar. It looked and felt rich. Ed wondered who owned the library. According to the film, if this world was built around his experiences, then, technically, the library was his. The film did not explain how the good folk at OmniCore select which area of the world to integrate a soul, and wondered why they chose an unfamiliar place for him. Why not integrate him into more familiar surroundings, like a re-creation of his apartment, or the house where he grew up? Why the library?

The integration dome was positioned behind an L-shaped sofa. Ed could see a woman lying on the sofa reading one of the books. From where Ed and the dome were situated, he could not see her face and couldn't tell if he knew the woman. According to the film strip, he should know her to some capacity.

Once fully integrated into his world, he walked up to the sofa and cleared his throat. The woman held up a finger and said, "Hang on. This part is good."

Ed looked at the cover, but couldn't make out the title. The print changed as if the letters couldn't decide which ones they were or from which alphabet they originated.

Ed decided to let her read in peace. He rounded the sofa and walked along the shelves of books. His library of books included every book he ever read and books he bought intending to read. On one end, the bottom couple of shelves were filled with children's books and picture books he recalled reading and re-reading as a toddler. It brought back fond memories of his parents and grandparents reading him bedtime stories. One of the books in the section did not look familiar, until he read the title, "Yertle the Fried Egg and Other Stories" printed on the spine. He gave a quiet chuckle and recalled the made up stories his babysitter had told him.

He continued browsing the books of his library. On another shelf were the middle books in off-white binding and printed in Times Roman font. These books were collections of his school essays and personal writings. Collections of periodicals and comic books filled other shelves of the library.

Like the books on the shelves in his apartment, some of the books stood upside down, but most of the books were shelved right-side up. He recognized most of the books and remembered the ones he read, started to read, or wanted to read. It made perfect sense to Ed. If the world was truly his, the books in his library would be ones with which he was familiar and shelved by his own method of cataloging of read-versus-unread books.

Ed picked one of the upside-down books from the shelf and flipped through it. All the pages had text, and the words were solid and unchanging. He half-expected unread books to have blank pages, since he never read them, but was pleasantly surprised to see they were populated with words. If OmniCore could recreate a world based on one person's experiences, he figured the details, like an unread book, could be completed by borrowing information from another soul's experiences. Maybe it wasn't too late to complete the tasks from the pages unfinished business in his Death Report.

"You were eaten by a dinosaur? How cool is that?" asked a voice behind him.

Ed turned around and saw the woman walking up behind him with her head down in his Death Report. He snatched the Report out of her hands and said, "Do you mind? That's private."

She looked up at him, and Ed gave a little jump. He did not expect to see a third eye centered on her forehead. All three of her eyes were dark brown like the last sip of coffee. His eyes stared at her third eye. He was certain he'd never met a three eyed girl in his life.

"Sorry," he said, "I wasn't expecting the, uh ... the ..."

"Third eye? Do you mind not staring at it? You're making me self conscious," she said.

Ed looked away from her third eye, but he kept drifting back to it. He said, "You probably already know this from reading my report, but I'm ..."

"Edwin James Black. Yes, I know you. Everyone here knows you. Or, should I say, everyone here knows of you. Not many people know you, know you. I mean, really know you. But, I do. I've read all your books. Well ... most of them. Did you know that most of your fictional books revolve around the same theme? Many of them deal with the main character falling through a hole from one world into the next. I call it the Alice Factor, as in Alice in

Wonderland."

"And, who are you?" Ed asked.

"Oh! I'm Emily. Emily Switzer. I took it upon myself to be your librarian. Did you know that some of the books have this weird thing they do. Most of the books are right side up, right? But, some of the books are upside down. When I try to shelve them right side up, they correct themselves and turn upside down again. Watch."

She pulled off a book that was upside down. She flipped the pages to show the book was indeed upside down. She turned the book around so that the words were right side up. Once she placed the book back up on the shelf standing right side up, the letters on the spine tumbled around like circus performers, and the book once again turned itself upside down.

"Weird, huh? It works the opposite way, too. If you turn another book upside down, it rights itself back up," she said.

Ed laughed. He found it ironic a woman with three eyes found something weird. He said, "That's because I haven't read it, yet. I put books I haven't read yet upside down so when I want to read a new book, I can quickly tell which ones I've read and which ones I haven't."

Emily stood back and stared. She said, "Huh. I never considered that. I figured you read them all. Why buy a book and never read it?"

Ed pointed to the sofa to the book she was reading.

"What's that book? It doesn't look familiar," he said.

"Oh. That's mine. Trashy romance novel."

"Why are the letters all jumbly?"

"It's written in Morphic."

"Morphic?" Ed asked.

"Yeah. The script of dreams. You know sometimes when you try to read something in a dream, but the words keep changing? It's like that. You read the story more by how it feels and what the story means – not by what the words actually are."

"Interesting," Ed said.

"Not as interesting as getting eaten by a dinosaur. Tell me about that. Did you travel back in time? You did, didn't you? Because, that's another theme with your books, time travel. Were you in some kind of prehistoric dinosaur land when it happened? Or, was it more like Jurassic Park?"

"I was not eaten by a dinosaur. Here. If you're the librarian, find someplace to shelve this," Ed said, and shoved his Death Report back into her hands.

"I thought you said it was private," she said, turning it carefully around in her hands.

"Sorry. Some of the report is a little embarrassing. Like the items from the Undone List."

"No worries. I won't read it. Not unless you want me to. If you don't mind me asking, if you weren't eaten by a dinosaur, then how did you end up here?" Emily asked.

She searched the shelves for the right section to add Ed's Death Report and stuck it between a

239

journal he tried, and failed, to keep as a teen and a bound collection of college essays.

Ed sat on the sofa and said, "I don't know. One moment I was sitting at home working on a puzzle; the next moment I was revived in the OmniCore medical facility."

"Sitting where?"

"In my apartment at the kitchen table."

"Did you choke on one of the puzzle pieces?"

"No. But, if I did, shouldn't the report say so? If you want to see something else odd about it, you should look at the piece of paper stuck in there," Ed said. Emily pulled the Report off the shelf again, then plopped down at the other end of the sofa. Emily flipped through the Report and stopped at Alaenia's handwritten notes.

"The thing about the pool boy and the playing card? What does that mean?"

"Don't know," Ed said, and leaned back into the cushions of the sofa. He surveyed the collection of books. He looked at where Emily had stuck his Death Report. Before pulling it off the shelf again, she stuck it among his own personal writings. Emily stared at Ed as if trying to read him like one of his books.

"What?" Ed asked, feeling self conscious.

"You're not how I remember you. You seem different," she said.

Ed's face reddened. He said, "I'm sorry. I would think I would remember a woman with three eyes. When did we meet?"

"You don't remember my dream?" she asked, sounding slightly disappointed.

"Oh. You're from a dream. That explains things. But, I've had a lot of dreams. What happened in your dream?" Ed asked.

"We were on a bus talking about goldfish swimming in liquids other than water. Sound familiar?"

Ed sat up straight. He searched his memory. The dream did sound familiar. He said, "Yeah. Then, the bus tipped over."

Emily said, "That's right! And, that's when you disappeared. I suppose you woke up."

Ed said, "No. I woke up into another dream. That was back when I still lived with my parents. The rest of the dream was me watching a news report about the overturned bus. Then, there was something about finding two tennis rackets, but not the tea set. I do remember that dream. What happened to you? Were you hurt in the accident?"

Emily waved her hand and said, "No. Not hurt. But, when they integrated me into your world, I had nothing to do. No job. I enjoyed our conversation so much, I set out to find out more about you. That's when I encountered your library and decided to become your librarian. I hope you don't mind."

Ed thought about Emily's dream, then suddenly something occurred to Ed. He stood up and examined the section of shelves with his personal writings. He went back and forth over the shelves, including the neighboring shelves above and below.

"It's not here," he said.

"Your report? It's over here by me," Emily said.

"No, not that."

"What are you looking for?" Emily asked.

"My journal," he said.

"That's where I keep your journals. Are you sure it's not there? I don't loan out your books. And, I'm sure every journal is-" she said, but stopped suddenly.

"Is what?" Ed asked. He turned and looked at Emily, whose three eyes looked up as if all three were searching her memory.

"No, there is one more journal, but I can't get it," she said.

"Is it a thick spiral notebook?" Ed asked.

"Yes. I think so," she said, tilting her head to the side and thinking hard, trying to remember.

"Wait. What did you mean you can't get it?" Ed asked.

"You have a museum of sorts. The journal I'm thinking of is encased behind glass, but I have no idea how to get it out," she said.

"Show me."

"Okay. Follow me to the garden."

CHAPTER THIRTEEN

Same Place, Different Name

The bathroom door attached snuggly into the frame of the bookcase. Glick's freestanding doorway stood off-center in the living room because the shelves that were perched on top of the Lazy Susan made the whole thing tall enough to collide with the ceiling fan. Since the ceiling fan had a light fixture and Glick needed to see, he couldn't dismantle it, too. Instead, the freestanding doorway stood swiveling and upright in the corner of the living room near the kitchen.

Glick surveyed the doorframe as if he carefully measured the perimeter. He picked up a black permanent marker from the cup of pencils and pens sitting on the kitchen counter next to the phone. He sat on the floor, uncapped the pen, and carefully began to write symbols up one side of the bookcase.

As Penny sat on the sofa and watched, she thought the symbols looked alien. Some almost appeared as recognizable alphabetic characters, while others resembled a child's squiggly alphabet. Whatever he wrote around the swiveling doorframe was complete nonsense to Penny.

Although she had many questions and wanted to ask what it said, Penny sat quietly on the sofa and watched. While moving and lifting the bookcase-door contraption, she asked Glick more about what happened to Ed, but he did not provide any more details. She also did not get a clear idea of how his door contraption would work. Glick was very analytical, but he did not appear to be annoyed with her questions. In fact, he was very honest with his answers. At times, almost too honest. Even though he seemed honest, he was not overly generous with information. Only when she asked specific enough questions did he offer information. Because this person looked like her friend Ed but was clearly not Ed, she was determined to keep an eye on him until he answered her questions to her satisfaction.

Like Penny, Oscar-Frank kept a curious, but cautious, eye on Glick. He kept his distance but regularly ventured forth to inspect Glick and his doorway with a series of methodical sniffs. Not once did Glick attempt to pet him, which confused and frustrated him even more. Every inspection ended with a sigh followed by him cuddling next to Penny.

Someone knocked at the door. Glick stopped writing and opened his bookcase door and peeked through the case. Penny shook her head, pointed, and said, "Apartment door."

Glick continued writing on the bookcase. Penny wasn't sure if she should expose any more people to Ed-not-Ed, but realized that whoever knocked on the door sounded persistent enough to not give up until someone opened it, so she decided she had better answer it. She stood up and walked to the door to the apartment.

"Who is it?" she asked through the door.

"Max," answered a voice from the other side.

Penny had been introduced to most of the people at the Egg at one time or another. She wasn't one hundred percent, but she thought she remembered someone named Max. Or, was it Matt? Maybe Ed had been expecting him. Or, if this Max was from the Egg, maybe it was some kind of emergency. Plus, the voice did not sound threatening. She decided it couldn't hurt to open the door to see who it was and what he wanted.

The door's chain lock was broken. The track the latch locked into was bent to the point it was no longer useful. She planted a foot firmly behind the door to help brace it, and then unlocked the door and opened it a crack. A lanky man with frazzled hair stood on the other side. He seemed friendly, but unfamiliar.

She asked, "Yes? Can I help you?"

The man asked, "Is this the home of Edwin James Black?"

Penny took a second to consider how to answer that question. Technically, yes, the apartment was leased to Ed, but, also technically, no, he wasn't really at home. She said, "Er ... Yes?"

The man asked, "May I come in?"

"I don't know if this is a good time. Is he

expecting you?" Penny asked.

"I have traveled a long way to see him. I'm hoping he can help me," he said.

"He's not exactly himself today," she said, which wasn't a lie.

"Please, I must speak to him," he said. He firmly but gently pushed open the door, taking Penny with it, and entered the apartment asking, "Where is he?"

"Excuse you," she said, "What do you think you're doing? Do you normally barge into people's apartments unannounced? Didn't your mother teach you anything?"

"Sorry," the stranger said. He walked back to Penny, shook her hand, and said, "Hi. I'm Max, and I don't have a mother."

Thinking Max meant his mother died, Penny said, "I'm sorry to hear that. I have two moms. Maybe you can borrow one of mine."

Penny didn't know how much more weird she could take this evening. She might as well throw a party and invite in more weirdos. Just in case, she mentally reviewed her self defense moves.

Max walked around the bookcase, smiled broadly, and said, "You're here! At long last! I found you!"

Glick paused in his writing, looked Max up and down, and said, "Who are you?"

"It's Max. I sell portable pools? Remember?"

Penny looked at Glick, who appeared to be searching his memory and possibly Ed's, too.

Nothing registered. He said, "No," and continued to write.

Max brushed the answer aside, and said, "You dreamt of me? Anything?"

Penny looked both confused and worried. Was this a side of Ed she had never known? Days of college experimentation, perhaps?

"No," said Glick, and continued to write.

Max looked crestfallen and said, "But ... You created me."

Not knowing what that could possibly mean, Penny asked, "He *created* you?"

Max turned to Penny and said, "Yes. He dreamt me into existence. How were you created?"

Penny shrugged and said, "You know ... the old-fashioned way ... with my biological parents."

Max said, "Oh. One of those," then returned his attention to Glick.

Glick set down the pen and approached Max. He examined him up and down, and asked, "Where are you from?"

Max said, "Your world."

Glick asked, "You are from Jaiu?"

Max squinted and said, "Not exactly. I'm from your world, which is one of the OmniCore worlds."

Glick muttered to himself, "My world, meaning Ed's world. OmniCore. Not Jaiu."

Max overheard Glick's muttering and said, "The world is in Jaiu. At least, that's the old name for it."

Glick looked at Max more closely. His stiffness

247

eased, and Penny could swear he seemed more excited than robotic. Glick asked, "How did you get here?"

"I climbed through a hole and got stuck."

"Does the hole still exist between Outworld and the other world?" Glick asked.

"No. That's how I got stuck."

"How did the hole open between worlds?"

"If I'm not mistaken, my scissors opened it."

"I assume since you are stuck, the scissors are on the other side of the hole."

"Bingo," Max said.

"Oh," Glick said. He appeared to calculate something in his mind with his eyes shifting rapidly as if trying to solve a tough equation in his head.

"Hello. Clueless neighbor here," Penny said, "Can someone please explain what the Hell you two are talking about?"

Max was about to recount his story to Penny, when Glick interrupted him.

"Explain later. We stick to the original plan. The door to the Zephyrus is nearly complete," Glick said, then continued writing on the bookcase.

"What is the Zephyrus?" Max said, leaning over to whisper to Penny.

"It's a marketplace," she said, glad to know something someone else didn't. "At least that's what this guy claims. Also, that is not Ed, and I'm sticking to him until I find the real Ed," Penny whispered back.

"Sure it's Ed. He looks just like him," Max

whispered.

"No, it's not," Penny said.

"If that's not Ed, then who is it?"

Penny shrugged. She and Max exchanged looks, then turned their attention to Ed-not-Ed. Penny returned to her spot on the sofa, and Max joined her. She appreciated Max giving her space by sitting at the other end. Max smiled at Oscar-Frank and ruffled his ears, who showed his appreciation by licking Max's hand in return.

"What did you mean when you said Ed created you? It sounds Frankenstein," Penny said.

"Long ago, Ed had a dream. That dream was the first moment of my existence."

"Oh, come on," Penny scoffed, "How can someone dream a person into existence?"

"That's how I was born. Ed dreamed of me. OmniCore reconstructed me and integrated me into his world," Max said.

"What's OmniCore? Some kind of corporation or something?"

Max wobbled his head from side to side, "Kind of, but not really. They make worlds. I was living in Edwin James Black's world."

"People have their own worlds? How is that possible?" Penny asked.

"OmniCore provides a world for every soul based on its experiences. I'm one of the dream experiences from Ed's world. They gave me a soul, and one day I will integrate into my own world. Since I'm stuck in this world, I don't know what will happen to me," Max said with a frown.

"I thought people went to Heaven and Hell," Penny said.

"Haven't been to Hell. Not much business there. Oh, but I love Slice of Heaven, especially their cherry pie. Have you been?" Max asked.

"No, I haven't, because I'm not dead," Penny said.

"Dead? What are you talking about?" Max asked.

"What are you talking about?" Penny asked.

"The Slice of Heaven. It's a diner in Ed's world. They have the best pies. And the Wednesday Night open mic poetry readings are fun, too. What did you think I was talking about?"

"I thought people went to Heaven or Hell when they die. People claim that good souls go to Heaven; the bad ones go to Hell," Penny said.

"What you say is an old legend. That was the soul division measure in times before Jaiu," Glick said.

Penny and Max jumped. Glick had been quietly writing on the doorway; they both forgot he was there.

"I thought Jaiu was a place, not a person," Penny said.

"A place named after its creator," Glick said. The conversation did nothing to distract him from his writing.

"Some people still refer to where the worlds are as Jaiu, but that's old school. It's all OmniCore now,"

Max said.

"This OmniCore of which you speak defies logic. Giving a soul to a dream also defies logic," Glick said.

"I've seen a lot of illogical things lately, like how a spirit inhabiting my friend's stereo can steal his body," Penny said, glaring at Glick.

"And yet it happened," Glick said.

Glick continued to write, despite the glaring look of hatred from Penny. The room got quiet. The only sounds, which seemed extra loud, were the marker squeaking against the flat surface of the bookcase and Oscar-Frank licking himself, oblivious to his surroundings.

Max cleared his throat to break the tension and get Penny's attention. He asked, "Is that what happened to Ed?"

"Yes," Penny said, "And, a pixie stole his soul."

"Collected," Glick said.

"Whatever," Penny spat.

"If his soul was collected, then that's good," Max said.

"How is that good?" Penny asked, trying not to pout.

"He's trying to get to Jaiu or OmniCore. That's where the soul collector came from and took Ed's soul. If we stick with him, maybe we can find this pixie who took his soul and somehow get it back into Ed's body," Max said.

"Maybe," Penny said. It sounded like a crazy plan, and she wasn't very hopeful. Then again, her whole evening was full of crazy, and she didn't know what else to do.

Glick eyed his writing and continued adding more symbols to the sides of the bookcase. When he was done, he double checked his writing. Satisfied with his work, he nodded. He capped the pen and said, "It is done."

"Great! Let's get going!" Max said, and stood up.

Glick turned to Penny.

"Two things. One, turn on the television to channel 138. Two, tell me which direction is north," Glick commanded.

"Why?" Penny said.

"To get to the Zephyrus," Glick said.

"Please?" Max asked in a kind voice. "It will help us find Ed."

"Fine," she said, stomping over to the entertainment stand for the TV remote.

"You want the weather station?" she asked, turning on the TV. Glick nodded.

She switched on the weather station. The screen cycled between the local, statewide, nationwide, and worldwide Doppler radars of precipitation.

"And, north?" Glick asked.

Penny got her bearings. She mentally pictured the sun rising and setting on her apartment. Since Ed's apartment was adjacent to hers on the same side of the complex, it would be the same.

"Towards that corner of the kitchen," she said with certainty.

252

Glick swiveled the door to point north. He looked at the TV, then adjusted the door to point more northwestwardly. He looked back at the TV and adjusted the doorway a little more. He reminded Penny of someone adjusting rabbit ear antennas on an old television set trying to get the picture just right. With the door positioned to his liking, Glick braced it with four makeshift doorstops of Ed's shoes placed strategically around the base of the Lazy Susan.

"What is he doing?" Max whispered to Penny, but she just threw her hands up and shook her head.

Oscar-Frank barked at Glick and his doorway from on top of the kitchen table. He pawed at the puzzle pieces and sniffed at the partially eaten cookie.

"Oscar! What are you doing up there?" Penny said, and pulled him down from the table. "Don't you eat that!"

Penny snagged the half cookie, gave a sigh, and tossed it into the garbage can in the kitchen. She returned to the kitchen table, scooped up Oscar-Frank, and set him down on the floor. Taken away from his delicious discovery and banished to the floor, Oscar-Frank returned to the sofa for more pets from Max.

Glick muttered something quietly to himself. To Penny, it sounded like no language she had ever heard. It was as strange as the writing all over the bookcase frame. She thought it sounded ancient and melodic and imagined it to be a musical language of the faery people. Glick completed his chant and looked at the makeshift doorway expectantly. When it did nothing, his shoulders slumped. He calculated again, then said, "Ah!"

He pulled out the shoe-doorstops, spun the door 180 degrees, and locked it into place. Before he could slide the last two doorstops into place, the letters and symbols on the door glowed a purplish hue like a black light. He gave a satisfactory nod and stood back.

Penny backed away from the door with her mouth open. She glanced at Max, who had Oscar-Frank next to him getting belly rubs. Max looked at the door with mild interest and had a tired, almost bored, expression on his face. She had seen her moms work "magic" before, but nothing like this. Her moms' magic was not much different from cooking or a poetry reading with a display of symbolic props and gestures. This was the real kind of magic she knew existed somewhere in the world. Who would have thought she would discover it in her neighbor's apartment?

Glick's doorway rattled the same way a closed door does when the air conditioner kicks on and creates greater pressure on one side of the door. A cool breeze blew across the floor to her sandaled feet.

Glick opened the door. Impossible sunlight shone through the doorway at an angle that had never hit the inside of Ed's apartment. Without hesitating, Max stood up and followed Glick through the doorway.

Max stopped on the other side, turned to Penny, and asked, "Aren't you coming?"

Penny's heart raced. She looked down at Oscar-Frank, and asked, "Well? What do you think?"

Oscar-Frank barked once and trotted through the door after Max. He looked up at Max and wagged his tail as if expecting a treat or more ear scratches.

Penny had no choice. Her dog had befriended a complete stranger and followed him through an even stranger door. Her friend's spirit-possessed body had just built an impossibly strange doorway to some strange place he called the "Zephyrus" and walked through it on some kind of strange mission to get home. Despite her better judgement telling her to run home, lock herself in her apartment, and pretend none of this had ever happened, she, too, stepped through the doorway. For Penny, things were about to get a lot stranger.

CHAPTER FOURTEEN

A Tale of Two Cities

Emily lead Ed through part of Black Manor. She wound them down halls and through room after room. Emily seemed right at home, but Ed certainly could have easily meandered endlessly through the maze of rooms. It reminded Ed of the vacations with his parents when he explored the hotels they visited. With a whole afterlife ahead of him, he imagined the hours he could spend exploring Black Manor.

Each room they passed through had its own unique style. One living room was decorated in a 60's style of furniture and shag carpet. They passed one room that looked built for a family with several children; it contained a jumbled fort of bunk beds, platforms, slides, and tunnels. Another room they passed had no furniture but was painted blood red. At the corner of the hallway stood the doorway to a bathroom as big, or bigger than, a living room they had passed through earlier. The layout defied logic but had a unique and natural flow.

As they walked from room to room, Emily explained Black Manor was an organic house.

Occasionally, the Manor would give birth to a closet or cupboard. This area would grow into a small room and develop its own decor. Some of the older rooms would either be pushed upwards or downwards by new rooms until they became mostly forgotten and declined either into basements or attics. The more people lived in a room, the less chance it would decline into obscurity. Because Emily practically lived in the library, that room had become a permanent fixture to the Manor.

"Here we are," Emily said, reaching for the handle of a door to the backyard.

Inside the Manor, they stood in a small greenhouse with dirty, misted windows. It wasn't until Emily opened the door that Ed could see into the backyard. He gasped when he saw the garden. His eyes lit up and his jaw dropped. Ed's legs felt weak as he stepped out the door and into a place he knew very well but had not visited in a long time.

"This is my garden," he gasped.

"Of course it is," Emily said, "the whole world is yours."

"I get that, but I *know* this garden," he said.

Emily looked at the garden, then back at Ed. She tried to read his expression. "This garden seems extra special to you. Why is it so special? I don't remember reading anything about it. And, I'm fairly certain you never wrote anything about it. I'm sure I would remember reading about a garden like this," she said.

"Back in college, I read this book about modern

shamanism," Ed said.

"I know that book. I started reading it, but never finished it. Not my cup of tea," she said, and wrinkled her nose.

"Anyway," Ed continued, "The book described how to imagine yourself in your mental garden in order to help deal with various situations and stresses. This is my mental garden." Ed looked over the physical form of his mental creation.

"You have a brilliant mental garden," Emily said, "I love reading here, especially by the fountain."

"Thank you. Throughout college, I'd meditate and mentally visit my garden. It's been years, but I used to mentally visit it probably hundreds of times. Come on, let's go explore it together."

He held her hand and led her down the path to the fountain in the center of the garden. Ed couldn't believe his eyes. The garden was better than he ever imagined it. It was so real! The garden he and Emily walked through was that same garden. Only instead of imagining being there, he was actually there. It felt like imagining a place he had always wanted to visit and traveling there only to discover how much better it was.

The gurgling three-tiered fountain – the feature Emily enjoyed the most – stood in the center of the garden. Ed explained its waters washed away his pain and stress. A ring of grey bricks encircled the fountain. Connected to the brick rings, multiple paths stretched away from the fountain like legs from a squashed octopus. On the far side, white tiles lead to a towering spiral staircase, which swirled upwards into the clouds high above and downwards deep into the ground. He knew that high above the stairs led to a Heaven of sorts where he could obtain sage advice. Deep below the garden, the stairs spiraled downward to a form of Hell, where he could picture himself solving difficult problems and battling internal demons. On one side, a gravel path wound up a short hill to a structure resembling a portion of ancient Rome with a crumbling grove of pillars of varying heights and diameters. Ghosts, looking like transparent-white ski masks, lazily floated around and among the structure's pillars; they could answer only yes or no kind of questions – like a game of 20 Questions.

The garden also had other, unfamiliar features. On another side, a red-bricked path ran to a square platform. The center of the platform held up a section of wall with a white door. Another path of cement wound a little ways off to a white picket fence that ran several feet in either direction before sinking lower and lower into the tall grasses beyond the garden. Another path, like a wooden pier, led to a gigantic oak tree, which shaded part of the house, and had a wooden door built into the base of its trunk.

Besides the additional, unfamiliar structures in the garden, flowers of all sorts of vibrant shades grew along the path. The fragrance from the flowers wasn't overpowering. The smell reminded Ed of summer bike rides and picnics in the park. In the distance, Ed could hear the crashing of waves and the chirping of birds in the branches of the towering oak tree.

Emily led Ed to the door in the oak tree. Ed imagined a family of badgers living within, speaking proper English and wearing old fashioned clothing.

"This, I call the Family Tree," she said, and opened the door. Ed stooped to enter the tree door, and Emily followed him inside.

The inside of the tree was definitely much larger than the outside. A yellow, sunny light illuminated the inside of the tree from an unknown source. Inside was a tall, cylindrical room disappearing high up the trunk of the tree. Two spiral staircases crisscrossed upwards, with hallways taking off into various branches of the tree limbs. Along the stairs and down some of the more visible hallways, Ed saw glass display cases with plaques like ones found in a museum.

"This case is yours," Emily said, indicating the largest case at the base of the stairs. Inside, the case held Ed's most favored possessions. His tattered, yellow, baby blanket given up long ago, but never forgotten. An old door knob on a string he carried around as a good luck charm. Leaning on a small easel inside the case was something he knew very well.

"My journal," he said.

"Unfortunately, I've never been able to get inside the case. No lock and key. No hinges. Just

260

solid glass," she said. She knocked on the glass with her knuckle to prove how solid the case was.

Ed approached the case to inspect how one might get in. He placed his hand on the top, but it slipped through the glass as if the case was made of water. When his hand touched the glass, the surface wavered and rippled. Emily tried again but still met resistance, even though the glass rippled below her fingers.

Ed reached for his journal and easily pulled it out of the case through the glass. No sirens or flashing lights went off.

"Hm," she said, "The case must know you're the owner."

Ed took the journal and walked out to the garden. He sat down on the rim of the fountain and leafed through the journal. Emily followed and sat beside him, peeking over his shoulder, trying to catch glimpses of one of the few books of Ed's she had never read.

Not far from the front of the journal, written in pencil, he found the entry he was looking for. It read, "Max's Portable Pools; Checkered Scissors".

Ed showed Emily the entry.

"Oh! Max! I know of him," Emily said.

"You do? Where can I find him?" Ed said.

"I said I know *of* Max. I don't know where in your world he could be, but I remember reading about him in the news. Something about a boy who paralyzed himself diving into his pool. The boy dove and missed."

Ed winced.

"There was another story about a shark that bit a wrestler in one of his portable pools, too."

"Two leads," Ed said.

"One lead. They've already held a funeral for the wrestler," she said.

"Ok. One lead. Do you remember the name of the boy?"

"No, but I know where we can look up his name. We can check the news archives in the City."

"I don't suppose you'll be wanting to take the bus into town, huh?" Ed asked.

"No. I don't ride the bus anymore. Not since that one time. These days, I walk. But, since the City is a long walk, I prefer to go by water."

"Is there some kind of shuttle boat?" Ed asked.

"Nope. Canoe," she said.

Emily leaned over the fountain. She touched the surface of the water with her index finger and drew a symbol, creating tiny wakes in its path. She stood up and looked expectantly at the fountain as if she were waiting for a bus.

Ed stood up and looked at the fountain. He could see nothing but the trickling water.

He turned toward her and asked, "What's that supposed to do?"

She pointed at the fountain. When Ed turned to look, an elderly man paddled a canoe from somewhere behind the fountain. He had no idea where it came from. The canoe seemed to barely fit in the fountain. The hull of the canoe bent in a slight banana shape to follow the curve of the circular fountain.

The old man stopped the canoe in front of Emily and pulled his paddle from the water. He bowed to Emily and she bowed back. The man turned to Ed and bowed.

"Well? He's inviting you into the canoe," she said, carefully climbing in.

Ed bowed his head, followed Emily into the canoe, and sat behind her. The canoe was sturdier than the ones Ed remembered from his summer camp days.

"Take us to the City, please," she said.

The man nodded. He slid his paddle into the narrow water between his canoe and the side of the fountain. He swept it backwards and the canoe departed. He slowly followed the curve of the fountain.

Ed thought this was ridiculous. It reminded him of being on a children's carnival ride. He wondered how in his world would this ever take them to the city. Then, he thought, on the other hand, he had no idea where the man and his canoe appeared from either.

As they circled the fountain, a quick, thick fog arose from the tranquil water. In seconds, a blanket of fog shrouded the canoe and its passengers. Ed could no longer see beyond the confines of the canoe. Even though he could not see, it no longer felt like they were paddling slowly in a circle. Somehow, they flowed in the swift moving current of an open stream.

The old paddle man switched the paddle from side to side and propelled the canoe like it was second nature. The canoe traveled quickly, but it rocked very little, if at all. The only reason Ed felt they were traveling swiftly was a strong sensation that he had of being pulled forward. Otherwise, everything else was calm. Even the fog hung lazily in the air around them.

The pulling sensation loosened its grip as the fog lifted. They no longer paddled around the circumference of the garden fountain, but they were somewhere else. It appeared to be a rocky canyon. The canoe drifted between large rock formations towering around them on either side. Ed caught a brief glimpse through the lifting fog of something very large crawling across the surface of one of the rocks.

"What was that?" Ed asked.

Emily leaned back and said, "It's nothing to worry about. It's only the fountain dragons."

"Dragons?" Ed asked, not concealing the nervousness from his voice.

The fog lifted completely. The old man brought the canoe to a halt beside the edge of a massive fountain. They were no longer in Ed's garden. Instead, a strange and beautiful city encompassed them.

"Welcome to the City," Emily said.

Ed's mouth hung open as wide as his eyes. He mouthed, "Wow."

✂ ✂ ✂

Penny stood in the doorway and stared. Her mind told her what she saw was impossible, but her eyes put up a good argument. Behind her, she clearly saw Ed's apartment through the doorway. The other side of the doorway was completely different. She raised her hand to her mouth.

"In or out?" Glick asked.

Penny had a hard time thinking. Her mind spun as she tried to take in the scenery. She focused on Glick and said, "Huh?"

"In? Or, out?" Glick asked again, "I assume you do not want strangers entering Ed's apartment. I must close the door and take the knob so no one else can use this door but us."

"Oh," she muttered, and stepped out of his way, completely through the door, and into this wonderfully, strange new place.

As Glick shut the door and worked at pulling off the knob, Penny stared at the Zephyrus. Such a place only existed in dreams and stories. She didn't believe a floating city could be real.

Glick's doorway stood on the outer edge of the city. A narrow, wooden pier with a rope railing served as the only barrier separating them from a drop of thousands of feet to the ground below. Clouds billowed around the edges of the Zephyrus. Breaks in the cloud coverage exposed the Earth far below. Currently, the Zephyrus hung over green farmlands.

She expected the temperature to be much colder

so high up in the air, yet it felt comfortable. The exposed sun above them felt warm, but not baking. Also, after experiencing a sudden altitude change, she thought it would be harder to breathe. It did not feel any different from being at ground level.

"Beautiful, isn't it?" Max asked. Penny felt comforted knowing neither Max nor Glick were disturbed by the new surroundings. Even Oscar-Frank seemed somewhat in his element as he approached the railing to sniff around. Max knelt down to scratch Oscar-Frank behind his floppy ears.

Penny laughed nervously and nodded. The Zephyrus was a beautiful floating city. The wooden piers, each plank separated by a tiny gap, were worn smooth by years of people walking from place to place. Small buildings lined the walkways in neat horizontal and vertical cross-sections. Many of the buildings housed open shops on the first floor, with what appeared might be living quarters above. Each shop had a single, glass front door and large windows exposing the shop's display. The rows of shops felt familiar to her, which comforted her nerves. Thoughts of floating high above the ground kept her worried. That, and two strangers accompanied her to this impossible place.

Finally pulling the knob from the door, Glick said, "Come."

Glick threaded the doorknob with a loop of string and hung it from his neck.

"Where are we going now?" Max asked.

"To the book trader," Glick said.

"You're looking for a book? I thought you were looking for a way home," Penny said.

"Are you surprised that I know how to read? Or, is this your way of asking which book am I looking for?" Glick asked in response.

"After taking Ed's body and performing that doorway trick, I doubt you could surprise me any longer. I guess my question is how a book is going to help you get home?" Penny asked.

"The book I am looking for is an old guidebook written in an ancient dialect. In its pages, it instructs one how to enter Jaiu."

"How do you know it's here?" Penny asked.

"Logic. If any place has a book as old as the one I seek, it most likely would be in an old place that deals in old books. The oldest book trader I know of is here in the Zephyrus."

"Next question ... How do you even know about this place, much less what kind of shops are here?"

"The Zephyrus is older than the book that I seek. It hasn't always been called the Zephyrus and hasn't always been airborne. In the early days, it traveled on the backs of large, land creatures."

"You mean, like elephants?"

"No. What you call dinosaurs."

Penny chuckled in disbelief.

"Since humans claimed ownership of the land, the city took to the skies and its name changed. Now it goes where the winds take it. After I studied weather patterns and aircraft flight paths, a simple

267

deduction pinpointed the Zephyrus's whereabouts."

"Flight paths?"

"The inhabitants of the Zephyrus would prefer not to have aircraft collide with the city, and so they have taken precautions to deter such disasters."

"Precautions?"

"Though it has nothing to do with either Bermuda or triangles, aircraft and their passengers have been confiscated in extreme circumstances."

Penny thought Glick was a living conspiracy theory. Everything about him was a tabloid reporter's dream. A spirit inhabiting someone's stereo possesses the owner, then constructs a magic door to a floating city in the clouds in order to find an ancient magical tome? Who makes up this kind of stuff? She seriously considered sending in the story to a tabloid. Too bad she didn't remember to bring her camera for proof. Yet, wasn't that always the way of urban legends?

"If you've been trapped in Ed's stereo, how do you know all this?" Penny asked with skepticism.

"The stereo had a superb transmitter and receiver. While the music was off, I listened to the world and learned a lot," Glick said, and walked away.

Penny clinched her fists and growled, "He's impossible."

"Yes. But, right now, he's our only way home. I suggest we go with the flow," Max said, and followed Glick. He turned his head, smiled, and encouraged Penny to follow, too. Penny looked at the closed door without a knob and realized Max was right.

Max and Oscar-Frank followed Glick onto the main walkway of the Zephyrus. Penny had a difficult time moving as she was suddenly hit by a panic attack. Of course, one of the two men looked like her friend and neighbor, but he no longer acted the same. As if chanting a mantra, she told herself over and over, "He isn't Ed. He isn't Ed." Even though he looked the same, he acted nothing like the man she knew. He expressed none of his humor and none of his charm. If it wasn't Ed, why, oh why, did she follow him through that impossible doorway? Why didn't she call her moms? She wondered if her moms could do anything to help her now. Most likely, this situation was way beyond them, too. She patted her pockets and realized she left both her wallet and cell phone in her apartment. She had her keys, but both her apartment and car were far away and far below. She hadn't figured she would be going out, especially this far out, and this panicked her even more. And now, this stranger had the only way back again hanging around his neck.

And, what about the other, impossible man? Max seemed to be a very eccentric person, who not only said he knew Ed, but also he claimed Ed created him. Was he serious? Max was friendly enough for Oscar-Frank to take a sudden liking to him. Penny found it odd that he trotted along happily beside Max. He never followed strangers before — whether or not they gave him pets. Even her dog suddenly seemed strange to her. Yet, Oscar-Frank was still a good judge of character. Agreeing with her dog's intuition, Penny also trusted Max and remained confused and leery of Glick.

Where in the world was she? The Zephyrus? A city in the clouds? It sounded like something out of a fairy tale. What kept them airborne?

Penny felt herself on the verge of a massive panic attack, but forced herself to relax. She breathed deeply and focused on the man who once was Ed. He was her only chance of returning to the world she once knew. She figured, if she wanted to get back home, she needed to stick with him. Penny leaned against one of the buildings. She swallowed her fear and willed her feet to move, slowly at first, after the two men walking with her dog.

"First time here?" asked an elderly woman poking her head out of the shop Penny leaned upon.

Penny nodded her head as she breathed.

"You're doing fine, dear. It is a bit intimidating. Keep breathing, and you'll get your air-legs," the woman said. She smiled and returned to her shop.

It was not difficult for Penny to keep an eye on Glick, Max, or even Oscar-Frank. People came and went from shop to shop, but the Zephyrus certainly was not the crowded, busy streets of a metropolis. The local mall had more people, and that's not including the teens hanging out. It seemed not many other people had heard of the Zephyrus either. It surprised her to see anyone else here at all.

Penny caught up and followed a close distance

behind them. She kept one eye on Glick and the other on the shops they passed. One shop had beautiful, flowing dresses that made her think of hippies and flower power. They passed a deli that made her mouth water and stomach gurgle. The shops and people were all very earthly. She half-expected some kind of magical creature or talking animal being in such a wondrous place. If it wasn't for floating so high off the ground, she would have thought the Zephyrus was any small town of shops.

They passed another shop, which sold potpourri and fragrances with various dried flowers and plants in the windows. She was about to say to Ed the fragrance store was the ghost of a florist shop, but remembered he was no longer Ed. Despite her animosity towards the inhabitant in her friend's body, she felt the mention of ghosts might be disrespectful. Plus, the fact remained, she still needed him to get home again.

Glick opened the door to a bookshop, or as he referred to it, a book trader. The bell above the door jingled as they entered. Even though he lived in a small apartment, Ed had quite a lot of books. Even her moms' house had many books. However, this shop had more books than Penny had ever seen at a public library or local book store. She worried the weight of all the books might bog down the rest of the Zephyrus, and whatever kept them afloat must be working extra hard because of this shop. There were even books piled high on all the shelves and counter space.

An old man sitting on the tall stool behind the counter left a valley in the stacks so he could see his customers. He sucked at the tip of a large, ostrich plume quill. His lips and hands were spotted with dots of black ink. His glasses had small circular lenses, one of which was cracked. His hair could have evenly matched Max's in a contest for messiest hair. The man's button-down shirt was also splattered with spots and smudges of ink.

"Welcome," the old book trader said, and waved his quill at the three as they entered his shop. He peeked over the books on the counter and smiled down at Oscar-Frank and said, "Hello, doggies."

Oscar-Frank looked up at the old man peeping at him from over the counter. He barked once, then sat down on his hind legs. With his floppy tongue hanging out of his mouth, he smiled at the old book trader.

Penny smiled, too. The man didn't seem to mind a wiener dog in his shop. She wondered about his eyesight though. Doggies, plural? Oscar-Frank may have two names, but he was clearly one dog. No other dog followed them in.

Glick approached the counter and asked, "Could you tell me ...?"

The old man swept him aside. He was more interested in Penny's dog than dealing another book.

"What's their names?" he asked, waving his fingers to let Penny know he wanted a closer look.

She bent down, picked up her dog, and set him on a sturdier pile of books on the counter.

272

"His name is Oscar-Frank," she said.

"Oscar and Frank. Perfect names," the book trader said, scratching her dog's ears.

"No. It's just Oscar-Frank. Hyphenated. Both hotdog references. You know, because he's a wiener dog," she said, and petted her happy puppy, too.

"You've got yourself more than just a wiener dog. This one looks as if it's from a much older breed. I bet he gets into all sorts of mischief when your back is turned, doesn't he?" said the book trader.

"All the time. It's like he's in two places at once," she said.

"Ah. Then you do know of his talent," the book trader said, looking at Penny over the top of his glasses.

"What talent?" she asked.

The old man chuckled. He scratched his chin and said, "You ever heard of Schrödinger's cat?"

"The one that deals with quantum physics? Something about the cat being in two states at once?" she asked.

"Unobserved," the man added, waggling his finger, "That's the key. The kitty is in more than one state while unobserved. Same with this little guy."

"Are you saying my dog can be in two places at once while I'm not looking?" Penny asked.

"Yes," the man said with the same amount of certainty that he might claim his store was full of books.

"Oscar-Frank is some kind of quantum wiener

273

dog?" Penny asked, barely masking the skepticism in her voice. Her moms told her a lot of odd tales, but this story was hard to swallow.

The old man chuckled again, and said, "In a manner of speaking, yes. It's really a variety of Bellman's Dingo."

"No. Not dingo. Oscar-Frank is pure bred dachshund. Although, it would explain a lot if he could be in two places at once. Wouldn't it?" she said this last part in baby talk and ruffled Oscar-Frank's ears.

"I bet it would. But, my dear, Bellman's Dingo is the modern term for his behavior – not really a breed. And, I'm certain this one has it in him."

Penny smiled at the book trader and shook her head, still skeptical.

"I'm sure you've heard the story about the boy who cried wolf. It's one of the earliest stories of someone witnessing the behavior. It was a dingo, not a wolf. And, it wasn't a boy, it was the town cryer. On watch one night, out of the corner of his eye, he spotted several dingos and rang the bell to warn the town. When the shepherds came running to protect their flocks, all they could see was a single mutt. After they ignored his warning, they couldn't believe the carnage the following morning was from one dingo. That's how the term became Bellman's Dingo," the man said.

"Now then, what can I tell you, good sir?" the man said, finally turning to Glick, who waited patiently. Glick stood so quiet and still, Penny forgot

274

he was standing right next to her.

"I'm looking for an old tome. The translation would be The Jaiuian Way. Do you carry it?" Glick asked.

"My, my. That is old school, isn't it?" the old man said.

"Do you carry it?" Glick asked again.

"No," the old man said. Penny thought when this old book trader gave an answer, it was solid and definite.

"You sound certain. You have not looked around. How do you know you do not have it?" Glick asked.

The old man grimaced and said, "I know for certain, because it is at today's auction. I wanted to be at that auction to purchase that very same book. If it wasn't for my assistant being ill today, I'd be there to bid upon it. I cannot close up shop, because today is delivery day, and I'm expecting several new books."

Penny looked around. If there was a shipment of books due, she didn't know where the man would store them. There were already so many books that the Zephyrus should be anchored to the ground.

"We could attend the auction for you," said Max, poking his head around one of the book cases. Penny forgot he was there, too.

"This is true," said Glick, "Let us go to the auction and purchase the book in your place. We will do this if I can use it briefly. I only need it for a short while."

The old man stroked his chin, and said, "Since this young lady is with you, and she has these charming little dogs, I will front the money if you bid for it on my behalf. Tell the auction house you represent Gulliver's Book Traders. My limit is 10,000."

Glick nodded, and, with the same certainty as the book trader, he said, "Yes."

"My dear, I'm afraid the auction house will not allow our little friends inside. Do you mind if they keep me company in my shop until you return?"

"Well," Penny hesitated. Not only was she in a strange place among strangers, but now she was asked to leave her dog with another complete stranger. Not to mention, this stranger believed she owned a quantum wiener dog.

"Consider it collateral until you return with the book," the old man said. Oscar-Frank squirmed around on his back as the old man rubbed his belly.

Penny looked at Oscar-Frank. Her dog obviously didn't mind, and the book trader seemed friendly enough. For a dachshund, Oscar-Frank was generally a good judge of character. Penny faulted herself for being too trusting at times. Oscar-Frank played the role of Penny's personality litmus test. Oscar-Frank didn't hold back on people he didn't trust, and Penny valued his opinion. Oscar-Frank liked the book trader and Max, but didn't have a strong opinion of Glick. If she had a chance of returning home, she needed to stick close to him. She didn't want him out of her sight. Glick did not seem untrustworthy, but didn't seem to care who he trampled to get what he wanted. He had a deal with the book trader, and Penny felt he would return to uphold his end of the bargain.

Penny sighed, and said, "Okay. Hopefully, he's not any trouble."

"No trouble at all. I assure you," the book trader said.

The old man wrote a brief letter to the auction house, folded it in half, and gave it to Glick. He gave them directions to the auction house and wished them luck.

Penny glanced back to see Oscar-Frank sitting on the counter, smiling at her with tongue flopped out and tail wagging. The book trader waved them farewell with one hand and pet her dog with the other.

✂   ✂   ✂

Penny may have thought the Zephyrus was impressive, but the Zephyrus couldn't compare to the metropolis at which Ed gawked. The city was an explosion of sensory overload. The fountain dragons crawled across the rock formations and blasted each other with jets of water. None of the buildings matched, as if the architects perpetually outdid each other in artistic style and structure. Some of the abstract architecture made one's eyes cross to look at and bent the mind to think about. Pedestrians walking down the sidewalks were a freakish blend of TV and movie personalities, cartoons, puppets, claymation, and people Ed knew from his past.

Other citizens traveled down the streets in anything that could carry them, from normal cars and trucks, to the backs of dinosaurs, and even a magic carpet taxi. In the distant skyline, a towering crab monster demolished buildings and crushed fleeing citizens. Emily assured Ed the crab monster was nothing to fear as it was a permanent fixture in the city's background – no matter where one was in the city.

Whichever direction Ed faced, his view was crammed with wondrous and highly active creations born from some portion of his mind. He had a hard time fathoming that everything he saw was either a figment of his own imagination or something he experienced in his lifetime. Buses with tiger legs instead of wheels ran down the street to pick up or drop off passengers. A man in a purple suit pedaling what looked like a half-bicycle, half-streetlamp whizzed by them as they climbed out of the canoe to the rim of the fountain.

"You'll get used to it and learn to block it all out after a while," Emily said, noticing Ed's open-mouthed gape at the city and all its wonders.

Emily led the way down the street towards the news archives. They passed shops, restaurants, and arcades of Ed's past. One place they passed, Hallucinatapes, was a kind of video rental store, but sold what seemed to be virtual reality daydreams. Another building held an indoor, grassy park with people sitting on park benches and kids playing on playground equipment surrounded by walls painted like a blue, summer sky.

As Ed took in the overwhelming scenery, he began to notice many of the people noticing him. Most smiled and a few waved. One man walked up to him, shook his hand, and thanked him – for what he had not idea. Ed felt out of sorts. During his life in Outworld, he wasn't noticed any more than most other people. Suddenly, in the City, he achieved celebrity status.

"Why are so many people gawking at me?" he whispered to Penny.

She rolled her eyes and said, "You're the world's owner. You created this place. Remember?"

"I'm not used to so much attention," he said, then tried to not look at the people looking at him, which was hard. He looked down at his feet and followed Emily, keeping an eye on her with his peripheral vision. Looking down also helped block out much of the scenery, too. He found it difficult not to look up now and then to see the sights, or to glance toward someone calling out his name.

The gawkers continued around the corner and up another block. The onlookers subsided when Ed and Emily arrived at the news archives and went inside. They entered through a set of glass doors beneath a sign in big block letters reading "Tellis Communications".

A grid of televisions checkered the back wall of the lobby, each displaying a different channel. Ed recognized many of the shows as sitcoms and movies he watched throughout his life. A few had new shows he had never seen before. A couple of the screens presented the news. Ed wondered if either one was the same station that covered news of the overturned bus of his dream of Emily. During commercial breaks, heads of different people appeared on some of the televisions. The head looked down at the people walking through the lobby, and the moment a person looked at the head watching, it disappeared and the show continued. Ed caught a couple of the channels watching him out of the corner of his eye.

Ed never had a moment of fame in his life. If he did, it was fleeting. Everyone who watched him, including the heads on the monitors, made him feel uncomfortable and self-conscious. He preferred to live an anonymous life. He had heard stories of celebrities wearing disguises and considered doing the same. Until he could travel incognito, he did his best to block the people out and focused on why he and Emily came to the City.

Emily approached the front desk with Ed at her side. A stiff, robotic, woman sat at the desk, and as they approached asked, "Yes? How may I help you?"

"We'd like to access the news archives," Emily said.

The woman click-clacked at her keyboard and said, "Booth 53."

"Thank you," Emily said.

The woman tilted her head in a barely perceptible nod.

Emily walked to a doorway at the left side of the lobby. A short hallway led them to a maze of office cubes, each with a computer and a bench wide enough for two people. People of the other occupied booths watched anything from television reruns, archived news reports, and even something resembling home movies. Emily led Ed among the cubes until they found the vacant one tagged "53".

Emily took a seat and patted the bench. Ed sat down beside her. Within seconds, Emily pulled up several archived clips regarding Maximilian Spyne, the Portable Pool Salesman. A few of the clips were commercials, which surprisingly contained little, if any, contact information. Ed thought the lack of contact information was odd. How could Max be so successful if people couldn't get in touch with him? Most of the clips regarded the two tragedies that crippled Max's Portable Pool enterprise. Sorting through the news clips, they finally found one clip that mentioned the paralyzed teen's name to be Daniel Halfunt. Using the computer's internet connection, they pulled up the Halfunt family's address. Beside the media archive computers, each booth provided a courtesy pad of paper and pen with the Tellis Communications name and logo. Emily jotted the address down.

The other news clips regarding Max detailed the tragic death of wrestler Dirk Juggernaut. The details of how Dirk actually died were confusing. The news talked about a shark attack in Dirk's swimming pool and him losing an arm fending off the attack. Other footage from his last wrestling match showed the arm being pulled off from another wrestler. Both scenarios claimed Dirk bled to death and had complications due to losing an arm. And, both claimed Dirk Juggernaut to be dead.

"I guess that lead is a dead end," Ed said, then added, "No pun intended."

"None taken. At least we can seek out the Halfunts and see if they've had any further contact with Max," Emily said.

"Sounds good. But, while we're here, the news about the wrestler mentioned a memorial service. Can you pull up any footage of Dirk Juggernaut's funeral?"

"Sure," Emily said. In seconds, they watched the archive of the special presentation of the wrestler's memorial. The footage had many of Dirk's friends and family talking about his life. Each person stood at the podium and shared his or her favorite moments. A large picture of the smiling wrestler stood on an easel centered behind a closed casket. Then, at the end of the presentation, the camera focused on the casket lowering slowly into the ground as a choir sang a mournful song and the credits rolled.

"Hm," Ed said.

"Sad, isn't it," Emily said.

"Yes. It was a good service, but I wonder something."

"What's that?"

"I mean the man no disrespect, but is this for real?" Ed asked.

"Of course it's real. As real as you or me. Why?

282

You think he faked his death?" Emily asked.

"Maybe. It's just that televised wrestlers put on an act for their matches. The memorial service wasn't presented by the news. It was produced by the wrestling organization. It said so in the credits. It would be interesting if Dirk's memorial service was not an actual funeral, but more of an elaborate way to retire the wrestler as a character. If we really want to look into it, I suppose there are probably official records documenting his death," Ed said, "I think we got enough to go on for now. Let's go meet the Halfunts."

They made their way through the cube farm back towards the lobby. Ed added an item to his mental checklist of things to do, which was to one day return to the archives and skim over any major news events that might be important. Apparently, while he lived his life, the world created for him took on a life of its own. Even though he created the place, he felt like an alien in his own world. Maybe, like Emily suggested, in time he would grow more accustomed to it. Ed wondered if he would feel better once OmniCore figured out how to reconnect him.

"Back to the fountain?" Ed asked.

Emily looked at the address written on the slip of paper and shook her head.

"I don't know if there is a water source near this address. We might need to take the televator," she said, and frowned.

"I'm sorry. The what?" Ed asked.

"The televator," she said, sounding defeated. "It's like an elevator, but it's not just vertical. You tell it where you want to go, and it takes you just about anywhere."

"You sound like you don't want to go by televator," Ed said.

"The canoe is fine. It's foggy, but open. The televator brings back memories of the bus, and I'm just not that crazy about enclosed places."

"Where is it we're going? Is it far? Can we walk there? Can we get a map and see if there's water nearby where we're going?"

Emily smiled and shook her head. "I don't get out much, other than to the City, but I don't know of a map of your world. I've heard people have tried to map it, but they get frustrated, and give up. It's a world the size of your imagination. It's an enormous place. Plus, there's all these overlaps and shortcuts. Cartography is a difficult profession here."

No maps? A televator? Ed felt like a tourist lost in his own world. Again, he wondered if he was connected to it, would he have better insight on where to go and how to get there? He felt helpless and dependent on Emily for guidance, but even she admitted her narrow scope of his world.

"What do you suggest?" he asked.

She thought about it. Ed could sense her internal struggle about what she wanted to do. Finally, rubbing her third eye with her finger, she sighed and said, "We can go by televator. You'll be with me. With company, I might be okay. No more

284

disappearing acts, okay?"

"What? I woke up into another dream. I couldn't help it," Ed said.

"No excuse," she said, "Come on."

The two walked through the city down another couple of blocks towards the televator station. Walking and talking with Emily, Ed already began to tune out the chaos bubbling all around him. It brought back memories of walking down the streets of New York City when he visited years ago, or visiting Downtown Houston as a teen on trips with his parents to the theatre. Except, instead of the cities he remembered, this was like a city architected by the minds of Walt Disney, Salvador Dali, and Terry Gilliam.

They arrived at the televator station, which had two, narrow, parallel structures, each with a set of five elevator doors. The structures mirrored each other with a line of backless benches running between them. Emily took a ticket from a dispenser and paced up and down the benches. Other people also waited on the benches for their televator to arrive. As other people's numbers appeared on the panel above the door, they entered the televators and disappeared behind the sliding double doors.

Ed sat on one of the benches. He kept his head down to make himself more inconspicuous. Emily anxiously looked from the ticket to the numbers above the televator doors. As she passed Ed, he reached up and grabbed hold of her arm.

"Relax," he told her, and coaxed her into sitting

285

next to him on the bench.

Emily sat down, then began nibbling her fingernails and tapping her foot. Ed watched the people entering and exiting the station. He saw a familiar young woman with her friends exit one of the televators. They laughed at a private joke as they exited, but the young woman's humorous spirit faded when she saw Ed. The woman excused herself from her friends, stormed over to Ed, and glared down at him.

She folded her arms and said, "How dare you!"

"Um. What?" Ed asked.

"Don't um-what me," she said, "How dare you treat me the way you did!"

Ed was confused. He remembered working with the woman a couple of jobs before Hammond Eggs, but could not think of anything he could have done or said to offend her. He remembered asking her out during his singlehood before Lydia, but didn't think she would be offended at that.

"Do you even remember who I am?" she asked.

"Yes," Ed said. "You're Karen. We worked together at Flexters."

She gave an icy snort and said, "The name is Kara, and that's not all we did. Or, don't you remember?"

Emily stopped biting her nails and watched the exchange between Ed and his ex-coworker. Ed shook his head and shrugged his shoulders.

Kara turned to Emily and said, "I'd watch out for your little friend here. He'll use you for a bit of fun and then throw you away and never call."

Ed racked his brains. He couldn't remember doing anything with her. He asked her out and she rejected him. That was the end of it.

"I'm sorry. I don't remember what we did," Ed said.

Glaring at Ed once again, Kara said, "Oh, you know what you did. We did you know what, then you disappeared, and never called me again. That's what."

Ed shook his head. He never did anything with this woman because she never agreed to go out with him. How could they ever ...?

That's when it hit him. He remembered the dream of her. In a dream, he got intimate with Kara in one of the meeting rooms. When things got really steamy, he woke up. He never called her again because he never dreamed of her again.

"But, that wasn't real," Ed said, then realized too late, he had said the wrong thing.

"Wasn't real?" Kara said, and slapped him. "Wasn't *real*? I thought I was special. I thought you wanted me."

Kara slapped him again and started to cry.

"I didn't mean that. It meant it was just a dream," he said.

Emily bit her lip and shook her head. She turned her face away, not watching Ed dig himself deeper.

Kara wiped away her tears and said, "Yes, it was a dream. *My* dream. I once thought it was a beautiful dream. I thought we had something special. Apparently, I meant nothing to you. I finally run into you after all this time, and you couldn't even remember."

"I'm sorry," Ed said.

Kara slapped him a third time, harder, and said, "At least now I know what I meant to you."

She returned to her group of friends, who comforted her and scowled over their shoulders at Ed.

A televator dinged, and Emily quietly said, "That one's ours. Ready?"

"Yes," he said, nursing his cheeks.

He followed Emily into the televator. The televator resembled an elevator, except for the panel beside the door. A small keyboard replaced the buttons representing the floor numbers. Instead of the panel showing the floor numbers, a small display screen was centered above the door. Emily entered the address into the keyboard, and the display showed the nearest televator stop. As the double doors slid closed, the destination blinked, then disappeared from the screen. They were on their way. Instinctively, Emily took hold of Ed's hand and held it tightly as the televator began to move.

"I didn't mean to hurt her. It was just a dream. I couldn't remember it," he said.

"It's not just a dream. For many people in this world, it's their birth. It's how you defined them as who they are in this world," Emily said.

The televator dropped. The movement made

288

Ed's stomach feel even worse. The drop slowed, and then the televator lurched to the right. It changed directions before slowing, then ascended once again. There were no windows, but Ed could picture their little televator car zipping along various underground tunnels like a personal subway. And all the way, Emily crushed his hand in hers.

"Geez, I feel like such a jerk," he said. "I must have made her feel like I defined her as a piece of meat."

"Pretty much," Emily said.

"I need to watch what I say," Ed said.

"Yep. Pretty much," Emily agreed.

Ed stood in silence for a while, feeling the televator pull them in different directions. He watched the display above the door cycle through various symbols and pictures.

"I've always experienced dreams differently. In Outworld, they tell us dreams are like our minds cleaning out our brains at night, purging information from our subconscious. I never really had control over what I dreamt about. I just ... dreamt. To me, some dreams are more powerful and more meaningful, but others are just fleeting moments. I'm so sorry if I made you feel bad about your dream," Ed said.

"I'm fine," Emily said, "I was pleased you even remembered my dream."

After another moment of reflection, Ed asked, "And, we never ... You-know-what ... In your dream ... Right? Did we?"

289

"You mean, you don't remember?" Emily asked, and shot him a wicked smile.

"Uh," Ed said, and tried to recall the full dream of him and Emily on the bus.

She shook her head. "No. We never did you-know-what. You were a perfect gentleman," she said, and grinned. "Just curious, though, exactly how many women did you you-know-what in your dreams?"

Ed's face turned pink with embarrassment. "I don't know. Lots, I guess?"

"That might make this an interesting little excursion. I wonder how many other exes we might run into," Emily said.

Ed wondered, too. Not all his dreams were good. Who or what else might they encounter? Ed gulped.

The televator slowed to a stop. The door chimed, then slid open again to reveal another completely different but familiar looking landscape. A suburban area replaced the cityscape. Emily exited the televator and sighed with relief, while Ed nursed life back into his crushed hand.

Ed looked up and down the streets and said, "I know this place. Let me see that address."

Emily handed him the slip of paper with the address printed on it. She said, "You should know it. You created it."

The televator doors slid closed and the box sank into the sidewalk leaving nothing but pavement.

"No. I didn't imagine this area. This is the

neighborhood where I grew up."

"Are you sure?"

"Positive. When I was a kid, my friend and I rode our bikes all over the neighborhood. I even helped him with his paper route. I'm positive this is it. It's been a while, so I'm a little rusty on the street names, but if I'm not mistaken, this address should be on the next block."

"Then, let's go," Emily said.

They walked down the sidewalk and Ed marveled at the detail in his world. The neighborhood was better than he remembered and was so familiar to the one he knew as a kid. It had been years since he'd seen his old house. The last time he saw it, he helped his parents move out.

He imagined now, how much the real neighborhood should have grown. Bigger trees. Newer families. Remodeled homes. Different paint jobs. This neighborhood – the neighborhood of his world – was recreated from a snapshot of his past. A time when childhood Ed rode his bike up and down all the streets like a rat in a maze.

Emily checked the address again. Verifying the house as the right address, they walked up to the front door. Ed rang the doorbell and took a step back. Inside, a small dog yipped at the visitors.

A woman answered the door. She had greying hair mostly pulled back into a ponytail with frazzled strands sticking out. The woman wore a well-worn shirt and sweatpants. She had the small dog tucked under one arm.

"Yeah?" the woman said.

"Ms. Halfunt?" Ed asked.

"Yeah?" she said again. She looked Emily and Ed up and down and didn't look impressed with either of them.

Ed sensed the woman was in the middle of something important she wanted to get back to. He said, "I'm sorry to disturb you. I was wondering if I might take a moment of your time to ask you a few questions."

"Look, I've already told the press everything. I wish people'd leave poor Danny alone, alright?"

"The question isn't really about Danny. It's about Max. I was wondering if he keeps in touch with you, and, if so, if you could let us know how to contact him."

"Mom! It's ready!" called a voice from somewhere within the house.

"Be there in a second!" Ms. Halfunt called back. She looked at Ed and Emily and said, "Max has been more than generous taking care of Danny's medical bills. But, he ain't here taking care of my son day in, day out. If he really cared, he'd lend a hand more often. Let a poor woman rest once in a while."

"Do you know how we might contact him?" Emily asked.

"I've tried calling him. He ain't answering. Hasn't returned calls in weeks, neither."

"Mom! Hurry up!"

"In a second!" she barked, "Max is usually good about returning calls. Maybe he just got tired of

292

dealing with us. Maybe he just dropped off the face of the world."

Ed and Emily looked at each other.

"Do you have his number?" Ed asked.

"Mom!"

Ms. Halfunt said, "I've gotta get back. If you see him, send him our way."

"Sure thing," Ed said.

"Mom!"

"I'm coming!" she yelled, and slammed the door.

Ed and Emily walked down the path to the sidewalk.

"That's a dead end. Now what?" Emily asked.

"We follow the other lead," Ed said.

"The other lead is another dead end. He was killed by a shark. How is that a lead?"

"His buddies attended his funeral. They might know how to contact Max."

"His buddies? You mean those TV wrestlers?"

"Those are the ones. Let's go to TV Land and talk to some wrestlers."

Emily stopped walking. She looked more nervous than before getting into the televator.

"What's wrong?" Ed asked.

"You want to go to TV Land?"

"Yeah. Let's take the televator down to the studio and get some info out of those wrasslers."

"Now?"

"No. *Sunday! Sunday! Sunday!* Yes, of course, right now. What's wrong?"

"TV Land. I don't know what it is about TVs and TV Land, but that place gives me the willies."

"What's so bad about TV Land? That's where the magic happens," Ed said.

"It's the magic of TV Land that gives me the willies."

CHAPTER FIFTEEN

Book Bidding

People trickled into the Quartermain Auction House. Generations ago, the Quartermain family bought the old Zephyrus Theatre, which was abandoned after the audience destroyed the seats beyond repair in the theatre's final production. It happened opening night of a poorly-cast production featuring an obscure, all-yodeling musical called *Go Yell It on the Mountain*. The theatre remained boarded up for decades, until the Quartermains bought it, touched up the paint, mended the curtains, and fixed a few holes in the stage. The Quartermains preserved the theatre's original style other than the auditorium seating area, in which they carpeted the floor and brought in straight-backed chairs. When the remodeling was complete, they reopened the building as the city's auction house.

Glick, Max, and Penny followed the crowd into the auction house and walked down the aisles of padded, straight-backed chairs. Most of the seats were already occupied in the front five rows. The nearest the three could find enough seats together was halfway down on the far side of the auditorium.

"I've never been to an auction," Max said.

"I have. My moms used to go quite a bit when I was young. They'd take me along. I remember thinking it felt haunted. A bunch of old people buying old things. After a while, something about them seemed, I don't know, magical."

"Silence. The auction begins," Glick said.

Penny and Max looked at each other. Max nodded his head in Glick's direction and rolled his eyes. Penny stifled a laugh.

A woman in an elegant, but plain, dark blue dress stood at the podium. She wore white, cloth gloves for when she was required to handle one of the auction items. She presented each item with a brief description, then requested a starting bid.

Item after item, they waited. What once seemed scary, and then magical, Penny now found slow and tedious. The chairs were comfortable. After a long day of work and an evening of watching Glick build his doorway, her mind began to wander as she drifted to sleep. She dreamt of exploring more of the Zephyrus, but instead of the marketplace, she was in a castle in the clouds. After climbing a tower and looking through the crenellations at the world below, someone snuck up behind her and pushed her over. As she fell, she saw Ed laughing maniacally from the top of the tower.

She slid off someone's arm and fell forward in her chair, snorting herself awake. Looking around, she realized she had fallen asleep on Max's arm.

"Sorry. I didn't mean to. Sorry," she said.

"You're okay. You had a good little nap and slept on my arm. I hated to wake you," Max whispered.

"How long was I out?" she asked.

"Almost an hour and a half," he said, "I almost joined you a couple of times myself. This auction seems to be going on forever."

Penny sat up straighter. Realizing she fell asleep in a strange place in the company of strangers and having a decent nap reenergized her. She watched each of the items up for sale, even though over half of them she had no idea what they were or did. Penny fidgeted in her chair and sighed. She wanted to stand up and stretch her legs, but she didn't want to stand up and walk around. For one, she didn't want to lose sight of Glick. She also feared that by standing up, she might accidentally bid on something she could not afford.

She looked around at the rich blend of people attending the auction. Not rich as in wealthy – rich as in very diverse. The crowd represented people of every nationality and age group. Everyone in attendance appeared to have a mission. A short, pudgy albino man mostly bid on the clocks. An extremely elderly woman in a wheelchair, accompanied by her much younger nurse, bid on many, but not all, of the books. A set of Asian twins focused their bids on furniture.

"When is our book?" Penny asked Max.

Max scanned the bidding itinerary and said,

"Soon."

As the crowd bid upon a brass instrument that resembled a trumpet and a slide whistle, Max whispered to her, "Tell me about yourself. Tell me what you do."

"I was tired of answering phones for tech support and decided to pursue one of my passions. I'm studying to become either a chef or a baker. I haven't decided which. Right now, I work in a daycare and help plan three meals for the kids: breakfast, lunch, and afternoon snack. What about you? Something about selling swimming pools?" she whispered.

"Not just swimming pools. Portable pools. I made them and sold them for years. Then, I got stuck. After that, I washed dishes and busted tables at a diner, then worked with a traveling theatre as the assistant costumer," he whispered.

"How do you make a pool portable?" she asked.

"I cut them with a pair of scissors," he said.

"And, those are the scissors you used when you got stuck here?"

"Yes, but I didn't use them. I don't know who cut the hole in the world, or how," Max whispered, and shrugged.

Penny thought about someone very real coming from a world of someone else's dreams. Since coming to the Zephyrus, she found the concept of holes in the world and portable swimming pools much less impossible. She understood how Max felt getting stuck in another world. She felt a bit stuck herself sitting in an auction in a floating city. At least for her, she could take the doorknob from Glick and return home, although she wasn't sure if it would work for her. For Max, it must be like locking his keys in his car, and leaving his car parked on the moon with no one to call and no one to help him.

"Do you miss Ed's world?" she asked.

"Very much so," Max whispered with a faraway sigh, "It's a beautiful place filled with wonderful people." His shoulders slumped and he muttered with a shutter, "And customers."

Penny chuckled and asked, "You don't like your customers?"

"I like people, but not when they turn into customers. But, traveling around Ed's world and seeing the sights ... That makes it all worth it."

"I bet. That's one thing I love about Ed. He's so creative. He and his buddy started a company based on building people's dreams and ideas."

"Yes. I do love the dreams he built," Max whispered.

"And, I loved him," Penny whispered.

They both sighed, then sat up straight when the next item came up for bid. The auction caller's assistant brought out a large, leather-bound book. He held it out for the audience to see, and everyone in the room seemed drawn to the book as the caller described it.

"That is the tome," Glick said.

"We shall start the bid at one thousand," the

caller said.

Before Glick could raise his hand, an ancient looking woman sitting in a wheelchair in the front row gracefully raised a wrinkled hand.

"We have a starting bid at one thousand. Do we have two thousand?"

Again, before Glick could think to raise his hand, a bald man wearing round sunglasses raised his hand and said, "Twenty-five hundred."

"The bid is now twenty-five hundred. Do I have three thousand?"

"Four thousand," croaked the old woman.

"Five thousand," the bald man said.

"What's the matter? Get in there and bid on that book," Penny said to Glick.

Glick raised his hand, and said, "Six–."

"Seven thousand five hundred," the woman said.

"Eight thousand," the bald man said.

"Nine thousand," Glick said.

"Nine thousand five hundred," the bald man said.

"Ten thousand," Glick said.

"Fifteen thousand" the woman said.

The bald man cursed and said, "Twenty thousand."

"I guess that's the end of that," Max said.

"They've passed our limit," Penny said.

"Twenty-five thousand," the woman said.

Glick raised his hand and said, "One Owe-Me."

The audience broke into an uproar. The old

woman said something very unladylike and shot another unladylike gesture at Glick. The bald man, too, had few choice words to spew forth.

Max sat back, laughed, and said, "Ha! They didn't see that one coming."

"What's an Owe-Me?" Penny asked.

"The bid is at one Owe-Me. Do I hear more? Going once ...?" the auction caller said.

"An Owe-Me is a very old bartering currency. Basically, one person owes the other one a favor. Sometimes, they can be little favors. Glick just bid one that is worth over twenty-five thousand."

Penny whistled and said, "That's a pretty big favor."

Max nodded.

"Going twice ...?"

They looked at the old woman, who shook her head sadly. They turned to look at the bald gentleman, who was still steaming.

"One Owe-Me. Ten-K." the bald man said. He looked smug.

"The bid has been raised to One Owe-Me, plus ten thousand. Any more bids? Going once?"

"I think he knows your limit," Penny said.

"Going twice?"

Glick sat in silence. His eyes darted back and forth. Penny could see that he thought hard, pushing Ed's brains to their limits.

"Three Owe-Mes!"

The audience gasped. Everyone turned towards Max and stared.

"Three Owe-Mes?!" Glick said to Max.

"Are you insane?" Penny said.

"Going once!"

Max whispered to Glick and Penny, "There's three of us. Three Owe-Mes. One for each of us to complete."

"Speak for yourself," Penny said.

"Going twice!"

"Since you aren't as familiar with Owe-Mes, one of us can help you with yours. Plus, you don't have to be indebted for these. I'm the one who bid; I'm ultimately responsible for settling them. We can do this."

"This is sound logic," Glick said.

"Sold to the gentleman for three Owe-Mes," the caller said, and banged her gavel on the podium.

Penny had no idea what was in store for the three of them. She had two strangers against her. The situation was far out of her hands. She didn't know what she might have to do for that amount of money. That was more money than she had ever seen at one time, and she wasn't sure what form of currency it was. What was going to be expected of her? At least, if she failed at the task, she would not be the one indebted to the auction house. It would be Max – not her.

Max went to the auction house's accounting office to receive his Owe-Me assignments, while Penny waited in the lobby with Glick. Penny fidgeted and bit at her cuticles. The Owe-Me made her nervous. What if they split up the three of them,

302

and what if Max and Glick left her behind in this strange, floating marketplace? Max didn't seem like the kind of guy to leave her behind. Glick, on the other hand, she wasn't so sure about. He looked like Ed, which should comfort her. But, it was Glick's personality. He was so cold and calculating, almost as if Ed had turned into a robot.

"I hope we're not doing this for nothing," Penny said.

"The book is authentic. It will contain the right steps for opening a door to Jaiu," Glick said.

"What is it with you and doors?" Penny asked.

"A door is the simplest form of travel between two locations," Glick said.

"Whatever," Penny said.

Several minutes later, Max returned with three index cards in hand. He picked out two cards and handed them to Glick. He said, "You two take these, and I'll take this one. We'll meet back here at the auction house to settle the tab and collect the book."

"I'm going with Ed, er, Glick," Penny said.

Glick looked over the two cards and nodded. He said, "Acceptable."

Max waved goodbye and disappeared into the crowd exiting the auction house.

"What do we have to do?" Penny asked, trying to see around Glick to the cards.

"Transfer cargo and feed a plant," Glick said.

"The cargo might be a little strenuous. What's so bad about feeding a plant?" Penny asked.

"Indeed," Glick said, "What kind of plant could

be worth so much?"

CHAPTER SIXTEEN

Visiting the Dead

Compared to Ed, Emily was a bigger bookworm. She rarely watched TV and preferred to read the book instead of seeing the movie, when possible. The televisions in Ed's world made her nervous. When she told Ed this, he could sympathize. He thought back to the lobby of the news archives, where he swore the faces on the monitors watched him while he looked the other way, which he agreed was creepy. Ed, on the other hand, was a mediaworm. He loved to read, watch TV, watch movies, listen to music, and play video games. He told Emily he believed it was because of his overactive imagination, and all that activity needed food.

Walking through the arches to TV Land, Ed thought Emily was completely justified for her nervousness and lack of desire to travel to TV Land. If one wall of suspicious monitors at the City's archives weren't enough, TV Land was a city, at least the outside portion, made almost entirely of a maze of television sets in various sizes and shapes. Emily

305

and Ed walked through the arch of television sets, each displaying a portion of stone archway, including the engraved words reading, "Welcome to TV Land". The pavement, the buildings, the courtyard statue of the town founder, even the sky was made of a mosaic of screens. Because the borders of each screen broke the feeling of openness, TV Land made them both feel claustrophobic.

Ed became disoriented walking among a maze of televisions. He felt nauseous and could see Emily was queasy and on edge, too. They walked down the televised sidewalk, looking at the electric signs above the store fronts. People appeared on the stacked screens making up the walls of buildings. The televised citizens of TV Land waved as they passed, then continued on their way. Even birds flew by on the sky television screens.

Finally, they reached the TV Land visitors' center. Ed pushed open the doorway made of three flat panel screens with Emily close behind him. They walked into the visitors' center and both sighed from relief. Once again, they stood in a normal-looking room. The visitors' center room resembled a typical waiting room at the Department of Motor Vehicles. A queue of people waited in a simple maze of ropes to talk to the woman behind the counter. On the wall, a couple of monitors rotated between some basic information, historical details, and a map of TV Land. Ed took his place in line. He stepped forward when it was his turn, while Emily clung close behind him.

"I need some information regarding one of your TV personalities," Ed said.

"We do not dispense personal information concerning any of our clients. If you want an autograph, I can provide the studio's address," the woman said with a heavy sigh. Ed wondered how many times a day tourists asked her a similar question.

"Actually, I was going to ask something related to Dirk Juggernaut," Ed said.

"The wrestler?" the woman asked, glancing quickly over Ed's shoulder to the wall beyond the queue.

Ed nodded. He turned around, but could not tell what the woman glanced at.

"Mr. Juggernaut is deceased."

"So I've heard," Ed said, "My question is not really about him, but whom I might talk to regarding his swimming pool. I'd like to get in touch with the gentleman who sold him the pool."

"You want Max of Max's Portable Pools. Did you try calling Max's number?" the woman asked.

"Yes. There was no answer," Emily lied.

The woman peeked around Ed to Emily, then back to Ed. Ed thought she looked like she was having an internal debate.

"One moment. Let me talk to my supervisor," the woman said. She slid off her chair, shuffled across the room, and disappeared through a door at the back of the room.

"You called him?" Ed asked.

"No," she whispered, "No contact information, remember?"

"I remember. Why would a traveling salesman create a commercial with no way to contact him?" Ed asked.

"I don't think he left it off. I think it was removed," Emily whispered even quieter.

The woman returned and sat down quicker than when she left. She glanced up at the monitors posted up on the walls, then down to her desk. She picked up a pen and notepad and scribbled a quick note.

The woman slid the note across the counter to Ed, and said, "Here. Go find the gentleman who lives in this area. He will help you find what you're looking for."

Ed read the note. The only thing written on the note was, "Faun Valley".

"Who is Faun Valley?" Ed said.

The woman shushed Ed and said, "It's not a who. It's a place. I'm sorry, but I really can't help you any further," she barked. She nervously glanced at the monitors again, then called for the next person in line.

"Who am I supposed to find in Faun Valley?" Ed pressed.

"Please. I've helped you all I can. Next!" she said. She looked up at the monitors, gulped, and gawked.

In a dry, hoarse whisper, she said, "Oh no."

Ed turned to see what the woman looked at on

the monitors and why she should be afraid. The information from the screens was no longer presented. The screens showed white rooms. On the screen, at the far side of the white room, Ed saw a tiny thing hopping like a bunny. He walked closer to see better, and realized it wasn't a bunny but some kind of toy-like man.

The man had big, cartoonish, black shoes that were attached to springs for legs. His body was a polka-dotted box that resembled a bright colored present. Two clownish arms sprouted from opposite sides of the box body. In one white-gloved hand, the toy-like man held an enormous mallet. Perched on top of the box was the man's head, which had wild, untamed hair and a very bushy mustache with matching bushy eyebrows. His dark hair matched the blackness of his large, onyx eyes.

The man bounced closer and closer on the screen at a steady, hypnotizing pace. Ed took a step back, and a similar man with a different colored and patterned box body bounced on the other monitor. The two men bounced steadily closer and closer.

One of TV Land's tourists standing in line pointed at the screen and yelled, "Bouncers!" That triggered a chaotic flurry of panic in the visitors' center. The woman at the counter quickly put up a closed sign, then fled to the office door beyond the desk.

"Come on!" Emily said, and grabbed Ed around the wrist. The mob pushing through the doorway blocked their exit. Emily yelling at them to "Go!"

and "Move!" did little to help the situation.

Confused at what all the commotion was about, his heart raced from all the excitement. Ed turned towards the monitors again. The entire screens were filled with the Bouncers' bodies. They crouched down as much as they could compress their spring legs, then released. With a crackle of static, the Bouncers jumped out of the monitors and into the room.

One of the Bouncers pointed to the counter, then leapt over it with a metallic *ka-ching*! The other Bouncer bobbled on the spot and turned towards the fleeing tourists. It pointed its oversized mallet at Ed and grinned.

"Let's go!" Emily said, and pulled Ed out the door and into the street of television screens.

Behind them, they heard "Ka-ching! Thunk!" Glancing over his shoulder, Ed saw the boxy body of the Bouncer get stopped by the narrow doorway.

They ran down the street with the other fleeing tourists towards the main entrance to TV Land. The virtual people in the background of the screens making up TV Land froze. Their bodies changed as they grew into other Bouncers. The umbrella held by one virtual person and a bag of groceries carried by another turned into the Bouncers' mallets. Running as fast as the mob would allow, they pushed on faster, especially when they heard the crackle of static signaling the arrival of more Bouncers.

Ed didn't know about Emily, but passing the screens of TV Land so quickly made him feel more nauseous. He swallowed down his upset stomach and continued to run. Finally, they broke through the archway to TV Land and into the world not hidden behind glass screens. They didn't slow down until they were clear of TV Land.

Emily panted, "Okay. We're okay."

Ed slowed his pace, "What were those things?"

When she caught her breath, she said, "Bouncers. TV Land's law enforcement. The Bouncers have no jurisdiction beyond TV Land. I think we're safe. They must not have liked what the woman said. What did she write on that note?"

Ed shrugged and panted, "All it says is 'Faun Valley'. Here, read for yourself."

Ed handed the slip of paper to Emily. She took the note and examined it.

"I've heard of Faun Valley, but I've never been. I don't know who lives there, but it doesn't seem like they want you to go," Emily said, handing the note back to Ed.

Ed took the slip of paper and slid it into his pocket. "What do you know about Faun Valley?"

"Not much. Something about goats. If it is a valley, maybe a river runs through it. And, if that's the case, we might be able to use the Paddleman," Emily said.

"Great. Let's go," Ed said, ready to put more distance between himself and TV Land.

Emily was relieved to take a conveyance more to her liking. Ed, on the other hand, was on the fence about which method of travel he preferred:

Paddleman's canoe or the televator. Didn't anyone drive a normal car with wheels and an engine in his world? Ed wondered where was his car? For that matter, where was his apartment? If this world was based upon his life, where was anything normal from Outworld? The closest thing he found to the real world were the Halfunts living in a clone from his childhood neighborhood, and even that felt more like time travel than visiting something tangible from his present life.

Emily led Ed to the closest water source, which happened to be a pond with koi fish of various sizes, colors, and patterns. They called upon the Paddleman to take them to Faun Valley. Something about the valley tickled the back of Ed's memory. If only he connected to his world, he should, in theory, be able to recall more information about the valley and what it was about the valley that nagged at him.

Ed was too lost in thought trying to remember what nagged him about Faun Valley to notice where the Paddleman appeared from in the small pond. Once again, they climbed aboard the Paddleman's canoe, and he took them through the fog and connected to a stream that ran through the valley. They disembarked the canoe and watched as the Paddleman disappeared over a short waterfall.

Ed had no idea who they were supposed to find in this valley or where he lived. The Paddleman had taken them ashore by a wooded area with many tall pines and aspens. In the distance, Ed heard a low roar, almost like the faint cheering of a crowd at a football game from far outside the stadium. They looked up and down the stream, and headed downstream in the direction of the rumbling sound.

Walking downstream, they rounded a boulder blocking the path of the stream. Ed and Emily stopped where the trees ended at a massive clearing at the base of the valley. They froze and gawked at the violent battle raging in the base of the valley. They were too in shock to go any farther.

Mountain goats and mythological faun fought a bloody war. The faun had the advantage of being able to carry spears, blades, and clubs in their hands. Many of the faun also had short, but sharp, horns protruding from their heads. The mountain goats had the advantage of strength and stability of four legs. It also appeared both their fore and hind hooves packed a punch for anything getting too close.

Emily tugged at Ed's shirt and whispered, "We should turn back."

Ed agreed, but as he turned away from the battlefield to head back upstream, a sight caught his eye. In the distance, across the raging battle, he spotted a log cabin. He couldn't make out all the details, but it appeared an elderly man sat on the porch and watched the battle.

Ed pointed out the cabin to Emily and said, "Do you think that's who we're supposed to find?"

Emily shrugged and said, "Don't know. Don't care. We should go."

Ed pointed behind the cabin, farther up the side

of the valley, and said, "Look. We can go up and around. We should be able to walk up in the tree line there and come down behind the cabin. If that's who we need to find, I'd like to give it a try."

"Or, we can go back to the Manor where it's quiet and safe, not worry about finding Max, and let you get on with the rest of your afterlife," she said.

Ed gave her a pleading look.

"Alright. Let's just get back to the trees before we're spotted," she said.

Not that anyone fighting paid much attention. They stooped and crept back to the trees. From there, they climbed up the valley hillside and walked up and around the battle below, doing their best to keep the cabin in sight.

They covered half the distance between the stream and the cabin, and paused a moment to catch their breath. Emily sat down on a boulder, while Ed leaned against a tree. The air was noticeably thinner here, and Ed guessed they were up in the mountains at a higher elevation.

The tree Ed leaned on disappeared. It shrank into the ground in a second, leaving him leaning against nothing. Ed stumbled and flapped his arms to regain his footing. The tree shot back out of the ground, farther up the hill. Ed completely lost his footing when two branches of the same tree shoved him down the hill. The thought bouncing around his head as he tumbled down the hill was, "Did that tree push me?"

"Ed!" Emily yelled.

Ed toppled over backwards and the world spun out of control around him. He thought other trees would stop his tumbling, but like the tree that pushed him, they disappeared out of his way, and he picked up momentum.

He could just make out Emily reaching for him and stumbling down the hill after him. She skidded to a stop. When Ed finally tumbled to a stop, too, it took him a moment to realize something was different. The valley was too quiet.

Laying face down in the grass of the valley, Ed raised his head to armies of goats and faun staring at him.

One of the faun roared, "Get them!"

Ed dropped his face back to the grass and blacked out.

>< >< ><

When Ed opened his eyes, he was suspended above the ground surrounded by a webbing of ropes and a canopy of tree branches. He wasn't sure what had happened, but had the impression he was laying in some kind of hammock. Above him, a canopy of bushy green pine needles fluttered in the wind. Below him, he heard arguing mixed with cheers and taunts. Cocooned by the ropes, Ed wiggled enough around until he faced downward. Rope nets suspended him and Emily twenty or so feet above the ground. Below, the faun army argued the prisoners were rightfully theirs, while the mountain goats bleated in protest.

"He charged at us from behind. You must have

sent them as a surprise attack. They are our prisoners," one of the faun proclaimed.

Another mountain goat bleated another protest.

"No!" the faun roared, "Just because they were on our side of the stream does not mean they are on our side. And besides, our side is the valley, while your kind belong farther up in the mountains."

The faun cheered, while the mountain goats growled and bleated angrily.

Ed looked at Emily. She shook her head and sighed. Emily looked over at Ed and said, "They've been arguing over and over about who we side with."

"We're not on either side," Ed said.

"Quiet you!" called one of the faun, and poked Ed in the belly with the blunt end of his spear.

Emily rolled her three eyes.

"It's not our fault your food source is running low. This is our valley. It is called Faun Valley," the faun said.

Again, the goats protested.

"Maybe, if I tell them who I am, they'll let us go," Ed said to Emily, risking another belly poke.

Poke!

"I don't think that's such a good ...," Emily said.

"Do you know who I am?" Ed asked aloud.

The faun and goat looked up at Ed.

"I am Edwin Black, your creator," Ed said.

Emily groaned.

For a brief moment, both armies looked confused. Confusion turned to realization, and the valley erupted in screams of rage. More angry faun poked Ed in the belly with the blunt ends of their spears. The mountain goats bleated loud and long.

"Silence!" yelled a voice from the side, and the valley fell quiet again.

Ed twisted around to see who yelled, but his wiggling seemed to tighten the rope netting around him. Out of the corner of his eye, he saw the old man on the porch looking out over the crowd. The man took a long pipe from his mouth and pointed the end at the crowd. He rocked back and forth in his rocking chair and straightened the blanket on his lap with his free hand.

"Thank you, sir," Ed said.

The old man looked up at Ed and said, "What do you have to say for yourself?"

Ed said, "I think you are the one I was told I should see. I want to know more about Dirk Juggernaut and his swimming pool. And, more importantly, I want to know how I can get in touch with Max, the pool man."

Emily said, "Ed, I don't think this is who that TV Land woman was talking about."

"Quite right, little lady," the old man said, then turned to Ed. "You should listen to this one. Quite right and quite smart."

With some effort, the old man pushed himself to stand up. The blanket fell off his lap, onto the porch, around the base of his rocking chair. Beneath the blanket were the two greying legs of an elderly faun. He stepped forward and used the arm rail to make his way slowly and carefully down the steps of the cabin. The army of faun parted and bowed their heads as the old faun approached Ed.

"That's better. Now I don't have to yell," he said. "What is this nonsense about juggernauts and swimming pools? When I asked what do you have to say for yourself, I meant about the battle for this valley."

"I ... I'm not sure what this battle is all about," Ed stammered.

"For years, the faun and the goats have fought over this valley. Much blood has been shed, and many from both sides have been lost. The fight for Faun Valley has perpetuated, on again and off again, as far as any of us remember. If you are our creator, then you are charged with warmongering, for instigating a war between two species. If, however, you are not who you claim to be, and are not our creator, then the charge is blasphemy for pretending to be a higher authority you are not. Now, what do you have to say for yourself?"

Ed did not know how to get out of this. This was a damned if you do or don't situation. He tried to think back to when he could have started this battle between goat and faun. Ed said he was their creator to stop them from bickering long enough to try to get him and Emily down. He didn't actually remember creating them. Something told him this wasn't a dream, but a concept. Why would he create such a thing that he couldn't remember?

And, then ... He thought of it.

318

"Mr. Kelso," Ed said.

"More nonsense?" the old faun asked.

"No. Mr. Kelso, my fourth grade teacher. He had these toys, a faun from the set of mythological figures, and a mountain goat which, for some reason, was mixed in with the farm animal toys. He used the two to explain racism. He said the two had their differences, but essentially were the same. He said they fought over their differences but struggled with the similarities, because each refused to accept they were anything like the other. I must not have paid complete attention. I must have been daydreaming about fauns fighting goats."

The old faun nodded his head and chewed on the stump of his pipe. He pulled the pipe from his mouth and said, "In that case, the charge is inadvertent warmongering."

The old faun turned towards Emily and said, "And, as right as you are, you have also done wrong. You are charged with cavorting with a notorious warmonger."

"What?! You can't be serious!" Emily said.

The old faun smirked. "Oh, but I am. In a moment, you will find out how deadly serious I can be."

The faun took the pipe from his mouth and pointed it at Ed. "Cut him down, boys."

A couple of the faun "soldiers" pulled out their blades and sliced through the ropes holding Ed above the ground, between the trees. Ed oofed to the ground like a pillow case filled with lumpy, day-old oatmeal. The fauns surrounded him with their blades and spears so that Ed laid helpless on the ground.

"The time for talk is over. Now is the time for action," the old faun said, "Execute him."

"Wait! You can't kill me. I am your creator! You can't kill me. You can't kill your creator. Can they?" Ed asked, this last question aimed at Emily.

If Emily could, she would have shrugged.

A burly faun stepped forward with a sword hefted upon his bare shoulder. The other faun stepped aside as their bigger brother walked to Ed's side and raised the sword high above his head in order to behead Ed.

"Stop!" boomed a voice from the back of the crowd where mountain goats stood among the faun.

The elder faun held up his hand to delay the execution. He squinted across the crowd to the source of the bellowing voice. Whoever, or whatever, the source of the voice, nothing could stop it from reaching the scene of Ed's near execution. The owner of the voice tossed aside mountain goats and faun like stuffed animals and rag dolls.

A large man, twice the size and girth of the burly executioner, appeared before the crowd. The portion of his chest visible from underneath the green cloak wrapped around his torso was covered in a vest of tree bark. The man wrapped his legs in dense fleece. Not that he was knocking his hero-of-the-moment, but Ed thought he looked like two sheep glued to the trunk of a tree.

320

"Let them be," the man said.

"You, and what army?" the old faun said.

"Just me. I fight my own battles," he said.

The old faun stared at the large man, then motioned for everyone to back away from Ed. While Ed released himself, stood up, and dusted himself off, the man stood between the trees where Emily hung, raised one massive hand beneath her, then nodded his head to a faun who chopped her ropes and freed her. Single-handedly and carefully, the man set Emily down.

"Your quarrel is not with them. They are in my care, now," the man said.

The old faun bowed his head and let the three leave in peace.

Ed and Emily followed the man through the crowd of faun and goats. Ed was taller than Emily, but not by much, and the man who rescued them stood at least a foot and a half taller than Ed.

"Thank you for saving us," Ed said.

"Yes, thank you," Emily said.

The man said nothing. He kept walking across the valley with Ed and Emily following behind.

"What is your name?" Ed asked.

The man said, "Quiet."

"Your name is 'Quiet'?" Ed asked.

"No. I want you to shut up," the man said.

"Oh," Ed said, and then was quiet.

At least, he was quiet for another minute and a half before he asked, "Where are we going?"

"Somewhere we can talk. Now, hush," the man

321

said.

"Oh," Ed said again. This time, Ed stayed quiet until they arrived at the man's home.

The old faun's cabin looked like a home to Ed. This guy's "home" was more like a fully furnished studio apartment carved out of the side of a mountain. Ed thought it was very Flintstones-esque. The cave-room had a long sofa and a comfortable, wooden rocking chair. A coffee table of a different kind of wood stood before the sofa. Along the back of the cave stood a propane stove, a standalone basin with a jug of water, and a set of shelves. It was very rustic, but comfortable.

"Have a seat," the man said pointing to the sofa.

Ed and Emily obediently sat on down. Neither of them had the nerve to argue with the man.

"Do you know who I am?" the man said.

Ed thought he looked familiar but couldn't place the face.

In a whisper, the man said, "I am Dirk Juggernaut."

He untied his cloak and showed them he only had one arm, which he used to wave "Hello" to them.

They gasped. Ed could see it now. It was Dirk Juggernaut. The wrestler in brief news videos had a shaved head and no facial hair. This man, the man who rescued them, was covered in long hair, a long beard, and a bushy mustache. Of course Ed didn't recognize him. Now it made sense why the lady at the information desk sent him here.

"I knew it!" Ed said, and smiled broadly at Emily.

"Yeah, yeah, yeah," she said.

"Knew what?" Dirk asked.

"I had a feeling your death was faked," Ed said.

"Why is that?"

"All wrestling on TV is fake," Ed said.

"The shark that did this to me wasn't fake," Dirk said, pointing to where his other arm no longer was.

"But, the other wrestler pulling your arm off was fake," Ed said.

"Yeah. After the shark bit it off, my wrestling career was over. I worked with the writers to create a dramatic ending for my character. We even pulled the news media in on the story. I retired to the mountains while the rest of the world still thinks I'm really dead. But, who told you I was here?" Dirk said.

"The woman at TV Land's information desk," Emily said.

Dirk roared with laughter. "Oh, Henrietta. I knew she couldn't keep my secret forever."

"It's not that funny," Emily said, "Last time we saw her, they sent the Bouncers after her."

The humor in Dirk's face instantly dropped. "Bouncers? Why would they go after her?"

"She sent us here to find you. I think someone didn't want us to find you," Ed said.

"Why did she send you to see me?"

"We were actually looking for Max, the pool

man. While looking at news reels related to Max and his portable pools, you were one of our two leads. Even though we thought you were dead, we figured someone who knew you might know how to contact Max," Emily said.

"Then, Henrietta did right. She's one of the few people who knows about Max and me."

"What about you and Max?" Ed asked.

"He's my closest friend. After the shark incident, Max felt really bad and we went out for drinks. I told Max I had no hard feelings about the shark. It could have happened to anyone, but it happened to me. Best thing that ever happened to me."

Emily and Ed looked surprised.

"You're glad you lost your arm?" Emily asked.

"Well, no. That part not so much. But, look what it brought me. It brought me my new best buddy, Max. It brought me an early retirement in the mountains. And, the best part is it broke me free of Tellis Pripen and TV Land," Dirk said, and shuddered.

"Since you know Max, do you know how to get a hold of him?" Ed asked.

"Nope. Not since he disappeared," Dirk said.

"What do you mean he disappeared?" Ed said.

"Like, 'poof!' Out of existence," Dirk said.

"What?" Emily said, "That's impossible."

"What isn't impossible here? I've only been here a short while, and I've seen some pretty impossible things," Ed said. "Why don't you tell us why you think he disappeared out of this world?"

"It happened a while back. I went to meet Max for drinks. I was running late. When I got there, Jackie said he was gone. At first, I thought that was very unlike Max not to wait for me. Jackie said they never saw him leave. He went to one of the back rooms to make a pool for a client. They checked on him later, and he was gone. He left behind the partially built pool, but no Max."

"He must be somewhere, right?" Ed said.

"I've never heard of anyone or anything disappearing like that," Emily said.

"What else can you tell us?" Ed asked.

Dirk shrugged and said, "Like I said, I wasn't there. But, you can go talk to Jackie yourself. They'll tell you all they know. It's the Jack of Diamonds Pub just outside of the City."

Emily nudged Ed. He turned to her and nodded. They were on the right trail.

"Dirk, thanks for all your help. No worries, your secret is safe with us," Ed said, and shook Dirk's bone snapping hand.

Dirk gave Emily directions to the Jack of Diamonds Pub. He gave her a one arm bear hug, which made her blush. He waved them off from the mouth of his cave home.

Down in the valley, the battle raged once again. This time, Ed and Emily were more cautious to avoid the fighting. Ed led the way back to the stream while Emily poked behind.

Ed turned around and saw Emily shuffling

behind him. He stopped, turned, and waited for her to catch up.

"What's wrong?" he asked.

"At first, I thought it might be fun tracking down Max. Dirk said he disappeared. I'm wondering why we're still doing this. We've almost been thumped by Bouncers. We were captured by two warring mobs of goats and goat people. I feel like we're headed towards another dead end. I'm tired, hungry, and wondering if this is worth all the trouble."

Ed opened his arms and she moved closer to him. He gave her a fatherly hug and said, "I'm sorry you feel that way. I think this is a great adventure. I appreciate and enjoy your company through this crazy world of mine. Besides, I'm getting hungry, too. The next place is a pub. We should be able to get some food there."

They made their way to the stream once again to take the Paddleman back to the City. Instead of arriving in the Dragon Fountain, the Paddleman arrived in the city in a stream of run-off water from a car wash near the edge of town closest to the pub. The citizens of the City drove their vehicles into the car wash. Windows on the sides allowed onlookers to watch the vehicles get washed by a variety of hoses and sprayers. As some of the vehicles exited the car wash, they shook off excess water like a wet dog, then drove away.

The Jack of Diamonds Pub was less than a block away. From the outside, it was a cube of a building with a front porch. The sun still hung high, but the sky grew dark like dusk was approaching, or like someone turned down the sun's dimmer switch. The light through the pub's windows were warm and inviting in the evening light, like the solitary house party on the block.

Ed was not used to the random fluctuations of time in his world. At times, it gave the impression he was living, or after-living, one very long day. At other times, weeks seemed to rush by. There appeared to be no logical flow. It gave him a false sense of urgency at one time, and at other times like he had all the time in the world. No telling how much time passed in Outworld.

They opened the front door of the pub and walked right in. The pub looked like what Ed would expect with the bartender wiping down glasses behind the bar. People mingled, laughed, or sobbed their drinks away at the various tables and booths around the place. The only difference between this world's pub and the Outworld pubs Ed rarely went to was the clientele. Jackie, the playing card bartender, greeted Ed and Emily with an amicable nod as they entered.

Ed never was much of a drinker. In Outworld, he accompanied Burt as his designated driver. Emily joined Ed at the bar.

"An Arnold Palmer, please," Ed ordered, then realized he had no idea what kind of currency people used in his world.

"A bloody bunny for me. Plus, I'll have an order

of gator eggs. Do you want anything?" Emily asked. Ed had never heard of that drink or food before, but the bartender acknowledged her order without question. Ed shook his head.

"I can share if you're hungry," she said.

Ed's stomach growled. He said, "Maybe I'll have a little."

Ed looked around the bar. Cartoon characters Ed remembered from his childhood Saturday mornings occupied a table on the far side of the room. They dressed in cartoon street clothes, which was out of character from the shows. More people sat at the other tables, and each one seemed familiar to Ed, but he couldn't always pinpoint where or how he knew them. Seeing old co-workers, school friends, and TV personalities mixed together and mingling didn't help. One thing for sure, with what he already experienced in the time he spent traveling with Emily, he grew more accustomed to his world.

"You're Ed, the creator, aren't you?" Jackie asked as she served Ed his tea and lemonade.

After the incident at Faun Valley, Ed wasn't sure if he should answer the question.

"Yes, I am," Ed said with confidence, and took a guilty sip of his drink. It was the best Arnold Palmer he ever tasted, which made him feel worse about not knowing how to pay for it.

Jack, on the other side of the card, flipped around and asked, "What brings you to town?"

"We've been looking for Max, the pool man," Emily said. Jack delivered Emily her drink. It looked like a glass of tomato juice with a wave of soy sauce swirled in with several carrot rings perched in a semicircle around the rim. Emily removed one of the carrot rings and dunked it in her drink before taking a bite.

"We've been looking for him, too," Jack said.

"So, he did disappear?" Emily asked.

"Like he walked right out of existence," Jack said.

"Weird," Emily said.

"Wait. What do you mean he 'walked' out of existence?" Ed asked.

Jack lowered his voice and made sure no one was listening. "We had it on our video surveillance, but Tellis Pripen confiscated it."

Jackie flipped around and whispered, "I think that fella he was with had something to do with it."

"He's a holomorph," Jack said from the other side.

"If not him, then Pinkerton had something to do with it," she argued.

"That's true," Jack said, as they flipped around.

"Who is Pinkerton?" Ed asked.

Jack starred at Ed. "You're not from around here, are you?"

"I'm new in town," Ed said. "Who is he?"

"Only one of the most powerful people in this world," Jack said.

"What makes him so powerful?" Ed asked.

"Money," Emily said, sipping at her drink.

Jackie flipped around. "That, and he is very

persuasive ... In an intimidating kind of way."

"What? Like the mob?" Ed asked.

"No. Like the devil," Jackie whispered, barely audible above the noise in the pub.

"I take it Max worked on a pool for Pinkerton before he stepped outside?" Ed asked.

Jack flipped around. "Something like that, yeah. And, Pinkerton's right hand asked him to do it."

Ed started to get lost in the conversation. He assumed Jack meant someone working for Pinkerton asked Max to build the pool, and not that Pinkerton had a talking hand, which ordered him to leave the world. Although, in this world, he was sure either could be correct.

"And, who's that?"

"A squirrely fellow by the name of Kasper works for Pinkerton. He was in here the night Max disappeared."

"He's not actually a squirrel, is he?" Ed asked. He wasn't sure of that either.

"No. But, he could be. He's a shape changer," Jack said.

A waitress walked out of the back rooms with Emily's gator eggs. There were about a dozen arranged in a heap on the plate with two cups of sauce on the side. The gator eggs looked like donut holes, but a bit larger. There was a thick, dark purplish sauce and a creamy yellow sauce in the cups. They smelled of chicken, bacon, fried batter, and deliciousness. It made Ed's mouth water.

Emily picked one up, but dropped it quickly

due to the heat. She said, "Help yourself."

"Kasper asked Max to step out of the world?" Ed asked.

"What? No! Kasper asked Max to make the pool," Jack said.

"And, instead of making a pool, Max made a hole in the world?" Emily asked.

"No. Look. You're getting me all confused," Jack said.

Jackie flipped around. "Let me explain."

"If we still had the surveillance tape, we could just show him," said Jack from behind Jackie.

Jackie rolled her eyes and pointed a thumb at her flip side. "Here's what we know. Max was here having a drink when Kasper hired him to make a pool for Pinkerton. We let Max use the Hilltop room so he could cut a pool in private."

Emily nudged Ed, and Ed nodded. She dipped a gator egg into the purple sauce and took a bite.

Jackie continued, "On the video, Kasper left the room, and Max rested a bit. That's when these hands appeared out of the floor and cut a hole in the world."

"Hands? Whose hands?" Ed asked.

"I don't know. Just hands. They stretched out of the walls," Jackie said.

"If this Kasper can change shape, could the hands belong to him?" Ed asked.

"No. Kasper is a holomorph. A holographic shape changer. He can't even hold his liquor, so to say. The hands couldn't have been his. Whoever the

331

hands belonged to used Max's scissors and cut a hole in the world. Max got up and walked through the hole. The hole closed behind him. No more Max. Haven't seen him since. Kasper left, but returned with someone for the partially cut pool and the security tape."

"And, Max's scissors?" Emily asked.

"The hands took them," Jackie said.

"Thank you," Ed said to Jackie.

Emily looked at Ed. "What now? Kasper and Pinkerton? Or, hands with scissors? Because seriously, I'm thinking of dropping this whole thing, heading back to the manor, and curling up with a good book. Or, a bad one. Either will do."

Ed sat and slowly bobbed on his bar stool. He chewed his lip, then said, "I'm thinking Pinkerton took the surveillance tapes for the scissors. He might not want anyone else to know about the hole in the world, and wants the scissors for himself. We don't know anything about those hands or where they went. If Pinkerton has the footage, he might know, and could be going after those scissors himself. All signs point to Pinkerton."

Emily choked a bit on one of the eggs. "Are you serious? We're just going to walk right into the monster's den and ask him to hand over the scissors?"

"Not exactly. If he's the devil, we need to peek at what cards the devil's holding," Ed said. He finished off his Arnold Palmer in one gulp and asked, "How much do we owe you?"

"You're the only two who care what happened to Max. If you can figure out what happened to him and bring him back, we'd appreciate it. Consider the drinks and eggs on the house," Jackie said.

"Oy!" said Jack.

"What? It's for Max!" Jackie said.

"Bah. Ok," Jack said.

Ed and Emily thanked Jack-Jackie, and said they would do their best bringing back Max. Ed and Emily chatted with Jack and Jackie a bit more while they finished off the gator eggs. Ed thought the eggs were delicious and liked the creamy mustard sauce better. Ed and Emily listened as Jack and Jackie reminisced about their favorite Max stories.

Ed stood up and wiped the crumbs from his clothes. He shook Jack's hand and Jackie leaned out of her card frame to give him a hug.

"If you can, bring Max home, okay?" Jackie asked.

"I'll do my best," Ed promised.

As they walked out the door, Jackie whispered, "Good luck. You're gonna need it." Jack nodded solemnly.

CHAPTER SEVENTEEN

Feeding Time

Penny helped Glick find the place where they would complete their first task. The address led them to a large, domed greenhouse on the outskirts of the Zephyrus. The greenhouse sat atop a cylindrical, one-story home, like a crystal egg in a nest.

The greenhouse was massive. Penny thought watering plants might be time consuming, but relatively easy. Growing up, she helped her moms water and weed their backyard garden all the time. How hard could it be?

Penny knocked on the door. She heard the shuffling of footsteps from within the house. An old man answered the door. The man did not look like he got many visitors. His hair was matted down as if it were wet or greasy. His clothes were baggy and worn with splotches of dirt as if he wiped his hands on them. He tilted his head back and squinted at Penny and Glick.

"Yeah?" he said.

"Mr. Upton?" Penny asked.

"Yeah?" he said.

"I've come to help you feed your plants," Penny said.

The old man sneered and looked Penny up and down. "You?"

"Yes. That's what the Owe-Me says," Penny said. She showed him the card from the auction house.

"You think you're up for it?" he asked.

"I help my moms with their garden all the time," she said.

"Huh," he said, and chuckled quietly to himself. "Bet your moms never grew plants like this."

"Uh," Penny said. She opened her mouth, then closed it. She couldn't imagine what kind of plant it could be and didn't know how to respond.

"Better come in," the man said. He stood back from the door to let Penny and Glick inside. Inside was a narrow, but pleasant and clean little home, the opposite of the man's personal appearance. A light was on over the kitchen table where Mr. Upton had been working on a crossword puzzle in the daily paper before being interrupted.

"You need gloves?" the old man asked Penny.

"Yes, please, if you have some."

"You?" he asked Glick. Glick shook his head. "Suit yourself."

The old man led them up a wide spiral staircase to a platform in the center of the greenhouse. The long platform divided the greenhouse across the diameter and stood about a dozen feet above the greenhouse floor. Penny could see greenery through the windows, but the automated watering misters fogged the windows.

Mr. Upton rummaged in a cabinet and pulled out two pairs of large rubber gloves and two aprons. The gloves fit Penny up to her elbows, and the apron hung down to her knees. The old man donned the same outfit. Glick quietly refused a third pair still folded in the cabinet.

"The plant you'll be feeding them is on this side," he said. He slid open a panel in the dividing wall and exposed a steep slope down to the greenhouse floor. Penny peered down the chute. "Trust me. You want to be careful not to slide down there."

The man crossed to the other wall. "Press this button. That'll call one of the monkeys. When the light turns green, pull the lever, and the monkey will appear in the bin. This handle, here, opens the bin. Take the monkey out of the bin and slide it down the chute there."

"Did you say 'monkeys'?" Penny asked.

"Of course," the man said, "That's what the plant eats."

"What kind of plant eats monkeys?!" Penny asked, her eyes wide in horror. She looked at Glick, but his look offered her no comfort.

"The kind of plant that keeps this place afloat. Better feed the plant about twenty monkeys. It's nearing the blooming season."

"Why monkeys?" Penny asked.

"Previous caretakers tried all kinds of animals, but the plant favors monkeys. It also loves pigs, but pigs stink something awful. And, they aren't stupid enough to come when they're called. We think it's because pigs and monkeys marinate themselves in their own filth making them nice and tasty for the plant."

"I don't think I can kill a monkey to feed to a plant," Penny said.

"Who said anything about killing them? The plant eats them alive."

Penny shuddered. "I think I'm gonna be sick."

"If you are, I've got a bucket for that over there," Mr. Upton said, and pointed to a large plastic bucket next to the cabinet.

"Guess I'll leave you to it," Mr. Upton said, "One more thing. Don't get too attached to the plant food." He chuckled as he disappeared down the stairs.

Penny looked at Glick, and asked, "Do I have to do this?"

"Yes."

"What if I don't?"

"Max remains indebted to the auction house. We don't get the book. I'm not leaving the Zephyrus without the book. And, you have no chance to see Ed again."

Penny sighed and pressed the button. A red light turned on above the bin. In less than a minute, the light turned green. She pulled the lever and heard thumping behind the bin door. She slid open the bin door and a monkey, covered in rust-brown fur, climbed from the bin and clung to Penny's side like a toddler wanting to be held by its mommy. One of the monkey's hands reached up and played with Penny's hair.

"I can't," Penny said.

"You can, and you will. Slide it down the chute," Glick said.

"Aw. But, it's so cute," Penny said.

"Don't get attached to the food. Slide it down the chute," Glick said with the infinite patience of an automaton.

Penny choked back a sob and crossed the platform to the chute. She shook away tears and closed her eyes as she dropped the monkey onto the chute. The monkey, thinking the slide was great fun, grabbed its feet and tumbled down the slide into the plant chamber.

Penny heard the monkey chatter playfully to itself. Then, she heard the rustling of the vines of the carnivorous plant as they stretched across the floor and grabbed the monkey. Penny heard more rustling and the creaking of wood and branches. Her eyes popped open again when the monkey howled in terror as the vines snagged it and pulled it in. Penny ran to the chute and peered down, but could not see a thing.

"That's one. Nineteen to go. Another," Glick said.

"This is so cruel. I can't do this," Penny said, trying to block the sounds of screaming monkey

338

from her mind.

"Another," Glick said.

She crossed the platform, shut the bin door, and pressed the button, all the while tears streaming down her cheeks. In seconds, the light turned green and she pulled the lever. Another monkey thunked into the bin. She opened the door and another monkey climbed out, unaware it was about to meet its doom.

Penny closed the bin, carried the monkey to the chute, and pushed it down. This monkey sensed something wrong at the bottom of the chute and reached out its hand to Penny. Guilt consumed Penny, and she reached back to save the monkey. The monkey was too strong and pulled her, too, down the chute towards the carnivorous plant.

"Help!" Penny screamed as she tumbled down the chute after the monkey.

Glick walked to the chute and looked down. He said, "I'll get Mr. Upton," and walked off.

"Hurry!" Penny yelled.

A quarter wedge of domed glass enclosed the plant chamber. Automatic sprayers coated the white floors with a slick layer of moisture. In the middle of the room, a gapping pit, built into the floor, housed the plant. Flower buds sprouted all over the vines. None were yet in bloom, but Penny could see by the closed lips of the soon-to-be-flowers, they were going to be a crayon box of various bright, vibrant colors.

Vines, more snakelike than plant, slithered

across the floor toward Penny and the monkey. The monkey climbed up Penny for safety. With the screeching monkey clung around her head, she could not see or hear anything around her.

The vines slid up her leg, and she froze with fear. They crossed her back and began to wrap themselves around the monkey. The vine tugged at the monkey as she pried it off her head. The monkey scrambled to free itself from the vines, but slid helplessly across the floor towards the pit. As some vines pulled the monkey closer to the pit, more vines reached out to her.

She looked around. There was no sign of the first monkey, other than its screams still echoing in her head.

Penny backed herself up and into the steep slope of the chute. She did not want to turn away from the vines creeping towards her. She pushed herself up the chute on her hands and bottom. When her feet got to the chute, she lost traction, because the soles of her shoes were slick with moisture.

The monkey pried itself loose from the vines and pulled itself out of the pit by tugging on the vines reaching for Penny. The monkey's legs were gone as if something had melted them away. Reaching the top of the pit, it hobbled on stumps towards Penny and the chute. Penny was too terrified to be nauseous. She wanted nothing to do with whatever kind of nightmare plant could melt a monkey's legs clean off.

The vines slithered away from Penny, for the

moment, and returned to finish what was presently on its plate. The plant engulfed the monkey and pulled it back to the pit.

The slight delay gave Penny the break she needed. Quickly, she kicked off her slick shoes and socks and climbed the chute with her bare hands and feet. The chute was steep, but she gained enough traction to climb back up. She peeked behind her and saw the vines had returned and were inspecting her discarded socks and shoes.

Hands grabbed at Penny's arms, and she screamed. Mr. Upton and Glick pulled her the rest of the way out of the chute.

"Didn't I say you don't want to go down there?" Mr. Upton asked, and chuckled.

Penny slumped down against the wall opposite of the chute.

"Call me if you need me," Mr. Upton said, and excused himself from the platform.

Glick stood with the same infinite patience of his spirit waiting in the stereo to claim Ed's body and soul.

"Why do I have to do this?" Penny sobbed.

"By volunteering to complete this Owe-Me, you are bound to Max by the Owe-Me contract to fulfill the deed," Glick said, looking down at her without judgement.

"Can't you help me?" she pleaded.

"You agreed to feed the plant. That is your contract."

"And, what if I break the contract?"

"An Owe-Me contract never breaks. You are indebted until the contract is fulfilled."

Penny sat. In her mind, she cursed herself for being so foolish. Why did she feel such an obligation to stick close to Glick? This man was dangerous and there was too much she didn't know about him. She knew much more about Ed, but Ed was no longer home, only the stranger within.

"You are going to help me," Penny said, and stood up.

"The contract dictates–"

"The contract said that I am bound to feed the plant. It doesn't say anything about the monkeys. You help me get the monkeys, and I'll ..." she took a deep breath and fought down her tears and her fears, "I'll slide them down the chute to feed the plant. Let's do this."

"Agreed," Glick said, and pushed the button to summon the next monkey.

Several minutes passed before the next monkey entered the bin. Penny was disgusted with the job and herself. This was one of the worst experiences she had ever endured. It was nearly impossible to not think about what would happen to each monkey. The vision of the legless monkey down in the plant chamber was an image that would haunt her for a long time.

She pushed all these thoughts aside and focused on completing the Owe-Me. She thought about Oscar-Frank keeping the book trader company. She looked at Glick and imagined he was still Ed. She daydreamed about finding the real Ed and giving him a big hug, then telling him all about her crazy adventures. She wondered where the real Ed was and what he might be doing. After talking with Max, it didn't sound like Ed would be in either Heaven or Hell. She wondered what kind of world he created and where in that world he might be. Maybe, one day, she might visit his world, especially if they could get Max back home, too.

The more monkeys she handled, the more Penny wanted to get back home for a long, hot shower to wash off the monkey stink. She looked at Glick and realized that's what Glick worked towards, too. He was someone who wanted to get back home. She couldn't imagine being imprisoned so long; he might not have a home to go back to. She began to better understand and felt a bit sorry for him, but only a bit. He still had stolen her friend's body and she didn't know if she could ever get over that. It wasn't like having a friend murdered. It was more like watching a friend get turned into a zombie. The shell of Ed remained as a constant reminder of what had happened.

Before long, Penny slid her last monkey down the chute. As she pulled the gloves from her hands, Mr. Upton trudged up the staircase.

"You did it, girl. Color me impressed," Mr. Upton said as Penny removed the apron.

"That's a horrible way to feed a plant," she said.

"I know. I still find it hard," Mr. Upton said. He opened his arms and embraced Penny. Penny broke down into more tears. He whispered quietly to her, "It's hard. You did so good, and now you're all done. Can you imagine doing that for the rest of your life?"

Penny shook her head into his shoulder and sobbed. Mr. Upton patted her back.

"That's the debt I owe the Zephyrus. Thank you for giving an old man a break," Mr. Upton said.

Penny stood back and looked at Mr. Upton, and asked "You're indebted to the Zephyrus? Why?"

Mr. Upton shook his head, and said, "That was a long time ago. It doesn't matter."

He signed the card and handed it back to Penny. "Whatever your friend bought from the Quartermain, I hope it's worth it."

"Me too," Penny said. She gave Mr. Upton another quick hug and a peck on the cheek before saying goodbye.

"One down," Penny said to Glick as they walked through the Zephyrus to get to Glick's Owe-Me.

"One to go," Glick added.

"Thank you for your help. If I can, I'll try to help you, too," Penny said.

"That is not necessary," Glick said.

"I know," she said. She thought about the trio at the Zephyrus, all trying to find their ways home. "I know."

CHAPTER EIGHTEEN

Pinkerton Mansion

Pinkerton hated visitors. He isolated himself as much as he could from the world he wanted no part of. His mansion rested on an island in a sea of molten cheese far up the mountains. The bubbling queso prevented the televator from coming too close to the mansion or within the mansion itself. The closest water source was a stream from a mountain runoff several miles away, so the Paddleman could not get any closer. Pinkerton only traveled in and out of his mansion via a tube from the island to the far shore of the queso.

Ed and Emily trudged through the tube towards the mansion. A large dome encased the mansion. The clear dome was forged from the same substance preventing Ed and Emily's feet from burning in the blorping and glurping melted cheese. Being so close to the extreme heat of molten cheese made Ed's feet itch and his stomach growl, and the thought of he and Emily walking through the tube made him understand what it must be like to be a gerbil in a Habitrail system of pipes.

The mansion loomed above them through the transparent tubes. Ed could not tell if it was the curvature of the tube and dome combined with the heat waves outside, but he swore the mansion moved.

"Is it just me, or is the mansion tilting and shifting?" Ed asked.

Emily looked up, and said, "It's your imagination. Speaking of which, why did you dream this place up?"

"I don't think I did. I don't remember dreaming up half the stuff I've seen."

Traveling through his world, Ed recalled bits and pieces, and he had a constant feeling of déjà vu, but this place was beyond him. One thing Ed had not fully grasped is that once people were born into his world, they took on a life of their own. The people and creatures from his life experiences were given a chance to create and add to his world. Ed had a feeling this was not his creation, but Pinkerton's. If Pinkerton could create something this massive, he did have power, whether it was money or influence. Pinkerton was powerful enough to build a fortress in the mountains surrounded by a moat of molten cheese, and that intimidated Ed.

"Are you sure you want to go through with this?" Emily asked, "We can always turn around and go home. I won't hold it against you."

Ed was having second thoughts, but continued walking towards the mansion. "Must keep going. Face the fear."

They reached the end of the tube and arrived on the island. The island felt spongy and rubbery beneath their feet. At the mansion, they realized it wasn't just a dome covering the mansion, but an entire sphere of transparent material. Ed could see down and around the edges of the monstrous globe encasing the mansion.

He walked up to the door and pressed the bell. A faint "bing bong" rang throughout the inside of the house.

The ground shifted and tilted.

"See? It is moving," Ed said.

"Is it an earthquake? Did you cause this?" Emily said.

"All I did was push the door bell."

"Well, don't push it again."

Ed and Emily held out their arms to balance themselves. At times they thought they were going to bump into the house, and other times they thought they would fall over the edge of the island into the bottom of the sphere. The ground stopped moving, and the front door opened up. Mr. Pinkerton, sitting in his wheelchair, filled the doorway.

"Yes? What are you doing here?" he said.

Ed looked down and saw a man in a wheelchair. He thought of Jackie calling this man the devil, but didn't see that in him. He looked more punk than devil with the horns on the sides of his shaved head and the fishhook for an earring. The metallic rings around Mr. Pinkerton's eyes and his mechanical arm and hand made Ed think of the people dressed in steampunk at comic conventions. Pinkerton's appearance gave Ed more of an impression he was a wheelchair-bound, eccentric rockstar. He did not seem intimidating or evil, and Ed wondered why others feared him.

"Mr. Pinkerton?" Ed asked.

"Yes?"

"A while back, a man, by the name of Max, made a pool for you. We were wondering if you've seen him."

"No," Pinkerton said, and started closing the door.

"Wait!" Ed said and held the door with his hand. Pinkerton looked at Ed's hand, then scowled at him.

"Sorry," Ed said, and removed his hand from the door. "Do you mind if I look at your pool? It's been a while since I've seen one."

Pinkerton continued to scowl at Ed.

"I'm considering having Max make one for me. I've been told you were his last customer. Apparently, his pools are really out of this world," Ed said with a grin. Out of the corner of his eye, he caught Emily's glare.

In an instant, as if Mr. Pinkerton were suddenly swapped with another person, he had a big smile, and said, "Of course. Won't you come in?"

"I appreciate it. I won't take up much of your time," Ed said.

Emily followed quietly close behind Ed into Mr.

Pinkerton's mansion. As Mr. Pinkerton propelled his wheelchair, they felt the ground shift again.

"Do you get these earthquakes often being out here?" Ed asked.

Pinkerton chuckled, and said, "No. It's not earthquakes, foolish boy. It's the mansion. The mansion tilts to help me move my wheelchair."

"That is so cool. Don't you think?" Ed said. Emily nodded, but kept quiet.

"I find it much easier than always exerting myself," Pinkerton said. He led them through the house. For a large house, it was sparsely furnished.

"Did my assistant tell you about the pool?"

"Your assistant?"

"Kasper. Did he tell you?"

"No. I heard it from a friend," Ed lied. If this man was powerful enough to find a way to move his mansion for the sake of laziness, Ed felt he shouldn't give away too much information. He already hinted enough at what he knew to get invited into the place.

"Did your friend tell you the pool is not finished?" Pinkerton asked.

"No, I don't think they said. What happened?"

"Max started cutting the pool, then walked out on the job. Just disappeared and left it unfinished," Pinkerton said.

"How unusual," Ed said. He couldn't believe how close Pinkerton skirted the truth of Max's disappearance. "What do you think happened to him?"

"I don't know. I guess he got frustrated and left.

Some people just have to get out, you know?" Pinkerton said.

They followed Pinkerton into the gallery. All the way, with the tilting of the house, it felt like walking downhill. As lazy as it was, tilting the house made it much easier for Pinkerton to get around.

Ed looked around the gallery and smiled. He glanced at all the displays along the walls, but the swimming pool in the center of the room pulled his eyes towards it. Even though it was unfinished, with the sparkling, blue water, the pool was an amazing piece of work.

"Wow," he and Emily said.

Ed and Emily walked over to the wedge of the unfinished pool. The water curled up and held to the surface in a very unwater-like way. Ed reached up and touched the water with his fingers. It rippled to his touch and felt cool and inviting. Max's portable pool made Ed want to jump right in.

"Out of this world, huh?" Pinkerton said.

"Yeah, it is," Ed said.

"It's beautiful," Emily said.

"Makes you wonder how it's done. Like he slices into a world of water," Pinkerton said.

"Then, peels away a piece of the fabric of space," Emily added. "How does Max do it?"

"Who knows? It must be cutting edge technology," Pinkerton said.

Ed sensed Pinkerton deliberately threw out the "cutting" remark to get a reaction, but Ed kept his poker face clear.

"You know, you've met me once before," Pinkerton said, "Do you recall our encounter?"

Ed took his eyes off the pool and looked at Pinkerton again. Pinkerton did look slightly familiar, but Ed couldn't recall. He tried to think of the man up and walking around in a time before he was wheelchair-bound, but drew a blank.

"I'm sure we have met, but it must have been a long time ago. Sorry," Ed said.

"Oh, yes, it was years and years ago. At the mall. Ring any bells?" Pinkerton asked.

Ed shook his head. He couldn't think of where he knew Pinkerton. He tried to recall a moment in Outworld he would have met, or in a dream he had, but could not recall.

"Like this pool, I have some unfinished business," Pinkerton said.

Pinkerton swung his chair around and faced Ed, who was still admiring the beauty of the pool. He inched his wheelchair closer to Ed. Ed felt the room tilt lightly and saw, out of the corner of his eye, Pinkerton staring at him. Ed felt a chill down his spine.

Something about the way Pinkerton stared at him triggered Pinkerton's birth dream. Or, in Pinkerton's case, his birth nightmare. It was many years ago, Ed had a nightmare of Pinkerton chasing him through a department store in the mall. He remembered Pinkerton demanding something from him but couldn't recollect what it was. The one image he did remember – the detail that stuck out in his mind – was the set of rotating blades Pinkerton chased him with. He could still hear the whirring motor and the buzzing sound of the blade cutting through the racks of clothing shelves of products to get to him as he tried to hide in his dream. Unlike some nightmares, which would awaken Ed the instant something bad happened, he remembered this nightmare had held onto him, like it refused to grant him permission to wake up.

Although his appearance changed, Ed was sure this Pinkerton and the man in the wheelchair from his nightmare were the same. What he thought were the eccentric decorations of a rocker now appeared more like the self mutilations of a deranged psychopath. Sensing him close in on him, Ed didn't want to find out if he was the same man or if he still had the same whirring blades.

"Yes," said Ed, stepping out of Pinkerton's way, and swept Emily away from the pool. "Unfinished business. I, too, have something I must attend to. Thank you so much for your time. I hope we didn't bother you too much. Come on. Let's leave Mr. Pinkerton be."

"Very busy, indeed. No time to kill. Perhaps another time," Pinkerton said, and stared into Ed's eyes with an icy gaze.

"Don't get up," Ed chuckled awkwardly with cruel irony, "We can show ourselves out."

Pinkerton continued to stare as Ed and Emily walked briskly from the gallery, down the hall, through the foyer, and out the front door.

Once outside and back in the tube, Emily said, "I know the guy's a creep, but what's the sudden rush?"

"While we were looking at the pool, I remembered how Pinkerton was created. I had a nightmare when I was a teen about a man in the wheelchair. He's not just creepy; he's a monster."

"I don't know if I'd go that far. Intimidating, a bit. Wealthy, obviously. But, a monster?" Emily said.

Ed walked faster. Emily had a difficult time keeping up with him. Ed wanted more distance between him and Pinkerton. He couldn't remember all the details of the dream, but he knew Pinkerton had something to do with him having a nightmare. He couldn't even put a finger on why the dream scared him so much.

"Slow down," Emily panted.

"Did you notice anything unusual about the room with the pool?" Ed asked.

"You mean the random art collection?"

"That wasn't art. And, those items weren't random," Ed said.

"What do you mean?" Emily said.

"The toll booth and little car? The big, blue box? The large, wooden cabinet? There were several other similar items, too."

"So?"

"So?! Each of those items were portals to other worlds. Pinkerton is trying to find a way out."

"What are you talking about?"

"I think Jack and Jackie were right. I think

353

Pinkerton does know about Max's scissors. He's the only one who said Max *cut* pools. Everyone else says that Max *makes* pools. I'd bet anything Pinkerton has the scissors, and he's trying to figure out how to use them to leave this world."

"If he has the scissors, why didn't you ask about them?" Emily said.

"It's not like he's going to just hand them over. Besides, we don't want to poke the monster with the stick. Asking about Max and the pool is too close to the subject. He probably already knows we know. We need to go back to the mansion and look for those scissors," Ed said.

"Are you out of your mind?!"

"I've been out of my body, might as well go out of my mind, too."

Emily stopped. "What do we do, now? We can't just go strolling back up the tube and ring the bell, again. If he knows we know about the scissors, he'll be expecting us to come back for them."

"That's why we need to find a way to sneak in."

Ed continued walking away from the mansion. Emily stood and stared at him. "Where are you going? If we're going in, the mansion is the other way."

"I know. I'm thinking. But, I don't want to stop in this tube. And, I don't want to march back there without a plan. Let's head back to Black Manor, or whatever you call the place, and come up with a plan."

Emily shrugged. "Black Manor works for me."

✂   ✂   ✂

On the way back to the mountain stream, Ed had an idea. When he was in middle school, he found an old, brass doorknob laying in the gutter near a field with no doors around, a place one wouldn't expect to find a doorknob. He took it home, cleaned it up, and kept it as a good luck charm. He figured if a doorknob could wind up in a place where there wasn't a door in sight, maybe it would bring him enough luck to take him far, too. He remembered day dreaming that it could be a magical doorknob that could transport him to other places if he could turn it just the right way. Over the years, he had lost track of his good luck charm, but he figured if he could find it here, in this world, maybe it actually could transport a person from one place to another. If so, he might be able to use it as a bargaining chip with Pinkerton to trade for the scissors.

It would be a hard sell, though. He didn't know if the doorknob actually worked the way he imagined it would, while the scissors likely worked. And, Pinkerton, in theory, had the surveillance videos to prove it.

Maybe the doorknob did work. Since his arrival, Ed had seen so many other fascinating creations, many of which he didn't remember dreaming up. Surely the doorknob would work, too. Ed wasn't too sure. His dreams were obviously brought to life. He wasn't sure if what he imagined was given life, too. He couldn't remember if the orientation film mentioned daydreams. Were daydreams considered something from his life experiences?

He decided to look for the doorknob and try it anyway. For the moment, it was the only idea that came to mind.

CHAPTER NINETEEN

Long Distance Call

Ed returned to Black Manor and visited his garden. He stepped out of the family treehouse carrying the doorknob. He threaded the doorknob through loop of string and wore it around his neck. He held the doorknob and turned it in his hands.

"I figure we spread a rumor about this doorknob that it's magical," Ed said.

"Magical? Seriously?" Emily snorted.

"Or, not. Whatever. We spread a rumor that it opened a door to Outworld. The rumor will spread to Pinkerton, and we can offer this knob as a trade for the scissors."

Emily shook her head. "It'll never work. He already knows the scissors work. Why would he believe rumors about the doorknob? Besides, how long is it going to take to spread this rumor? And, what if he wants to see it demonstrated before the trade?"

"Maybe we should try it out and see if it really does work," Ed said.

"I guess," Emily said. "How does it work? Do

you draw a door on the wall and stick the doorknob to it, or what?"

"I don't know. I only imagined it taking me to other places, I didn't really imagine how it worked. I guess I just stuck it out in front of me and turned it."

"Ok," Emily shrugged. "Give that a try."

Ed took the doorknob from around his neck, grabbed the knob firmly, stuck it out in front of him, proclaimed he wanted to go to his apartment, and gave it a good turn, but nothing happened.

"Maybe you need to replace an actual doorknob with your magic one," Emily suggested.

Ed looked around. He didn't want to use the door to the family treehouse. Too many valuable possessions and memories were inside, and he didn't want to leave this personal museum too vulnerable. He saw the freestanding door in the garden.

"What about that door?" Ed asks. "Where does it go, anyway?"

"I don't know. It never opened for me. As far as I know, it's always been locked," Emily said.

"Shall we try again?" Ed asked.

"Knock yourself out," Emily said.

Ed placed the doorknob around his neck and walked over to the freestanding door. He walked around it. There was nothing on either side. It was a simple door frame attached to a platform of red bricks. He grabbed the knob of the freestanding door. "Here goes something."

The knob turned easily in his hand and opened smoothly inward. A dark room stood somewhere on the other side. Ed peered around to the other side and saw the freestanding door closed on the opposite side. He returned to the front, and the door was still open to the dark room within.

"Come on. Let's check it out," Ed said and looked into the dark room.

Emily was wary. Out of all the times she had tried the door, the knob had never turned and the door had never opened. Why would it open now?

"Are you sure we should go in?" she asked, and cautiously approached the doorway.

"Why not?" We've been to all sorts of other places without much worry. Why does this one make you nervous?" he asked.

"It's never opened before, and now, it opens so easily. Why now? Why do I feel like you're being lured inside?" she said.

"Maybe it's like the case in the museum. Maybe it only opens for me. Come on. Don't be such a three-eyed chicken."

Ed opened the door wider and walked inside. The room was dark, except for a large bay window on the far side. Ed walked over to the window and peered out. The view outside the window swooped back and forth high above the clouds. The movement made the view seem like the room they were in swung somewhere in the sky, but Ed could not feel any motion. They saw a giant set of arms and a massive lower body through the window. They realized what they were looking through the eyes of a person swinging back and forth as if riding a swing set in the sky. Below the swinger was a wide net like one might see in a circus below the trapeze.

"Are you ready for the next one?" a voice called out.

"Who said that?" Ed whispered.

"It sounded like you," Emily whispered back.

"It wasn't me," Ed said.

The window swiveled around and showed a loading dock platform. A woman stacked a crate with her back to the window.

"Penny?" Ed asked.

As if he called to her, she turned around to face the window. It was Penny. Her hair and clothes were a mess, and she appeared a little banged up. Ed was very happy to see her just the same. He couldn't tell if it had been days or weeks, but it felt like longer since he last saw her at a time when he was still alive.

"Penny!" he called.

Ed wanted to know how to open the window to call out to her where she could hear him, but the window wouldn't open. He banged on the window with his hands hoping she could hear him.

Penny's face looked concerned. Ed wondered if she did hear him. Penny asked a question, but her voice was too muffled for Ed to hear.

"Penny, it's me!" he called.

"I hear a voice in my head, and it's not my own," the voice said.

Penny mouthed another question.

"It said, 'Penny, it's me'," the voice said.

Ed was frustrated that he could only hear half of the conversation. He wanted to hear Penny's voice again. He didn't realize how much he missed her.

"One moment. I'll ask," the voice said, then asked aloud, "Who is the owner of the voice in my head?"

"I think it means you," Emily said.

"I figured that," Ed said to Emily, then to the voice, "We are Ed and Emily. Who are you?"

"Glick," the voice said.

"Glick?" Ed asked. Why did that sound familiar? Who was Glick?

And then it hit him. That was the name given by Penny's divining board on the night of the seance. Did the spirit in his stereo succeed at stealing his body? Or, was this a duplicate representation in his world? Ed couldn't possibly be looking out a window into Outworld ... could he? If Max had a pair of scissors that cut from his world into Outworld, could this window somehow be a connection to his body in Outworld?

"Are you the spirit that claimed Edwin Black's body?" Ed asked.

Emily looked at him like he was crazy.

"Yes," Glick said.

"Then, that means I have somehow found my way back inside my own mind," Ed said.

"You are Edwin Black," Glick said in a way that sounded both like a question and a statement.

"Yes," Ed said.

"I don't believe it. How in the world are we in

your head in Outworld?" Emily asked.

"It is a valid question." Glick said.

"First, I want to know a few things. You claimed my body with music, right?"

"Correct."

"Am I also correct that you are using my body to find your way back to Jaiu?"

"Correct."

"Then, tell me, how are you using my body to get you back to Jaiu?"

"My original intent was to use your soul to create a connection back to Jaiu, but your soul was harvested. If your soul was harvested, how did you find your way back into your mind?"

"I am in my own world, which is a part of Jaiu," Ed said.

"What do you mean by your own world?" Glick asked.

"I mean a world created by my experiences. It was all explained in the filmstrip," Ed said.

"I do not know of this filmstrip of which you speak," Glick said.

"The orientation filmstrip. Put together by OmniCorp," Ed said.

"I know nothing of what you speak, but if you are able to bridge the connection between Jaiu and Outworld, then there is a chance that I may find my way home," Glick said.

"I'd like to get back to Outworld, too," Ed said. "What do we do?"

"I am in the middle of my next plan to connect

to Jaiu. And you? How do you plan to get to Outworld?" Glick asked.

"There is someone here who we think has a way to get to Outworld, but we are trying to figure out a way to get it from him," Ed said.

"Then, let us proceed with our current plans," Glick said.

"Fair enough," Ed said. "Good luck."

"The same to you."

"One thing before I go," Ed said, "Where are you? And, can you promise me Penny is safe with you?"

"The Zephyrus," Glick said.

"Where is the Zephyrus?" Ed said.

"It is part of the plan," Glick said.

Ed turned to Emily and asked, "Have you ever heard of the Zephyrus?"

Emily shook her head.

"What about Penny? Is she safe with you?"

"At the moment, Penny is safe."

"At the moment? What does that mean?" Ed asked.

"She has completed her part of the bargain, and for that, she is safe. She is helping me with my part of the bargain. My intent is to complete all tasks required for the plan to succeed."

Ed had no idea what bargain she was part of, but it sounded like he was keeping her safe, as if he needed her for something. He hoped she could still stay a necessary part of his plan.

"As long as she is safe," Ed said. "I'll be back,

hopefully with a way to bridge our worlds."

Ed and Emily left the dark room and shut the door behind them. Emily tried the door, but once again it was locked.

Ed was quiet. He was concerned about Penny but couldn't do anything from where he was. She looked a little stressed but was alive and well.

"What was that?" she asked, breaking Ed's moment of silence.

Ed looked at the door and then at his garden. If he could talk to Glick inside his own mind in Outworld, he had a guess as to what this door was.

"I told you this garden used to be a place I went to meditate, right?" Ed said.

Emily nodded.

"I think this door is how I arrived in my garden. First, I relaxed, then I imagined myself entering the garden. I guess, in this world, this doorway represents that connection between my meditating body and the garden I imagined myself in. Somehow, there must actually still be a connection between this world and my body in Outworld. This world must not be connected to me, because it's not completely disconnected from out there."

Emily sighed. "Weird. I guess we can head back to Pinkerton's. It may not be the doorknob that works, but we do have a doorway that connects to Outworld."

"No way," Ed said, "If this door is connected to the old me in Outworld, I don't want him to know about this door at all."

"Then, what do you suggest we do?" Emily said.

"We're going back to Pinkerton's, but not through the front door. If we return too soon, he's going to know something is up. I have another idea," Ed said.

✄ ✄ ✄

In Outworld, Glick hung by the harness holding him above the safety net and much higher above the ground far below.

"Are you okay to continue?" Penny asked.

"Yes," Glick said. "Let us continue."

"No more voices in your head?" she asked.

"No. The voices are gone."

"Are you sure? You were quiet an awful long time. You must have had quite a conversation. What did the voices say?" Penny asked.

"Like myself, they are looking for a way home."

"Then, why did the voices say my name? Why did you say the voices said, 'Penny, it's me.' Me who?"

"The voices said a lot of things. Let us continue my task," Glick said.

Glick built up a good swing and grabbed the pole on the opened hatch of the zeppelin's cargo bay. He grabbed another crate and swung it out to Penny. She enjoyed working on this task with Glick. It was hard work moving boxes and crates from the zeppelin's cargo bay to the Zephyrus bay, but swinging so high above the Earth below, it was the closest she could get to flying, and she told this to

365

Glick.

With Penny's help, the two were finished in no time. Glick may have pushed her hard for her task, but she appreciated his help and patient motivation to finish her own that she felt obligated to help Glick with his. Glick may have lacked the emotion to adequately express his thanks, but the calculating and analytical side appreciated the rate at which they were approaching another step closer to home.

What also satisfied the logical side of Glick was if the voice in his head really was Edwin Black, and Edwin Black was looking for a way from Jaiu to Outworld, the probability increased of finding his way home. He did not understand how Edwin Black was able to project his voice into the mind space Glick presently occupied. Edwin Black's soul was harvested, and from his experience, consumed. He did not know what Edwin meant by being in his own world, nor what he meant by something explained in a filmstrip. If it was Edwin Black, those statements seemed to be false. In which case, the probability of him finding his way home was exactly the same as before he had heard Edwin Black's voice. On the other hand, the things Edwin Black said were similar to what Max spoke about. Was the voice an imagined extension of Max's words? To Glick, the most logical answer was that the voice in his head may not have been Edwin Black, but Edwin Black's brain firing random thoughts into Glick's mind, much like projecting a dream. Either way, Glick stayed his course and continued working towards his plan, which, logically, would be the most successful of the two plans, and so he continued to transfer cargo from the zeppelin to the Zephyrus.

Many people lived in the Zephyrus and rarely walked upon the Earth below, and a few of the younger Zephyrians had never set foot on the ground at all. The cargo transferred by Glick and Penny was the monthly shipment to sustain life on the Zephyrus. The crates were packed with food (not grown in the greenhouses), monkey food (also not grown in the greenhouses), supplies (both medical and clerical), and of course packages from loved ones who refused to travel to see friends and family.

Glick swung the last of the crates to Penny, who swung back to the platform where she placed the crate neatly on the stacks with the others. Eighty crates in all were transferred to the Zephyrus, while thirty-eight bundles of trash and forty-seven crates of goods were shipped from the Zephyrus. All one hundred sixty-five items were transferred by Glick and his assistant, Penny.

When they were done, Penny swung out and grabbed Glick with one hand and gave him the secondary loading tether with her other hand. When he had secured the secondary tether, she swung back to the loading platform, attached the safety tether, and detached her loading tether. She stood at the edge of the platform waiting to help him onto the loading area. Glick detached his original loading tether, swung above the safety net, and landed awkwardly on the platform where Penny helped

367

steady him. She attached a safety tether to his harness; then they both stood back for the loading bay door to close. With the door closed and the safety signal lit, they were able to slip out of their harnesses, leaving the safety tethers still attached for the next person to wear.

As they walked across the boardwalk, Penny said, "That was incredible! I felt like I was flying! Much better than those stupid poop-flingers."

"Who's flinging poop?" Max asked, appearing in the small crowd of people around them. Max carried a wide, flat box tied with string under his arm that he did not have when they departed.

"Oh!" Penny said, surprised by Max's sudden appearance.

"Monkeys," Glick said. "Did you finish your task?"

"Yes, I did," Max said to Glick. To Penny, he asked, "What's this about poop-flinging monkeys?"

"Ugh. I had to feed monkeys to a carnivorous plant. Totally disgusting."

"You got monkeys? Aw, no fair," Max said, and pouted.

"Why? What did you get?" Penny asked.

"I had to cut five hundred swatches for a dress maker," Max said, bored.

"Cutting swatches? That is what's not fair. Next time, I pick the first Owe-Me," Penny said.

"Yeah, it took me about twenty minutes," Max said.

"You cut five hundred swatches of fabric in

twenty minutes?" Penny asked.

Max nodded.

"Impossible. That's like ..." Penny said, pausing to work out the math in her head, "That's like one swatch every two and a half seconds."

"What can I say? I'm good with scissors. That's why I took the job."

"Our Owe-Mes took several hours. What did you do the rest of the time?" Penny asked.

"Flora – that's the name of the dressmaker – she and I talked for a while. I helped her cut patterns for some dresses she was working on, and helped her clean up a bit around her shop. Now, she owes me an Owe-Me," Max said, and smiled. "Oh! I forgot. I have something for you."

Max took the box from under his arm and handed it to Penny. Penny smirked at Max. She untied the string and carefully opened the box. She gasped with her hand over her mouth and nearly dropped the box and its contents.

"Oh, Max. It's beautiful," she said.

She pulled a light summer dress with spaghetti straps from the box. The dress a swirl of the brightest and boldest colors. The material felt thin, soft, and extremely comfortable.

"Thank you!" she said, and threw her arms around Max.

"You smell like monkeys," he said tilting his head away from her.

She let go, sniffed herself, and crinkled up her nose. "Sorry."

"The book?" Glick said.

"Oh, yes. Let's go claim your book," Max said.

Glick walked down the boardwalk towards the auction house, where they could now turn in their Owe-Mes and collect the book that would bring him one step closer to home.

Max waited next to Penny as she tried to quickly and carefully fold her dress back into the box. She tied the box together again, scooped it up in her fingers, and gave him another half hug. "I can't wait to try it on."

"I'm glad you like it," Max said. The two walked quickly to catch up with Glick.

At the auction house, they turned in the three signed slips of paper declaring the Owe-Mes were complete: one from Mr. Upton, the greenhouse keeper; one from Mr. Rigby, the loading bay manager; and one from Flora Delany, the dressmaker. In exchange for the slips of paper, the auction house manager gave them the old tome, which Glick claimed and bowed his head with thanks.

The three returned to the book trader, who was extremely pleased to see Glick carrying the old tome. Oscar-Frank stood on the counter, keeping the book trader company. The dog rested his chin along the edge of the book as the old man read.

"Whatcha reading, Oscar-Frank?" Penny asked, and the dog stood up and wagged its tail, happy to see his owner once again.

"They and I are reading a cookbook, trying to

find a recipe for my lady friend. They have been perfectly well-behaved. Are you sure you don't want to part with them?" the book trader asked.

"No. I love my doggie," Penny said.

"If they ever become too much for you, please let me know, and I'll take them off your hands," the book trader said with a wink. "Now then ... to business. I'm impressed with your ingenuity. Three Owe-Mes? And, completed so quickly? My, my."

"Eh. It was nothing," Max said. Penny glared at Max.

"Before we hand it over, you agreed to let us borrow the book. Since no money from the book shop was used, I think you'll find this more than fair," Glick said.

"Certainly. You deserve it," the old man said.

"Before we go," Glick said, "I would like you to verify its authenticity."

"Of course." The book trader pulled on his cotton gloves he kept under the counter to handle the older texts. He didn't want the oils from his fingers harming the pages.

He ran his gloved fingers across the spine and covers, both back and front. He opened the tome to three sections and skimmed the text on two of the three and scrutinized a picture on another. He gently closed the book again and said, "This one is not the original. It's a copy, but a well-made copy. It is as close to authentic as you are going to get, and should still be useful to you. I assume you are doing some old, old school magic?"

"Opening a door," Glick said.

"Another one?" Penny asked.

Glick nodded.

"If you say so," the book trader said, "Good reading."

"The same to you," Glick said.

Glick picked up the old tome, Max held the box for Penny, and Penny scooped up Oscar-Frank into her arms. The three headed back to Ed's apartment so that Glick could work on his next door, and Penny could wash up and try on her new dress.

CHAPTER TWENTY

Paddling about the Pool

"I have an idea, but I don't know if it will work. Do you have one of Max's pools?" Ed asked Emily.

"No, I'm not much of a swimmer," she said.

"Then, we need to borrow someone's. Summon the Paddleman, please," Ed said.

"Now where are we going?" Emily asked.

They walked to the fountain, and Emily called upon the Paddleman. In a moment, he mysteriously appeared around the base of the fountain, again.

"We're heading back to Dirk's," Ed said.

Emily gave the instructions to the Paddleman, who held his hand up and nodded as if he remembered and did not need to be told again. They climbed into his canoe and returned to the mountain stream near the Valley of the Faun.

Knowing where to go, they took more caution the return trip to the other side of the valley to Dirk's cave. Dirk, sitting outside his cave in a wood-carved chair, was surprised to see them again.

"What brings you back?" Dirk asked.

"Do you still have your pool? And, if so, may

we borrow it?" Ed asked.

"Yes and yes," Dirk said.

"Does it still have the shark in it?" Emily asked.

"Could be," Dirk said, "After getting bit, the rest of that day was a blur."

Dirk got up from his chair with a grunt. "Wait here."

Ed and Emily waited outside his cave. They looked down at the valley, where the faun and mountain goats still fought. Ed felt guilty at creating such a bloody battle. It started when he was a school kid and it still raged today. If fighting was all these creatures were created for, is fighting all they'll ever do? Or, will they eventually come to peace?

"Got it," Dirk said, walking out from his cave and waving the rolled up pool over his head. "Can I ask what you need it for?"

"I have an idea of how to sneak into Pinkerton's mansion," Ed said.

"With a swimming pool?" Emily said.

"Yeah, this I've got to see," Dirk agreed. "I'm a little out of shape, but if you're sneaking into Pinkerton's, you might need a bit of muscle. I'm coming with you."

Ed looked him up and down. He was pretty big and didn't look out of shape to Ed. Ed wasn't sure if he'd fit into his plan, but it couldn't hurt to have him by their side, especially when dealing with Pinkerton.

"Sure. Come on," Ed said.

"Now where?" Emily asked.

"Back to the Paddleman," Ed said, marching across the edge of the valley, back towards the mountain stream.

Emily called the Paddleman, and without fail, he appeared again. Ed wondered, if they were his only passengers, was there more than one Paddleman? If there were more than one, all the Paddlemen all looked very similar. Were Ed and his group the only ones to travel by Paddleman? It was unusual and uncanny that he promptly showed up whenever they called him.

"Where do you want to go?" Emily asked.

Ed walked up to the Paddleman. He unrolled a foot of Dirk's pool and held it out to the Paddleman.

"Are these pools connected to your waterways?" Ed asked.

The Paddleman dipped his index and middle fingers into the pool and swirled them around in a counterclockwise circle. He withdrew his fingers and shook his head.

"Are the pools connected to each other?" Ed asked.

The Paddleman nodded.

"Could you travel between pools?" Ed asked.

The Paddleman motioned, and Ed understood that he was asking for the pool. Ed placed Dirk's rolled up pool in the Paddleman's outreached hands. The Paddleman unrolled more of the pool across his lap. With both his hands, he drew a series of complex symbols with his fingertips in the pool's water.

"What are you thinking, Ed?" Emily asked.

"If all the portable pools are connected like the waterways of this world are connected, then we may have our found our way to sneak into Pinkerton's mansion," Ed said.

Emily gasped and said, "His partially built pool."

"Exactly," Ed said.

"Brilliant," Dirk said.

They looked over at the Paddleman, who was rolling the pool back up. He handed the pool to Ed who passed it along to Dirk.

"Will it work?" Ed asked.

The Paddleman nodded and motioned to spread the pool out on the ground. Dirk unrolled the pool along one of the paths. It was at a slight angle but would work. As the Paddleman carefully stepped out of the canoe onto solid ground, Ed wondered how often he walked anywhere. Ed and the Paddleman carried the canoe, which was very light for its size, and placed it at the top of Dirk's unrolled pool.

"Wait. Do we even know where the scissors are?" Emily asked.

Ed shook his head. "I don't recall seeing them in the room with the pool. We'll have to look around. Unfortunately, they might be where Pinkerton is. Since our visit, I'm guessing he will work harder at getting them to work, if he hasn't figured out how to use them by now anyway."

"We don't even know he has them. I think we're going in blind, without much of a plan. It's too dangerous," Emily said.

"What choice do we have?" Ed said. "We have to get those scissors back?"

"Get them back? We never had them in the first place. They were never yours. They belonged to some guy who used them to make pools. And, he's gone. He fell through a hole into Outworld. I say the choice is we leave this matter alone. We drop it. If Pinkerton has the scissors, and he is looking for a way out, let him. This world would be better off without him," Emily said. She folded her arms and turned her back on Ed. "Why do you want those scissors so much? Do you want to leave, too?"

A heavy silence hung in the air. Dirk and the Paddleman stood awkwardly nearby and looked at each other, then at Ed and Emily.

"Yes," Ed said. "When I saw Penny, I realized how much I miss her. We could have started a new life together, but we'll never know, because I was taken from that world. I'd love to get back to her in that world. Plus, there's someone out there, Max, who probably wants to get back to this world. Finding those scissors is the only way I know to set things right."

"What about me?" Emily said. "Couldn't we've started a new afterlife together?"

"We had a wonderful dream together. You know so much about me, but I hardly know anything about you. The only thing I know about you is that you know a lot about me. Too much at times. I'm flattered. A little creeped out, but very flattered. I've had amazing adventures exploring my world with you. You've made Black Manor a home, and I need you to help guide me back to that home, so I don't get lost. I'm still new to this world. I do need you by my side, but I'm not ready for a relationship with you. Sorry."

Emily faced Ed and stared at him. "I need you, too," she said, and sniffled. She turned away, walked toward the canoe, drew a deep breath, and composed herself. "Let's go."

The Paddleman entered the rear of the canoe and steadied it with his paddle as the others climbed in. Even with Dirk's bulk, the four sat comfortably in the canoe. When they were seated, the Paddleman pushed off the side of the portable pool and began to paddle.

Instead of the fog that accompanied them on their other trips with the Paddleman, an instant darkness enfolded them. Ed could not see Emily in front of him; he turned around and could not see Dirk or the Paddleman behind him. He could sense the others tensing and reaffirming their grip on the seats of the canoe as they felt it move across the darkened waters. Ed tried not to lean too much, but even over the edge of the canoe, the crystal blue water of the pool faded to an inky blue-black. In the distance, they could hear people laughing, playing, splashing, and swimming in what Ed could only assume were other portable pools.

The journey seemed to take a long time, longer than it had compared to their other trips. Maybe it was the darkness. To Ed, it was the uncomfortable silence that followed his confession to Emily. He liked her and enjoyed seeing his world with her by his side. Penny, on the other hand, was someone he had built a stronger bond with over the years. He wanted to get back to her, and hoped that he could travel through the world with her, whether that world was his, hers, or Outworld.

And, then it was over. Their eyes grew accustomed to the bright lights of Pinkerton's mansion. The canoe, now slightly banana-shaped because of the curvature of Pinkerton's half-constructed pool, rested in the wedge of pool in the same gallery Ed and Emily saw earlier. They each stepped out of the canoe and dropped to the floor as quietly as they could.

"Wait here," Ed whispered to the Paddleman, "We'll try to be back as soon as we can. But, if there is any trouble, leave. We don't want anything to happen to you. Okay?"

The Paddleman nodded.

"Should we split up?" Dirk whispered.

Ed and Emily both said, "No."

"We stick together," Ed said.

"Where do we look?" Emily asked.

"I don't know," Ed said. "Follow me."

They walked as quietly as they could through Pinkerton's mansion. They left the gallery and passed the front door and foyer, where they had been on their last visit. The mansion seemed impressive before but was actually quite small. The

379

rooms were enormous, but there weren't that many of them. The first room they encountered was a bedroom with a king-sized four-poster bed, a closet, and a low set of drawers. Ed imagined Pinkerton sleeping in there and wondered what gave him nightmares. Ed searched the closet, Dirk combed through the drawers, and Emily lifted the covers to find there was nothing under the bed. The box spring and mattress rested on the floor. Coming up short, they headed to the next room.

They walked into the kitchen. Ed did not think the scissors were in the kitchen, but they searched the drawers, pantry, and cupboards anyway. In his apartment, he had kept scissors in the kitchen drawer, but if these were special scissors, he didn't think they would be stuffed in a drawer with spatulas, spoons, and other kitchen gadgets.

The kitchen tilted and they stumbled. Emily fell into the pantry and knocked several food packages from the shelves. Ed braced himself on the kitchen sink. Dirk stood his ground.

"Pink's on the move," Ed whispered.

The kitchen tilted again and all three stumbled again. Emily was caught by the pantry door, but Ed tripped and fell through the kitchen door and into the hallway.

"I know I'm so close to a breakthrough," Pinkerton said.

"You'll get those scissors to work, sir," Kasper said.

Ed heard their voices coming from further

down the hall and around the corner. Ed steadied himself against the wall across from the kitchen.

"At least there's no more water," Pinkerton said.

He and Kasper appeared around the corner. Pinkerton wore a white lab coat, while Kasper looked like a garden gnome in a Prom dress.

"You!" Pinkerton spat.

The tilting stopped, and Ed stood his ground before Pinkerton.

"Where are Max's scissors, Pink?" Ed said.

"The name is Pinkerton. Kasper, why is this fool of a man who broke into my house demanding to know about things that do not concern him?"

Kasper said, "Considering it is his world, I would assume everything concerns him."

"Wrong answer," Pinkerton said, and slapped a button on his chair. Kasper crumbled to the floor, writhed in pain, and cycled through a series of different tortured creatures. Pinkerton pressed another button, and said, "Get him."

Kasper, panting and looking like a cartoon fish on dry land, said, "I can't, sir. I'm a hologram."

"Not you," Pinkerton said, "The Yabowak!"

Wooden hands and arms stretched out of the wood-paneled walls and grabbed Ed. Dirk burst through the kitchen door and exerted his strength to pry apart the Yabowak's grip on Ed. Other hands grew out of the Yabowak's arms and clasped Dirk's hands.

Emily walked through the kitchen door. "What's going on out here? Oh!"

"Run!" Ed yelled.

"Stop them!" Pinkerton bellowed.

Emily turned to run but tripped. A metallic tentacle reaching out from Pinkerton's chair wrapped around her feet.

Dirk managed to free Ed, but got himself entangled in the Yabowak's hands and arms in the process. The tentacle around Emily's feet pulled her closer to Pinkerton.

"Emily!" Ed said. Hands in the wall flailed at Ed and he dodged them.

"I'll save her. Run!" Dirk said.

"But," Ed said. He took a step towards Emily and reached out for her.

"Run!" Dirk said.

Ed turned around and ran back down the hall towards the gallery.

"That's right. Run for your life, coward," Pinkerton said and laughed.

"I know you have the scissors, and I'll be back for them," Ed said.

"They won't be here when you return, and neither will I," Pinkerton said.

"Emily, give me your hand," he heard Dirk say as he passed into the gallery. Ed hated leaving behind Emily and Dirk, but if Dirk could free him, he had faith he could free Emily, too.

Ed saw the Paddleman waiting patiently in his canoe in the pool. He stood next to the pool and waited for Dirk and Emily.

"Dirk! No!" Emily screamed, "Ed! Help me!"

Her scream was muffled, then drowned by the cold laughter of Pinkerton.

The gallery titled and Ed nearly fell over backwards into the pool.

"Dirk? Emily?" Ed called. Pinkerton's laughter grew colder and closer.

"They can't hear you," Pinkerton said in a sing-song tone.

"What have you done with them?" Ed hollered, but Pinkerton only laughed.

The Paddleman reached down and grabbed Ed from under one arm. He hoisted him up to the canoe. For an elderly looking man who paddled a canoe and did not much else, he was surprisingly strong.

Pinkerton rolled into the entrance of the gallery; he pointed at Ed, pressed a button, and said, "Get him!"

A wave of arms and hands rose from the floor and charged across the gallery towards the swimming pool. Hands splashed into the floor as new ones grew and stretched out of the floor.

Ed pulled himself into a sitting position.

"Back to the valley! Go!" yelled Ed.

The Paddleman nodded and slid his paddle into the pool as the wave of hands towered over the canoe. The world plunged into darkness, and there was a bump that nearly capsized the canoe as it propelled forth into the darkness of the waterway of pools.

Ed panted as he managed to catch his breath. He knew where the scissors were. Pinkerton confirmed that. Unfortunately, Pinkerton knew Ed was after the scissors, too. Pinkerton also had Emily and Dirk. The world thought Dirk was already dead; he hoped this myth wouldn't end up as truth. As concerned as he was about Dirk, Ed was more concerned about Emily. She knew a lot about Ed, and if Pinkerton knew this about her, the situation could get much worse for Ed. He still wanted the scissors to get back to the home he lost, but if he didn't get Emily away from Pinkerton, he could lose this world, too.

Ed felt horrible at leaving Dirk and Emily behind. Neither deserved to be left behind with Pinkerton. He only hoped Dirk could take care of both of them and come home safely.

CHAPTER TWENTY-ONE

Knocking on the Door

Glick, Penny, and Max returned to Ed's apartment. Glick spun the doorway to break the connection to the Zephyrus. Penny excused herself to wash the monkey off her and try on her new dress. Since Glick returned them safely from the Zephyrus, she figured she could turn her back on Glick for a few minutes to get a quick shower. Besides, she left Oscar-Frank behind to keep an eye on them.

She returned to Ed's apartment a half hour later. The door was still unlocked, and she let herself into Ed's apartment. Glick sat at the kitchen table in the same seat where he had stolen Ed's body. Max lay sprawled on the sofa with his feet dangling up and over the arm of the sofa.

"What do you think?" Penny asked with a twirl. Her new dress fit her perfectly and complimented her figure.

"What do I think about what?" Glick asked without looking up from the book.

"My new dress," she said twirling again.

"As beautiful as the woman wearing it," Max said.

"Thank you for the compliment and the dress," Penny said with a curtsey. She glided across the room, stepping lightly around the mess, and sat with Glick at the kitchen table. Max fiddled with Ed's Rubik's Cube, while Oscar-Frank lay curled up on Max's stomach, fast asleep. Glick had the old tome in front of him and carefully flipped through the pages. Penny looked at the puzzle pieces she made and sighed. They were swept to the side, and some spilled on one of the other chairs and floor. Penny sat adjacent to Glick and wished Ed was somewhere still inside. She looked down at the strange, old book, but could not make out any of the writing.

"What language is that written in?" Penny asked.

"It is written in Static, which is a form of Morphic," Glick said.

"Static? Morphic? What languages are those?"

"They are not languages," Glick said, and flipped through the book.

"Morphic is a style of writing," Max said quietly, so as not to disturb the dog's slumber. "Emotion and feeling are poured into the writing, and that's how you read it, by feeling it."

"Yes," said Glick. "Static is the non-dream form of Morphic."

"Huh," said Penny.

"How do you know so much about this stuff?" Penny asked Glick.

Glick continued to turn pages. "Experience. I am very old."

"How old?" Penny asked.

"Over a millennia," Glick said. He stopped on a page, examined it more closely, then continued turning pages.

"How did you end up in Ed's stereo?"

"You ask a lot of questions, Penelope Nichols," Glick said.

"Sorry," she said, and slumped in her chair. "I'm curious."

"You ask a lot of questions, but I do not mind answering them," Glick said. "I was stranded a long time ago, before the Between was tamed."

"The Between?" Penny asked.

"The Between is the layer between Outworld and Jaiu," Glick said.

"Jaiu is now known as OmniCore," Max said.

"I am unfamiliar with OmniCore," Glick said.

"Then, Glick is pretty damn old if this happened before OmniCore," Max said.

"Before the Between was tamed, I collected souls, much like the woman who collected Ed's soul ..." Glick began.

✂   ✂   ✂

In a time before OmniCore existed and shortly after the Great Music War, in a place where angels and demons worked and sometimes fought for the souls of mortals, Glick and his apprentice traveled to the Between to collect a soul. It should have been a routine collection, but it went horribly wrong.

387

Glick was a Risen Demon, meaning he took a demotion to learn from the demons so that he could become a better angel. He fell, became a damned good demon, then worked even harder to prove his way back upward again. As a Risen Demon, he worked to be one of the best soul collectors, if not *the* best.

As one of Jaiu's best, his assignment was to train a difficult newbie to harvest souls from the Between, the unseen, untamed world of the souls of mortals. Some Outworlders could see behind the veil into the Between, and some Jaiuians could influence Outworld from the Between. Glick could both influence Outworld from the Between and show himself to Outworlders as he pleased. As impressive and influential as Glick was with his set of skills, one trainee proved difficult for anyone to train. If anyone could get through to this cadet collector, the powers that be figured Glick could.

In the collector's embarkment area, Glick and Florn, the newbie, prepared for collection. Glick pulled on his gloves and slid the satchel over his shoulder. "While we are out there, you must do exactly what I tell you. Do you understand?"

Florn mumbled something as he fiddled with a clockwork project on Glick's work table. Glick pulled it from Florn's hands, lifted his chin, and asked again, "Do you understand?"

"Yes, sir," Florn spat.

It wasn't that Florn hated working with a Risen Demon, though he used that as an excuse. The fact was Florn hated work. Glick thought he would make a good demon, influencing and taunting mortals, but Florn thought demons were beneath him, pun unintentional.

"Good. Follow me," Glick said.

Glick opened a portal from Jaiu to the Between and stepped through. Florn, after some hesitation, did as he was told and followed Glick. In the olden days, the Between was a fuzzy, out of focus, view of Outworld, like looking at the world underwater without goggles, but with more mobility. Only those with keen vision could bring Outworld into focus. Over the years, the connections between worlds became tighter, providing a much clearer, accurate view of the different layers.

Lying ahead of them were the bodies of the souls they were sent to collect. Four humans and five boar lay dead on the ground after a tragic ending to a hunting party. In this time, the souls were harvested together. There was no segregation between types of souls in these days. They were all collected and delivered together.

Glick knelt down beside one of the dead. "The first thing you do is reach into ... Where are your gloves?"

Florn exaggerated a sigh and pulled out his gloves from his pouch, as if it was obvious to everyone where they were.

"Put them on," Glick said.

Florn sighed again, rolled his eyes, and then put on the gloves.

"Good. The first thing is ..." Glick said and froze. He stared past Florn, into the distance.

"You already said that. What's the first thing?" Florn asked.

"Beanies," Glick whispered.

"What?" Florn asked sounding bored and annoyed.

Glick pointed slowly and carefully to what he was keeping a steady gaze upon. Florn rolled his eyes and turned around.

Hovering above the field, but still a ways off, a solitary beanie hovered above the ground. Beanie, the creature, was kin to the jelly fish, but were flesh-eating scavengers that lived in the Between. Similar to the beanie hat, four, stubby propeller-like tentacles protruded from the top of the beanie's dome-shaped body. Several, thin tendrils hung down from the center underneath the beanie's body. The tendrils numbed their victims with euphoric thoughts. Then, the bodies attached to the victim to consume their flesh while they were alive. Beanies left next to nothing behind. They even consumed the soul's outer shell, leaving behind an invisible imprint behind to forever drift in the Between. The propellered hat originated as a morbid joke derived from this vile creature.

As vile of a creature as the beanies were, their means of reproduction was interesting, but also incredibly dangerous. Like the quantum states of a Bellman's Dingo, once a beanie realized they were noticed by a victim, they became impregnated. The moment eye contact was broken, they gave birth. As a seasoned collector, Glick knew this behavior of the beanies, and barely survived a beanie at an earlier hunt, which was why he didn't take his eyes off it.

"I want you to keep your eyes on the beanie while I finish collecting the souls," Glick said quietly.

Florn looked at it with boredom and asked, "Why am I looking at that thing?"

Glick gathered the souls as quickly and gently as he could and said quietly, "It's a beanie. Didn't you pay attention in class when they talked about them?"

Florn rolled his eyes and looked back at the beanie. Now there were two. "What in Jaiu?"

Glick looked up and saw the two beanies lazily drifting closer to them.

"They've doubled, but don't panic. We still have time to collect the souls. Whatever you do, don't break eye contact."

Florn, not daring to blink, stared at the two beanies. As they approached, they drifted farther and farther apart to divide and conquer.

"They're separating! They're separating!" Florn said, panic rising in his voice.

"Keep your voice down and don't panic!" Glick said. "You watch that one. I'll watch this one. We'll be okay.

Glick fumbled around on the ground for the remaining bodies to finish gathering the souls. He kept constant gaze on his beanie, but broke eye contact when Florn stepped backwards into his field of vision between him and the beanie. Emerging on the other side were two beanies.

"There's too many of them. We need to abandon the souls and leave now," Glick said.

"Why?" Florn asked, and turned his head to take a quick glance at the two beanies drifting behind him. When he turned back, there were two beanies in front of him. Now there were four.

Florn panicked and ran. He broke eye contact with the two. Now there were six. Two of the beanies drifted after Florn, while the remaining ones circled Glick. Florn crossed over into Jaiu, leaving Glick behind. The two beanies chasing him drifted back to join the others.

It was impossible to keep an eye on all the beanies, so Glick closed his eyes. If he couldn't look at them, they couldn't reproduce. Unfortunately, he had a hard time defending himself from what he couldn't see.

Glick flailed about trying to bat them away with gloved hands. His hands were protected, but his arms were exposed. Thin tendrils reached out and stung his arm. An instant of pain was replaced by an overpowering feeling of goodness. Glick tried to shake the feeling of how wonderful the universe was and the urge to open his eyes and bask in all its beauty. He lost the urge to fight and embraced the beanies' stings.

In seconds, he was numbed into submission. After several minutes, his flesh and soul were consumed. Glick was nothing but a thought drifting in the Between like a beanie.

He sensed the rescue party that appeared later to look for him. There was not enough left of him to call out for help and nothing left of him for them to find. They gave up their rescue, and Glick was left alone.

To Glick, time became a series of events, one after another, with no idea of how much time passed in between events. He sensed the massive hunt, which nearly brought the beanies to extinction. Unknown to Glick, the last few beanies were collected by OmniCore to be used in world cleansing.

Every once in a while, he sensed a collector arriving to take a soul. Mostly, it was a whole lot of nothing but his own thoughts.

Then, one day in Outworld, humans cleared the field Glick hovered over and built an apartment complex. People came and went in the apartment. They listened to their human music. Some of the softer more melodic music reminded Glick of the days he fought in the Great Music War. Styles of music came and went with each new tenant in the apartment. Glick was attracted to the music and drifted as close to its source as he could get.

When Ed moved into the apartment, Glick appreciated Ed's variety of music. When he upgraded to the CD changer, Glick discovered he had a library of music at his disposal. In time, he realized he could pick and chose among his favorite songs.

If music could be used to influence the enemy in the Great Music War, Glick experimented to see if music could influence the listener. Through experimentation and patience, Glick established a more solid connection to Ed's mind and was able to influence him through carefully selected music.

>< >< ><

"... Eventually, the connection was strong enough to control Ed's actions. With the last connection, I completely took over his body. It disconnected his soul from his body. One body, one soul. My soul, although no longer visible, was the only soul that could occupy his body. A collector took his abandoned soul back to Jaiu," Glick said.

Penny was in tears after listening to Glick's story. "That is so sad. To be lost and abandoned all that time. No wonder you want to get home so much. I'll do anything to help you get home. You just tell me what you need me to do."

"I do not desire to go home. I will go home because it is the logical thing to do," Glick said.

"Of course, you desire to go home. Desire must be what motivates you," Penny said.

"No. All I am is thought using a body as a vessel. I desire nothing. I feel nothing."

"Is that why you are so cold?" Penny asked.

"It is not my intention to be cold. I am cold because I lack the emotion to be otherwise. I am thought," Glick said.

Glick searched the tome for the spell he wanted. Penny sat and watched him. Penny still felt strange to see Ed acting so unusual. She had been spending so much time with him that she was beginning to think of this person more as Glick and not Ed. And, that made her miss Ed even more.

Max wandered around Ed's apartment examining every little knickknack, gadget or possession, from the chewed pencil next to the phone to the partially melted spatula in the kitchen drawer.

"Do you mind? We're all strangers in this apartment. It doesn't feel right that you are messing with Ed's things," Penny said to Max.

"Technically, according to his story, Glick was here first," Max said, and continued to rummage and snoop.

Penny looked at the old tome as Glick flipped through the pages. She asked, "What are you looking for in there, anyway?"

"I am no longer looking. I have found," Glick said.

"Okay. What did you find?" Penny said.

"A way to open the door to Jaiu," Glick said.

"Great. How?" Max asked, sniffing a jar of olives from Ed's fridge.

"Similar to the portal to the Zephyrus," Glick said. He grabbed the permanent marker, walked to the closet door, and pulled off the cap.

"Wait!" Penny said.

Glick stopped, turned, and stared at Penny.

"Before you go graffitiing more of Ed's apartment, can't we reuse that door?" she said, pointing to the freestanding doorway in the middle of the apartment's living room.

"We are borrowing the book. We will need that door to return the book to the Zephyrus," Glick said.

He turned and began writing on the closet doorframe before Penny could protest further. With the book in one hand and the marker in the other, he wrote and wrote. The symbols were similar to the ones in both the book and the other doorway, but there were at least eight times as many. After writing the last of the symbols, they began to glow purple as if lit by black light from within.

Glick closed the book, set it on the kitchen table, and returned to the closet door. Penny held her breath. What was on the other side? She'd already seen an improbable floating city. What would the afterlife look like? Supposedly, Max came from there. Was it another world? Was it like a parallel universe?

Glick opened the door. Instead of the closet with Ed's jackets, shoes, vacuum cleaner, umbrella, and other belongings, there was blackness. Was nothingness what the other side looked like? Glick pressed a hand against a black barrier that looked as if it were made of rubber.

A voice resonated out of the barrier. It said, "All personal barriers to and from OmniCore must be cleared by management. All OmniCore employees must consult their local transportal representative for proper forms and schedules for all multiplane travel. Thank you, and a peaceful existence to you."

Glick stood and looked confused. He pressed

his hand harder into the flexible, black barrier. Again, the voice said, "All personal barriers to and from ..."

Glick shut the door. The voice continued, muffled from the other side of the closed door.

"Now what?" Max said. He looked depressed. He was hoping to get back to his home, too.

Glick didn't look depressed. He looked broken.

"I do not understand. This should have worked. OmniCore has broken the portal," Glick said.

"Just fill out the forms and schedules. Where is the nearest transportation representative?" Penny said.

"Trans*portal* representative. And, I have no idea where that could be," Glick said. He sat down at the kitchen table and stared at nothing in particular. Penny looked at Max, who shrugged and shook his head.

"Guess this means I'm staying a while longer," Max said, and stretched out again on the sofa.

"There must be another way," Glick said.

"Could the Zephyrus have a rep?"

"Even if they did, I am not an OmniCore employee," Glick said.

"Don't look at me. I'm just a dreamizen," Max said.

"Move over," Penny said to Max. Max dropped his feet to the floor so that he could still lie on the sofa, only not as comfortable. Penny slumped down on the sofa and pouted. She began to doubt she would ever see Ed again. Part of her wondered if she should go home, forget any of this happened, and try to get on with her life. The other part of her – the part that kept her with two strangers – wanted to see the Ed she knew and refused to give up.

"Ed, where are you?" she asked under her breath.

Glick sat up straighter, pointed to his head, and said, "He's in here."

CHAPTER TWENTY-TWO

Another Bad Idea

Back in his garden, alone, Ed tumbled out of the canoe. He knew where the scissors were, but the person who had them had this grabby-hand-watchdog thing. The worst part is that he abandoned Emily and Dirk. He trusted Dirk to save Emily, but he had no idea what had happened to either of them. He didn't have a plan for going back and rescuing Emily, Dirk, or the scissors. Since he had failed, Ed figured he better tell Glick. Perhaps Glick had better news.

Ed opened the door and walked into the darkened room. Out the window, he saw his apartment. Glick was sitting at the kitchen table. Glick sat in the same chair Ed was last sitting when his body was stolen. Shivers ran down Ed's spine.

"Glick?" Ed asked.

The view from the window changed a bit, as if Glick sat up straighter.

"Is this Edward Black?" Glick's voice said.

"Yes."

"He's in here," Glick said. Ed could tell he had

said this aloud because there was a muffled echo from the window.

"Is Penny there?" Ed asked.

"Yes," Glick's voice said. The view swirled around and revealed Penny on the sofa sitting next to the portable pool salesman. Ed also saw a huge mess of books in his apartment and the furniture pushed out of the way to make room for a freestanding door similar to the one in his garden. The door cluttering up his apartment was affixed to one of his new bookcases. He saw it was attached to his lazy Susan and had writing all over it.

Penny was talking to Glick, but Glick ignored her. Her voice was too muffled for Ed to hear what she was saying. Ed was too busy looking at the person sitting next to her to concentrate on what she was trying to say to him.

"That's who we've been looking for," Ed said.

"Penelope? Or, Maxwell?" Glick asked.

"Max," Ed said, "What is he doing there?"

"He tracked you down, and has been following Penny and me since," Glick said.

"Tell Max we know where his scissors are," Ed said.

There was a muffled conversation as Glick and Max talked. Max's eyes lit up, and he mouthed some words.

"Max wants to know if the hands still have them," Glick said.

"No, tell him Pinkerton has them. Both the scissors and the hands," Ed said.

400

Glick repeated this, and Max's excitement vanished.

"Who is Pinkerton?" Glick asked aloud.

Ed couldn't hear what Max called him, but Ed said, "He's a nightmare. I don't know how I can get them back. Pinkerton's also taken two friends who were helping me find them. What about you? Any luck?"

"No," Glick said. "They have shut the portals in and out of Jaiu."

"Is that why there's a doorway in my living room?" Ed asked.

"No. That doorway is to the Zephyrus," Glick said. The view changed slightly to show Ed's graffitied closet door. "That door was the attempted portal to Jaiu."

Ed paused a moment to think. He thought about Pinkerton looking for a way out, the graffitied doors in his apartment, and the freestanding door in his garden.

"What if I could provide you a portal to Jaiu?" Ed asked.

"How so?" Glick said.

"Somehow, there is a connection between my world to Outworld through either my old mind or old body. That's how we're communicating. Right?"

"True," Glick said.

"There is a freestanding doorway in part of my world, and when I walk through it, I'm in this area where I can communicate with you."

"True. You are a voice in my mind," Glick said.

401

"Maybe my old mind or body in Outworld is still connected to this world, which is part of Jaiu. You tried to connect a doorway to Jaiu from Outworld. Maybe there is some way to connect your door to Jaiu with the door here in my world. Do you think you can do that? I mean, it's not really Jaiu, but it is part of it. And, if you get here, maybe you and Max can help get his scissors back."

"I will try," Glick said. "You will need to be on the right side of the door to not be trapped in your old head."

"Good point," Ed said. "I will wait outside. See you soon."

"See you on the other side," Glick said.

Ed left the room to his old mind and shut the door behind him. He may have just found a loophole to get himself home.

✂   ✂   ✂

To Glick, this was the most logical plan. If Max found a hole from Ed's world to Outworld, and there was a communications channel between that same world and the body Glick occupied, then chances were good he could adjust his doorway to Jaiu to connect to Ed's world.

Unfortunately, he needed Ed's body to stay connected to the doorway so he could pass through the door to the other side. This would allow the connection to stay complete and uninterrupted. He needed to disconnect from Ed's body to travel through the door.

Once disconnected from Ed's body, the body

would become a soulless automaton. He needed someone with the greatest connection to Ed to influence his body to stay connected to the door's frame. Although Ed did create Max at one time, he was merely a character in one of Ed's fleeting dreams. The Ed in Outworld barely remembered the original dream. On the other hand, he had known Penny for years as a friend and neighbor. And, Penny had deep feelings for Ed. The connection between Outworld Ed and Penny was much greater. Glick needed to occupy Penny's body. For that, he would need music.

Glick searched Ed's mind, and then his apartment. He pulled out a dented trumpet and plastic recorder. Glick opted for the recorder and returned to the living room.

"What are you doing?" Penny asked. "What did Ed say?"

"We may have found a use for the doorway, but I will need your help," Glick said.

"Of course! Anything!" Penny said.

"I want you to sit back on the sofa, relax, and concentrate on Ed," Glick said.

Obediently, she did what he asked of her. Penny closed her eyes and took deep breaths. She tried to relax, but could not help smiling. She had no idea her body was about to be taken the way Ed's body was taken from him. If it worked the same; her soul would be collected, and she would be revived in her own world, like Ed was in his.

With Penny relaxed on the sofa and thinking of

Ed, Glick thought this would be easier than it was with Ed. Thoughts of Ed would help Glick find the way to Penny's mind. Relaxation is her acceptance to be put into a trance. And the sofa will prevent her from collapsing to the floor during the transition, the way Ed's crumpled earlier. To prevent Ed's body from collapsing too far, Glick sat on the floor with his back pressed up against the bookcase frame of the Zephyrus door.

"What do I do?" Max asked.

"Sit quietly. I will need your help soon," Glick said.

Max nodded. He sat back on the sofa and relaxed, too.

Max sat back on the sofa, laced his fingers behind his head, and closed his eyes.

Glick pulled out the recorder and began to play. Ed never got the hang of playing the recorder, except for *Mary Had a Little Lamb*. Glick found the recorder similar to the flutes he played in the Great Music War. Although it was not his optimal choice of musical instrument, it would suffice. It was not the stereo, either. He had much more control over the music with the recorder than he did with Ed's selection of music.

A happy, haunting tune filled the apartment. Penny breathed deeply and sighed. Glick engulfed her in the music and reached out to her mind. He sensed her thinking of Ed. He nearly lost the connection when her mind strayed to work, her dog, or her moms, but the connection solidified when her

404

mind wandered back to Ed and how much he meant to her. Her strong emotions for Ed made it so much easier for Glick to take over her body.

Glick opened Penny's eyes in time to see Ed's body slump over sideways. Because he was familiar with controlling Ed's body, it took no time to control Penny's body. He liked Penny's body better. Her small hands with slender fingers reminded him of his own so very long ago.

Glick tapped Max on the leg and woke Max from his brief nap. Max awoke with a jerk and a snort. Glick stood up from the sofa and was careful not to touch Penny's soul.

"Let's get to work," Glick in Penny's body said.

"Glick?" Max said.

"Yes. Now is your turn to help," Glick said.

Max looked at Penny, and then at Ed like a discarded doll on the floor. "How do you do that? You aren't taking my body, too, are you?"

"No. I need you to help move Ed's body over to the closet," Glick said.

Max stood up and said, "Right. Hide the body in the closet. What is that?"

Glick saw that Max was pointing at Penny's soul hovering above the sofa.

"You can see that?" Glick asked.

Max nodded. "What is it? It's so beautiful." Max reached out to touch it.

"Don't touch it! That is Penny's soul. Someone will be along to collect it soon."

Max withdrew his hand. He and Glick knelt

down to pick up Ed's body and carry it to the closet. Glick held up Ed's body by the feet while Max carried him under his arms.

"He's still alive," Max said.

"Yes," Glick said.

"I thought he'd be dead," Max said.

"He is soulless, not dead."

"Oh," Max said, and looked back at Penny's soul above the sofa.

Glick propped up Ed's body against the wall next to the closet door. He grabbed Ed's head, opened his eyelids, and looked into Ed's vacant stare.

"I know you can hear me. Ed is off in another world. I want you to concentrate on him," Glick told Ed.

The soulless, ex-body of Ed nodded in acknowledgement.

"I also want you to keep your arm, from elbow down to your hand, touching the doorframe," Glick said. He helped Ed position his arm along the doorframe. Ed, like a mannequin, obeyed.

Glick grabbed the marker and looked at the symbols already written along the doorframe. Ed's arm blocked part of the letters. He pulled off the cap and wrote along Ed's hand and arm, and Ed's body didn't care a bit.

"What's that?" Max asked.

Glick looked, and Max was pointing at the air wavering in the corner of the room. Oscar-Frank cowered into the cushions on the sofa and whined.

"They've come to collect Penny's soul," Glick said, and went back to write on Ed's arm.

Alaenia, on her dolphin, splashed into the room. Max watched in surprise as the petite woman on a dolphin circled the room. Glick stood up. Alaenia was staring between the two people standing in the apartment where she had just been only a couple of days before. With more urgency than before, Alaenia swooped over the sofa to claim Penny's soul.

Glick turned Penny's back to Alaenia and knocked on the closet door. The door opened. Ed stood in his garden on the other side of the doorway.

CHAPTER TWENTY-THREE

One Perturbed Pixie

As soon as Penny walked through the door into Ed's garden, Ed threw his arms around her and gave her a big hug. He suspected a problem when she didn't hug him back.

"What's the matter?" Ed asked, pulling away.

"You are expecting to hug Penelope Nichols. I am not Penelope Nichols. I am Glick."

"You're not ... But, I thought ... What happened to my body?" Ed asked.

Glick pointed to Ed's old body sitting on the floor on the other side of the doorway.

"Excuse me. Sorry," Max said as he tripped over Ed's old body and stumbled through the doorway after Glick.

"If you're Glick, where's Penny?" Ed said.

"I do not know. She was taken," Glick said and closed the door behind him, leaving Oscar-Frank alone in Ed's apartment.

"First you take my body, then you take Penny's body! How could you?!" Ed yelled at Glick. He felt so conflicted. He wanted to shove or hit Glick, but he would never harm Penny. Instead, he walked over to Max, shoved him, and asked, "How could you have let this happen?"

"How could you have let Pinkerton take my scissors?" Max asked.

"I didn't give them to him. He already had them when I got there," Ed spat. He took a breath and kept his anger in check. He reminded himself that he wasn't mad at Max. He was furious at Glick.

"Got there?" Max asked, "You went to Pinkerton's and lived to tell about it?"

Ed sighed, "Twice. Only, the second time, I barely escaped."

"Damn," Max said. Ed could tell from Max's expression he was thinking Ed either did something amazing or amazingly foolish.

"That's not the worst part. I left two of my friends behind at Pinkerton's."

"One," said a deep voice. Dirk walked up the hill to the garden. Ed's jaw dropped.

"How did you ...? I thought that ... What happened?" Ed asked, at a loss for words upon seeing Dirk alive and well.

"Pinkerton captured Emily. I tried to save her, but those hands overwhelmed us. At my first opportunity, I played dead. I didn't know what else to do. If I couldn't fight off the hands, I took the fight out of the hands."

"Hands? You mean the ones that stretch out of walls and floors?" Max asked.

"Yes. They took Emily. I couldn't fight them

all," Dirk said.

"All? How many are there? I've only seen one, maybe two," Max said, trying to remember. He was more concerned about being stuck in Outworld than doing a hand check. What he remembered most was the one hand waving to him as the hole between worlds sealed itself shut.

"He's got dozens of those hands," Dirk said.

"Not only can Pinkerton control them, it sounds like he can duplicate them, too," Ed said.

"What is that?" Glick said.

Sharing notes about Pinkerton, they had ignored Glick, who was looking at something behind them. Ed rolled his eyes. He still hadn't decided how to deal with Glick, but he looked in the direction of where Glick was looking. A black sphere grew out of thin air.

"Get back! It could be dangerous!" Dirk said, protecting the group with his one good arm.

"Did Pinkerton send that?" Max asked, wincing.

Ed stepped around Dirk and approached the sphere. The sphere grew to about a ten foot diameter, and then stopped growing.

"I think it's from OmniCore. I arrived in something like this when I was acclimated to this world. This must be what it looks like on the outside. Maybe it's Penny."

The bubble grew clearer and popped much more rapidly than the one in which Ed had arrived in his world. In the middle of the bubble was an irate fairy, surrounded by a pack of burly demons wearing OmniCore security uniforms.

"Take that one," Alaenia said, pointing to Penny. Two of the demons rushed over, threw Penny's body to the ground, and restrained her. Then, they slapped a small disc over her mouth. Glick tried to speak, but the disc over Penny's mouth silenced all sound from her.

Ed threw up his hands but said, "Hey! Be careful with her!"

Max and Dirk followed suit and raised their hands, too. Max raised his arms to their full extent, hands high above his head, while Dirk placed his one hand on his head.

Alaenia walked over to Penny, looked down, and said, "OmniCore places you under arrest. The charge is two accounts of reckless abandonment of two souls and for the theft of two OmniCore Outworld vessels. The punishment is purging. A trial will be held as your only chance to redeem yourself. Do you understand?"

Glick nodded.

"Take him away," Alaenia said to the two demons. A bubble formed around the two guards holding Penny's body. It was like watching a large, bubble slowly unpop itself. The bubble turned black, shrank, and disappeared.

"What's going to happen?" Ed asked.

"A purge, meaning he will be erased from existence. Which could happen to you and your world if someone can't help me understand what in

Jaiu is going on around here," Alaenia said.

"Is Penny okay?" Ed asked.

Alaenia calmed down, and said, "She's fine. She's going through the same thing you went through. We're creating a new body for her now."

"And, you," Alaenia said, turning on Max, "Explain all the holes you're punching in Ed's world. How did you get out, and how did you get back in?"

"I didn't do it. I, personally, haven't made any holes. I make swimming pools, and I don't even dig holes for those," Max said. He went on to explain the hole he crawled through and the hands stretching from the floor. He and Ed tried to explain the door in Ed's garden that connected Ed's world with his apartment, but said that was mostly Glick's doing.

"The door will need to be sealed," Alaenia said.

Ed nodded. He looked forward to traveling between Outworld and his world. It would make his apartment much larger. But, he mainly wanted to get back to Outworld for Penny, who was now taken from there, too.

"What happens to our bodies? My Outworld body is sitting there on the other side of the door. You just hauled off Penny's body. What happens to them?"

Alaenia walked to the door and asked, "Do you mind if I have a look?"

Ed shook his head and motioned to the door. When Alaenia tried the door, it appeared to be locked.

"I think it only opens for me," Ed said. He

walked to the door, and it opened without a problem.

Alaenia stepped into the apartment and bent down to Ed's old body sitting on the floor, still holding his hand up to the doorframe. She examined the body like a visitor viewing a statue in a museum. She stood up and said, "I need Connections to come look at this."

"Why?" Ed asked.

"I think it's still connected to this world," she said, "which would explain why there's been an issue connecting your new body to this world. If I'm right, we might be able to reuse this vessel and Penny's with duplicate souls. I'm not guaranteeing anything, but there doesn't seem to be any damage other than swapping out one soul for another."

"So, what? I can go back to living in Outworld?" Ed asked.

"No. You stay here. A duplicate soul drives this body until it breaks down. The duplicate soul will build upon your world until the connection is terminated. In other words, this body's death. Then, you take over the connection to your world."

"Okay. I'm cool with that," Ed said.

"Same for Penny," she added.

"Excuse me," Dirk said. "There's a damsel in distress who needs to be saved."

"Not to mention getting my scissors back," Max added.

Alaenia and Ed exited Outworld, and Ed shut the door behind him.

413

"You know where the scissors are?" Alaenia asked.

"Of course. I've been looking for them. I thought that's why you left me the notes," Ed said.

"Notes? What notes?" Alaenia asked.

"You know, the notes that said something about security videos, finding the pool boy and his scissors, the Jack of diamonds? Any of that ring a bell?" Ed said.

Alaenia slapped the sides of her face and groaned. "I left those notes in your death report, didn't I?"

"Yeppers," Ed said.

"I was supposed to investigate that, but I got side tracked, then couldn't find my notes," she said.

Ed pointed to the manor. "They're in there, in the library, if you need them. I don't think you do. There's Max."

"Hi there," Max said.

"And, we were talking about where the scissors are before you stormed in," Ed said.

"Well, then, my work is nearly done. Good work. Are you planning on retrieving them?" she asked.

"Yes," Max said.

"And, Emily," Dirk added.

"Her, too," Ed said.

"Okay. You get the scissors and try not to cause any more holes in the world, and I will go deal with the stolen vessels," Alaenia said.

"Excuse me, ma'am," Max said, "Go easy on

414

Glick."

"Glick? Who is Glick?" Alaenia asked.

"He's the spirit inside of the woman's body, or vessel, or whatever you want to call it. Listen to his story. Just don't let him break out into a musical number."

"Glick is the name of the spirit that haunted my stereo. He must have used my own music to take over my body," Ed said.

"And, he played a recorder to take over his friend's body, too. He said he fought in some kind of musical war. Or, was it a musical about a war?" Max said.

"The Great Music War?" Alaenia asked.

"That's the one," Max confirmed.

"That was a long, long time ago. Like, ancient history. I learned about that in training when I was a little girl. How did he end up haunting your stereo?" Alaenia said.

"Just listen to his story," Max said, "Like me, he just wanted to get home."

"He violated a law ... twice."

"If he's as old as that ancient war, he might have existed before those laws. Maybe he can be grandfathered in? Or, great, great-grandfathered in?" Max said.

"I will see what I can do. No promises. Do your best to find those scissors before any more holes appear. I wouldn't want this world to be purged," Alaenia said.

They all agreed to find the scissors. They stood

around the garden and watched as Alaenia disappeared into another bubble.

"I hope Glick will be okay," Max said.

"I don't know what to think about Glick," Ed said, "Right now, I'm too concerned about saving Emily and getting your scissors away from Pinkerton. I think I have a plan. Dirk, you're going to need your swimming pool again."

"He'll be expecting us if we travel that way again," Dirk said.

"We're not using it for travel."

"Ok. Sure," Dirk said. Ed handed him his rolled up, portable pool.

"Max," Ed said, "I want you to walk right up to his mansion."

Max gulped and shook his head.

"It's okay. He's not expecting you to still be in this world," Ed said.

"Aw, man. What about you?" Max asked.

"Dirk will sneak in with me, since we're both expected. I think I know of another way into Pinkerton's place, but I need to talk with the Paddleman."

"What about those hands?" Dirk asked.

"Pinkerton has some kind of device on his chair that controls the hands. If we can neutralize his chair, we might be able to stop the hands."

"How are we going to do that?" Dirk asked.

"I don't know, yet. I'll think of something," Ed said.

"And, when that fails, then what?" Max said.

"Have a little faith in your creator. If we can't subdue him, then I'll try to bargain with him," Ed said. He pulled the doorknob out of his pocket.

"A doorknob? Seriously?" Max said.

"Pinkerton said something about no longer cutting water. He must be getting close to knowing how to use them. I figure if he did know how to use the scissors, he wouldn't be in the world anymore. But, he is. So, if he can't get the scissors to work, he might have his doubts that the scissors actually work or be frustrated with them. Especially when he sees you walking up to his mansion, he'll doubt they can cut to some place outside of my world. Whether or not the scissors work, we can tell him we have a door linked directly to Outworld to set him free."

"We don't even know where he keeps the scissors," Dirk said.

"Pinkerton and his buddy were further down the hall. There must be some room where they are experimenting with the scissors. My guess is that is where he has Emily, too," Ed said.

"What do you think?" Max asked Dirk.

"It's risky, but we have to," Dirk said.

"Okay. Let's go," Max said.

Ed ran into the manor. He said he needed a couple of supplies. While he gathered things, Dirk and Max summoned the Paddleman. One of Ed's supplies was a book from his shelves, which he showed to the Paddleman. The Paddleman dipped his fingers into the fountain, then nodded his head. They climbed into the canoe and were off on their double rescue mission.

CHAPTER TWENTY-FOUR
The Elaborate Plan

"I'll ask you one more time. What do you know about the scissors?" Pinkerton asked, looking down upon Emily. He perched upon a stool like a vulture over its helpless victim. Multiple hands of the Yabowak strapped Emily to a metal operating table.

"Even children know how to cut and paste. I'm surprised an evil genius like yourself can't figure out a simple pair of scissors," she said.

"It pleases me that you recognize my genius, but don't get smart with me, girl. I know there's more to these scissors than cutting paper. I know there is more than cutting pools. If these scissors can do what I know they can, I want to know why you and your friend are looking for them," Pinkerton said.

"You seem to know so much. Why don't you tell me?" Emily mocked.

"And, you seem to be so foolish. There you are, helplessly strapped to a table holding on to your last bit of courage. Do you know what kind of table this is? It's an operating table. I'm not only an evil genius; I'm also a bit of a mad scientist. You want to hear about one of my crazy schemes?"

Emily tried to shake her head, but the metal hand of the Yabowak made her nod her head instead. Another metal hand sprouted out of the table and clamped her mouth shut.

"I was bored one day and thought I would graft parts of one animal onto other animals. It was terrific fun," Pinkerton said. He reached for a scalpel and twirled it in his fingers about her head. "If you'd like to have terrific fun, too, I'd be happy to arrange it."

Emily's three eyes grew with fear.

In a quiet voice, he said, "Why don't you tell me what I want to hear? The scissors. What do you know?"

Emily mumbled. The Yabowak loosened its grip on her mouth and she repeated herself. "All I know is the scissors belong to Max. He used them to make portable swimming pools. We were looking for Max, but he disappeared. Somehow, Max left this world, and Ed speculates it was the scissors. He figures if he can find the scissors, he can leave this world, too."

"Good," Pinkerton said. "About Ed, is he the real Ed, or another one of the fakes?"

"He's real. I welcomed him into his world," she said.

Pinkerton tilted his head and said, "Isn't that sweet. You welcome him, and he leaves you behind with me."

"He didn't leave me behind. He'll be back to stop you," Emily said.

"Aw," Pinkerton said, then tisked Emily. "You were doing so well, then you had to go and spoil the fun with threats. Time to cease the idle chitchat and commence with the terrific fun!"

Pinkerton lowered the scalpel towards Emily's face. A metallic hand clamped her mouth shut so she couldn't scream. Pinkerton paused, then said, "Let's pause a moment. I just thought of something. I am an evil genius. That means I must explain my evil plot before being thwarted by the hero. You want to hear what terrific fun I have in store for us today?"

Again, Emily tried to shake her head, but the Yabowak made her nod.

"Excellent," Pinkerton said. He set the scalpel down on a nearby surgical tray. Pinkerton held the sides of Emily's head with his hands. Emily flinched at his touch. "Has anyone told you, that you have beautiful eyes? I wish I could have eyes as beautiful as yours. Oh, wait. I can. But, I'm going to give you something in return."

He picked up something that looked like a ball attached to a wire. He held the ball so the connector at the end of the wire dangled down towards her face. "You see this? Unfortunately, you won't for long. This is a special new eye for you. What makes it special is that I'll be able to see what you see. You see? Say cheese!" He smiled and pretended to take a picture, then frowned at Emily and said, "Oh. That's right. You can't smile."

He set down the one artificial eye and picked up a billiard ball, that was smaller than standard billiard balls. He turned it in his fingers so that she could see the number.

"This, in case you didn't know, is an eight-ball. It's to remind you that as long as I'm stuck in this world, you will always be behind it. What? Can't speak? Cat got your tongue? Yes, that is an excellent idea, but we don't want to have all our terrific fun at once. You hold your tongue a little longer. Kitty can wait."

Pinkerton set down the eight-ball and picked up the scalpel again. As two of the Yabowak's hands held her eyes open wide, Pinkerton lowered the scalpel.

✂   ✂   ✂

Dirk needed supplies. After dropping off Max as close as possible to Pinkerton's, the Paddleman dropped Dirk off at a lakeside, the scene comprising various horror and camping movies. From the lake, Dirk joined a touring group of elementary school children on a field trip as they headed towards Toonville, a small cartoon subdivision of TV Land. Whenever the children started staring at him, Dirk barked, "Face front!" or "Pay attention!" and the children would immediately turn away with wide-eyed terror.

Once in Toonville, Dirk visited a cartoon mouse. In the days when Dirk still wrestled, he and the mouse did a commercial together for promoting health and fitness.

"What can I do for you, mi amigo?" the mouse asked, his Spanish accent faded over the years.

Dirk looked around, bent down, and whispered into the mouse's large ear.

The mouse disappeared in a cloud of dust and returned before Dirk fanned the dust away with his hands.

He pulled a black, rubbery disk from under his cartoon sombrero and handed it to Dirk. Dirk tucked the disk into his satchel and pulled out a block of sharp cheddar cheese. He handed the cheese to the mouse and thanked him.

The cartoon deeply sniffed the block of cheese and said, "Mmm. I love the real stuff. Gracias, mi amigo."

Dirk made one more stop in TV Land at a hardware store. The store was a composite of hardware stores featured in various sitcoms. He purchased a few items and tucked them into his satchel. Finally, he was ready to head to Pinkerton's.

Once outside of TV Land, Dirk took a short hike up a nearby hill and called upon another friend. A large, dark figure descended from the sky and landed before Dirk. The figure looked half human and half crow. Fine feathers as dark as a midnight shadow covered its body, except for parts of its face, feet, and hands. Instead of bird talons, its feet resembled strong gorilla pads. A matching pair, equally as strong, attached at the ends of each wing, almost giving the bird-man a more bat-like appearance.

"Hello, Raven," Dirk said.

"I guess you need a lift?" Raven asked.

"How did you guess? I owe you another one. What's that make? Two? Three?"

"Eleven, Dirk. But, who's counting," Raven said. He cocked his head and watched a cloud in the shape of an elephant in a sailboat drift across the sky. "Where this time?"

"Pinkerton mansion. In the queso fields of– ..."

"I know where. Are you sure you want to go there?" Raven asked.

"Do you mind taking me? Or, do I need to find another way?" Dirk asked.

"I will take you. After this, no more," Raven said.

"Fair enough," Dirk said.

Raven flapped his wide wings and took flight. He hovered low over Dirk's head. Dirk lifted his arms straight out to the sides, and Raven grabbed him under the arms. Raven flapped hard, lifting Dirk off the ground.

"You've lost weight," Raven said.

"Thanks," said Dirk, "I've been taking more hikes. That battle will be the death of me."

Raven and Dirk flew high over Ed's world. TV Land disappeared behind them as the land scrolled by beneath them. Fields and forests. Hills, mountains, and deserts. It all whooshed by.

Several minutes later, Raven circled the heat thermals rising from the bubbling queso near Pinkerton's mansion.

"Set me down on top of the dome," Dirk said.

Raven nodded his head. Raven adjusted his

424

grip on Dirk, and Dirk held tightly to his sack of supplies.

Dirk touched down gently on top of the smooth surface of the glass dome. Raven fluttered to a rest beside him. His wings flapped and twitched since his sweaty feet could not grasp a good hold on the slick surface.

Raven, with his voice deep and raspy, asked, "Should I wait?"

"No. Go on," Dirk said, "And, thank you ... Again."

Dirk watched his friend fly away. He crouched down, opened the sack, and rummaged for the first item. He pushed aside his rolled up pool and a length of tube and removed the floppy disk he got from his cartoon amigo. The disk was as black as Raven, but rubbery and floppy, and felt like a circular shower mat. He rolled up the disk and held it in his hands.

He looked down at the tube extending away from the mansion far to the hills in the distance. Connected to the dome, the tube looked like the stick of a clear, spherical lollipop with a house trapped within its candy shell. Dirk kept a steady gaze on the tube and waited patiently for Max to walk up the path within.

✂   ✂   ✂

Max looked at the directions Ed gave him on how to get to Pinkerton's mansion and rolled his eyes. He didn't know why Ed gave him the directions. The only people who knew Ed's world better than Max were the architects who helped piece it together, but not by much. Max folded the instructions into a paper crane and let it fly away in the breeze. He watched the paper crane fly away and join a passing flock of pizza slices.

He realized he was procrastinating, and he couldn't hesitate any longer. The others would be waiting for him. It wasn't Max's fear of Pinkerton slowing his progress to the mansion. It was his scissors. He worried that getting the scissors back meant a future of constructing a never ending line of custom, portable pools. He wasn't sure that was the future he wanted. Spending a stretch of time in Outworld away from portable pools was refreshing and freeing. It's not that he hated creating pools. He was born to cut pools. It was comforting to know he didn't have to spend the rest of his life creating pools. If he got the scissors back, he worried he would fall into his old ways and wind up cutting pools where he left off.

One thought did propel him forward, and that was the thought of Emily. During his pool cutting career, he had met so many people. He had no idea if Emily was ever one of those people he met. It didn't matter who Emily was. She was left behind and trapped at Pinkerton's. He didn't blame Ed or Dirk for leaving her behind, but no one deserved to deal with the insane force of Pinkerton.

Max took different shortcuts, which would bring him closer to Pinkerton's mansion than Ed's direction. From the City, Max took a televator to the clover fields of Framington. The televator left him at the base of the clover fields near the cliff. He heard the distant waves crashing against the rocks at the base of the cliffs. Neither the sea nor the cliff was what he needed.

Max looked up at the many floating patches of clovers suspended above the cliff. From below, it looked like abstract patches of dirt hanging down with a hint of clover growing over the upper edges. He scanned the floating fields for one in particular, shaped like a folded banana. He spotted it suspended over the cliff, above the sea, about three layers up.

He pulled a large, red balloon from his pocket and inflated it until its diameter matched the height of his torso. He tied off the balloon, and then pulled a shoelace from his other pocket. The shoelace was one he kept from a costume emergency before a full-house performance of Roaming Thunder. He tied the shoelace into a loop and attached it to the balloon.

Pushing the balloon down with both hands, Max slipped his right foot into the loop of shoelace. He waddled to the edge of the cliff and stepped off. Instead of him plummeting to his death, as one would expect in Outworld, the balloon supported his weight and lifted him up. With both hands holding the top of the balloon, he steered it towards the floating field shaped like a folded banana.

Once above the field, he touched down and freed his balloon from the loop of shoelace. With a safety pin, another Roaming Thunder souvenir, he popped the balloon and crammed everything back into his pocket.

At the point of the fold, hovering three feet off the ground, a picture frame hung in the air. The picture in the frame was a child's crayon drawing of a domed island with a solitary palm tree and squiggly, blue waves. Carved into the left edge of the frame was a small, bald head a little larger than a golf ball.

"Welcome to the Framington Clover Fields!" the small carved head said.

"Thank you. Show me the Pinkerton mansion," Max said.

"The portrait of Pinkerton mansion is no longer in our gallery," the head said.

"Fine. Show me the Queso Fields," Max requested.

"Which one? The Harrison? Or, the Reitlinger?" asked the head.

"The Harrison, please," Max said.

"Certainly," the head said.

The crayon drawing of the island faded from the frame to a blank, off-white canvas. In its place, a watercolor picture appeared of the bubbling queso fields in a time before Pinkerton built his mansion.

"Thank you," Max said.

The head began to educate Max about the history of Walter Harrison and his watercolor painting entitled *Hot Cheese*. Max rolled his eyes and shook his head. He took several steps back to the far edge of the floating clover patch. He took a few deep breaths and focused on the painting. Exhaling one last deep breath, he sprinted towards the painting, then leapt at the picture in a horizontal dive. Max's fingers entered the painting first, followed by the rest of his flying body. A blurry watercolor Max appeared in the painting, as the real Max transported himself to the actual queso fields.

In the valley of the queso fields, Max tumbled into a roll and stopped himself from skidding into the molten cheese. He stood up, dusted himself off, and looked around. A short walk away, Max found the entrance and took the lonely walk up the tube, over the sea of molten cheese, towards Pinkerton's mansion.

Ed assumed Pinkerton would disable his partially built pool as a way to get into his mansion by rolling it up as Dirk had done to his. It's what he would do if the roles were reversed. If it wasn't disabled, then most likely it would be closely guarded. It didn't matter. Ed knew of another way to sneak into Pinkerton's mansion.

After the Paddleman dropped off Max and Dirk, he returned to Black Manor for Ed. Ed did a bit of research in his library of books and met the Paddleman in his garden fountain. Ed showed the Paddleman a drawing of a map from one of his books and asked him if the canoe could take him there. Since Ed read and reread his favorite books, parts of the worlds he imagined existed as real places in his world. The Paddleman confirmed Ed's hunch that the sea in the book was connected to the waterways of the rest of his world. Once there, he asked one of the inhabitants for directions to the lamppost. Eventually, he found a squirrel who was busy chopping wood who knew they way.

Ed followed the squirrel's poorly described directions, got lost in the forest, but eventually found the lamppost. Along the way, he found a rusted short sword and shield abandoned from a long ago battle. He took both in case he needed to defend himself against Pinkerton. He didn't think he could kill the man, but figured he never knew what he might have to do to save Emily or survive another encounter. From the lamppost, he found his way through the wardrobe, which stood as an exhibit in one of Pinkerton's failed attempts to leave the world. The long path through the wardrobe was stripped clean. Only a few bent coat hangers remained on the clothes racks above, which Ed banged his head upon a couple of times. The wardrobe was big enough for children to climb through, but not a lanky adult.

In the distance ahead, Ed saw the rectangle of light coming from the edges of the wardrobe door. He opened the door a crack and peaked into the exhibit room of Pinkerton's mansion. As he suspected, Kasper, looking like a chameleon in a prom dress, watched over the pool, which was not rolled up. The good news was Kasper had his back to the wardrobe and could not see Ed peeking through the slightly cracked door. The bad news was that Kasper stood between the wardrobe and both the pool and exhibit room door to the rest of the mansion. Kasper's two independently mobile eyes watched the pool. When Ed thought it was safe enough to exit the wardrobe, he pushed the door open wider and caused a loud creak in the process.

Kasper's chameleon eyes swiveled around to the wardrobe. Ed instinctively closed the wardrobe door with another loud creak. Without the fur coats, there was nowhere to hide within the wardrobe. If he ran back, Kasper would hear his footsteps on the wood floor of the inside of the wardrobe. Ed stood perfectly still, hoping Kasper would ... What? Go away? No. Then things would be worse. Kasper might run off to tell Pinkerton of his arrival. Ed figured he better face his fears.

As Ed reached forward to push open the door of the wardrobe again, the large, round, lizard face with two swiveling eyes of Kasper poked through the door. He spotted Ed and quickly withdrew.

Ed pushed open the door and leapt into the room, which tilted out from under him. Already, Pinkerton was on the move. He tumbled over and tried to gain his footing.

Kasper turned from a chameleon into a plaid kangaroo. Before Kasper could hop away to inform Pinkerton, Ed said, a little louder than he should have, "Wait! Don't go!"

✂   ✂   ✂

High atop the glass-domed fortress, Dirk

431

spotted Max walking up the tube and went into action. He looked down to make sure his sack was secured to his back. He scooted down the opposite side of the dome, away from the tube, and in an area with the fewest windows. He turned over onto his belly and slid face first down the ever steepening slope of the dome. Nearing the bottom, he flipped open the floppy disk still clutched in his hand and slapped it against the glass of the dome. Instantly, where the disk touched the glass, the glass disappeared and left a clean, circular hole. The portable hole from Toonville worked as Ed said it should.

Dirk gripped the rim of the hole and slowed his face-forward slide from the outside of the dome, through the hole, to the inside of the dome. Passing through the lip of the circle, he caught himself with his legs and feet. Once again, Ed was right in that the glass was not a dome, but a sphere. Once inside the dome, Dirk slid to the base of the ball encasing Pinkerton's mansion. He was a little concerned the portion of dome buried beneath bubbling cheese would be hot, but it was actually cool to the touch. Dirk slid the rest of the way down to the base of the sphere.

Once at the bottom, Dirk opened his sack and pulled out his portable pool and a siphon. He placed the pool higher up on the curve of the sphere, plugged a hose of the siphon into the pool, and let the other end drop to the floor. Once he got the water flowing out of the pool, the inside of the sphere began to fill. With the water siphoning from one pool of water to another, Dirk opened his sack again and pulled out two inflatable inner tubes and a hand pump. One of the tubes was for his portable pool and siphon to keep it elevated from the water collecting in the base of the sphere, while the other was for himself, so that he did not need to tread water as it got deeper.

With the pool and siphon on one tube and himself seated on the other, Dirk waited for the water to get high enough. He watched the mansion above him. For a while, it remained steady; then it began to tilt and shift. Dirk figured Max must have arrived.

✂   ✂   ✂

Max stood at the front door practicing in his head what he was going to say to Pinkerton. He wanted to get it right, so that he didn't put his foot in his mouth and make things worse. He figured he would start by apologizing for not completing the pool earlier. Then what? When was it acceptable to demand Pinkerton hand over Emily? Since he had never met Emily, how would he know if Pinkerton handed over the right person?

Pinkerton opened the door. Based on his expression, Max could tell Pinkerton was surprised to see him.

Pinkerton said, "It's you!"

"Hello," Max said. As to Ed's apartment, Max took initiative and invited himself into the scary man's mansion, but then was seized by the tile-floored arms of the Yabowak for his intrusion.

"How did you get here?" Pinkerton demanded.

"I walked through the door," Max said.

Max could tell Pinkerton was clearly frustrated with his answer. When Max said he used the door, he did not mean the door to Pinkerton's mansion. He honestly meant the door in Ed's garden.

Pinkerton held up the scissors to Max. "Hey! My scissors! There they are!" He would have reached out to take them, but his arms were pinned by the Yabowak.

"I know you used these scissors to go to another world. What I'm asking is how did you use these? And, how did you get back without them?" Pinkerton asked.

"To answer your second question first, like I said, I walked through the door. To answer your first question second, they're scissors. They cut. Instead of paper, they cut into the fabric of space and make pools. And, one time, they cut a hole to another world," Max said.

"I know that, but how?" Pinkerton demanded.

"I don't know. They're scissors. Just point and cut!" Max said.

"Here," Pinkerton said, and he thrust the scissors into Max's pinned down hand. "Show me how they work."

The Yabowak freed Max's hands. Pinkerton moved his chair backwards. Max doubted Pinkerton moved back to give him more room to work but figured it was more out of fear of being stabbed by the scissors.

It had been a while, but Max went through the motions like it was a natural part of his daily routine. And, for many years, it was. With one hand, he grasped at nothing, and with the other he cut. As always, clear, blue pool water shimmered on the other side.

Pinkerton growled. "I meant, show me how to cut a hole to another world!" he spat.

"I don't know! I can't work them like that! All I know is pools!" Max said.

Max mentally kicked himself for walking into this trap. Since he was in a stand off with this crazy person and his holey obsession, was now the right time to ask about Emily?

The Yabowak's hands slid around Max's hands. Max thought his arms would be pinned down again, but something was different. The Yabowak slid around Max's hands like a living glove and controlled their movement. Like cutting a pool, it made him grasp at reality with the one hand. Instead of feeling where to cut a pool, the Yabowak showed Max how to feel deeper and into other worlds. It felt like searching a woven network of vines to prune a single strand. Instead of the firm, leafiness of a vine, the strands were soft – like cooked spaghetti. The Yabowak caused Max to gently grasp one of the strands, and then cut at it with the scissors in his other hand. Sure enough, instead of another pool, a small hole was cut from one world into another.

Max's eyes grew wide, but not as wide as

435

Pinkerton's. Pinkerton laughed at his success and wiped away tears of joy on his sleeve. He took the scissors from Max as Kasper leapt into the room.

"He's here!" Kasper said.

"Excellent," said Pinkerton, "He arrived just in time for my departure. Yabowak, once you are done taking out this trash, return to my side and show me how you cut a hole in the world."

Pinkerton followed Kasper into the exhibit room. The Yabowak opened the mansion's front door and tossed Max outside. Max missed the pathway and tumbled sideways off the path and onto the sides of the sphere. He slid down a short steep slope and splashed into the water, which was a couple feet away from the base of the mansion. The water Dirk pumped out of his portable pool was quickly filling up the sphere surrounding Pinkerton's mansion.

Dirk, lounging in his tube, paddled over to Max and said, "Come on in, pool boy. The water's just about right."

✄　✄　✄

Ed followed Kasper, but Kasper moved too rapidly for him to keep up. By the time Ed pushed open the wardrobe and stepped to the floor of the exhibit room, Kasper was already gone. Ed wanted to follow him because Kasper could take him to Pinkerton. Pinkerton was either with Emily, the scissors, or Max. Ed thought any combination of the three would be good.

He clutched the sword and shield. It felt awkward in his hands. Then again, the sword and

436

shield were most likely built for an animal – not for a human.

Ed heard voices from the hallway and walked quietly toward to door. The room tilted and Pinkerton rolled into the room and blocked the door.

"Kasper told me we have a guest. Sorry I have to cut out early," Pinkerton twirled the scissors in his hand.

"Where's Emily?" Ed asked.

"The three-eyed girl? Well," Pinkerton said, and chuckled to himself, "We may need a recount."

"What have you done to her?" Ed demanded.

"Me? Would I do anything to harm her? She can't wait to see you," Pinkerton said with a smile.

Ed shifted the shield to the hand with the sword so he could take out the doorknob. He held it out for Pinkerton and said, "I've come to make you an offer. I'll trade you this for Emily and the scissors. This is the doorknob that helped Max get back into this world. Attach it to any door, and you can leave the world. That's what you want, don't you?"

"I've got what I want right here," Pinkerton said and held up the scissors. "As soon as my helping hands dispose of Max, they're going to show me to the exit. Now, if you'll excuse me."

Pinkerton grasped the control on his chair to tilt the mansion so he could exit. The mansion did not respond to Pinkerton's controls; it bobbed and weaved like boat on the water instead. Very much like a boat on the water.

Ed smiled. The plan was working. He readied

the sword and shield in his hands and walked towards Pinkerton in his immobile chair. Sure enough, Dirk and Max, both dripping wet, appeared behind Pinkerton.

"Having trouble going anywhere?" Dirk said.

"Yeah. If I were you, I'd consider moving. It seems your mansion has a little water damage," Max said.

The smile disappeared from Ed's face. Although he was glad to see two out of three of his friends were okay, he was surprised by Pinkerton's chair. Pinkerton slapped a button on the controls, and four spider legs unfolded from underneath the chair.

"Oh look," Max said, "Pinkerton's got legs. I guess he can walk after all. At least, his chair can."

One leg of the chair slipped in the water pooling on the floor from the drip-drying Max and Dirk. A hand reached out of the floor and helped steady it.

"And, look! He's got hands, too," Max said.

"Before I cut a hole in the world, let me introduce the rest of my family," Pinkerton said. He activated the controls, and the Yabowak reached out of the floor to throw a switch on the wall. Along the other walls displaying Pinkerton's exhibit of portals, the walls swiveled around to reveal a small zoo of caged animals. The Yabowak threw another switch on the wall, and the cages popped open.

"Meet my other collection," Pinkerton said.

Creatures emerged from their cages, some hesitant and some ready for a taste of freedom (if not

438

a taste for something else). Ed turned around. His jaw dropped, and he carefully stepped away from the strangest menagerie of animals creeping towards them.

CHAPTER TWENTY-FIVE

Departure

Monstrous animals spilled out of their cages. They were the hidden collection of Pinkerton's animal experimentation in which he had frankensteined bits of different animals together. Ed wondered … If someone was genius enough, or crazy enough, to piece together a zoo of mismatched animals, why couldn't he give himself new legs in order to walk? He also wondered if Pinkerton created a zoo of monsters to make himself appear less monstrous in comparison? Yet, the act of piecing together animals made Pinkerton more of a monster. Did he do it as a hobby or out of boredom? Was it a trial run to build up the courage to operate on himself?

Ed had no idea if Pinkerton bothered to name his creations, or if they were labeled "Experiment #12" or "Creature X". He surveyed the group to decide which was the most dangerous. They all looked creepy and dangerous in their own ways. Which should he be prepared to fend off first?

Starting on Ed's left, there was the parrilla with

a gorilla head perched atop the body of an enormous parrot. Where did Pinkerton find a parrot large enough to attach a gorilla head? With wings, it could fly, which it chose to do. It perched itself on the roof of a cage. Birds have eyes on either side of their head for a wider field of vision. Ed figured that the gorilla head, with its front-facing vision, gave itself a much greater blind spot.

The next animal Ed named the centishark. The creature had the body of a shark with multiple pairs of legs attached down the sides. The centishark had the toothy mouth of a shark but still didn't seem fully coordinated with all its legs and feet. The shark body wanted to swish from side to side, while propelling itself with its tail. The legs couldn't keep up, which caused it to stumble. Plus, the numerous legs appeared to keep it weighted to the ground. If Ed could gain some height, the centishark might not be much trouble.

Like the centishark, the next was the hippospider. This one might be tricky. The enormous head of a hippopotamus had four pairs of chimpanzee arms and hands protruding symmetrically on either side of a spherical body. Hippos in Outworld were known to be very territorial. The strength of eight chimp hands gave it better mobility to climb and grasp. The wide mouth with sledgehammer-sized teeth were also intimidating.

At first, the fist-snake did not seem too threatening. The snake looked mostly normal, except for a human hand at the tail end. The hand, dragging behind, impeded the snake's slithery movement. When one of the other creatures came too close to the fist-snake, the hand on the tail lashed out to slap the other creature away.

The porcubat also looked relatively harmless if Ed could keep his distance. This was a smaller creature about the shape and size of a normal bat. The only difference was the porcupine quills protruding from its back. This creature seemed to want nothing to do with anyone in the room. It searched for the darkest place to hide and go back to sleep.

Finally, there was Quirk, who was not in the zoo, but entered the room to see what it was missing. It tried to jump up into Pinkerton's lap. When he pushed Quirk from his lap, its chicken head pecked at Pinkerton's mechanical hand.

The centishark, stumbling a bit, circled the room. It worked at herding Ed and his friends into a tighter circle. The parrilla watched from its cage, while the hippospider grunted at each pass of the centishark.

The hippospider crept towards Ed on its chimp legs. It opened its hippo mouth and grunted at Ed. Slamming its mouth shut, it charged. With one watchful eye on the circling centishark, Ed gripped the sword and shield and stood his ground.

Dirk watched the circling centishark and groaned, "Not another one."

Max stepped away from the slither-crawling

fist-snake and backed up against Dirk behind him. Max said, "Seriously. What is it with you and sharks?"

Dirk shrugged.

The fist-snake flattened its hand on the floor and coiled around it. Its eyes kept a steady gaze on Max. With the help of its hand, it pushed off the floor and leapt at Max. Instinctively, Max jumped aside, and the fist-snake grabbed ahold of Dirk's ankle instead. Max twisted sideways to avoid the oncoming centishark and skidded to a halt by the toy tollbooth, which crashed to the floor and frightened the centishark away.

As carefully as he could, Dirk reached down and quickly grabbed hold of the snake's head. With the fist still clutched to his ankle, Dirk tugged at the snake trying to free it from his leg.

As territorial as a real hippo, Pinkerton's creation lunged at Ed over and over. With the circling centishark, the partially built swimming pool, and the others fending off the other monstrous creations, there was little chance of Ed vacating the hippospider's newly claimed territory.

Over by the door to the room, Pinkerton laughed as he watched his creatures close in on Ed. The Yabowak had returned and was sliding the floor up around Pinkerton's hand like a living glove as it did for Max.

"What's so funny?" Ed asked over his shoulder.

"I don't know what to do. Do I finally leave your forsaken world behind? Or, do I stick around a bit to watch you die by one of my creations? Decisions, decisions," Pinkerton said, and laughed again. "It's not that I'm squeamish, but I can't wait to leave this world behind. I guess this is goodbye."

"Yeah. Goodbye for me, too," Kasper added, looking like a uniformed football player with a horse's head.

"Where do you think you're going?" Pinkerton asked Kasper.

"With you," Kasper said, disillusioned.

"No. Not you. You're part of this world and would be a constant reminder of what I'm trying so desperately to leave behind. You're staying here," Pinkerton said, and chuckled coldly at Kasper.

"But," Kasper said. He said nothing else, as he watched Pinkerton's hand hover over the button on his chair. "No. Please don't press that. I'll stay."

"Good boy," Pinkerton said, "Back to business. Yabowak, show me how to cut a hole to another world."

The Yabowak did as it was told and cut a hole, connecting Ed's world to another. They made the hole large enough for Pinkerton to climb through on his spidery mechanical chair. It looked like a peaceful scene with a field of grass and the remnants of a rainbow arching across the sky. Pinkerton's chair stepped through to the other world, so that it was half in and half out of the world.

Teddy bears hopped down from trees growing lollipops and plastic wrapped candies. They began singing and dancing and asked Pinkerton in high-pitched, child-like voices, "Do you want to play with us?"

"No, I don't!" Pinkerton said, and quickly backed through the hole returning to Ed's world.

"Seal it up," he demanded. The Yabowak obliged. The hole began to heal itself shut, but not before the centishark leapt through and began chasing teddy bears back up the candy trees.

Pinkerton chuckled and said, "There! Play with that!"

The hole closed to the screams of teddy bear carnage.

"Let's try again," Pinkerton said.

The next hole, he stopped cutting shortly after he began. The other world was an extremely painful and nauseating color of ultra-pink.

"What do you think, Pink?" Kasper asked, and laughed, but stopped when Pinkerton shot him a cold look and his hand reached for the button.

The next hole was to a world comprised of all sky, trees, and birds. The parrilla noticed this world and launched himself through the hole before it could be sealed. The last Pinkerton saw of the parrilla was it flying off with a flock of toucans.

"I want a world where I can live in peace!" Pinkerton demanded.

"I'll take those," Max said reaching from behind Pinkerton and taking the Checkered Scissors.

"What the …?" Pinkerton asked, looking at Max with disbelief. The centishark and the parrilla disappeared into other worlds. Ed wounded one of the hippospider's chimpanzee arms, and it was curled in a ball nursing its arm with its large hippo tongue. Ed nicked it with the sword he brought from Narnia. The porcubat hung from the ceiling and did its best to ignore the commotion below, while the fist-snake grabbed hold of Dirk's leg and tried to bite him. Ed left the hippospider to help Dirk. That left Max holding the scissors.

"Please. I'm begging you. I just want to leave this world and start a new life. I don't want to be someone's nightmare. I don't want to be here anymore. Please. Help me," Pinkerton begged.

"You want out of here?" Max asked. Learning from his experience with the Yabowak, he plucked at reality and cut a hole in the world. On the other side was the Void, a place of nothingness beyond the Jaiuian wall of worlds. "There you go. Clean slate. Have fun."

"I don't want *nothing*," Pinkerton spat. "Give me those scissors. I'll do it myself."

The spider legs of Pinkerton's chair leapt into life. It steadied itself, and then charged at Max, who backed himself out of the way.

"No, you don't," Dirk's voice roared, and he charged Pinkerton's chair.

Ed chopped the head off of the fist-snake, freeing Dirk except for the dead fist end still clutched to his ankle. Max tripped backwards over Quirk, who was grooming his horns. The scissors slipped from his hand, only to be snagged by Pinkerton. As Dirk tackled Pinkerton off his chair, he stumbled on the remaining bit of dangling snake still grabbing his leg.

Dirk and Pinkerton tumbled through the hole into the Void and floated weightlessly away. The force of Dirk's collision with Pinkerton caused them to spiral away, drifting farther and farther from the hole and each other, helpless to return. Dirk flailed his arm towards Pinkerton, desperately trying to reach the scissors. Pinkerton did not float away as fast, but laughed maniacally with the scissors still clutched in his hand.

"Give me back my scissors," Max said.

"Not a chance. Once I figure out how to use these, I can go anywhere and wreak havoc on anything I please," Pinkerton yelled, and laughed even harder. The hole to the Void was already slowly starting to close. Pinkerton twirled the scissors around a finger of one hand and waved goodbye to Ed's world with the other. All the while, he laughed.

"Do something!" Max said, turning to Ed, pleading his creator to do something. Anything.

Ed thought quickly. Pinkerton was no longer in his chair, which was on its side, on the floor. With the controls damaged and no one to operate them, Ed figured the Yabowak was free.

"Yabowak," Ed called.

In response, a hand reached out of the floor. Ed pointed through the hole in the world, and said, "There go the scissors. Fetch!"

Obediently, the Yabowak stretched its hand through the hole. It reached as far as it could, then stretched some more. When it was close enough, it pulled the scissors free of Pinkerton's finger. Floating helplessly, it was impossible for Pinkerton to get them back. The Yabowak pulled its hand and the scissors back through the hole.

"N–!" Pinkerton began to shout, as the hole sealed itself closed.

"Do you think he was about to yell, 'Noodles'?" Max asked.

Ed chuckled and said, "I don't think so."

The Yabowak placed the scissors into Max's hand and closed Max's fingers around them. The Yabowak placed a gentle hand to Max's chest. As if reading the Yabowak's mind, if it had one, both Max and Ed understood this as the Yabowak's way of telling Max the scissors were his, to keep them safe, and, in its own way, apologizing for taking them.

"Thank you," Max said.

The Yabowak sunk into the floor, but kept a hand stretched out as if it still wanted to see what happened next.

Sharing the same thought, Max asked, "What now?"

"We need to find Emily and make sure she's okay," Ed said.

Kasper walked up. He looked like Ed, but wore brightly colored clothing. He asked, "What about me?"

"What about you?" Max asked.

"Pink's gone. What do I do now?"

"I'm sure Max could use the scissors to find you

a new home," Ed said.

Max wagged the scissors at Kasper.

"No, thank you," Kasper said, "I like this world."

"Thanks. I made it myself. If you like my world, then why did you want to leave?" Ed asked.

"Pink accepted me. He made me feel wanted and important," Kasper said. "Sometimes."

"Yeah, until his sudden departure," Max said.

Kasper smirked. "Yeah. Until then."

"Look. If you want to stay, feel free to tag along with me," Ed said.

Max shook his head and shot Ed a look of concern.

"You mean it?" Kasper said.

"Of course. Just do us one favor," Ed said.

Kasper, aiming to please his creator, said, "Anything! What do you need?"

Ed said, "Help us find Emily."

The Yabowak's hand snapped in two at the wrist. The stump slowly sunk into the tile floor, while the hand steadied itself on its fingertips and crawled across the floor. The Yabowak's hand tugged at Max's pants. Max bent down and scooped it up in his free hand. The Yabowak crawled up his arm and perched itself on Max's shoulder.

"What do you think? Can I keep it?" Max asked.

"Yes, the Yabowak can come, too," Ed said.

The Yabowak on Max's shoulder did a little four-finger-one-thumb jig, then settled down.

"Follow me," said Kasper, "She should be this way."

✂ ✂ ✂

Kasper lead the way through Pinkerton's mansion to his laboratory, where they found Emily. Emily was on the floor, in the corner, with her arms clutching her legs and her head tucked between her knees. They could hear her sobbing.

"Emily?" Ed asked, "Are you okay?"

"No," she sobbed, "Everyone left me."

"But, we came back for you. Max is here. And he has his scissors, too," Ed said. He crouched beside her and placed his arms around her shoulder.

"Don't touch me!" Emily said, slapping Ed's arm away. "Don't look at me, either."

Ed stood up as Max crouched beside Emily. He kept his hands to himself but said gently to her, "It's nice to meet you, Emily. Thank you for looking for me."

Emily curled up into a tighter ball. "Go away." She sniffed, then added, "I'm glad you got your scissors back."

"Eh. They're just scissors. I came here to make sure you were okay," Max said.

"Really? But, you don't even know me," she said.

"No. I don't know you. But, I know of Pinkerton. And, I know nobody should be left alone with him," Max said.

"Where is he?" she asked.

"Pinkerton?" Max said, and chuckled, "He got

450

knocked clean out of this world, thanks to Dirk."

"Where's Dirk?" Emily asked.

"Unfortunately, he's out of this world, too," Ed said.

"Well," she said, "Thanks for coming back for me."

"Are you ready to get out of here?" Ed asked.

"Yes. But," Emily said, "I don't want anyone to look at me. I'm hideous."

Ed's feeling of relief at finding Emily switched to concern. "What did he do to you?"

"Let us see," Max said. He placed his hand on the sides of her head and lifted it slowly.

Dried, bloody tears encrusted Emily's face from the corners of her eyes down to her cheeks. Deep crimson stains spotted her pants. Ed and Max both gasped when they saw her eyes. The left eye was replaced with an 8-ball, and the right one was replaced with what looked like a glass eye as blue as one of Max's pools. The third eye on her forehead was left untouched. Ed could read her pained facial expressions as Emily blinked her three strange eyes. She lifted her head and gazed upon Max for the first time with sad, mutilated eyes.

"I've seen a lot of things traveling around Ed's world selling pools ... But, I've never seen-," Max started to say.

"Anything as hideous as me?" she said, finishing his sentence.

"No. I was going to say, I've never seen anything as beautiful as you," Max said and smiled.

451

"Stop it. You'll make me cry, again. And, it really hurts to cry right now," she said, smiling back at Max.

Emily and Max took an instant liking to each other. Emily allowed Max to pick her up and carry her from Pinkerton's lab. Max taking care of Emily reminded Ed of Penny. He had seen her again briefly, and it wasn't even her. With Glick inhabiting her body, Ed wasn't sure Penny could be rescued.

CHAPTER TWENTY-SIX

What Now, Boss?

Everyone crashed on the sofas in the library of the Black Manor library. Emily cuddled up with Max at one end of the sofa. They talked all the way back and discovered they had a lot in common. Max explored most of Ed's world, and Emily knew much about Ed from his library. Kasper sat at the other end of the sofa near Ed, who was sprawled out on the adjacent sofa. He no longer looked like Ed, but held the image of a depressed man in a grey suit. For Kasper, he looked almost normal, except that he blurred as he slowly melted into the sofa. The Yabowak, still as a detached hand, curled up on the top of the cushion near Max.

"What now, boss?" Kasper asked. Since losing his former employer, it was the first thing he had said since leaving Pinkerton's mansion behind. He did nothing to mask the overtone of hope and desperation from his voice.

"I'm not your boss. You are your own boss," Ed said.

"I mean, what happens now?" Kasper asked.

"I'll tell you what happens now," said a female voice from across the room. Everyone sat up. Alaenia was back in Ed's world, and still seemed annoyed.

"The higher ups are furious about the two counts of cross-world pollination and two people found drifting in the Void. Not to mention the whole Glick mess. This whole fiasco has them itching to purge," she said.

Max sat up straighter, breaking free of Emily's embrace. "They can't do that, can they? Dirk was only trying to stop Pinkerton and get the scissors away from him."

"Speaking of which, they also wanted those scissors of yours destroyed," Alaenia added.

"Not Max's scissors," Emily said.

"Hold on. They aren't destroying anything," she said, "Yet. They chose not to purge Glick, because he is considered an endangered race. Reconstruction is figuring out how to build him a new body. It's been too long since his last body, and his essence has been tarnished by borrowing Ed's and Penny's bodies. While he still occupied Penny's body, he pleaded to return to work, no matter who was running the show. We've never seen such dedication to a job, even centuries after being stranded."

"And, the scissors? They can't destroy them. Even after the troubles they've caused, they could still be useful," said Emily. Max grimaced at the mention of them.

"As for the scissors," Alaenia said. "They want

to destroy the scissors, but I talked them out of it. You can keep them for now, but on one condition."

"What condition?" Max asked. "They want free pools?"

"No," Alaenia said, smiling, "Part of the condition is that Ed will be the keeper of the scissors, and not Max."

"Yes," Max rejoiced.

"Okay. What's the other part of the condition?" Ed asked.

"The other part of the condition is that you now work for OmniCore with me as your supervisor," she said.

"Doing what?" Ed asked.

"I work in the Special Investigations Department. My job keeps me busy enough without you adding to it. Plus, I could use a hand. But, you're not the only new member of my team," Alaenia said.

"Penny?" Ed said, hopeful.

"No," she said, "Glick. Once he is reconstructed and goes through orientation, he will be your partner."

"What about Penny? Or, the other me? What about Outworld? Do I live here, in my world? Am I allowed to go back to Outworld?"

"You are to live here. You and Penny are both considered dead. You live in your world. She lives in hers," Alaenia said.

"What about her body missing from Outworld? What about mine hooked up to a doorway?" Ed said.

"Funny you should ask. Your first assignment is to help Glick clean up his mess," she said.

"What happens when people start questioning where they've disappeared to?" Ed asked.

"They won't be missing. Once you and Glick have cleaned up, a new Ed and new Penny will pick up their lives where they left off. False memories will fill in the holes of the past few days. They will never know anything happened."

"Why create new bodies? Why can't we go back to living out our lives in Outworld?" Ed asked.

"The body you occupy now is conditioned for your OmniCorp world, not Outworld. That, and we must restore the natural balance of Outworld by new replacement vessels. Now, unfortunately, that means you are not to return to Outworld, at least not without permission. Whenever you do return to Outworld, you are not to cross paths with yourselves, and you are not allowed to interfere with the lives of your other selves."

"Do our other selves get their own worlds?" Ed asked.

"No. There will only be one world per individual. One for Penny, one for you. The vessel housing the clone of your soul is temporary. When the vessel in Outworld expires, control will switch to you. In order for your world to keep growing, the connection will need to remain in Outworld for the extent of your other's life. The same applies to Penny."

"What about Mr. Pinkerton?" Kasper asked.

456

"And, Dirk?" Emily added.

"They were found floating in the Void. Like Edwin, here, they have been sent back to their own worlds," Alaenia said.

"Won't Pinkerton's world have a copy of the scissors?" Ed asked.

"We considered that. The architects have hidden them well within his world. And, if he ever finds them, a flag has been set on his world to alert us if any holes should open. Any other questions?" Alaenia said.

"When do I start work?" Ed asked.

"After Glick has finished his orientation," Alaenia said.

"What about the rest of us?" Max asked.

"Yeah. What do we do?" Emily asked.

"I could use all the help I can get," Ed said. He looked at Alaenia.

She waffled a bit, then said, "Okay. Sure. They can help, too."

"And, me?" Kasper asked.

Alaenia sighed, and said, "I suppose."

The Yabowak raised its hand. Alaenia couldn't help but smile. "Yes, you, too."

The Yabowak gave Alaenia the thumbs up, and everyone laughed.

"Looks like you've built yourself quite a team," Ed said.

Alaenia shrugged and said, "They just said you and Glick are to work for me. They never said you couldn't ask for help. Besides, it will be nice having a good team of people working with me for once."

Before she returned to OmniCore, Ed asked his new boss for one small favor. Under the circumstances, she obliged.

✂   ✂   ✂

Alaenia fell into the chair at her desk and breathed a sigh of relief. Penelope Nichol's Death Report sat nearly finished on her desk. It rested on top of a handful of messages from others requesting her attention, but those could wait until another time. Any moment, Penny was to be integrated into her world and would need her report.

As she hurried to finish the last few entries, she stole a couple of glances at the family picture on her desk. She scribbled the last entry in the Report, closed it, and picked up the picture. She kissed her fingertips and pressed them against the picture of her husband.

"Very soon, my love," she said, "It may be a long shot, but I think I found someone to help me find you."

She brushed a tear from her eye, scooped up the report, and walked out of her office. She planned to visit Glick, her newest recruit, in Reconstruction after escorting Penny to integration.

Vern was telling Penny about his favorite creations when Alaenia walked through the door. Alaenia rolled her eyes at him.

"What? She asked," Vern said.

Alaenia grinned, shook her head, and asked Penny, "Are you ready to go?"

"Yes, ma'am," Penny said. She turned to Vern, gave him a hug, and said, "Thank you for my dress. It's perfect. Keep up the good work."

Vern blushed. "Go on. Get yourself out of here."

Alaenia walked Penny to Integration. Penny asked, "Did you escort Ed to his world?"

"Yes, I did," she said.

"Is he okay?" Penny asked.

"He's in good hands," Alaenia said.

"Will I see him again?"

"In your world, there is an Ed who exists who was created by you for you."

"But, he's not the same one who was taken from me, is he?"

Alaenia was silent. She could relate to Penny. She had lost her husband. Penny had lost her friend. They both wanted to find what was lost. After a bit, she said, "No, he's not."

"Will I ever see my Ed again?"

Alaenia quietly said, "One never knows what the future holds."

In the Integration room, Penny stood before the door to her world. Before walking through it, she bent over and gave Alaenia a hug. She said, "Thank you."

"For what?" Alaenia asked.

"For taking care of lost souls, like myself and Ed."

Alaenia thought of all her lost souls: Penny, Ed, Glick, Dirk, Pinkerton, Max, her husband. In their own way, they were all lost souls, trying to find their way home to the ones they love.

"It's what I do," Alaenia said, and waved goodbye to Penny as she entered the integration chamber.

✂ ✂ ✂

As Ed had done before, Penny sat on the floor of her new world surrounded by the black integration bubble. Like Ed, and so many others before them, she sat and read her Death Report, waiting for the bubble to break and preparing herself to start her new afterlife.

Submerged in her Death Report, she did not hear the person walk up behind her. A familiar voice asked her, "How did you die?"

"It says here, 'Unicorn poisoning', but I know it was the music that got me," Penny said.

"Mine claimed I was eaten by a dinosaur."

Penny stood up and turned around. She stepped forward and gave Ed a hug. When they broke apart, she said, "If I had any emotions right now, I know I would be really happy to see you."

"I know," Ed said, smiling. From his pocket, he pulled a pair of scissors covered from handle to point in a checkerboard pattern. He had cut a slit between Penny's world and another.

"Come on," Ed said, "we have things to do and places to go."

Postface

The idea for *Checkered Scissors* originated in a dream. In 1989, I awoke from the dream, jotted down a note of it, and became determined to write the story about those scissors. I started and stopped writing several iterations of the story because I couldn't find the right version to tell. The years passed, but I never gave up on the story. I knew it was in my head somewhere. Decades later, I finally captured the right story and caged it with my word processor.

In 2000, I met the love of my life, Julie. The magic of our new relationship energized me. She inspired me! After a few more failed attempts and false starts, I finished my first complete draft!

I'll be the first to admit the first draft was horrible.

I told an author friend, and she recommended the book *The 38 Most Common Fiction Writing Mistakes*. After reading the book, I realized why the story was so horrible. I had committed at least a dozen, if not half, of the mistakes listed in that book.

Around this time, I shared the first chapter with Turkey City, or as I call it, the "Boot Camp of Peer Reviewing". As I was the new kid in the group, they were kind enough to share their brutal honesty with me, and reserved the brutal and painful honesty for the recurring members. The feedback was hard to swallow. It was harsh enough to break my spirit and force me to give up writing fiction.

But, I didn't give up.

Instead, I studied other books on the craft of writing. Also, I wrote several short stories to help me find my voice and improve my writing skills. I attended Slug Tribe, a milder peer review session with excellent critiques. Not only did I learn to embrace what author peers said about my writing, but I also learned from what they said of other people's stories, too. More time passed, and I attempted another draft of *Checkered Scissors*.

In 2011, around the time of losing both my dog and my job, I completed the next, first draft. I don't count the first-first draft because the story changed so much it evolved into a new and better story. As other authors suggested, I set this new, first draft aside and returned to it months later with a fresh mind.

After several months of ignoring my creation, I loaded *Checkered Scissors* into my e-reader to read my story with a fresh mind. I took notes as I read, but saved the edits and revisions for another time. When I finished, the story felt more right. I enjoyed reading what I had written.

When I write documentation and specifications for work, I know the intended audience will consist of my co-workers and customers. When I write fiction, typically my intended audience is me, or people who read what I like to read. I enjoy a little light reading each night to wind down at the end of the day. I like to lose myself in an adventure where I don't have to wrestle with the language. If I find myself wrestling big, fancy words or flowery language, I tend to stumble and fall out of the book. Many times, I set those kinds of books down, limp away, and rarely return to finish them.

My favorite novels are the ones in which the protagonist stumbles through a hole into another world. *Checkered Scissors* embraces this theme. What happens when someone stumbles upon another world? Will that person find their way back? What if he/she gets stuck so long and becomes so desperate that nothing and no one will stand in their way? What happens when someone becomes completely obsessed with searching for a hole between worlds all that person can think about is how to escape the world in which that person exists?

Checkered Scissors explores what happens to the characters who accidentally end up so far from home there may not be a way back. Do they think about all the things they left behind? Can they find and latch onto the tiniest glimmer of hope of finding their way back?

And, what happens to the friends and family left

behind when someone falls through a crack into another world? The hero typically meets new characters in the other world. These characters are the ones who encourage the hero to stick with the search. Or, when all else fails, they adopt the hero into their family.

Speaking of family... I tweaked and refined the story some more, and then shared *Checkered Scissors* with my family. Because they are family, I take their feedback with a grain of salt. My dad, who typically gravitates towards books with capitol buildings or smoking guns (or occasionally a smoking capitol building), rarely reads fantasy novels, and he enjoyed my story. My mom, who gave up on *Harry Potter and the Sorcerer's Stone* when she encountered the word "muggle," also enjoyed my story. And, my sister, with a Master's degree in English and Philosophy, and whose massive collection of books rivals her equally intimidating Pez collection, was impressed her brother wrote an entire novel. She, too, enjoyed reading my story.

I liked my story, and my family liked my story. Was it ready for the general public? When I decided the story was ready for publication, I researched how to publish it. On the one hand, I could stick with tradition, find an agent who would help this story find a publisher, and maybe years down the road the story sells and I receive some amount of advance. On the other hand, I could hire a freelance editor and a cover artist to help bring it to completion, distribute it through various e-publishing channels, market it myself, and hope for the best. Both paths require a lot of effort, and neither appear any more right or more wrong than the other. After weighing the pros and cons, I decided to attempt the self-publishing route. After all, before this book hits the virtual shelves, I've already pleased the target audience and his family.

Like the characters in the story, I've traveled a long way to bring this tale to you. At times, I struggled with it, but I enjoyed every step of the journey. I appreciate you for considering *Checkered Scissors*, and thank you for the time you spend reading it.

Douglas Schwartz

About the Author

Douglas Schwartz funnels his creativity in numerous ways. He designs games and puzzles for his company, Pegamoose Games. The first short story he presented to a peer writing group, "Glovebox of a UFO", was web-published on RevolutionSF soon afterward. Sometimes, he draws, folds origami, or constructs LEGO creations, too. Despite his ever-flowing creativity and demanding day job in the field of computer software, he always makes time for his wife and kids.

If you would like to contact Douglas, you may find him at any of the following:

www.checkeredscissors.com
www.pegamoosegames.com
http://www.facebook.com/pages/Checkered-Scissors

Twitter: @CheckerScissors

He welcomes feedback, both positive and negative, and criticism, as long as it's constructive and not destructive. If you have a chance, please post a review online and let others know what you think of this story.

Acknowledgements

There are many great people to thank...

First, I would like to thank Douglas Adams, Stephen King, Neil Gaiman, and Terry Pratchett for their excellent works of fiction, which I have enjoyed several times throughout the years. Other authors provided the gift of reading great stories. These four authors inspired me to pursue my writing my own stories, and I am lucky to have met three of the four. I'll leave it to you to speculate the one I have not yet had the honor to meet.

To my wife, Julie, thank you for putting up with me and reading multiple versions of this story. I understand my stories aren't always your choice of book. Thank you for your support and encouragement.

Also, I want to thank my family and closest friends. They have offered their love and support of every creative project I've pursued. I have bounced ideas off them and treated them as my personal Guinea pigs for testing my creations. At times, they help me find a focus and bring what I start to completion. And, most importantly, they are the ones brave enough to tell me when I need to rethink an idea.

Many thanks go to the good people of Slug Tribe, Turkey City, and the Armadillo Con Writer's

Workshop for helping cultivate and improve my writing skills. Through you, I have learned to take constructive criticism head on and not to heart. I've learned to discover what is considered good writing and why. And, I've learned that critiques are also listening to what people haven't said, too.

A big thanks to my editor, Leanna of Studio Z Publishing. She edited my novel page by page, on budget, and within my desired timeframe. She spent the time to go over the consistent mistakes, why they were mistakes, and how to fix them. She also paid me one of the best compliments on my writing.

Thank you all!

www.ingramcontent.com/pod-product-compliance
Lightning Source LLC
Chambersburg PA
CBHW071340020726
47502CB00001B/186